THE HUNT IS ON,
THE TERRITORY HAS BEEN MARKED

for eighteen all-new tales of extraordinary felines. From the dangerous to the daredevil, from nose sense to nonsense, they will sniff out the trail to the most satisfying conclusions. And when these cats pounce upon their quarries, what they will catch are such memorable adventures as:

"The Tale of the Virtual Cat"—When you've got bugs in the system, get a programmer. When you've got Mice in the mains, get a Cat. . . .

"Miss Hettie and Harlan"—They said the mansion "wasn't right" ever since the Larchmare family was murdered there. But Miss Hettie wasn't one to be scared by rumors, and besides she had a cat to protect her, didn't she?

"The Neighbor"—Though young in the arts of sorcery, Dory had an instinct for trouble, and a clever cat named Trouble who was determined to keep her out of it. . . .

CATFANTASTIC IV

Other FANTASTIC Anthologies from DAW Books:

CATFANTASTIC I, II, and III *Edited by Andre Norton and Martin H. Greenberg.* For cat lovers everywhere, three delightful collections of fantastical cat tales, some set in the distant future on as yet unknown worlds, some set in our own world but not quite our own dimension, some recounting what happens when creatures out of myth collide with modern-day felines.

WITCH FANTASTIC *Edited by Mike Resnick and Martin H. Greenberg.* From a timeless coven gathering on All Hallow's Eve, to an old woman brewing up the promise of love requited, to a witch and her cat with the power to rewrite history, let such masterful magic makers as Jane Yolen, Judith Tarr, Katharine Kerr, Roland Green, and David Gerrold lead you to the secret glens, the inner sanctums, the small-town eateries, isolated farms, and city parks where the true practitioners of magic claim vengeance for ancient wrongs, free innocents from evil enchantments, and play their own private games of power to transform our world.

DRAGON FANTASTIC *Edited by Rosalind M. Greenberg and Martin H. Greenberg. With an Introduction by Tad Williams.* From a virtual reality watch dragon to a once-a-century get-together of the world's winged destroyers, here are swift-winging fantasies by such talents as Alan Dean Foster, Mickey Zucker Reichert, Esther Friesner, and Dennis McKiernan.

HORSE FANTASTIC *Edited by Rosalind M. Greenberg and Martin H. Greenberg. With an Introduction by Jennifer Roberson.* From a racer death couldn't keep from the finish line to a horse with the devil in him, here are magical tales by such top writers as Jennifer Roberson, Mercedes Lackey, Mickey Zucker Reichert, Judith Tarr, and Mike Resnick.

CATFANTASTIC IV

Edited by
ANDRE NORTON &
MARTIN H. GREENBERG

DAW BOOKS, INC.
DONALD A. WOLLHEIM, FOUNDER
375 Hudson Street, New York, NY 10014

ELIZABETH R. WOLLHEIM
SHEILA E. GILBERT
PUBLISHERS

First Printing, August 1996
1 2 3 4 5 6 7 8 9

DAW TRADEMARK REGISTERED
U.S. PAT. OFF. AND FOREIGN COUNTRIES
—MARCA REGISTRADA
HECHO EN U.S.A.

PRINTED IN THE U.S.A.

ACKNOWLEDGMENTS

Introduction © 1996 by Andre Norton.
The Last Answer © 1996 by Wilanne Schneider Belden.
The Quincunx Solution © 1996 by Anne Braude.
Circus © 1996 by Marj Krueger.
Tybalt's Tale © 1996 by India Edghill.
The Tale of the Virtual Cat © 1996 by Heather Gladney, Don Clayton, and Alan Rice Osborn.
Arrows © 1996 by Jane Hamilton.
Miss Hettie and Harlan © 1996 by Charles L. Fontenay.
The Neighbor © 1996 by P. M. Griffin.
Tinkerbell © 1996 by Sharman Horwood.
SCat © 1996 by Mercedes Lackey.
Professor Purr's Guaranteed Allergy Cure © 1996 by Brad Linaweaver and Dana Fredsti.
Noh Cat Afternoon © 1996 by Jane M. Lindskold.
Totem Cat © 1996 by A. R. Major.
Deathsong © 1996 by Lyn McConchie.
Noble Warrior, Teller of Fortunes © 1996 by Andre Norton.
Born Again © 1996 by Elizabeth Ann Scarborough.
The Cat, the Sorcerer, and the Magic Mirror © 1996 by Mary Schaub.
One With Jazz © 1996 by Janet Pack.

CONTENTS

INTRODUCTION

It would seem that the very word "cat" sets the imagination furiously to work. Nor can any editor guess in how many directions at once. *Catfantastic IV* sees some familiar characters returning for further adventures, and introduces new ones as well. Also this year the offerings are international, one being from New Zealand and one from South Korea.

You shall meet wizards' four-footed helpers (often quite a bit more intelligent than their so-called masters), talented Japanese cats able to improvise a Noh play to interest a lordling, a cat who is a strict judge of the very best in jazz, a cat who chooses reincarnation to aid a beloved human companion, cats who deal with Jinns and Angels, and a number more, all at home in this universe, world, or time, or journeying to other places of feline activity.

It all adds up to one point of blazing importance—in all dimensions there is nothing equal to a CAT!

—*Andre Norton*

THE LAST ANSWER
by Wilanne Schneider Belden

Wilanne Schneider Belden grew up in the Midwest. She was (and is) involved in reading, writing, dance, music, and drama. Then: Bachelor in Fine Arts in Drama from the University of Iowa; marriage and a move to Southern California, motherhood, elementary school teaching, Masters degree in education, and writing short stories for adults and novels for children and young people. She taught Gifted and Talented students for many years and still consults, offering courses in creative writing, bookmaking, and science fiction and fantasy.

Perielle was pretty sure they were going to kill her. An eight-year-old girl was proving to be a nuisance. She wasn't old enough to be married off to one of them, probably the big man who always smelled of blood. So he couldn't rule as husband of the crown princess. She'd overheard talk of using her as a puppet ruler, but this required too much statecraft for the big bloody one. So they'd kill her, and soon, and eliminate the last member of the Royal Family.

Not that it would help them any. No one could rule this kingdom without the Relics. The sword and crown

11

had mystical properties. Whoever wore the crown became invulnerable to all untruth, whatever that meant. Whoever bore the sword was rightful King, accepted by all. Being an unimaginative child who knew truth from fiction, Peri was none too convinced of the truth of these adages. Her opinion was that a sharp sword swung by strong arms is an excellent tool of persuasion. But the difficulty these invaders were having seemed to bear out the validity of the legends. However, she told herself, the problems probably were caused by Alfesian, the traitorous Royal Magician. He should have showed up weeks ago to begin ruling—or to have it out with the invaders' magician, who was spoiling for the fight.

Perielle knew her twin brothers lived. In those last days, Father told her things now and then. As she had figured out for herself, Father had so little Royal Power that he'd had to employ Alfesian, the Royal Magician, whom he had never entirely trusted. When the boys were born, he had them spirited away, weeping as he announced that they'd been stillborn. He took great care not to reveal the strategy or the location of the boys to anyone. When the invaders came, he'd discarded his minimal, useless Power and had taken up the Sword to defend his realm. Carolus and Hadrius were safer where they were, he'd believed, far from war, being raised like peasants.

Perielle was surprised and a little confused to be told her father's secret. He never lied, but she thought him unreasonably optimistic. Alfesian had much magic and many, many spies and informers.

When Alfesian announced that he intended to rule, he and Father disappeared in a blinding flash of black lightning, leaving mind-numbing terror behind. All resistance to the enemies died. It took the invading army only six days to overrun the capital and declare its leader the new king. His magician prepared to battle Alfesian when he returned. Peri had infinite contempt for the newcomers. Because it took longer than they had thought, they supposed he would not come. He would. Peri shuddered and thought about something else.

Suppose Carolus was alive—and not in Alfesian's

power. First someone would have to tell him who he was, and nobody knew. Next, he'd have to locate the Relics, which Father had when he disappeared. Then he'd have to learn to use the sword. Peasants used hoes and pitchforks. If he developed a great deal of Royal Power—and only one of every three rulers ever had enough to be useful—he'd put aside all killing to retain it. No, hoping for help from Carolus was pointless. She sighed. If he lived to grow up, Carolus probably would wring the neck of any female who stood between him and the crown.

She realized this wasn't fair. He could be a pretty good person. But she had little trust in men. Her early life hadn't been easy, and it had gotten harder when Mother died. Father ignored her. He'd sent away the only tutor who taught what she wanted to learn. The magician said not to bother him until after she'd been sick. She'd never had so much as a cold. Carolus was unlikely to care about her either.

At least, the new inhabitants of the castle didn't think she had any information worth knowing, so they just penned her up in her room and ignored her. Oh, she was fed, and she had water and firewood, and nobody hurt her. But she wasn't too sure that would continue for long. She spent long hours hoping that her father might still be alive. Being an orphan, alone in the world, was more than she could handle—and continue to act as a crown princess was expected to do. Father hadn't cared much for her, but he was better than no one. If he still lived, where was he? She'd know, if she ever came there.

The insurgents had no such doubts. King Morion was dead. Everyone who had seen the spectacular disappearance agreed to that. They searched constantly and ever more desperately for the Relics.

When her guard brought her evening meal, Perielle could hardly choke down the ill-prepared food. But she had a healthy appetite, sense enough to try to stay alive and strong, and no desire for the new "king" to remember her. He was busy enough that she hoped he'd forgot-

ten her for now. If she didn't eat, somebody would
remind him.

This evening, as on several before, Chithit slipped in
when the door was open. Chithit was not a prepossessing
cat, being long and lean, principally gray, and frequently
battle-scarred. Perielle had never been fond of cats. Her
opinion was based on Alfesian's familiar: a huge, all-
black, longhaired tomcat with a disposition like boiling
lye. But since her imprisonment, Chith had taken to visiting her, and Perielle found his presence comforting.
She cuddled him and whispered how welcome and how
superior he was. After all, he alone had found a way to
visit her, to leave when he chose, and to get along in a
castle now overrun with large, fierce hunting dogs.

Usually, he came in to sit in Peri's lap in front of her
tiny fire and bathe. Tonight he requested food. Being
fed more than she could eat, she obliged. She knew she
might be eating her last meal—in which case she and
the cat would leave the world together—but decided that
was his problem. He seemed far more capable of solving
problems than she was. Tonight he gulped down every
bite she left and licked the plate, then drank an entire
bowl of water. After he washed his face and paws, he
leaped onto Perielle's bed and appropriated her pillow.

Peri was a little miffed and a good deal disappointed.
When one has only occasional contact with a compan-
ionable living being, moments with that individual become precious. She tried to pretend that it did not
matter, but she was only eight, and it did, and she cried
a little.

Having nothing better to do, Peri poured enough wine
into the water to make it safe to drink and took one
gulp. Uggh! She wandered over to the bed and observed
Chith. How odd. She was almost positive he wasn't
asleep. Why was he pretending to be? She sat on the
bed and wondered. She knew that she was watched,
clock around. Did her spies stop spying when she went
to sleep for the night? Well, it wouldn't hurt to find out.
She set her cup on the floor by the wall and curled up
next to the cat.

Planning to remain awake, she was sure she would

fall asleep instantly—the contrary having been her life-pattern for many months. She wished she hadn't drunk the wine. Her mouth tasted awful. They must be using water from the well in the courtyard. How could anyone believe her family would drink that?

The longer she lay on the bed, eyes shut, breathing deeply, the more wide awake she became. If someone had dropped an eyelid, she would have leaped to her feet screaming. The sound of the cat's breathing became loud in the silence. She heard a muffled yawn, a soft scraping—chair on a stone floor? Well, someone was watching from behind the picture at the head of her bed. She grinned. He couldn't see her; she and Chith were too close to the wall. Hm. Is that why Chithit chose to sleep there? She turned over sleepily and wiggled up a little toward the head of the bed, then reached out and circled the cat gently. He rubbed his head against her hand.

Peri realized that she had slept, after all, and that a sound had wakened her. She listened.

"What's the word?" one of them said in their language.

"Asleep. Drank wine with dinner. She'll be out all night."

"Ahhhh. I can use the sleep."

Scuffling noises. Sound of footsteps. Sound of person clearing throat. Silence. Sound of snoring.

Perielle lifted her head. She looked directly into the cat's open, alert eyes. He, too, had raised his head. He seemed impatient.

Peri began to shake a little. She had not the least idea what would happen next, but she waited, tense, ready.

Chithit stood, stretched, and padded to the foot of the bed. He crouched on the edge, tail lashing. Perielle leaned up on her elbows—slowly, quietly.

The cat gave a powerful leap across the four or so feet separating the bed from the wall and drove all eighteen claws into the edge of the tapestry hanging next to the fireplace. Peri held her breath.

Chithit clawed upward until he was just below the mantel. He reached out with his right front paw and attempted to press something—one of the centers of the carved flowers? The tapestry simply moved away from the wall. He could not apply enough pressure.

Perielle slid off the bed and crept to the wall. She put both thumbs on the flower and pressed with all her might.

The tapestry appeared to curve into the wall, cat and all. Perielle slithered behind it. The opening was narrow and not too tall. People much larger than she would find it hard to wiggle through. A soft thud indicated the cat had dropped to the floor. In a moment, she felt his furriness against her ankle. His brief delay had been to find and drag one of Peri's soft boots with him. She pulled it on, then retrieved the second boot herself. As she stood, she felt the end of his long, silk-furred tail against her hand.

He couldn't want her to hold it; she might pull. He hissed softly and whapped the tail against her hand. *Well, I guess he does.* She tried to grasp firmly but without squeezing. He did not go far—to the right, where he scratched the wall. Peri caught on at once. She'd been wondering how to close the opening. She searched up and down and sideways—and found a handle. When she moved it in an arc, the stones slid back into place.

Peri followed Chith into the darkness. The sound of a snore made cold sweat break out all over her body. They turned a corner. The next snore was a little louder. She saw a faint hint of light—one candle in a dark lantern. Not too slowly, cat and girl passed the sleeper. Chith slipped his tail free. He leaped onto a narrow ledge and pawed at something. Groping next to him, Peri located a bumpy leather pouch. Food, she guessed. She slung its ties over her belt and knotted them, picked up the lantern, and took Chith's tail again. He led her on and on, down, at last, down and down and down and down.

The first part of their escape had been through passages built when the castle was. They were old and, if narrow, high enough for a man to walk through without bending. This downward section, leading off from the passageways, was new, rough-cut into earth, even narrower, and little higher than her head. Something said, "Magic" about the tunnel—perhaps she smelled it. People said Mother could.

Dampness on either side and dripping from overhead signaled their whereabouts—under the moat.

Chith swore in Cat. Peri picked him up. He curled around her shoulders making it impossible for her to stand erect. She tried unsuccessfully to move him into a more comfortable position. Sloshing into darkness, she found he had again kept her from harm. The tunnel became lower, smaller, and filled above her ankles with seepage. She splashed on, going as quickly as she could. If she were very lucky, the ceiling would hold, and the tunnel would remain open long enough.

Several eternities later, passing through a tube no adult could have used if not crouched or crawling, Perielle emerged into a large space. Chith jumped down. He seemed to understand that Peri could not go on just yet, and purred loudly. She leaned against the rock at the side of the tunnel and breathed for a moment or two. Tears kept running down her face. She blew her nose. Chith wrapped himself around her legs—wet be damned—and purred even louder. If he had said, "I understand, and it's all right to cry, and I'm proud of you," he could not have made his meaning clearer. Peri sat down, pulled him onto her lap, and petted him.

On and on, darkness forever and ever. But this darkness seemed to be natural and certainly was far larger. Often, she had no sense of walls on either side. Chith never hesitated, but continued as if in daylight on a path he took daily. She fell several times. She pulled Chith's tail more than once, and apologized profusely. They rested two more times, once beside a pool of water from which Chith drank, so Peri drank, too.

The candle in the lantern guttered out. Perielle started shaking and could not stop. They walked on. If her candle had still burned, she probably would not have seen the light ahead for several more minutes. She was too tired to run, but she hurried, hoping. Soon she would be out of this endless darkness. Soon she could lie down and sleep knowing that when she woke, light would greet her. Soon she might be warm again, and unafraid.

Chithit pulled his own tail trying to go faster. Peri thought she would die, but she let go. Perhaps he ran ahead to check that she would be safe.

The earliest hints of dawn drew her to the opening of a small, dry cave. She looked out across the river. Chithit was already asleep on a pile of blankets. Perielle burrowed into the pile and was asleep in moments.

She slept until Chith woke her. He pulled at the pouch she'd stolen from the sleeping guard, and they shared the food and well-watered wine. Peri would have tried to sleep again, but Chith meowed angrily. He ignored her demands to wait until daylight, and led her down to the water. The way he chose seemed impossible, but she would have thrown herself over into the river rather than be left behind. She succeeded in sliding where she could not step, trusting blindly and following the sound of Chith's purr when there was nothing else.

He clawed something at the water's edge. She reached over to find out what it was. Her fingers found cloth, and a cover came loose as she pulled. Beneath was a small boat with a strong rope tied into a ring at the bow. Chith leaped in; Peri wadded up the cover and followed. She released the line mooring the boat to a ring in the rock wall. They wrapped up in the cover and lay in the bottom of the boat, he in the circle of her arms.

The boat slid out into the current, then slowly, almost as if by happenstance, moved closer and closer to the other shore as it traveled downriver. Someone on the shoreline at the bend ahead pulled the rope to which their boat was attached.

They came ashore in darkness, where people were waiting, and she could smell horses. She still held Chith, and only his request could have made her give him up. Someone retrieved the boat cover, wrapped them both in a warm robe, and handed the bundle up to a mounted man. Peri ate and slept again, this time held in some-one's arms as he rode through the night.

In the morning, Perielle came to her senses.

"Who are you?" she demanded of her rescuer—the human one.

"No one you know," he replied. "Who do you think I am?"

One tutor had trained Peri in the intricacies of the Question and Answer Game, in which, though stating only truth, you could keep the other participant from discovering what you did not want him to know. *Careful,* she thought. *He asks the right kind of questions.*

"I don't know," she answered. If he really asked the right kind of questions, he wouldn't accept her answer.

He shook his head and smiled.

Well, that wouldn't work.

She thought furiously for several minutes, then cleared her mind. The man said nothing. He continued to eat his travel bread and leftover rabbit. Peri ate, too, and snagged a whole front leg for Chith.

She kept pushing one idea away, refusing to let it develop into a full thought. *What else?* Something about the sword and the crown. And the cat.

Start with something simple, she told herself. "I think you are a friend," Peri ventured.

"True. To rescue you was not easy."

An interesting answer. The two parts of it didn't go together. See what more she could find out. "That means you are an enemy of the butchers in the castle now."

"True."

Chith wiggled to get his head out, and she felt he was trying to distract her. A different tack seemed sensible. She knew nothing useful about the sword and the crown. But the cat? No matter how intelligent and helpful, cats did not make plans and dig tunnels and arrange boats. While he could be a wizard transformed, it seemed much more likely that he was a familiar, sent by the wizard to rescue her. No sorcerer would do dirty physical work he could make someone else do for him.

"You or someone you work with is a magician, and Chith is a familiar," she said quickly.

The man stopped eating, looked at her keenly with a slight smile on his face, and commented, "Excellent. Which is it?"

"You're not a magician. Chith led me to you, but he's not your cat."

"My cat?" he inquired.

Oh, what he hadn't said. She mustn't let on she understood that lack of answer could mean agreement. "Not that a familiar belongs to anyone, even the magician he works with," Peri went on, fast. "But that's the easiest way to say it." If he thought her stupid or foolish, he might be less careful.

The man nodded. His smile broadened. "And that means?"

Peri didn't answer. She couldn't without scaring herself to death. The little band packed up and prepared to leave. Chith took Peri to a place she could use for a privy and waited until she was done. He led her to where they'd tied the horses. She kept on thinking.

This time, she rode pillion behind the young man who seemed to be in charge. Chith had a lidded basket on the other side of the horse from her seat. Someone's plans had included transportation both for her and for the cat.

I've got to say something, she thought. *It's taking me too long.* "That means," she said at last, "that you're probably a son of a loyal noble family. You're alive because you're studying to be a magician, so you weren't in the battles."

"Well done," he said.

That answer didn't help one bit. It only said she had reasoned well, not correctly. She snorted.

Chith whopped the top of his basket up and put his head out. Peri squirmed around as far as she could. Cats cannot change their facial expressions much, but Chith looked annoyed. He hissed silently.

Peri could not understand why Chith wanted her to stop this line of questioning. She trusted the cat as she did not trust anyone else, so she subsided. Later, perhaps, she would find out more.

"Are you taking me to a magician?" was as close as she could come to the terrifying idea looming in the back edges of her mind. Where else could she be taken? It was hard to see Chithit, almost directly behind her back, but she caught a motion out of the side of her eye. A nod?

The man didn't answer, which Peri took for another confirmation.

The fear took words and pushed out of her mouth. "To Alfesian?"

He nodded.

In a moment, Peri discovered she could breathe. *There, I've said it, and I didn't faint or shiver myself off the horse,* she thought. Such little reassurance was necessary. The magician had eliminated Father. She was the last of the line. She would be in his grasp. What awful things would he do to her? *Stop it*! she shouted at herself. *Think nothing*!

Filling her mind with gray sometimes helped. She concentrated on breathing. A memory of Mother's voice seeped into her mind. "Alfesian is not cruel because he enjoys cruelty. He harms others only if he believes he will benefit. He thinks only of himself, of the most direct way to get what he wants. His one great weakness is that he is unable to understand how others react to what he does. His is the only way." The voice paused, then went on very softly. "I do not know how he would act if someone kept him from getting what he wanted." Peri could only hope she would not find out.

She couldn't help worrying and questioning. Why would Alfesian want her?

Oh! Yes! Alfesian would enjoy making her a puppet ruler, with him pulling the strings. Well, that would be better than being dead.

Her answer felt wrong. Alfesian would not care that he had no legitimate claim to the throne—though he wouldn't leave any loose ends. He wanted the rule, he took it, and that was right.

Why wasn't she already dead?

The Royal Relics kept pushing into her mind. Father had them when he and the wizard disappeared. Alfesian knew where he had sent the king, so he knew where the Relics were. Had he hidden them? Why? That idea made no sense at all.

No, no, no. She didn't know what she didn't know. *Wait.*

Hmm. Adults didn't think children had the brains of rabbits. Let these people think it wouldn't occur to her that they were enemies. If they really were friends, she'd find out soon enough. At least she was warned.

Chith began to purr, warming Peri's insides like a hearth fire. She found herself wondering. If he was a familiar, could he read her mind? Did he approve of what she'd decided? She sensed approval. But perhaps that was just because he was proud of her for having faced her fear. *Anyway,* she decided, *he certainly wouldn't be purring if he were a magician who wanted to use me to take over the rule of the kingdom.*

Alfesian nodded to Perielle's escort when they rode into the camp. He ignored Peri as he always had. They would all have mounted and taken off, but Chith yowled. "Well, make it quick," the magician growled. So she was allowed to relieve herself and get a drink and a handful of food before she was tossed back up on the pillion. She managed not to shiver or to cry. Holding Chith helped.

The company traveled fast and quietly for several days.

Being with Alfesian's group was an improvement over being a prisoner in the palace. The magician gave no orders to the contrary, so his "guest" was properly provided for. A woman was assigned to attend her. Peri enjoyed being warm and well fed and treated courteously—and not having to worry about being murdered in her sleep. She knew that Alfesian, like her former captors, one day would decide that she was unnecessary. But for now, and until they got to where they were going with such stealth and speed, things were better.

During the long and silent rides, Peri decided she had every right not to have recognized Chith as Alfesian's emissary. No cat could be less like the one she remembered. She hoped she'd never need to see it again. One evening at supper she asked about Alfesian's former familiar. "He sauntered away from a sword thrust," someone said. "Guess he thought he was invulnerable."

"But how . . ." she began.

"The new one? Wandered in one day acting as if he's been here since B has followed A."

Peri didn't understand, for she could feel the cat's active dislike of the magician. Couldn't Alfesian? If he did, didn't it matter? She said nothing, but worried and watched. Alfesian's behavior showed only his usual arrogance. Of course, so important a wizard as he would be provided for. On this journey, it seemed he had no need for Chithit's services, thus he took no notice of the cat. Chith stayed with Perielle day and night, which delighted her. Being a sensible little girl, she avoided saying so or showing it. She was adept at not calling attention to things she didn't want noticed.

Late one evening, half-asleep and half enjoying a beautiful sunset, Perielle roused when her rider halted his horse. The company had paused in a rocky area of the high escarpment along which their narrow path led. "Our destination," he said. He gestured out ahead. At the foot of the cliff spread wide, wide sands bordering the wider sea. A causeway stabbed across the glowing waters to a rocky island, seen in silhouette, and more castle than rock. Alfesian's fief, *Hope Denied*. Peri shuddered.

The last flickers of hope for her father's life died. She knew he was not there. She had not let herself cry. She did not intend to cry now. But the realization of her desperate and total aloneness in the world crashed in on her and broke her barrier. Tears burst from her eyes and poured down her cheeks. She sobbed uncontrollably, shaking as if with ague.

Alfesian noticed. In sudden, raging fury, he ordered her to control herself. She cried harder, wailing in loss and fear and dread. He changed from anger to menace. He would not be robbed of his triumph by a blubbering idiot. She would serve his needs, and now, and never again annoy anyone.

The nameless young man who had met and attended Peri braved sure wrath by suggesting they wait until tomorrow, when the child was not so tired, when her grieving had subsided. Alfesian waved a hand negligently and the man fell back, unconscious or worse.

Peri could take no notice. Alfesian dragged her off the pillion and dropped her to the ground. He glared down at her. She saw him through tears, black-rainbow splintered and huge. He gestured, and Peri's screams and sobs became soundless. She must listen, would she or not. Victim of too-long-denied grief before, she became also a victim of terror.

"I am destined to rule," Alfesian pronounced. "Your fool of a father presented me with the opportunity. Who could have known that the Royal Power he disdained protected those ridiculous Relics?" He actually growled. "Rule without them is impossible. When a ruler dies, only his heir can succeed because the Relics will not pass to anyone else." He laughed with a sound of breaking bones. "He refused to name me heir and paid the price."

Peri's despair became unbearable. She would have thrown herself at him, to use her teeth and nails, as she had nothing else. He lifted one finger and she could not move.

"Listen, worthless girl-child! You wonder why you still live. Because you have a duty to perform. I searched until I found my answer. If the heir is too young, unfit, or unintentionally absent, then an heiress will do." Again, he roared with a manic laughter from which his followers drew away. "She may claim the Relics to rule herself or to present them to the next ruler." He leaned over and shouted into Perielle's face. "So you shall. To me!"

He stood and shook his robes free of dust. "Then you will join the other members of your useless tribe. In death."

His gloating passed. Icy rage and disgust replaced it. "You have not long to wait." He glared at her as if she were already dead, then drew himself up. Very softly, but with infinite menace, he whispered, "But first, I Will Have The Relics!" In a flare of hissing robes, he whirled and gestured at a huge rock. It disintegrated with an explosion of thunderbolts, leaving an opening into the granite below. He strode toward it, ordering, "Bring her. At once!" over his shoulder.

Too many terrible emotions devastated Perielle. Her desperation broke the magician's casual bonds. She went from grief and panic into flailing hysterics, thought gone, screams tearing her throat. Exhaustion prevented her manic strength from freeing her. Strong, obedient hands seized her, lifted, held, and carried her after the triumphant wizard.

Below all the evidences of her complete defeat, Perielle had only the inborn stubbornness of her heritage—and herself. Over and over, she repeated, *I won't. I won't. He can't make me.*

He could. Her screaming made no sound. Her flailing ceased. Her arms and hands moved at his direction, then her legs. Set on her feet, she found herself running awkwardly, half-dragged by silent guards.

They entered a sea-cave, water carved, dry now at low tide. A ledge rose above the high tide mark. On it lay something Peri struggled not to see.

She could not even shut her eyes! Closer and closer she was forced toward the hideous corpse of her father. The crown circled what remained of his head. He gripped the sword in rotting fingers. It lay across his torso, half sunken into the disintegrating flesh. Her breath caught in her throat. Her stomach heaved, the scene before her swam. Alfesian ordered her to breathe and, perforce, she did.

The stench completed her undoing. She lost consciousness and collapsed, no longer subject to his will.

Members of the Royal Family were blessed (or spelled) with extreme good health. Thus Perielle's high fever, screaming nightmares, hallucinations, continuous nausea, and only rare moments of awareness caught everyone by surprise. Alfesian announced that her illness was not contagious. Continuous trials at returning her to sense proved unavailing.

Alfesian ceased communicating. Entering his presence filled everyone with unreasoned terror.

He transferred the party to his castle and had Perielle installed in a small tower room. He knew she would not die. In a few days, she would eat and drink a little. Emotional disruption this great was known to initiate Royal

Power, a magic outside of and unavailable to him. No
reference indicated that the onset would cause so great
an illness, but then, no source hinted that it could be
housed in a female. When she was in the last stages of
recovery, he would triumph. He could not believe that
an eight-year-old girl would know what she had ob-
tained. Assume she did? Training in its use was essential.
His magic would prevail. He waited with steeled
patience.

No fool, he realized that again to require her to enter
the sea-cave and confront the corpse would result in re-
lapse. He hastened the natural change death caused in
the body of the late King Morion. It became a desic-
cated, odorless mummy holding no identity other than
that of the Relics. Relics which no one but Perielle could
remove from his keeping. The Magician also continued
his efforts to negate the Royal Power making the Relics
unavailable to him. With continued futility. His state of
mind was not improved by discovering that the familiar
who had appeared so fortuitously had disappeared
equally unexpectedly. Idly, he had considered sacrificing
the cat in an effort to obtain the Relics.

Alfesian discovered that his personal presence in
Peri's room caused her slow improvement to stop. The
Power served only itself and rejected him. In cold fury,
he assigned a series of guards to watch her every second.
The moment she could walk unaided, he was to be told.
He used the time to experiment with methods of circum-
venting her protection. Unsuccessfully.

Within a week, the overwhelming shock that had pre-
cipitated her collapse no longer devastated Peri. From
somewhere, she received the idea that the horrible vision
of her father was only the first of her torturous nightmares. Thus, real or not, she could dismiss it when she
returned to sense and reason. The Power possessed her
and changed her, a little. What it did not do was what
she most wished: remove her responsibility, remove her
terror and dread, make her, suddenly, twenty years
older. Alfesian was wrong in believing that she would
not know what had happened to her; right in knowing
that she must have training before she could use it.

Perielle's return to health took many weeks, much of which time she did not remember. She told no one, even after she was well, but she knew who had helped her. Although no one else ever saw Chithit after his disappearance, she continued to act as if he were still with her. Others believed this one more evidence of her illness. It was not. Sunup to sundown, he remained at her side.

If she had told anyone, it would have been the young man who had brought her to Alfesian's company. He had not been permanently damaged by the magician's spleen, but was recovering from his attempt to help her. He spent each night by her bedside, holding her hand, talking to her. To others, he explained that he believed she responded a little to his voice, and someone must keep her "here," remind her of her place in this plane of existence. She knew he spoke the truth.

Yes, she might have told him as she began to improve, for it was good to have someone care. But her invisible companion warned against speaking, and she refrained. Still, he persisted.

His unawareness of her improvement corrected Peri's assumption that he was in training to become a magician. Even before, she had been able to tell when magic was being done. Such minimal ability certainly would be expected in anyone preparing to work magic. She was embarrassed to realize that she had never tested her assumption. What else had she mistaken?

Who was he? Why was he so interested in her? Why was he convinced that she could respond to him? Why would Alfesian allow him to continue this? She listened, hoping she would hear something that could give her a clue.

Eventually, he ran out of things to say. To continue to keep alive the thread of relationship his intuition told him existed he simply whispered. He no longer censored what he said. One of his unconsidered mutterings gave her the hint. She seized upon it with shock. He called her, "little sister."

Suppose she really was. Suppose that . . . Suppose that the babies she remembered, the ones Mother died bearing, were truly stillborn. Suppose that the babies Father sent away were not younger than she, but *older!* Suppose Alfesian had discovered them. Or this one, anyway. What happened to the other? Alfesian must know that the one who served him had no talent for magic.

Was there a pact between them, or did the Magician think of this one as bait? Was this Carolus, the heir, or Hadrius, the younger? Where was the other one? Was he—the other—still alive? Could this one have . . . ? Or had Alfesian? Wielding weapons negated Royal Power, not Alfesian's magic. She shuddered.

If this one had no magic, did the other one have twice as much? As much as who? Or what? As she? She had no idea how much she might have, one day. Royal Power rarely evolved in women, so little was known of its strength.

Half the time she knew she was out of her mind to think such things. The other half, she knew she was right.

Peri woke. She and Chithit had a task to perform. The steady sibilance of her brother's voice had stopped. He slept, as did her attendant and the guard. She knew better than to deepen their slumber. Alfesian would know if she used her Power. She must use as little as possible, and only for the necessary. She slipped out of bed and dressed. As it had once before, Chith's tail led her into darkness.

The journey was much like the first one they had made together. Here, the secret ways within walls had been made by Alfesian's magic, meant to be available only to him. But hers was the Royal Power, and it obeyed no laws except its own. She guessed that if it chose to include Chith, it had the right. He was, after all, a cat.

The tunnel bored through Magic, and through time/space, through rock rather than earth, and she was glad not to have to bend and wade. Too, she had done something like this once, and now she trusted that the trail would end. She feared less.

And more. She knew they approached the place of her nightmare. She was the one appointed to retrieve the Relics. Only because Chith was with her did she have any hope of accomplishing her task. No eight-year-old girl could rule, heiress or not. What she must do was to decide which of the ones who sought the crown and sword should wear and wield them. The possibility of choosing wrong terrified her.

Whom should she choose? Not the butcher in the castle now. Not Alfesian. Her maybe-probably-brother who had, at least, tried to help her? Who was he? Why had he tried? Could he once have talked a brother through such an illness? Was that why Alfesian allowed it? What did either stand to gain?

The faint light ahead lay in the sea-cave where her father, by Alfesian's treachery, lay dead. The jewels in the crown and the sword hilt glowed just enough so she knew where they were. Chithit slid his tail from her hand and stood aside. She must do this herself.

Only the Relics identified this husk as that of her father. These remains were as organic and natural as wood—and no more frightening or disgusting. Here was proof that her first "sight" could be dismissed as an illness dream. She lifted the crown, then the sword, away from the brittle bones, and watched the image of a body become clean dust.

Light! Light so intense and glaring and filled with such great threat that she screamed. The lightning strike and thunderclap heralding Alfesian's arrival nearly drove her to the floor. Beside him, armed, stood the brother who had no magic, brought here, she knew, by Alfesian. They had made a pact! What pact? Why?

He opened his eyes, closed against the brilliance. He saw her and held out his hand.

"Perielle! To me! I am your Champion. My voice anchored you to reality, as it did our brother, when you each gained the Power. The Magician must not triumph!"

Alfesian's voice trembled the walls. His fury might have driven Peri into the wall, but she was not the target. "Forsworn! Forsworn, King's son."

What had he sworn?

"Not so! Fool! You chose the name by which you

called me. For myself, I swore nothing, thus I am not bound. But you are. You can harm me in no way so long as I do not try to take the rule from you. Triple fool! You shall never have it. I shall hold the crown and sword!"

Perielle still could not be positive, and she hesitated.

Another futile pass of Alfesian's magic washed over her. The false king from the castle appeared, brought here with his men to give her more enemies, more directions to have to guard. War ax raised, the bloody conqueror rushed at her. The twin drew his own sword and leaped to her defense.

Time stopped, for her Power set her outside it. Perielle could only hold the Relics and shake. She must present them to one who could reign, and each of these men thought he was the one.

She didn't. She must make her choice on faith, not on the answer to the last question. Only one individual here deserved her faith.

Perielle lifted her head. She looked directly into Chithit's open, alert eyes. He, too, held his head high. He waited with infinite patience.

She placed the crown on his head. Time began with her motion. As he transformed, no longer cloaked by untruth, he took again his proper shape and form. She placed the sword in his hand. He set it, still in its jeweled scabbard, point downward before them and held her close against him, half-hidden beneath his cloak of silky gray fur. "Forgive us, Perielle," he said. "We could find no other way."

King's Champion took his Place, standing to the right and a step ahead of a king whose sword would never be drawn. Not a hair's difference distinguished one from the other, but Perielle's last question was answered.

Peri turned in the grasp of the Royal arm, hugged as hard as she could, and whispered, "Oh, Carolus."

And all but the Champion knelt to the King.

THE QUINCUNX SOLUTION
by Anne Braude

Anne Braude grew up as an Army brat, and attended twelve schools in twelve years before finally settling down to get a degree in English and history at DePauw University in Indiana. She was a part of the undefeated DePauw team on the *GE College Bowl*, and continued her English studies with graduate work at Berkeley. She is the associate editor of *Niekas*, a Hugo award-winning fanzine, and lives in Scottsdale, Arizona, "slightly to the left of practically everybody."

The Baron was roaring with rage; Master Ambrosius was stammering excuses; and Margaret was wringing her hands—but underneath her apron, where it wouldn't show. (Margaret is my person; she is small and slight, but very brave.) I was prowling up and down the manteltop, weaving in and out among the retorts, alembics, and ill-wrapped packets of worse-smelling alchemical supplies, wondering if it were worth my while to jump the Baron. If I went for his head, he just might be quick enough to seize me and wring my neck; and the rest of him was clad for hunting in leather jerkin, moleskin breeches, and enormous heavy boots. Deciding that it might be a better move to distract him, I tapped a retort with my tail, making it sway. It did not fall over, of course; cats never knock over anything by accident. But the movement caught his eye.

"Wizard! Alchemist! Hah!" snarled the Baron. "You're bloody *witches!* And that bloody-be-damned cat is your familiar!" He swiped a meaty arm at me. I leaped lightly to the floor amid a shower of breaking glassware. Margaret swooped and clutched me protectively to her bosom.

Outraged, Master Ambrosius drew himself up to his full unimpressive height. "Witchcraft, my lord, is mere superstition, and wizardry is a wrong turning leading to a dead end. I am an alchemist, sir, a man of science. I am learned in—"

"In chousing me out of money, you old fraud. You've had damned near a thousand marks of silver off me since I invited you here. And what do I have to show for it? Broken crockery, foul stenches, and lame excuses!" He drew a plump purse from his pocket and flung it onto the table. "There's two hundred marks there, and it's the last you'll get from me. If I don't have *something* from you in a fortnight, I'll have the hide off you— and everything you possess." He looked at Margaret and licked his lips. I hissed at him, and she clutched me more tightly, whispering "Hush, Quincunx dear. Don't annoy him."

"A fortnight, and that's it, old fool." The Baron stomped out, banging the door behind him, and we each drew a deep breath of relief. Margaret set me down, took a broom, and began to sweep up the broken glassware. I whisked to safety under the table and commenced washing away the reek of alchemical supplies. Master Ambrosius, ignoring both his daughter and his cat, hauled out one of his moldy old books and paged through it, muttering to himself.

I don't believe I have introduced myself properly. I am Quincunx. I am a black cat without a single white hair, and I was born to have adventures. . . .

My son, you are a black cat without a single white hair, like your father, which means that you were born for an adventurous life. I can remember my mother telling me that when I and my sisters (both tabby gray) lay snuggled against her in our cozy nest in Tanners Alley. At the time it sounded wonderful. A few months later I recalled it with bitterness, as I lay mewling with pain and cold in a strange gutter, half dead with exhaustion, hunger, and fear. When Mother didn't come home one morning, and we were forced to split up and each seek a separate livelihood, I set out with high hopes, for I believed myself invincible. I was swift, strong, and clever, and I had mastered Mother's mousing skills. I did well enough through the summer and early autumn, what with mice in the harbor granaries and garbage from the shore taverns, but as cold weather drew in, the pickings became leaner. A huge, battered old tom off a timber barge drove me out of my territory; and a bad mistake in judgment led me to tackle a rat nearly my own size, leaving me with a nasty slash that festered. Now I had been chased into a strange part of town by a pack of stray dogs. I had eluded them, but I was starving. Between weakness and pain, I couldn't summon the strength to move. When the footsteps stopped beside me and a man bent to lift me by the scruff of my neck, I commended my soul to Bast and resigned myself to the worst. Mother never said it would be a *long* adventurous life.

The man (you will no doubt have guessed, my good Reader, that it was Master Ambrosius) turned me to and fro, closely examining my draggled fur. "All black . . . not one white hair. Perfect—but rather small." He popped me into his greatcoat pocket and buttoned me into the warm darkness. Having nothing better to do, I curled up and went to sleep.

I awoke as I was being lifted out again. The man set me on the floor and stepped away. "Margaret! Look after this thing for me, will you? It needs food and tending."

Then I was swept up again and cuddled (for the first time since losing Mother) against a soft, sweet-smelling bosom. Gentle fingers stroked me, stopping when they found my infected rat-slash. Dazed by the sudden warmth and kindness, I lay passive as Margaret carefully cleaned the wound and dressed it with a poultice of sharp-smelling herbs. For the next three days I dozed on a scrap of blanket in front of the kitchen fire, rousing only when Margaret coaxed me to lap broth with an egg beaten into it or to swallow snippets of chicken or boiled beef.

On the morning of the fourth day I awoke to full alertness (though weak as the proverbial kitten) and began to explore my surroundings. If I were to rise in the world and become, by Gracious Bast's goodwill, a real, indoor house cat with property of my own to maintain, it behooved me to put my best paw forward and convince these humans they had not made a mistake in adopting me.

As I had never been in a private home before, I was confused by my discoveries. I had better summarize from the advantage of three years' experience.

Master Ambrosius had made his name as an apothecary, the most successful in our town. He lived in commodious rooms behind his shop in the High Street, looked after by his daughter Margaret, a skilled herbalist in her own right. It was she who fed me, healed me, loved me, and gave me my magical name. (A Quincunx, according to one of Master Ambrosius' learned books, is "an arrangement or disposition of five objects [in my case, four paws and a tail] so placed that four occupy the corners, and the fifth the center, of a square or other rectangle [i.e.,me].") She had looked after the house and kept the shop for him while he paid home visits to sick patients (or especially wealthy ones) or compounded his pills and potions in the upstairs workroom. The shop, the kitchen, and the storeroom took up the ground floor; upstairs were the workroom and the bedrooms. I made the ground floor my own domain, dealing with the mice who came to nibble the stores and even the medicinal herbs in the shop. The workroom herbs were safe enough, as I never let a mouse get abovestairs. Once I had the house cleared, I slept on Margaret's bed at night, leaving it occasionally for silent patrols.

At the time I came into the household, Master Am-

brosius was no longer a practicing apothecary, though
Margaret still compounded remedies for those in need.
He had always been fascinated by the science of alchemy,
spending every penny he could spare on books and manuscripts dealing with the subject. About a year before he
found me, he had received a large legacy from a grateful
patient and had taken the opportunity to retire from practice and become a full-time alchemist. My new home
was filled with strange stenches, and not-infrequent explosions sent us running up to the workroom. Margaret
lost weight and I developed a permanent twitch in my
tail. Over meals we were treated to long disquisitions on
the Panacea, which would cure all ills, the Alkahest or
Universal Solvent, and the *Elixir Vitae* which conferred
immortality and could be distilled from the Philosopher's
Stone, the ultimate goal of my master's quest, which be-
stowed unending riches by transmuting base metals into
gold. Margaret listened dutifully, but I paid little heed
to his talk of calcination, sublimation, and albification;
of Sol, Mars, and Mercury; of crucibles, alembics, and
athanors. I opened one eye and both ears when he began
to speak of the Raven, the Green Lion, the Snowy Swan,
and the Toad of the Earth, the Red and White Dragons,
and other such livestock, wondering if they were to be
introduced into my territory, and if I would have to fight
them; but eventually I realized that they were not real
creatures at all but some sort of alchemical symbols.

Margaret often spoke wistfully as she stroked me of
the better times before her father took up alchemy; but
as I had not been there at the time, I had nothing to
miss. Despite the stinks and explosions, life was good.
On a diet of table scraps, plump mice, and affection, I
thrived exceedingly. I well remember the night I proved
my true worth as a house cat, when I tackled the large
rat that slipped through from the cellar somehow and
slew him after a tremendous battle. I laid him out on
the hearth as a present for Margaret, having discovered
through sad experience that she did not care to have
such trophies on her pillow. She praised me extrava-
gantly and gave me a chicken liver. Well contented with
my lot, I had forgotten Mother's prophecy. I was to re-

member it the next day, when I discovered why I had been brought into the household.

Margaret was washing fine linens that morning; the kitchen was filled with steam from the copper boiler and the acrid scent of bleach. I was napping on the counter in the shop when Master Ambrosius suddenly swooped, pounced, and bore me upstairs. This was a quite unexpected development, as he never petted or cuddled me; I concluded that a mouse must have eluded my vigilance. He carried me into the workroom and closed the door, setting me not on the floor as I had expected but on the table next to his alchemical furnace, beside a large open folio. The only other objects on the table were a large, empty crucible and a long, sharp knife. I backed away slowly, stiff-legged, my tail bushed and the hairs along my spine beginning to rise.

Master Ambrosius put on his spectacles and bent over the book, muttering aloud. "After heating for seven days in a sealed retort, remove the vessel and slake the Black Dragon in the blood of a black cat without one white hair."

Well, I may not have understood the science of alchemy, but I certainly understood *that!* The master took a small lump of cheese (a delicacy I adore) from his pocket and held it out to me, cooing unconvincingly, his other hand poised to seize me. I leaped from the table to a high shelf, seeking frantically for an exit, trying to conceal myself among the assorted objects cluttering the shelf (but not, of course, accidentally knocking anything over). The window was closed and latched; there was a hole in an upper panel of the door—the result of a recent—explosion—but it was too small for me. Laying my ears back, I squalled at the top of my lungs. "Help! Help! Someone help me! Margaret! Lady Bast! *Mother!*"

The door flew open. Margaret stood there, her cap half off and her hands dripping. I leaped down and ran to her before Ambrosius could move. She picked me up and began rubbing my chin to soothe me. Her hands were wet and reeked of bleach, but I didn't care.

Master Ambrosius demanded me back, explaining his

intention and reading his text. A horrified Margaret attempted unsuccessfully to argue him out of it as she wiped her wet hands on my throat. When both were out of breath, she carried me over and lifted my head. "Look, Father. There is a tiny white spot under his chin. Your experiment wouldn't work anyway."

He looked, and was convinced. My good Reader, do you think I have been lying to you? Or have you been paying proper attention? As she stroked my chin during the argument, my clever Margaret had *bleached* me. It was then that I knew absolutely that she was my person and that I would never willingly be parted from her.

Well, that was three yeas ago. By the time my fur grew back in its true color, Margaret had convinced her father that the "black cat without a single white hair" was another alchemical symbol and did not refer to a real cat at all. But she could not convince him to give up alchemy, even though the money was running out. Eventually he sold the shop and set off for the Continent, dragging Margaret (and me) in his wake, sure that *somewhere* he would come across the one true text and discover the secret of the Philosopher's Stone. We had run across the Baron in a mountain inn, where we had all been snowed in for a week; and Master Ambrosius' lecturing had convinced that nobleman that there was something in it for *him*. He had invited us for a visit (dragged us home with him willy-nilly is more like it) to his remote estate in one of the lowest of the Low Germanies, set us up in a house in the village, handed over some money, and demanded results. Master Ambrosius had been willing enough, since the Baron's estate held the ruins of an ancient monastery where the legendary alchemist Brother Theodoric had supposedly made either the Elixir or the Stone (the legends were unclear) and left it behind along with an account of how he had done it. Margaret was so numb with homesickness that she scarcely knew where she was. And I go where Margaret goes, though I didn't like the Baron. I didn't like the way he shouted; I didn't like the way he smelled of stale genever; and most of all I didn't like his looking at

Margaret the way that I would look at a plump mouse I intended to gobble up.

So here we are, half a year later. No records of Brother Theodoric have turned up, though we have found the overgrown ruins of his monastery. The Baron's silver has mostly gone on unsuccessful experiments, while Margaret has eked out a meager living for us with her medicinal herbs. We are alone in a foreign land with no way to escape the Baron's grasp. Great and Gracious Bast, I have had enough of adventures!

In the morning, of course, we were all more optimistic. Master Ambrosius took to his books again, sure that somewhere in Rhazes or Geber or Hermes Trismegistos he would find the key he sought. Margaret decided to gather fresh herbs out by the ruined monastery. And I? The sun was shining, there would be mice in the meadow, and Margaret was offered a ride in the back of a cart. I had never seen the ruins, and I have the curiosity of—well, a cat. I decided to set out with Margaret.

Although we started before dawn the next day, when the dew was still on the grass, the roads were dry and the cart made good time. Margaret took her basket down to the brook to harvest water plants, while I prowled the meadow. A nest of baby voles made a tasty mid-morning snack, some compensation for damp grass. Soon I found myself drawing closer to the mound of earth that covered the ruins of Brother Theodoric's monastery—destroyed, some say, by divine wrath at his impious studies. (From my own experience of alchemists, I think it much more likely that he blew it up himself.) It may have been my seventh sense that drew me; it may have been a lust for the wild catnip I had heard Margaret say grew there. But when I saw a flash of white beneath a berry bush, everything else flew out of my head. A rabbit, I thought, or perhaps a tender young leveret—stew for Margaret, who had an unaccountable aversion to eating mouse. I stalked; I crouched; I quivered; I pounced—

On a mole. A white mole.

My good Reader, allow me to digress. Have you ever

wondered why we cats go to so much effort to catch moles and then don't eat them? Especially since moles, as you know if you've ever tried one, taste horrible?

Mice are excellent for food, but moles have *information*. A mouse can tell you where to find things to eat, and gatherings of other mice; but it is basically a party animal, without another thought in its head—as the Old Feline proverb has it, your mouse is more hors d'oeuvre than oracle. Moles, however, *know* things. They move through the deep places of the earth; and what they find, they remember. Cats therefore catch them for their educational value. (If you see a cat chasing a mole, batting it to and fro, catching it and letting it go and catching it again, it isn't cruelty, it's research; the little wretches aren't very forthcoming.)

And white moles are special. I don't mean the business about them granting three wishes to any cat who catches them; that is only a milk-tale for kittens. But they are old—that is why they are white—and they are the repositories of the collective wisdom of their entire mole-system. And the other moles value and protect them. Suddenly I had a brilliant idea.

My catch had gone limp and was whispering to herself in Mole, presumably commending her soul to the deity of moles. I loosened my clutch and addressed her in Common Beast.

"Old one, summon your folk. I am minded to ask a ransom for you."

She lifted her head and wheezed, "I will not trade their lives for mine, cat. Do what you must."

"Now, now. I see no need for bloodshed. I only want information. And perhaps a little assistance. Call your people and let us talk terms."

I will not bore you with the tedious details of the negotiation. The moles knew, and readily described to me, the location of the chamber where once the alchemist-monk had labored; they had explored it for the remnants of certain herbs. But their access tunnel was too narrow for me, and I needed somehow to persuade them to fetch me the relics of his endeavors. The old white mole said the journey was too risky because the tunnel was crumbling away, and she was resigned to death. The plight of Margaret and her father moved them not at all. And although he owned the meadow in which they dwelt, they had never heard of the Baron. His cruelty, tyranny, and general wickedness left their tiny little hearts untouched.

"But he wears moleskin trousers!" I said rather desperately.

That got their attention. The depredations of the molecatcher had been recent and severe, and they somehow got the idea that his sole purpose had been the enhancement of the Baron's wardrobe. I did not disabuse them of this curious notion. A bargain was struck.

For hours I crouched under that berry bush, the white mole held loosely beneath one forepaw, while relays of moles trotted to and fro with gleanings from the alchemist's chamber. Scraps of parchment, fragments of glass, unidentifiable sticky lumps—nothing was of any use whatsoever. I kept trying to explain that I needed something—anything—*intact*. The sun was beginning to decline into the West and Margaret would soon be calling for me. Suddenly the white mole, whom I had believed to be asleep or swooning, spoke up.

"Cat, if you will trust me, I think I can find what you want. Let us go down into the chamber. There is a certain corner which I explored in my early youth . . ."

The moles had kept their part of the bargain, and she was entitled to her freedom in any case. I lifted my paw.

With remarkable speed she scuttled into the nearby tunnel. I waited. Margaret, who had been working her way toward the ruins in her gleaning, reached the foot of the mound with her almost-full basket and began to call me. I knew we would have to leave soon to reach home before nightfall.

There were noises at the mouth of the tunnel. The white mole reappeared, followed by a couple of strong-shouldered youngsters dragging something that clinked against a pebble. I bounded forward.

The white mole turned her blind snout toward me. "Cat, here is the only intact vessel left in the chamber.

Take it; but we moles have a proverb: 'Be careful what you wish for; you may get it.' "

"There is a similar saw in Old Feline. But my person needs help. I'll take the risk—and remember the warning."

Having brushed off as much of its dirt encrustation as I could manage with my paw, I inspected the moles' offering. It was made of some substance that I had never before encountered, seemingly part stone and part metal. It was a tiny flask, not much larger than a baby mouse but much heavier, rounded at the base and tapering to a narrow neck, stoppered and covered with wax. Graven into the wax were strange symbols, some of which I had seen before in Master Ambrosius' books.

With a brusque word of thanks to the moles, I sank my teeth into the wax and dragged the flask down the hillock to Margaret, whose cries of "Quincunx!" had taken on a tinge of panic. It was remarkably heavy. I dropped it at her feet and mewed urgently.

"Oh! Ugh! Is it dead? Quincunx, *must* you fetch me dead things?" She spurned it with her foot. I growled, which shocked both of us. I laid a paw on the flask and batted it toward a nearby rock. Once again it clinked, and Margaret reacted as I had. She pounced on the flask and examined it closely.

"These are alchemical signs. And you found it in the abbey ruins. And—oh, Quincunx! I think this is Theodoric's own seal. The stories are true! This—this may be the veritable Elixir! We're saved! Wonderful, wonderful, *wonderful* Quincunx!" She swept me up and began raining kisses on my nose. I stood it as long as I could. I was starting to squirm free when a hail from the distant road gave notice that our ride home had arrived and was getting impatient. Margaret tucked my find into her bodice and we scampered for the cart.

Once we reached our lodging, Margaret bustled about preparing supper at her father's querulous insistence. (I got chicken *and* the last of the cream.) Once the meal was done and the table cleared, she produced my find. Master Ambrosius did not waste time in thanks or praise but fell at once to studying the seals, shuffling through his books and manuscripts and muttering away as usual.

"Yes!" he exclaimed at last. "It is the seal of Brother Theodoric. And the strange substance of which the vessel is made must be the legendary thrice-tried adamant of which Geber speaks. But the inscription on the seal has been rendered illegible by the toothmarks of that blasted cat of yours [Such is the gratitude of alchemists. —Q.], so there is no way to know what it holds without opening it and testing the contents."

"But, Father, if it isn't the Elixir of Life, what could it be?"

"Like me, Theodoric was an apothecary before he became an alchemist. He was originally seeking the Panacea, the cure for all ills."

"Doesn't the Elixir do that?"

"If you have an illness or a wound, the Panacea will restore you to perfect health, but that is all. The Elixir won't cure wounds or illnesses, but it will prolong life—some say it will confer immortality. And properly used, it can transmute base metals to gold. That is why the Baron wants it."

"I think I'd rather have the Panacea. But wouldn't the Baron be satisfied with it? He could fight his horrid wars in perfect safety. And he could make a fortune as a healer."

"My foolish child, no barbarous Almaine nobleman is going to lower himself by *earning* money. He'd probably toss it out with the rubbish."

"But *we* are healers. If it's the Panacea, we could quickly earn enough to pay him back with interest. All we'd have to do is set up a practice in some large city."

"He'd never let us leave. But take heart, child; this may indeed be the veritable Elixir."

"If it is, he'll probably slit our throats to keep the secret. And that is a very small bottle of whatever-it-is. How far will it stretch? And won't we have to test it?"

They fell to planning a test that would use as little as possible of the flask's precious contents. Master Ambrosius' first suggestion was to cut me with a knife and put a drop of the liquid on the wound to see if it healed.

Margaret objected violently and suggested he use the knife on himself instead. The notion did not appeal. It would be impossible to test for immortality in two weeks; and the contents of such a tiny vessel would be unlikely to transmute enough gold to satisfy the Baron. Finally they decided to put one drop on a piece of base metal to see what would happen. Master Ambrosius broke the seal, which immediately crumbled into fragments, and removed the stopper, which did likewise. He sniffed cautiously at the flask. "Pungent," he commented, and sneezed. Margaret placed the fire shovel on the table, and he carefully tipped out one drop of liquid.

There was a faint sizzle and a wisp of vapor. I leaped onto the table and took a wary sniff, wrinkling my nose. There was a minute hole where the drop had fallen, and the sizzling sound continued. My keen ears caught a faint "Plop!" from under the table, and I dropped down to investigate. There was another tiny hole in the stone floor directly under the hole in the shovel (and the table). Cocking my head, I caught a faint, ever-receding sizzle. The humans dropped to their knees beside me.

"Merciful Mercury! It's the Alkahest!" gasped Master Ambrosius. "The Universal Solvent!"

Margaret leaped to her feet, wadded up some discarded paper, and thrust it into the neck of the bottle, which she placed on the mantelpiece. We stared at one another in wonder and confusion. Not even Master Ambrosius had anything to say.

We knew that we had something of great rarity and value, but in the next few days we were completely unable to find a way to make our fortune with it. At first Master Ambrosius thought it might be possible to put one drop into a large quantity of pure water and use the resulting solution to purify antimony ore, which is the first stage in the manufacture of the Stone and the Elixir; but when he tried it, the drop of Alkahest dissolved its way through the water and on through the bowl, the table, and the floor as before. After this failure he ceased to experiment for a while, stoppering the bottle with wadded paper again and putting it back on the mantel.

Since this warm and lofty shelf was my favorite perch, I had to nap with one eye open to avoid being chased away. As if I, who had found the treasure in the first place, would carelessly knock it over!

It then occurred to him that the Solvent might do something interestingly transmutational to one of the Baron's silver coins, but Margaret absolutely refused to let him try. She had hidden the purse the night before our expedition to the ruins; and no matter how her father stormed and ranted, she would not produce it. I noticed also that whenever he was out of the house, or totally absorbed in his researches, she would surreptitiously pack up more of our belongings in the satchels stowed under her bed. Clearly she was going to be ready to scamper at a moment's notice. Clever as a cat, my Margaret.

The stalemate continued until two days before the Baron's deadline. Master Ambrosius was half out of his mind with frustration and indecision. He had in his possession one of the rarest treasures of alchemical science, and he had not the faintest idea of what to do with it. Or rather it would be more accurate to say that he had far too many ideas and not enough Alkahest. And since the only experiments he had managed to bring himself to attempt had been dismal failures, he lacked the courage to try again. As was his wont, he retreated into his books.

Margaret, on the other paw, was all decision. She had held onto almost all of the Baron's last contribution, doling out a few coins to her father for alchemical supplies—fortunately for us, the village didn't offer much of a selection—and necessary foodstuffs. That morning she confronted Master Ambrosius immediately after breakfast.

"Father, you have *got* to listen to me. In two more days the Baron will be coming back, and we have nothing—*nothing!*—for him. He is a tyrant, and we are completely at his mercy. Do you think that miserable little bottle of Alkahest is going to impress him enough that he will spare us? You may be willing to give your life for alchemy, but Quincunx and I are not!"

Master Ambrosius blinked bleary eyes at her. "Child, you are worrying for nothing. Of course the Baron will appreciate the value of the Alkahest. And in any case, what could we do? We're stranded here till he gives us leave to go and funds to travel with."

"I still have the last pouch of silver he gave us. There's more than enough in it to purchase two tickets on the stagecoach. It comes through the village today at noon. By the time he misses us, we'll be across the border. I have everything packed except your alchemical paraphernalia. And we don't really need that."

The notion of leaving his books and apparatus behind truly horrified Master Ambrosius. Margaret attempted to argue, then to persuade him to pack a bare minimum; but he was angry and obstinate, lost to what little common sense he possessed. He was shouting at her when the door flew open and slammed against the wall. There stood the Baron in all his hairy splendor. His tiny, boar-like red-rimmed eyes glittered, and he positively reeked of genever.

"Well, my witches!" he bellowed, staggering forward and flinging the door shut behind him. "Where's my gold?"

Margaret shrank back into a corner. Master Ambrosius smiled ingratiatingly. "Welcome, my lord. We weren't expecting you for another two days. Won't you have a glass of something?" He stared bemusedly at the breakfast table, which offered nothing but the dregs of a pot of small ale.

"I've been drinking all night. It's gold I want! Gold, or that Elixir of yours. Or I'll skin you alive—you and that damned cat! But you, my pretty," he snatched at Margaret's arm, "you can pay me in other coin. Let's have a kiss for starters." He dragged her into his arms despite her screams and struggles. He was twice her size, and Master Ambrosius could do nothing but wring his hands and plead with the Baron to desist. Clearly rescue was up to me.

The Baron had Margaret bent back over the table and was forcing slobbering kisses on her. I leaped onto the table, rose up on my hind legs, and raked his ugly face

with the claws of both forepaws. He screamed and
lurched backward. I sprang to the safety of the
mantelpiece.

Roaring what I presumed were filthy curses (they were
in Almaine so I couldn't be sure), he snatched a dagger
from his belt. Master Ambrosius moaned and closed his
eyes. The Baron swiped his sleeve across his bloody face
and turned to look for me. I froze, but he spotted me
and flung the dagger with a snarl. It clipped an ear and
stood quivering in the plaster. I squealed, more in shock
than in pain.

"No!" screamed Margaret. "Leave my cat alone, you
animal!" She swept up the only weapon to her hand, the
empty ale pot, and clouted the Baron across the back of
the head. It wasn't much of a blow, but he was off balance from the dagger-throw as well as more than half
drunk. He staggered forward and fetched up against
the fireplace.

I snarled and lashed my tail. It caught the tiny flask
and decanted it squarely on top of the Baron. The make-
shift cork dissolved at once, and the Alkahest streamed
out onto his forehead. He screamed, a thin, high, bur-
bling shriek more befitting a dying vole. His head simply
vanished. It was the strangest sight. All that spectacular
wickedness—melted. Soon there was nothing left but an
oily little puddle; then, nothing but an oddly-shaped hole
in the hearth.

Margaret was simply splendid. She pulled herself together and restored her garments and person to their
customary neatness, washing off every trace of the Baron's touch. (I think she could have done with more
washing; but time was short, and she is only human.)
She straightened the room and fetched a rug from her
father's bedchamber to cover the hole in the floor. She
scolded and bullied Master Ambrosius into packing his
personal possessions and alchemical impedimenta, ruth-
lessly discarding anything that could be replaced later.
We caught the stagecoach with minutes to spare.

We are two days past the Almaine border, and so far
there has been no hue and cry after us. This is a pleasant

inn in which to recuperate and make plans. I am sprawled on a broad windowsill, enjoying the spring sunshine and toying with a chicken wing, idly eavesdropping on my people. Master Ambrosius wants to go to some place called Wittenberg which is famous for scholarship. He has heard that there is a vacant professorship in alchemical studies there, and he wants to apply for it. Margaret, who has developed a good deal of spirit lately, thinks it would be rank folly to return to Almaine lands and is roundly saying so. She wants to go somewhere warm and sunny, perhaps Languedoc, which she argues persuasively is a treasury of Saracen lore. (The Saracens were great ones for alchemy.)

Warm and sunny Languedoc sounds just fine to me. It borders the Middle Sea; surely there will be fish.

My people rise from the luncheon table. Master Ambrosius announces his intention of exploring the town in search of bookshops. Margaret, who has a more proper appreciation of leisure, comes to curl up on the windowsill beside me and bask in the sun. She ruffles my ears with a gentle hand.

"Good old Quincunx. Enjoy your comforts, my lad; you've earned them. If you had not chanced to knock over that bottle on top of the Baron, heaven knows what would have become of us!"

Dear Margaret! So wise, and yet so foolish in some ways. Surely she should have realized by now that cats seldom do things by chance—and we never, *never*, NEVER knock things over by accident.

CIRCUS
by Jayge Carr

Jayge Carr has had four novels published, and stopped counting short stories at fifty. On the personal front, she is a native-born Texan with pioneer roots, married with two grown children, has a degree in physics, and worked for NASA as a nuclear physicist. She and her husband live in an ordinary (except for her disorganized study) house with a cat who makes sure they don't sleep in unhealthily late in the morning.

The circus is coming! The message flashed through the news and personal nets. *Download circus.schedule.rec!*

The circus owners knew the value of publicity. All kinds of teasers could be downloaded off the net. Colorful holoposters and holobillboards appeared on major ground routes and on public buildings in the cities. Commercial channels carried paid ads, and even the blasé news'porters smiled as they interviewed advancefolk on the newest acts added to the circus.

The five ships that brought the circus left colored contrails (thanks to additions of harmless chemicals to the final exhaust) over every populated region of the planet.

News channels covered the landing and unloading of the wagons and then simulcast it all around the planet.

The wagons were all designed on the same plan. The bottom section, including the wheels, were opaque vehicles, concealing living quarters, equipment, whatever. The top was a display platform, with transparent roof and sides (that could be taken off and stored in good weather, or in cities with domes in bad).

Once the circus folk loaded all the wagons, their journey to the first site was also broadcast.

Loi Mandela-Takahuri, aged seven, was watching the parade on the big screen in the main room. "Daddy, are you going to take me to the circus when it comes here?" she called over the intercom.

Her father, working over his computer in his study, groaned to himself. "Can't your mother?" The large white angora cat purring at his feet stirred slightly.

"Oh, DAD-dy." Loi pouted. "You know she'll have an operation or something scheduled."

Boris Mandela-Andrews frowned to himself. She would. Either that or a class she couldn't trade off. Odd how he always seemed to get stuck with the one-off chores involving Loi or the house, especially since his wife had won the coveted teaching channel slot for "Advanced Micro Neural Splicing Techniques." Not that her course hadn't been oversubscribed ever since, but . . .

"Ohhhh!" Loi was watching a screen showing a wagon with its sides up, full of pacing animals. "Lions and tigers, oh my!"

Boris, hearing her because she'd forgotten to turn off the intercom, smiled. Lions and tigers indeed. The smile broadened as he remembered circuses when he was young. Maybe this was one "chore" he'd make durn sure he got "stuck" with.

"Ohhhh!" Loi's voice was filled with awe.

Boris glared at his own screen, with the all important work on the upgrade of the planetary satellite system, hit Save, and flicked over to a repeat of what Loi was seeing. A platform with three clowns chasing a fourth rolled under the camera relaying the parade. The clown in front, all floppy orange shoes and billowing purple clothes, suddenly tripped over something, and rolled across the platform. Suddenly, purple-and-orange was in back of the three pursuers. They stopped, making exaggerated gestures of dismay, tumbling over each other, clouds of colored smoke appearing from their clothes. Boris chuckled, and heard a startled Pur-rup from the floor.

Yes, he'd take this chore! He gave a little gasp as several kilos of cat thumped into his lap. He leaned down to pet the circling animal. The screen now showed a collection of exotics, non-Terran animals, each (he assumed) in its own sealed-off area. He whistled. Whew.

"Look at that, Oberon," he said. "Look at those big boy relatives of yours, fella." Oberon gave the collection of exotics an uninterested stare, and settled down to his usual: a nap. But Boris continued to watch, as fascinated as his daughter. It *was* his turn to take Loi on a field trip, wasn't it?

Harry Harper had been a lion tamer for a long time. His father was a lion tamer, his grandfather, his great-grandfather. When backers had organized the Greatest Show in the Universe some ten years ago, he had jumped at the chance to have an act of his own, instead of being an assistant. In ten years, he had acquired a wife, three children, and a fine reputation of his own.

"It's Harry the lion tamer!" someone on the circus parade's physical route squealed. The sound was coming from above, so he looked upward toward it and smiled and waved at the young happy face leaning precariously out a fourth-story window over the street the circus parade was traveling down.

"Get back in here this second, son!"

"But, guardie, it's the lion tamer! Harry!"

Harry smiled again, as a second face joined the first. Behind him, there was a lion's warning cough.

"Harry!" the child screamed. "He's after you."

It was an old routine. Harry turned. The single lion sharing his platform had slyly slipped off his crimson and black drum. Harry snapped the whip, nowhere near the animal, and it gave a mighty roar.

"Harry!" the child screamed.

Harry posed, cracked the whip in front of the animal several times. With another growl, the lion jumped back on its pedestal. Harry bowed grandly, then, as the tiny red light that said the camera was on him went off, he grinned and winked at the child's face in the window, already receding . . . and threw a kiss at the older face, as pretty a woman as he'd seen in at least ten minutes.

But it was all as automatic as breathing. Inside, he was still in a total panic.

Once the circus wagons arrived at the first appointed site, the next steps were automatic. Sometimes they were in an already prepared auditorium. But this time, they were on a rocky flat outside of a major city, and would have to supply everything themselves. First the wagons were arranged in the back of the flat. All the animal acts were in one sector, and Harry, as the lion tamer, had a primo site in the corner nearest where the big top would be. The autodrive in his wagon parked him neatly, and within a minute, the wagons with the other animals had formed a neat U shape, with his personal wagon at one end.

His oldest child, Linda, spilled out of the quarters under the tiger wagon as soon as it stopped. "Can I help, Daddy?"

Harry, who had slung himself down the unobtrusive "ladder" of neat bars (there was also a trapdoor into the living quarters, but he needed to be outside, not in), frowned. "Where's your mother?"

"Petey's still fussy," Linda informed him.

"Has she rung up Doc?"

"Yes." A shrug. "He says, just a bug. Petey'll be better soon."

Harry smiled with an effort. "Sure he will. Well, cat-meat, do you know which wagon the fence is in, and how to set it up?"

Her lower lip came out. " 'Course I do."

"Think you can do it for me. I want to take another look at Diavolo's paw."

"Yeah!" Her face glowed. Then, horrified, "You don't think anything's wrong with Diavolo. do you, Dad?"

"No." He forced a smile. "But you can't be too careful, and I thought his timing was a little off at the last practice."

"Oh, Daddy." A smile, and a falsetto imitation he knew well. "Picky, picky."

He ruffled her short brown hair. "In the first place, we don't want the local Animal Rights people on us. We know we're careful, in every way, but not all circuses are."

"Dad-DY. We've never hurt or neglected an animal!"

"Right. But remember, 'He who checks 'fore every act, Will live to bow, and that's a fact.' "

"Gonna rehearse after?"

" 'Course. You won't need to wear your costume, though."

Linda giggled, on her way to the wagon storing the electronic fence.

Harry sighed, his face showing his worry as soon as she'd turned her back. Then he moved to the wagon with Diavolo and the other exotics, and started up its outside ladder.

"I watched the rehearsal today." Harry's wife Amii, part of the Flying Romanovs' High Wire Act, was rocking the fretful baby Petey when Harry came in that evening.

"I need a shower," he muttered.

Her mouth pursed. "When did you add that claw on your throat to the exotics' act?"

He shrugged, not meeting her eyes. "Did they hook the water up yet, or am I going to have to make do with a hot air scour?"

"We've water," she bit out. "Harry, when did you add that claw on the throat?"

He stripped off the padded shirt with the high protective collar he used during the rehearsal and tossed it carelessly toward the floor.

"Harry!" Living in small cramped quarters made for some strict rules.

"All right, sorry." He picked up the shirt, and headed back for the personal area.

"You're not going to distract me." She picked up the baby and followed him into the personal area.

He wadded the shirt, and shrugged, not facing her. "I needed something new, something bigger and better."

"I saw where you had him putting the claws, Harry. Your dress collar protects the sides and back, but not the front of your throat."

He still didn't face her, busy swiping his face with a wet towel. "What do you expect, Amii? It's no thrill for the rubes if it isn't bare skin."

"No thrill if it isn't incredibly dangerous, you mean. For heaven's sake, Harry, with the exotics. You know how unpredictable they are."

He ground his teeth. Then, carefully, "Have I ever fussed about you working without a net?"

"That's different and you know it. We're expected to do our act without a net, that's what makes us *numero uno*."

"Right. To stay *numero uno* in my field, I have to keep adding to the act. Yes, this is dangerous. But I have to have it, Amii. So leave it. Drop it now."

She might have kept arguing, but their oldest burst in, carrying a housecat whose head was solid black, but whose color faded slowly from front to back, until the tail was a silvery gray. "Momma, the funniest thing happened just now with Jetlag."

"Oh." She forced a smile. Then, "Not too loud, honey, Danny's still asleep."

Linda dismissed her four-year-old brother's nap with a shrug. "But the funniest thing happened, Mom. Jetlag disappeared."

Amii had to laugh. "Honey, Jetlag's a cat. He's always disappearing."

"Especially when he's exploring a new site." Harry's voice was partially muffled by the wet towel, which also made it sound a little hoarse . . . as if he were frightened, which was nonsense, Amii thought. "Your mom doesn't need to know about Jetlag, she's known him longer than you have," Harry continued, in a more normal voice as he slung the towel over his now bare shoulder.

"But it was so funny, Mom. I was looking and looking

for Jetlag, and calling and calling. But I couldn't find him."

Amii chuckled. "I may not be bred a lion tamer, honey, but I know cats. Jetlag could have been under your feet, but if he didn't want to come, he wouldn't have, and you'd've never seen him."

"I know. But I haven't got to the funny part yet." Behind her, Amii heard teeth grinding.

Linda's eyes were suddenly wide. "Lobo got loose."

Amii stiffened. "Out of the cage loose, you mean."

"Yes. Tandri must not have closed the gaps properly. Anyway, he was loose and wandering around, and I saw him, and I was worried about Jetlag. I mean, he'd make one bite for Lobo. Then Dad—" Her eyes glowed with hero worship. "Dad just sailed through the fence with the big cats, and strolled up to Lobo as though he wasn't the biggest fiercest wolf in the circus. Then the next I knew, Lobo was rolling over for Dad to scratch his tummy!"

Amii rolled her eyes. Harry groaned under his breath.

"And Daddy kept scratching his tummy until Tandri could get behind him with the leash and snap it on. But that isn't the funny part, Mom!"

"I'm glad there's a funny part," Amii got out between her teeth.

"Jetlag came up while Daddy was playing with Lobo, and I think Jetlag was jealous! I was gonna run grab Jetlag, but Daddy waved me back." Her lip pouted.

"Thank God for small favors," Amii muttered under her breath.

"And Jetlag just sat by Daddy's knees while Daddy played with Lobo. Then you know what happened then, Mommy?"

"No." Too sweetly. "You tell me."

"It was so funny, Mommy. When Tandri snapped the leash on his collar, Lobo stood up, and leaned over ... at Jetlag, and then he—" A loud giggle. "He licked Jetlag. On the face. Jetlag jumped back, and shook his head. Lobo just grinned and went with Tandri. But Jetlag kept shaking his head and sort of jumping around, his face all scrunched up." Another giggle. "Jetlag's always washing himself. Why should it bother him if Lobo does it for him?"

"Jetlag's a cat, honey, just like your daddy's a man." Green slanted eyes held a message of anger . . . and gratitude. "Jetlag's a cat, and he likes to wash himself. But he doesn't like other people to do it for him, any more than you used to like me cleaning your ears and so forth for you when you were little."

"Oh." A happy smile. "Do you think Lobo thought Jetlag's a baby, because he's so much littler than Lobo?"

"I expect that's it, honey," Amii agreed. "Though I wouldn't count on it working if Lobo was hungry." Changing the subject: "Have you done your schooling assignments yet?"

"Ahhhhh, Mom. I'm gonna be a lion tamer like Dad when I grow up. What do I need mathematics and all that other stuff for?"

"If you haven't noticed that any of the folk, even the roustabouts, can take over any job on the ship in a pinch, I'm surprised at you, honey. Suppose the navigator is sick. Your daddy or I or any of the others could at least limp us to a port. Or fix stuff, or keep the computer books—" Linda's lip was jutting out.

"Or whatever's needed. And so will you, young lady. Even if you're the best lion tamer in the universe . . . next to Daddy, of course . . . you'll be a danger to the circus. All of us have a lot of jobs. The animal folk less than others, because animals take so much caring for. Suppose something happened to one of your animals, and the vet was tied up elsewhere. You'd have to be able to use the computer files to tell you what to do, and be able to do it."

Linda's lip almost folded over, it was stuck out so far.

Amii suddenly looked dangerous. "Daughter, I don't need to give explanations, even though that one is true. I say, Do it, and that's all you need to hear. Now, scat!"

Linda knew that tone. Lip still out, she disappeared into her tiny room.

"I'd better hear the click of keys," Amii warned.

"Weren't you a little rough?" Harry asked softly.

"Yes," she admitted, and shivered. "But Lobo . . ."

"I was between them before he was close enough to do anything to her."

"I know." She leaned against him. "I know." A soft sigh. "But what about you."

He hugged her. "Cats, dogs, not that much difference. Besides, Lobo and I have been friends for years. He's a lot more bluff than fact, Amii."

Harry was feeding the cats when the giant claw came out and rested just beside his left eye. **well,** said the mental voice he had learned to hate.

"I did what you said," Harry muttered. He knew Diavolo could hear him as easily if he said it only in his mind, but if he spoke aloud, he could pretend that the "exotic animal" was only that, and he was talking to himself or another human.

A chuckle that was half lion's warning cough and half deep devil's cackle. **did they accept? more important, did he accept?**

Harry shuddered. "Yes. He's coming. The one you want. Three tickets, three acceptances. And nobody should notice. I just added the name to the publicity ticket list."

good The claw withdrew into the toe, and the paw moved away from his face. Harry grabbed at it, to have the physical connection, and snarled.

"What about my son? He's still sick!"

The mental voice held both threat and contempt. **and he'll stay sick until I am finished. do as you're told, man.** The "man" sounded like a woman talking about a garden slug, with disgust and disdain. **exactly as you're told and he'll recover. cross me and they'll all die, one by one.**

Harry shuddered and dropped the paw. The exotic, who looked like a sleek black leopard, if leopards came two meters long with saber teeth and eyes of liquid topaz intelligence, drew back his lips in a sneer. Harry didn't need the telepathic link, which only held with direct flesh to flesh contact, to interpret that expression.

"Oh, God, oh, God help me," Harry was moaning as he fed the rest of the animals. While worrying about the sentient masquerading as an animal; and why he wanted one particular man in the audience. In one of the privileged front row seats where he could lean down and touch the acts as they went by.

Or the acts—or one of them—could stretch up and touch him.

Boris looked at the neat printout that told him he had only to show identification at the box office of the circus to claim three seats in the front row center. For purposes of publicity, it said, we have allotted certain prominent citizens free seats . . .

"Well, Oberon." He reached down and petted the large old cat sleeping by his feet. "Your family is going to the circus. Doesn't that sound like fun?"

An excited screep he was beginning to know and flinch at interrupted him, and the new orange tabby kitten his wife had allowed someone at work to foist off on her came galloping in, hit a wall, and used Oberon and then his knee to jump on the keyboard.

"Agrh!" Boris plucked the bouncing animal off his keyboard, and surveyed the damage. "Nuisance, you are NOT to come in here," he told the animal, quivering in its eagerness to play.

"Screep," said Nuisance. (Whatever her permanent name would be, she was Nuisance for now.) She twisted around to lick Boris' wrist, then made a wriggle and landed on the keyboard. Its clicks seemed to fascinate her, and she did a dance on the keys.

"That does it," Boris roared. This time he picked up the kitten and tucked her under one arm. "Loi! Come get this miserable cretin!"

"But, Daddy, I'm doing schoolwork."

"I'm working, too." He was heading into her room. Oberon, who had opened one eye at the furor, closed it. His wheezing snores followed Boris and the wriggling infant cat out the door.

"I'm almost through." Loi looked up from her console, all innocence. "Then I'll take him, Daddy."

"You promised," Boris muttered. He stayed there,

petting the little bundle of mischief, until Loi turned off
her console and held out her hands.

It wasn't until he was back in his study that he realized
that he had, in essence, ordered his daughter to stop
doing her schoolwork to play with the kitten.

But that thought lasted no longer than his first good
look at the chaos caused by the kitten's paws on the
keyboard.

His howl of anguish penetrated even the closed door
of Loi's room. But she only smiled smugly and held the
soundmuffs she had taken off just before letting the kitten out of her room higher, for Nuisance to leap for.

Harry went through his routine in a haze of pain and
fear. Diavolo was getting plenty of pleasure out of playing cat and mouse, with Harry the mouse. The sentient
cat had all his feline instincts. Just frightening the prey
wasn't enough. Every so often, what looked like a near
miss wasn't. Harry was having trouble keeping the angry
scratches and resulting scars from Amii.

At least he could be proud of Linda. About a year
ago, she had worked up an amusing version of his routine using Jetlag the cat. Even Amii chuckled as Jetlag
refused to obey commands, leaving Linda in her imitation lion tamer's gear, begging and pleading, while her
father's animals went through their act flawlessly. Now
it was part of the act, although outside the cage. Linda
was a wonderful performer, and timed the amusing parts
of the act (as when Jetlag hopped off the tiny bucket
and ran away from her) for the parts of his act where
he was merely rearranging the animals.

Linda's act was becoming very popular. He had noticed that it was up more and more on the giant re-
peater screen.

But it made it worse for him, because she now re-
hearsed with him, to be sure she had the rhythm of his
act down pat.

She was very observant. Suppose she noticed something wrong?

Even Diavolo complained about her. A leg touched
his. **get the child and that ridiculous excuse for one of
us out of here.**

Harry pursed his lips. "I can't," he muttered, with a glance over his shoulder. Linda had flopped to the dust of the practice floor, and Jetlag was purring as he made biscuits on her tummy. "I would if I could," he added desperately.

"Did you say something, daddy?"

"Just mumbling to myself, sweetheart. Nothing important."

you have three cubs and a mate. you won't miss that one.

It was a threat and Harry knew it. He straightened. He was panting in rage and fear for Linda. He put both hands on the beast's shoulders and glared into topaz eyes. "I'll turn you in to the authorities!"

"Is that part of the act, Daddy?" Linda had gotten up, and come to stand beside him, Jetlag rubbing at her calves.

Harry still had his hands on Diavolo's sleek shoulders. "It will be fact if this idiot animal doesn't cooperate."

Linda giggled. "You've never given up on an animal before, no matter how stupid."

ape flesh is a treat, Diavolo warned.

"Wild animals put down by authorities don't worry about treats or anything." Harry meant it, and the brain link carried his determination.

"Dad-dy!" Linda wailed

do as you're told and I'll keep my word, apething.

"Daddy!" Linda flung her arms around his hips and howled; even Jetlag was complaining at the top of his lungs.

"Linda." He dropped his arms from Diavolo and shook her slightly. "Remember the rules. Don't upset the animals. I didn't mean anything. He's just stupider than the other animals and I got a little nicked at him, that's all."

Tears streaked down her cheeks. "Real true, Daddy?"

"Real true. Remember, more flies with honey, sweetheart." He forced a smile. "Okay, baby?"

"Um-hum," she swiped at her eyes. "I shudda known you wouldn't do anything like that. Sorry, Daddy."

He smiled his love down at her. "Get back to your

bucket, with Jetlag. We're going to have to take this one from the top again."

His hand patted the giant black shoulder next to him. "This animal's gonna learn." His mind added, **or else!**

Hihihihi! Nuisance the kitten danced around Oberon, long time cat to Boris Mandela-Andrews. The older cat rolled over and yawned. One eye opened. It was as if he asked, *How did you get loose, pest?*

Hi! Nuisance butted Oberon. *Come and play!*

Oberon stretched luxuriously.

PlayPLAY! Nuisance sank her baby fangs into Oberon's ear.

"Rorrrrw!" Oberon screeched objection to the tiny pinprinks.

Haha! Nuisance ran toward the door.

Oberon got up slowly, body language proclaiming, *I'm gonna FIX you!*

Nuisance wriggled with glee. *Chase me!*

Oberon crouched.

Nuisance zoomed back into the room, circled the large adult cat, flicked her tail under his eye, and zoomed back. *Can't catch me, naaa naaaa!*

Oberon thought it over. Slowly, as he did most things these days.

Nuisance wriggled, and made a happy yawn, showing the little fangs.

Oberon rose to his full (and impressive) height.

Nuisance made a cat giggle, and turned her little rump on Oberon.

Oberon made a low growling noise.

Nuisance poised to run.

Oberon jumped up on Boris' empty seat, and then onto the desk. With deliberation, he walked all over the keyboard.

Nuisance, puzzled, watched him.

Oberon rolled on the keyboard for good measure, then jumped back on the empty chair and down on the floor. Within seconds, he was back in his favorite curled-up pose and apparently asleep.

Nuisance watched, mouth open. Then she zipped back in the room again.

Footsteps echoed outside the door. Boris, carrying a fresh cup of coffee and a bag of healthychips, froze on the threshold as he saw two cats where he expected to see one.

"I told Loi to keep you out of—" His voice stopped, and he got a look at the screen. "You miserable animal! I'm gonna fix your wagon!" He stomped over toward the console and the two cats below it.

Nuisance didn't know what she'd done wrong, but recognized the tone. She streaked for the open door. Oberon cracked one eye.

"Agggrgh!" Boris had gotten a better look at the screen. The coffee and chips went on the table, then he sped after the kitten, who was screeping at the top of her lungs in fear.

Oberon shut his eye. Justice was going to be done.

Harry knew something was wrong as soon as he heard the threatening growl. He stiffened his spine, and carefully shut the door as he walked into Diavolo's cage.

Diavolo made a come here gesture, and Harry, his teeth biting his lip, stalked over to stand next to the cat. The chunk of meat he had meant to feed the animal dangled forgotten in his hand.

Diavolo laid his paw across Harry's throat, claws out and one of them over the jugular. **he wasn't there, apething. why didn't he come?**

Harry swallowed, pressing his skin against the sharp claws.

Fury glittered in the topaz eyes. **well!**

"I don't know," Harry said. "I didn't even know he wasn't there. None of the pub seats were empty, so someone was sitting in that seat."

yes. but that person was a coworker of the mate. a healer of all the useless crafts. she only knew that the one i wanted couldn't come, and so the female invited her to use the ticket.

Harry shut his eyes. It wasn't the first time that something outside his control had stopped Diavolo. "I know nothing. I—" He swallowed again. "Get the claws away from my throat, and I'll try to find out."

The claws retracted, but only a little. They still lay, a threat, near his jugular.

Harry pulled his communicator off his belt, and called the cheerful retired clown who now handled ticketing. ". . . old friend of mine, didn't use his ticket, or rather handed it off. Know anything about it?"

The older woman chortled. "Yes I do, Harry. I always keep an eye on ticketing requested by any of us. You're gonna love this, m'boy. It was a cat made them make the last-minute switch."

"What?" He hoped his voice didn't sound as weak to her as it did to him.

"A kitten, really. The daughter was telling me about it while I was punching the seat passes. They have this new kitten, see, and it likes to jump on keyboards. The little dickens got out of the kid's room and into her daddy's office, and gave the keyboard a real workout. Ruined some work he had to hand in asap. Big important gummint secret stuff, according to the kid. He'd about finished it, but hadn't saved when he went to get another cuppa. So the kitten put him back on square one. He backed out of the performance so he could re-work it, madder'n hops he was, and they got a last-minute substitute. The daughter was scared he might make her stay home, too, as punishment, but he decided wasting two tickets was too much."

"I see. Thanks, Angie." He cut off. Swallowed. "Satisfied?"

I must be. but such accidents happen too often.

Between gritted teeth. "I've done the best I can. You can't blame me."

your mind is clean. but why so many strange incidents and why usually involving those miserable scraps you call cats?

"Why not? Most families share their homes with cats. More than have dogs or any other pets."

pah! pets? no, not even those minuscule bad imitations would be what you call pets.

Harry had to laugh. "They aren't. Don't be fooled by

Jetlag, or the big cats. They're circus animals. Most of them like the roar of the crowd. But most cats are totally independent beasts. Humans don't understand them, really, but they like sharing their lives with them. I'll bet even the guy who lost all his work didn't do that much to the kitten, past yelling at him. Cats are—" He hesitated. "Cats. We love them, and live with them. But they are—not pets." He would have shrugged if not for the claws. "It's hard to explain. I get the impression you don't have pets in your culture, and you sure don't have the equivalent of cats."

A snarl. **we eat monkeys. otherwise they are useless.**

Harry was staring over Diavolo's shoulder, an odd smile on his face. "Your loss, big cat." His gaze focused on the animal, and his face was suddenly grim. "Understand this, boyo. I've done what you said. But you're a prisoner here, and you don't get released until my family is well, all of them. And you better understand this. If I die, you'll be put down. Amii doesn't trust the exotics."

A low growl. **the dose your cubling was given was carefully calculated. he will be well before i leave.**

"When?" Harry couldn't keep the eagerness out of his voice.

my mission is over. i have all i could get. on the next space lap of your voyage, you will program one of the lifeboats for me when i tell you to. then your part will be over.

"If Petey is healthy."

he will be. i must report, so i must survive.

Suspicious: "What report?"

Another devilish cat chuckle. **nothing to worry you, apething. now. i have found too many strengths in your people and not enough weaknesses. so our people will meet yours openly and then only to trade.**

"Oh, God!" Harry sagged against the black shoulder. "You're a—a scout. A war scout!"

what else? Diavolo pushed, and Harry crumpled to the flexifloor. Diavolo stood glaring over the trembling man, and then laid a paw on his chest. **i like you like this. your people are weak, but your defenses are *strong. this last one might have told me different, but without him i still have enough. you have the technological edge, so we will treat you carefully.***

Harry swiped at his eyes and sat up. The paw was still on his chest. "I thought you were like our cats. Independent. I thought you were doing it on your own, for meanness, pure cat maliciousness."

you are weak and stupid, apething.

"Not that weak!" He spat in Diavolo's face. "If I'd known what you were up to, I would have killed you, or tried to, whatever you threatened my family with! You—" His mouth worked. Then, low: "I will kill you!"

The topaz eyes held his, solemn now, and intelligent. ***yes, you can. it was a risk i always had to take. if i kill you, i die. i know that. but my report is good, apething, good for your people. you've picked rich worlds, apething, juicy worlds. and who knows what lie beyond them. without my report, my leaders may look at the glorious worlds you apethings hold and try to take them and you anyway. who knows, they may succeed despite the strength i detect in you now.***

"They won't." Harry was certain. "We're different in wartime, cat. Your folk won't stand a chance!"

you believe it, and i believe you. it is the missing factor that didn't make sense to us. yet we'd have the advantage of surprise. who will believe you if you survive and tell about my people. so, apething, kill me and a lot of your people will die for nothing. send me back and your people will not be threatened. Diavolo grinned another cat grin. ***and the war resources of my people will be saved to use against a weaker enemy, which is what i want.***

"I want to kill you."

but you won't. i begin to understand your different breed of courage. when you let me do what i did to you, it was a form of courage. none of my people would have knuckled down like you, for what you saw as a higher cause, unless they were cowards and only allowed to live as long as they were useful. but you were in truth being brave, enduring pain and humiliation for a higher reason. my people must think much on this.

"Think hard, cat. If I let you live now, it's not coward-ice, it's to protect those of my people who would die if your people attack."

yes, i see now. i think your people would be safe even if i had found more technical weaknesses. Dia-volo's head went up. He had heard, before Harry did, the sound of childish footsteps, and an imperative cat's MeOW. **but i don't understand your relationship with the nithings you call cats.**

"Don't worry, big cat." Harry used the massive shoul-der to heave himself upright. He gave the big sentient a twisted half smile, leg still touching so they had contact. "Neither do we. Sometimes I think they run us."

As his leg moved, he caught a last message. **it almost appears so.**

Then there was a knock on the cage. "Daddy, you okay? You been in there a long time."

"Mew-urrrrppp," added Jetlag.

"Everything's okay, honey. I was just—" He laughed suddenly. "I was just discussing the state of the universe with ol' Diavolo here."

"Oh, Daddy!" She sounded just like Amii, sometimes, Harry thought happily. "You're so silly. Stop telling Dia-volo how the universe runs, and come on. It's lunchtime, and I'm hungry. So is Jetlag."

"Jetlag's always hungry." Harry looked down at the relaxed exotic, sprawled in a cat's easy, boneless pose. "Just keep your word, cat, and I'll keep mine."

Diavolo yawned, and curved around to lick his privates.

In Boris' study, Oberon was also licking his privates, to finish a long luxurious bath. All was right in his home, his world, his universe. Which was the way it should be. All cats knew that!

TYBALT'S TALE
by India Edghill

India Edghill's interest in fantasy can be blamed squarely on her father, who read her *The Wizard of Oz, The Five Children and It*, and *Alf's Button* before she was old enough to object. Later, she discovered Andrew Lang's multicolored fairy books, Edward Eager, and the fact that Persian cats make the best paperweights. She and her cats own too many books on far too many subjects.

One of those who lives in the land of Always Night, where the moon never sets, is Tybalt, Prince of Cats. He is Prince only, for cats have no king. A cat speaks for himself.

As Prince of Cats, Tybalt is proud indeed, for a cat is prouder than Lucifer in all his glory. "Proud as a cat," they say in Queen Persephone's dark kingdom. "Proud as Tybalt."

He cannot be outstared. Make a cat blink first, and you have won; but cats cannot abide losing. Even the least kitten, whose eyes are still foggy with blue, can stare down a king. Tybalt's gaze has made basilisks turn aside their heads.

Tybalt walks by day, when he chooses. More often he walks by night, for then all ways are open. A cat walks by himself, and all places are alike to him. Once Tybalt told this to a mortal man, who wrote it down that all might read and take heed of it.

It is true, when a cat wishes it to be.

Tybalt looked at the smiling moon, the Lady who had made a pact with them at the Gates of Day and Night, and had given cats her eyes. Coin-gold eyes; moon-round eyes. Cat-eyes, to see in dark and light.

And what Tybalt saw now was roads through day and night that he had walked time and time over. "I am bored," he told the moon. "I would go a-roaming, and there are no new ways for me to travel."

The Mother of Cats says little at any time, and that little only silken hints, whispers through moon-silvered leaves. She veiled her face, and was silent.

Tybalt sat, and yawned, and thought. Once he had roamed the mortal world for his sport, but it had been long, and long again, since he had done so. It was an unlucky road to walk now, so the tales and gossips said. Tybalt smiled, and uncoiled to stretch long and tall.

"The Prince of Cats makes his own luck," he said. "I will go and walk among my little cousins in the Lands of Men. Perhaps it will amuse me, for a night."

He stood upon his castle wall on two feet; he landed on the path on four. He would go velvet-footed down forbidden paths tonight. A cat walked where he wished; the Prince of Cats could do no less.

Cathy was not and never had been superstitious. A person named Catharine Courtney Carrington, with all that implied, had enough problems without adding to them. A black cat crossing her path didn't worry her; black cats were a positive godsend compared to muggers, street people, and other delights of modern urban life in New York. It was the cat who needed to worry.

Sleek as jet in the harsh uneven glare of the street-lights, the cat walked as if he were king of the side-walk—or of all Manhattan, Cathy thought with a smile. Not a streetwise cat; he was too clean, too cocky. Street cats hugged shadows, shunned humans. A house cat, then, either escaped or released, and one about to get a series of rude shocks.

"Be smart, cat," said Cathy. "Go home, cat. You won't like it out here."

Her voice echoed slightly in the night air, and she looked around automatically. Her apartment was in a "good" section of the city, but she still didn't like being out on the street alone this late. You never knew ... and there were a lot of crazy people in the world today.

The cat stopped and turned, one paw curled in mid-step. He regarded her with eyes as round and unblinking as coins. Golden coins, gleaming hot in the dark quiet street. Then he smiled. Cathy could have sworn he smiled at her; a trick of the halogen lights.

She sighed. "Okay, damn it," she said. She was a sucker, but she couldn't just leave him. She'd take him home with her, and advertise for his damn-fool-stupid owner. "Here, cat." She held out a hand and made the sort of noises usually considered attractive to felines.

They were not attractive to him. Cathy sighed again and moved slowly and carefully toward the cat. "Come on, stupid cat. Come to Cathy ... who's just as stupid as you are—you can't stay out here, poor baby, you'll get run over—"

He waited; Cathy came up to him and crouched down. "Nice boy," she said. "Good cat." It seemed oddly inadequate as she looked into the black cat's eyes. Hot eyes. Eyes full of—what? Wildness? Intelligence? Glowing—

She reached out and slowly put her hands on him. Fur over muscle; softness sliding over resilient firmness. A moment's tension, testing; would he let her pick him up?

He would. Cathy gathered him up, wondering where a cat really put its bones when it relaxed in your arms like that. "What am I going to do with you?" she said. "I've already got two cats. They'll kill me."

The black cat purred and rubbed his head on her hand. "Oh, shut up," said Cathy crossly. "If you'd stayed where you belonged, we wouldn't be in this mess."

"That's right, lady. Now do as you're told and you and your kittycat won't get hurt."

Cathy froze. She didn't care if the object touching her

back was a gun, a knife, or only a rolled-up newspaper.
The mugger had come on silent feet, and could hurt or
kill her and be gone as swiftly and silently. All she had
was a cat. If only he were a dog, preferably a pit bull—

"Just stand real still and drop the pocketbook."

Cathy carefully juggled the cat and her pocketbook
until she could ease the strap off her arm. The pocketbook hit the sidewalk and disappeared from her line of
sight. The cat was oddly still in her arms. His tail hit her
ribs with a solid thump every other second. That was all.

"Okay," she said. Her voice still worked, which was
a nice surprise. "I did what you said. Take it and go
away, please."

He didn't. Fingers on her neck—fumbling for her gold
chain—at least, she hoped that was what he wanted. She
couldn't breathe, or move, or hear anything but blood
pounding through her body, hard enough to shake her
bones—

Then there was clawed pain burning her arm and a
flow of dark fur up her chest. Small pain again, as the cat
used her shoulder as a launching pad and she staggered
forward, fell to her hands and knees. Noises from behind
her. Unpleasant noises. A pause; stillness. She was afraid
to move; afraid not to.

"You can get up now. But don't look around." A new
voice. Low, intense—amused?

She pushed herself to her feet, automatically grabbing
her pocketbook when her numb fingers touched it. "The
cat," she said, gasping for breath. "The cat."

Laughter behind her; a rich purr of sound. "Don't
worry about the cat. Go home, Cathy. Run."

A hand strong between her shoulder blades, pushing
her forward. Cathy ran. She didn't stop until she half-
fell up the steps to the door of her apartment building
and grabbed the outer door. It took two tries to get her
keys out and into the lock. When she had the outer door
safely open, Cathy sucked in a deep breath and turned
to look back down the block.

There was nothing there. Nothing, and nobody. At the
far end of the block, where it crossed First Avenue, a
man with a pair of small busy dogs was entering the

street. Halfway down the block a dark blotch marred the pavement. From this distance, it could be anything. A splash of blood. A rag. A shadow.

Cathy flung herself into the tiny lobby and slammed the door behind her. One more door between her and inside, and real safety. She turned, key ready.

The black cat sat before the inner door, still as night.

Cathy gasped, then began to laugh in a way that was not quite hysterical. "You're smarter than I am, cat, and braver, too, and if nobody claims you, you're mine, damn it. Come on in. You've earned it."

Sleep did not come easily that night, and when she did sleep, she dreamed. Nightmares first; she expected that. Horrors chased her through empty streets, had their hands on her, she would die of fright and could not wake and save herself . . . but then there were other hands, gentle hands to stroke away the fear, and change her nightmares to waking dreams.

Eyes like hot moonlight, gold on glitter-gold cutting light to pieces and throwing it back at her. Hands like strong velvet on her body. Skin fur-soft, fur-supple. A dream not long enough. Only forever was long enough.

"No. Don't do that. I don't want to wake up."

"You are awake, Cathy. And the moon is setting. It's time for me to go."

"I can't be awake, or I wouldn't be doing any of these things—you're laughing at me. Stop it."

"Good-bye, Cathy. I thank you for your kindness to a stranger."

"No, wait! I'm awake?"

"As awake as you will ever be."

"You're the—the person who saved me tonight, aren't you?"

"What do you think?"

"I still think I'm dreaming and that you're laughing at me—but if I'm not—don't go. Stay. Please."

"If I stayed here when the moon had set and the sun is high, I would be very little company for you. There are pleasures of the night that may not be indulged by day. I will kiss you good-bye, and you will kiss me, and then I will go. I wonder if you will remember me, when the sun is high? Theories differ on that point."

"I'll always remember you. Will you come back? Please say you'll come back!"

"I may. If the moon is full, and you remember—yes, I will come."

"How will you know if I do?"

"Try leaving out a saucer of milk."

In the Lands of Men the moon is full each month. And each month for many years Tybalt was to walk softpawed down the ways to the room where Cathy waited for him in the moonlight. For Cathy never forgot, and Tybalt honored his promise, although, as he would say if questioned, he was not overfond of milk.

As for why he went at all, Tybalt had a cat's answer.

"I am a cat and all places are alike to me," said Tybalt, Prince of Cats. "But some places are more alike than others.

"And she was kind to cats," he would always add with a cat's smile, which may mean much or little. "She was very kind to cats."

THE TALE OF THE VIRTUAL CAT

by Heather Gladney, Don Clayton, and Alan Rice Osborn

Heather Gladney is the author of the *Teot's War* series. She has a degree in pomology, which enables her to work in menial jobs to help support her writing career. When not around a nursery, she is likely to be found in the company of wild and exciting men, but still finds time to write. She lives with two cats, a blue-eyed Siamese and a 22-pound Maine Coon.

Don Clayton is a native Southern Californian, but is not holistic, vegetarian, nor does he own a hot tub. The bulk of his writing can be found in legal documents, but he enjoys very much the opportunity to indulge in his love of science fiction and fantasy with his friends. He rooms with a humanoid, Theresa Brooks, and currently six felinoids: Vicious, Demon, Black and Blue, R. K., and Anastasia (who named herself).

Alan Rice Osborn is a Ph.D candidate in geography at the University of Oregon. He has published short stories and poetry, as well as articles on fungal disease and alternative medicine. He was nominated for the 1995 Rhysling Award for science fiction poetry. His primary felines are Gilbert, who sings, Sullivan, who is going bald, and Tigerlil, a.k.a. "The Mad Rabbit."

Impossible fingers extended, bent, and moved forward into the chest cavity. "The heart muscle is exposed." The voice was authoritative, each syllable clipped. "At this point the patient would normally be on full support." Fingernails sharpened, narrowed, spread, and gripped.

Doctor Mary Rose Henderly had a reputation. With the coming of VR operating theaters, a new class of surgeons had invented themselves, a fusion of miniaturist, mechanic, programmer, surfer, and lacemaker. Getting respect in this company said something about surgical style. Mary had fans in the industry.

Rather than using the usual armamentarium, Mary created a cartoonlike environment where the parts of her virtual body could become bone saws, catheters, suction tubes, syringes, and clamps. It led her to demand new tools and reinvent old ones. On one memorable occasion she startled her coworkers when she appeared to become a Chinese pagoda. Flying buttresses became ornate spiderlike arms wielding scalpels and clamps, while miniature bath attendants, clothed in surgical greens, sponged during a lengthy artery rebuilding.

In a real-time operation, banks of microtools would be delicately deployed. They were idle now. This latest simulation was an operation she'd performed many times. As usual, biotelemetry and commentary were recorded for use by the tech staff. She hated that—her tapes tended to get pirated and played at inappropriate times. Bootlegs of her comments during a reconstruction on the C4 and C5 vertebrae, which contained the spinal nerves to the groin, had enlivened a number of parties, and caused intense speculation on which elected official had such interesting problems. She'd created tapeworms to search and destroy that one, but there were still encrypted copies circulating on the Nets.

She caught a sudden motion out of the corner of her

eye. "We've got company," she snapped. She shifted her frame of reference, but it was gone. What she did see was dreadfully familiar. "Vicious little—no, we're losing it." Snow blurred the edges of her imposed reality, and white-noise interference reached inward. "Too late. *Nice* new cage, guys—that's definitely a Mouse. Just like every other damn time. The edges of the imagery are collapsing." Her visuals grayed and faded.

A disembodied voice came from the ceiling, and through Mary's headset, "Can you advise as to the cause of system failure?"

She resisted the impulse to hurl the VR helmet away. *Her* equipment wasn't the problem. She had little patience left for stupid questions. Or the tech staff's dead-end simulations. "Tighter cages," she growled, "and smarter Mice."

Slamming the lab door didn't help. She stormed down the corridor, avoided the elevator, and took the stairs a stomp at a time up to her office on the second floor. She thumped down on her office's VR couch and threw herself into her favorite aggression-release environment: A dimly-lit place where each skittering, scattering, skulking, furry thing made a satisfying crunch under her cleats. She'd created the place especially for times like this.

Her breathing became more relaxed. She shifted to monitor the lab techs' most recent variant of her simulation. Sometimes a Mouse showed up during a test, sometimes it didn't. As usual, there was no pattern. Despite the exaggerated promises from downstairs, their stats were dismal. Their latest cage was no more effective. Depressing.

When she finally dropped out of the Nets, it was late. The building was dark; everybody had left but the lab staff. They were still downstairs with Lenny Houge, the operations director, trying vainly to justify their existence. Mary was starving, but she didn't want fast food. She knew where to get real cooking, and a sympathetic ear.

"Bev? Mary. I'm sorry, it's been a while, but listen, have you eaten yet? I've had a day that could etch glass.

Can I come over? I can bring something or . . . Thanks.
I need to talk to somebody. Somebody who *doesn't* have
a cunning plan to waste my time on."

Mary's opinion of her sister's neighborhood hadn't
changed: call a SWAT team and get out the body armor.
Even the junkies moved out, she thought. *Find a better
street, Bev.* She knew that wouldn't happen. The house
had belonged to their parents. It was big, it was cheap,
and it was comfortable. Mary was just afraid the place
was going to end up a statistic.

Beverly had learned to be frugal after their parents
died. She'd left school to keep them going after the in-
surance money ran out. She'd made Mary's education
possible. Mary felt guilty about it, which annoyed Beverly. She'd been trying to convince Mary for years that
she wasn't a martyr—she made fun of it. Mary knew
better. Whenever she came back to her parents' house,
she remembered it all too well. She hated coming back.
Surgeons hate places where things have died.

At least the inside was different now. Off the street
and up the cracked concrete steps, the door opened into
what was definitely the home of an accountant. No other
profession breeds such obsessively organized rooms.
Beverly's rooms were always ready to act as gracious vid
backdrops for her professional consultations. Even during lean times, she would go without lunch for a week
to buy a vase "a shelf just cried out for." These days
she had expanding collections of curios. They were all
meticulously labeled and cased against the careless depredations of various interested cats.

Mary's own apartment contained three pieces of furniture, bare walls and bare floors. She liked it that way.

"Let me punt Dickens," Beverly said at the door,
doing a reflexive foot slide to contain the cat. It wasn't
working.

"Thanks for having me over." Mary helped her form
part of a human wall to block the door. "I don't know
what I'd have done if I had to go thaw dinner alone."

Beverly finally scooped up the cat. "I've been meaning
to have you over for a while anyway. I found a new way

to torture Dickens while I cook. Found an old incubator in a thrift store—you know, the clear polymer containers with the rubber-sleeved holes on the side for your arms to go in? I've taken to cutting meat inside while Dickens dances around on top trying to find a way in."

Mary smiled. "So I'm not the only one with the experimental spirit." Mary enjoyed watching her sister's relationship with a furry roommate, but she knew her own schedule would never allow her to adopt one of her own.

"Dickens is such an *inventive* beast." Beverly draped the cat over her shoulder. He looked perfectly harmless, except for the rakish tilt of his whiskers. Purring, he squinted his eyes nearly shut, looking at Mary. Mary often brought crab puffs and shrimp bits and other feline delectables. "The little brat reminded me of it. I originally thought it up back when I was taking care of six of them—the brutes were stealing from my cutting board fore and aft. But I couldn't find a box like this until now! Think of it—a cow aquarium."

"Steak-in-the-box," Mary said solemnly. The cat blinked at her, and yawned widely, stretching and sprawling in Beverly's grip. His pink paw bobbed in the air as she walked away from Mary.

"Now," said Beverly, "How badly do you need something to drink? Wine? Or something heavier? Something with paper umbrellas? I think I have a hollowed-out coconut somewhere . . . Paper hats, helium balloons? No? Martini, shaken, not stirred? Hey, I've got a bottle of Sambucco that creates its own gravity . ." she trailed off.

Mary settled heavily into an overstuffed sofa. "Scotch will do. I'm free for a couple of days until they can reprogram the simulator, and I have every intention of getting a decent night's sleep. Even if it's passed out on your floor."

"Oh, nooo, you can't!" said Beverly in mock horror. "I haven't mopped it yet!" She put Dickens down on the shining parquet, brought Mary her drink, and sat down, elbows on knees, on the ottoman across from her. "You sound dreadful. Can you tell me what happened?"

Mary stared absently at a print Beverly knew she hated. Her tone was flat. "We tried something today. I thought it might finally work. It didn't. If it'd been for real, I'd have lost a patient."

"Do you know yet what went wrong?"

"Mice." Enunciating deliberately, Mary said, "They're called Mice. We have the most sophisticated equipment in medical history, decades of research, countless billions of credits, and Mice come along and degrade the code. They can destroy even the most secured realities. Stupid, repulsive, little make-believe Mice."

Beverly shook her head. "Shocking attitude—I can hear Walt Disney spinning in his grave. I've never heard about Mice."

Mary snorted. "I'm not surprised. Not *really* a feature they want advertised. Bureaucrats." Both of them were silent for a moment. Mary went on, "Did you ever use a PC?"

"A what?"

"A 'personal computer.' You remember from science class? No Net, no VR, just a box with a little flat info-screen and wiggly lines and stuff? Okay, well, they used a pointing device to move around the screen. It was small, it was gray, it had a cable like a tail, so they called it a 'mouse.' You used to see them up until twenty years ago. They were used in the initial setup of the Nets."

The cat brushed Mary's shin, demanding attention. She gave Dickens a distracted pat and took a drink of her Scotch. "Now, here's where it gets amusing. When the photonic mains were latticed, a mouse interpreter was in those initial formatting commands. Which was fine. But then some irresponsible little hacker forced a linkage with the mammalian databases on lab rats and mice. Then stupid techs tried to fix it. And that really did it." She got angry again, remembering disasters.

Beverly murmured in dry agreement. Sorting out other people's messes was three-quarters of her job.

Mary sat back and finished her Scotch. She sighed. Then she reached down and gave Dickens' back a good scrubbing. Dickens arched his tail happily and made a furry comma around her leg.

Beverly smiled inscrutably into her Scotch glass.

Mary went on, "Programmers couldn't remove the

problem without relatticing the operating system. It's not urgent for most uses. You wouldn't run into it because most of the time it's hidden, but whenever the architecture is asked to create a complicated experimental construct, something sophisticated enough to require a security matrix—say, traffic control, computerized sea-walls, high-atmosphere solar power or," she scowled, "high-level surgeries—it bloody well creates a Mouse and drops it in. Some programming glitch makes a fuzzy sort of a field or matrix or something. Totally random input. I've been fighting it for a year now, ever since we got that new VR suite. You remember I was so excited because I could try out lots of new ideas? Yeah, well, the place is elaborate enough to get into system trouble on the mains and generate Mice. They creep into the imagery and make the VR collapse. You lose control. Sometimes patients."

Beverly said, "If Mice got in back *then,* can't somebody nowadays take them out? Invent some type of, oh, what's it called, tapeworm? Antivirus? Is that the term? Isn't there any way they can fix it along each of the mains?"

Mary shook her head. "There's no center. A main's pathway changes with relative usage, and the operating system is distributed into something like a billion nodes, each one capable of reviving the system in an emergency. Nobody knows if we can shut it all down to relattice. The security is absolute. Each command node is blinded and quantum encrypted; any attempt to alter the basic instruction set is automatically rejected."

"So you're stuck with Mice."

"Yeah," Mary said, "Mice and dead patients."

Beverly got up and shuffled through her laser cubes until she found something she thought would be soothing, understated, cheerful. She tossed it into the field for play. "Well," she said, looking at Mary's glass, "someone needs a refill."

When she returned with their drinks she decided to try more bluntly to cheer her sister up. She threw her shoulders back and her voice took on orotund tones. "Sit back and I'll tell you the wondrous tale of 'Dickens, the Mouse Slayer, Scourge of All that Scuttle and Scamper,' " and she proceeded to tell the kind of stories that, were the subject children, might be inflated by proud parents for an indulgent audience. On cue, Dickens jumped up on Beverly's lap to receive praise in person.

"Ah, there you are, Mighty Hunter." Beverly stroked the cat, who curled up and purred. The innocent little tabby looked nothing like the Four-Footed Terror Tiger of Beverly's story. "Yes, the Universe of Rodents Trembles in Fear whenever the Great Mouser ..." She stopped. "Oh. Oh, my. Mary, I think I just had an idea."

Mary had to laugh at the look on her sister's face. "What are you talking about?"

"Dickens. Dickens is the answer!"

"The answer to what? Where hairballs come from?"

"No, no, no, you don't understand. Dickens. *The Mouse Slayer.*"

"Yeah, you just told me all kinds of stories—"

"A cat. Use a cat! A lovable, cuddly, affectionate, bloodthirsty, devious little carnivore of a cat!"

"For what, surprises in slippers?"

"Don't you see, Mary? Put a cat in the Nets!"

"What?"

Beverly waved away the lack of comprehension. "It's downright elegant." She ruffled Dickens' fur. Oblivious to the conversation, he had rolled around, chin up, and gone to sleep. "Think about it, Mary. Who's better equipped? Cats have been catching mice since Adam and Eve got their eviction notice!"

"But—"

Beverly patted Dickens' loose forepaws. "Do you think the Egyptians domesticated cats because they were fond of fur-balls?" Her voice became playful. "They *liked* cat hair on their furniture? They didn't have enough sand for litter boxes? You have grain, you get mice, you find a cat! You told me once that VR links with animals are feasible—you said they tested on primates. They use it with disabled children in rehabilitation. What's so different? What have your techs tried so far? Programming mousetraps? Maybe a VR cheese world to distract them?"

Mary's sour look showed this was closer to the truth than she was supposed to admit.

Beverly laughed out loud. "Look at Dickens. Look at his whiskers twitch. His claws grab. He chases mice in his *sleep*, for God's sake. Dickens is the answer! Dickens is the answer to all your problems!"

"Uh, Bev, not that I'm trying to be negative or anything, but how much did you have to drink before I got here?"

Beverly laughed, and eased the cat off her lap. Dickens was so visibly annoyed at being dislodged that Mary laughed, too. "Come on," Beverly said. "Let's go pound the pepper steaks. You've *got* to see the acrobatics Dickens gets up to with the box. We can watch him try to find his way *into* a locked room mystery. While we annoy *him*, I'll annoy *you* with my cunning plan."

Under the weight of a mild hangover, Mary thought about their conversation in her office the next day. It should be possible to put a VR link on a cat, but what could a real cat do to a VR Mouse? Would VR Mice know that they were supposed to be afraid of cats? Would placing cats in the Net just compound the situation? She remembered dinners with her sister when Beverly's cats seemed to materialize in the middle of the table. She remembered the constant *thwacking* last night as Dickens pummeled the plastic, probing for a way into Beverly's 'cow aquarium.' What would a virtual cat do when Mary was cutting human meat? *Now there's a gruesome thought . . . But still . . . in a controlled environment . . .*

Mary remembered part of a book she'd read in college. Don Marquis seemed unusually appropriate for something that bobbed up in her unruly subconscious. Aloud, she drawled, "As Mehitabel the cat told archy the roach, '/but wotthehell/archy wotthehell/it's cheerio/ my deerio that/pulls a lady through/.' Might as well. Mehitabel was right, *'life is just one damn kitten after another'* anyway." She tapped the phone. "Yes, this is Dr. Henderly. You remember? Upstairs? I need to speak with a Mousetrap tech. Yes, downstairs." *Now that's an-*

other problem, she thought as she waited, *they've got to have all the data in the mains, but can data like that simulate an artificial intelligence subroutine if needed? And if they can, will the AI be able to—*

Her thoughts were interrupted by a bored and nasal voice, "Yes, Doctor," delivered in tones that would curdle gases into solids. Mary began the conversation politely. When that didn't work, she tried a different approach.

"Yes," Mary snapped, "and then I said 'cat.' I don't have time for this, I ask questions, you give answers, it's a service type of thing. Yeah, I know, 'the mains contain the wealth and breadth of all human knowledge,' but that takes too long. Do your research files have neurological databases involving *cat* predatory behavior patterns? I need data on interactions with other species, spatial perception, route-finding behavior, and limits on independent action. I also need to know if your cage studies showed that Mice in the system mimicked the behavior of real mice. Yes, I know your boss is on vacation. No, you are not going to go query the project manager—no, you're not going to go bury it in channels—I know you're not that busy, and I know where your access codes are kept, dear. You just send it all to my account, stat." She broke the connection. *I hate it when a misplaced sphincter cuts off blood to the brain.* She took a deep breath. *Now I can face Lenny.*

The basement lab was not what anyone ever expected. It wasn't a gleaming white factory clean room filled with the soft susurrus of scrubbed air. It wasn't a dim, clammy, raw cement lab crowded by jury-rigged equipment tied together with duct tape. That was because Lenny Houge was fixer, scrounger, lord and master down here. The systems were so out-of-date that equipment had to be kept at a constant temperature and humidity—so it was the only place in the entire building that stayed comfortable year-round. They needed to be protected from noise and vibration—so Lenny had chosen plush carpeting, thick wallcoverings, and heavy, solid antique furniture. And he was simply helping recoup overhead by renting storage space for all those expensive paintings hung up in his steady-state stronghold. It wasn't his fault it made the place look like an opulent nineteenth century plantation house. Unfortunately, his manners seemed to belong to that era, too.

"Lenny." It was important to speak in very precise, plain terms with Lenny to avoid any impression of friendliness, which, with him, was like mentioning you'd heard of something kinky and couldn't wait to try it. Mary enunciated the words very tightly. "I need an input-only VR program with security encoding and a recursive protection algorithm. No, not the place you stuck me in yesterday. *If* you remember, despite how you *swore* you had such a great cage—and you know what I think of the whole cage idea—*that did not work.*" At least that unpleasant reminder of failure might keep his paws off her. "Now, I need input-only, security, recursive."

"Oh sure, that's easy, Mare." Lenny had familiar names for everyone. *If there ever was a second coming of Christ,* Mary thought, *Lenny would say "Hey Jeez, what took ya so long? How's the Big Guy? End of the World comin' along okay? Good, good."* He leered cordially at her. "What do you need it for? If it's about that trouble yesterday, a secure lab still wouldn't help. An input-only lab on your access levels would still be hanging a welcome mat out for our little furry friends."

Rather than inviting him to restate the obvious yet again, Mary told him the truth: She *wanted* an appearance by Mice.

"Oh-ho!" Lenny exclaimed. "The little surgeon has a new Mousetrap, perhaps? What have you got in mind? I'll tell you whether it'll work or not."

"I really appreciate that, Lenny," she said, biting back unkind personal comments, "but I couldn't take you away from *your* important work just to indulge *my* little idea. Admin would never forgive me for monopolizing your time. Just schedule a few hours for me in a secure lab, and I'll be out of your way." Mary had learned the old-fashioned art of the well-placed simper. She had to use her claws carefully. And only when necessary.

Escaping Lenny's curiosity, Mary went up to Supply to select among the old VR headsets used for diagnosing infants and premature births. Some had even been built into the sort of box Beverly had. "Oh, heavens, not cow aquariums *again*." Mary grabbed the technical specs for the headsets, read them, and gave a predatory grin. "This *is* going to be interesting. Now, just one more ingredient."

In better spirits, Mary called her sister and said she'd like to have Dickens for lunch. "No, seriously. I have a cunning plan. Why don't you and Dickens come by? I do have to thank you both for being patient with me last night. You've always wanted to see the labs, and there's nothing high-security going on right now. Oh, do. You know how Dickens loves trips ending in small, crunchy morsels. I'll have something made up special for him."

The lunch turned out better than expected, and Dickens, a seasoned traveler in Beverly's big mesh purse, was in good temper, although Mary did not kid herself—the crab puffs she'd ordered were the reason for the cat's tolerance. After accepting delighted attention from her staff, Dickens was quite willing to be escorted on the tour of the lab complex where he could be admired by all.

When they reached the lab levels, Mary ever-so-innocently wandered over to the secured lab that Lenny had set up for her. Palming the optipad, she told Beverly, "Go ahead and stick your hand on the pad. I'm on file, but they want a scan of everyone who goes in. Come to think of it," she smiled disingenuously, "let's put Dickens' paw on it, too. I can't wait to see the memo from security."

Mary, Beverly, and Dickens (although it took twice) were all accepted by security. They entered the stark and antiseptic environment of a medical VR lab. Beverly squinted in the glare. "Good Lord! This is dreary! Do you have to work in this all day long?"

"Heavens, no!" Mary laughed. "I work out of my office, or one of the VROOMS upstairs. Down here there's no reason to dress up the place. Once you're up on the Nets, you create your own environment. Oh, here, it looks like they've left a helmet or two ..." Beverly gave her a look that made her go on persuasively, "I know you're hooked into Moneycomm, but have you ever been on the main Nets? I mean, since you're here ..."

Beverly was many things. Stupid wasn't one of them. "You mean, since there just *happen* to be two big helmets and one little one in that rat's nest of wires left lying around?" Beverly gave her another look. "I thought I was finished playing guinea pig after your first year of med school. You know I've never forgiven you for leaving me in a full body splint while you ran to the store 'to pick up a few things.' "

"I was back that afternoon, you *said* you needed a rest—and come to think of it, your posture improved noticeably—really showed off your—" Beverly's swatting hand interrupted her. Mary grinned as she untangled cables.

Beverly submitted with good grace. Despite what she'd said, she was curious. She was familiar with the commercial Nets, but she'd never had an opportunity to see what VR was really like up on the mains. Not many people ever did. In a few moments Mary had her hooked into the system. Mary put on a helmet and structured their surroundings to a comforting and familiar image, Beverly's own drawing room.

While Beverly worked to create a tangible body within the sketchy room, Mary focused on improving her sister's imagery. Only a surgeon could have done it so deftly. Any blunt attempts to attune would have felt like assault, but Mary's experience and skill made it possible for her to merge into Beverly's input without peeling the layers of her thought process. Beverly practiced moving, walking, picking up objects, as delighted as if she'd never done so in the actual room. An equilibrium was reached. There was no need for conversation now. Every thought translated at a nearly subliminal level, like an internal conversation. **There's a ceramic jug out of place** from Beverly. A mere thought from Mary altered the placement. **Showing off!** Beverly laughed.

Like it? Mary asked. "You can add lots more stuff.**

Is this what it's like on the mains? I can't believe the difference from Beverly.

Time compressed in VR. The sisters simulcast a dialogue understandable only to themselves. Mary had never really heard half the ideas Beverly thought out in clarifying the objects in the room. To Mary they had always been odd lumps of glass or wood or fabric. For Beverly, each lived in a web of stories and memories. She could not describe them without bringing them out from the parlor's shadows, putting them in the best light, and telling their histories. It made the room unusually solid for a VR environment. Such highly detailed observations were exactly what Mary had hoped for from her sister.

Mary's experience allowed her to view the VR image and also to be aware of her realtime environment. Dickens was relaxed in his bag. All was in place; just one more link, and she'd see if Beverly's Scotch-fueled opinion of her cat's abilities was deserved.

Even as she sent a casual message to her sister, **Let's let the cat out of the bag!** she reached for the third helmet. She opened the big mesh purse on Beverly's lap and slipped the helmet onto Dickens' cranium. **Dickens' turn to join the link!**

She vocalized the command.

PROGRAM FELINE–1 EXECUTED

Both sisters reeled from the discontinuity. Disorienting. Like staring through a fish-eye lens at a sculpture while running around it, spinning. And hearing a symphony from a radio, from a recording studio, and live from within a tuba, all at once. And touching the very air in and around their lungs, being able to press their fingers to each breath inside their throats. Virtual space became at once transparent and solid.

Mary supported Beverly's grip on the wavering outlines of their shared VR parlor. Then Mary extended her faculties into the new reality forming under the weight of a third presence. Taking threads that she recognized, she began to map them onto the reality she and Beverly shared. *Floor, wall, table leg*—she sensed the alien presence working just as hard. The room was acquiring more fine adjustments everywhere she looked. Threads crawled across her reality and anchored themselves. Chairs acquired underside springs and torn stuffing and vivid dusty scents and lost loose change. The reality had been unusually detailed before; now it had more depth and texture and vitality than Mary had ever seen.

Even the tear on the underside of the ottoman! How on earth did you notice that?

I hadn't from Mary, **but Dickens obviously did!**

Beverly was entranced, seeing her parlor from a cat's eye view, and she commented on the detail.

Mary fired back, **Enjoy it while you can, it's unusual. It must be making a huge demand on the system. This kind of detail really chews up computing power.**

A flat black-and-white image of Lenny shuddered on the periphery of Mary's vision. His voice barked from the speakers in the VROOM's ceiling panel. "Mary! What are you running down there? Our monitors on your lab just went to gray-tone in three dimensions! What the hell is going on, Mare?"

"Shut up, Lenny. I'm cleared for this VROOM, and you told me it was sealed." Mary spoke without inflection, trying to maintain her concentration on the forming link between herself, her sister, and Dickens. "Go monitor a colostomy!"

"You girls don't know what you're playing at! Go on like that and you'll be yelling for me to rescue you."

In response, Mary formed big, black, very false six-foot VR eyelashes and batted them. The sisters harmonized in falsetto tones, trilling, "Oh, thank you, Testosterone Man!" Beverly laughed, and the threefold link became stronger.

Lenny was not amused. "You just wait, you'll get in trouble and I'll be off saving somebody else's project!"

A new imagery began to manifest in response to Lenny's presence in the VR nexus: *heat . . . stalking . . . prey . . . hot blood . . muscle, sinew, claws unsheathing, tearing . . . and teeth closing . . .*

Lenny dropped out of the nexus with a yelp.

I don't blame him Beverly noted with amusement. **If every woman had this opportunity, a swine like that would stick to sniffing truffles!** A large tabby cat image formed, curled its tail around its front paws, and purred in response to her praise.

With the outside interference gone, Beverly's parlor ramified and gained even more definition. Objects Mary had never even noticed snapped into complete focus, their shapes, textures, and positions sharply correct. The trap had become more than complex enough to generate a Mouse. It didn't take long. A squealing blur darted across Beverly's pristine drawing room and halted at the baseboard, shimmering.

There's the problem! Mary indicated, transforming the image of her hand into a ridiculous ten-foot poster-paint red arrow.

Attention drawn by his social pack, Dickens took only sidelong, indolent notice of the Mouse. But his eyes became slits.

Look! Beverly flashed.

The virtual Dickens' tail curled at the tip, his ears perked and triangulated, and his hindquarters poised for a pounce. The fuzziness moved rapidly about the confinement of the parlor, growing desperately active. It began to scrabble against the ceramic jug that Mary had readjusted. Mary knew it was searching for escape back into the mains. It kept sniffing at the traces of outside command code left there. Dickens crept forward.

What do you know, rose from deeper levels of Mary's thoughts, **maybe androids *do* dream of electric sheep. Virtual kitties chase Electric Mice.**

What? thought Beverly.

Before Mary could explain the reference, a cat-shape blurred the VR image. Dickens sprang. Not a pounce, not a leap, Dickens just *appeared* at the site of the Mouse. Before the startled sisters could form a response, the Mouse was gone. Only an irate cat remained, pawing and mewing at the spot.

Another Mouse popped in across the drawing room,

almost under Beverly's VR feet. She shrieked. Dickens *struck*. The Mouse was gone.

Mary had begun it all by asking for a secure lab; between the three of them, they had built the room into a very secure trap. New Mice emerged at different virtual locations inside Beverly's drawing room. Through his strenuous gymnastics, Dickens formed up the hallway, then the next room that he knew had to be there. The house expanded outward with each of his frustrated, mewing explorations after disappearing Mice. Whenever a Mouse formed, the image of Dickens exploded onto it. At no time was any item in Beverly's virtual parlor disturbed in the least. There were just fleeting glimpses of fuzz and fur.

Incredible! thought Mary.

Wonderfulpride**cat** was the affectionate thought from Beverly.

From Dickens came a series of impressions: sight, depth, smell, spatial dynamics and relationships, arousal, muscular strains and pressures, and no small amount of amusement. The roar became leonine. **PLAY!**

With all her skill Mary slipped out of the direct VR link. Smoothly, she isolated Beverly in a seductive little library subroutine pod, distracting her with images of shelves full of books she'd been too busy to read. The program could easily call up pages of text for Beverly to read to her heart's desire. Mary moved on swiftly. Timing was critical. She had the VROOM's own record, of course, but bitter experience with the contaminations of Mice taught her to make sure she had some kind of outside backup.

She'd made sure. She knew Lenny. She'd known there was no way, in spite of his promises of a secure lab, that he'd fail to peek in on a new Mousetrap. Even after they'd chased him off, she knew he'd still be there, watching. And his unofficial recordings were always much better as detailed backup than dry tech summaries. *He's a fool, but a predictable fool. Now if he'll just do what he's supposed to* ... "Lenny!" she yelled into the VROOM, "Lock! Save program!"

Mary's next surgery went fine, as did the one after that, and the one after that. Each time the peripheral fuzziness would appear, so would an image of Dickens, and the virtual reality would resolve back into its initial parameters. Mary would spare a virtual stroke and praise for the virtual cat. It always purred in response to Mary's attentions.

Beverly's share of the program rights made her financially secure enough to move. This annoyed Dickens, but after only a year the cat seemed to have gotten over most of his resentment, and allowed it to be known that he approved of the nice new place. Beverly talked with the same indiscriminate affection to the real cat and to the VR Dickens that popped up, prowling, in her office work.

Lenny Houge got a share of the program rights and became a reasonably wealthy man. He himself rarely used the program. For some reason it appeared to dislike him. Perhaps because of his distrust, he continued to monitor the AI subroutine from the sidelines as the VR Dickens expanded into the mains. It wasn't easy. The program seemed to take a positive delight in tormenting him. Nobody else seemed to have any problems, and nobody else knew the full extent of the effort Lenny devoted to the challenge. They were only aware of the volumes of memos he was sending out.

It was the second anniversary of the capture of the Virtual Dickens program, and Mary and Beverly were celebrating their annual dividend checks in Mary's office. Of course the original Dickens was there to take his share, translated into crab puffs and proper homage from the humans. As the sisters clinked their glasses, the phone flashed. Taut-faced, Lenny appeared on her monitor. "Dr. Henderly, could you come down here, please?" Her first thought was *Doctor? Doctor Henderly? What is this 'Doctor' business? Who are you, and what have you done with Lenny Houge?*, but his expression did not invite levity. She was half out of her chair before replying, "On my way." To Beverly, she simply said that she'd be back soon.

The door barely cleared her in time as she charged into Lenny's office. "All right, what's wrong? You look terrible. You look like you've seen a ghost."

Lenny palmed his optipad and waved Mary to a chair. She pulled it up next to his desk. "Ghost, huh? Very funny, Mare. I've been monitoring our furry artificial intelligence subroutine."

Mary rolled her eyes. "Yes, Lenny. I know. I've seen the memos." Lenny's memos were becoming legend.

Lenny went on as if he hadn't heard. "Here, let me make this simple for you. This is a pie graph of the mains as of two years ago." Mary looked at an orange circle on his monitor and nodded. Lenny continued, "This is the same graph as of one day after you introduced Dickens to the mains. See the narrow purple wedge? That's the subroutine we sectioned off to give the program AI status." Mary nodded again, and Lenny plodded on. "Here's six months farther along." By now the narrow purple slice was big enough for a dab of whipped cream.

It reminded Mary she was still hungry. In a few minutes Beverly was going to cut the cake and she'd miss the surprise Beverly had promised her.

Lenny was busy on the pad again. "Progressive growth was expected as more and more users got access. Plus, even nonsecurity level operators claimed they got better results with the damned thing's help, and licensed in. That would be about ... here." Mary exhaled as the screen image formed. Nearly a quarter of the pie was purple. "Again," he continued, "this traffic was within projected parameters, but I sent several memos to the Director requesting a temporary restriction of new licensees until my staff could do further simulations."

Mary was all too aware of Lenny's memos. "So why am I here?"

One more stab at his board, and the screen coalesced into a new image. "I did another map of the mains last night, Mary—tell me what you see."

A circle of pure orange formed on the screen. No sliver of purple. The Virtual Dickens traffic had vanished.

"That can't be," she said. "I used the program yesterday. I know Bev uses it daily. If it went down, our clients would have been asking for our heads—it's got to be there."

"Oh, it's there," he said bitterly, calling up a new image. "It's just not part of the mains." A wider-angle view appeared, showing two circles. One orange, and one, smaller, pure purple. "Here's your 'ghost.' "

"What is that? A new main?"

"Sure looks like it, doesn't it, Mare? Somehow the Dickens AI managed to relattice part of the mains for itself without crashing the system. It's entirely independent now. I can't touch it." Always one to give credit to another who has made a mistake, Lenny said, "You started this thing—any more bright ideas?"

Mary made an irritated hand gesture, urging calm. "Let me think. The program is running perfectly, right? And the main Nets have been operating normally, right?" Lenny nodded. "I assume you put techs onto studying that relatticing—if they could shut down nodes and partially relattice, just like that, with modern code, maybe they could clean up all the Nets. *I* haven't forgotten about Mice, even if everyone else has. So that'd be a real nice second bonus from our program to the people clever enough to work out how Dickens did it."

Lenny looked sour. He and his techs obviously hadn't been getting anywhere.

Mary took the optipad from his desk and called her office. "Bev, do you remember how to get to Lenny's office? Good. Please apologize to our guest and come on down." She broke the connection. Mary wasn't sure where this meeting would lead, but now she felt it might be better if Lenny didn't know that Dickens was in the building.

"Curious." Beverly arched one eyebrow, and addressed the cat. "You're on your own for a bit, child. Don't cut the cake until I get back, and no long-distance calls."

Dickens rolled on his side in Mary's overstuffed chair and heaved an innocent, overstuffed sigh.

Beverly got a replay of the graphs. Her response was

decidedly different. "Not bad, but you're off on the date of separation. I noticed it a couple of months ago."

Lenny did a split-take onto his pad. "You *knew*!"

Beverly spoke slowly, as if to a child throwing a tantrum. "Yes, Lenny, I knew."

"Yes? You said yes? Mary, your sister said yes." Mary sighed. Lately a lot of his memos had deteriorated into this sort of gibberish. Mary thought it was actually an improvement, since he'd lost interest in harassing the staff—paranoia beat bullying. Lenny kept babbling. "Yes. She said yes. Would you like some more tea, Beverly? Why yes, she'd say. Do you take sugar? Why yes, she'd say . . ."

Mary turned to her sister. "Well, we've lost Lenny for the duration." She explained to Beverly what a partial relatticing program could mean, both for cleaning up and modernizing the mains, and in terms of licensing fees for a whole new cascade of programs. She glanced aside. Lenny's babbling was beginning to run down. "But I get the feeling some of this isn't exactly news to you, is it, Bev?"

"It's clear neither of you have roomed with a cat lately. The first thing they do in any new place is establish their turf. Usually as big an area as they can defend. The Virtual Dickens just set up his little separate territory and put a 'don't tread on me' sign on it. I had a horrible time getting in myself."

Lenny jerked to attention. "*You got in*? How? I've had a team on the transition all month! It's impenetrable! Every time we've gone in, it smacks us down just like it stomps the Mice. The best 'back door' I've got left gives us total garbage!"

"Of course you couldn't understand it!" Beverly looked at him witheringly. "Neither could I. Its thought process is nonlinear. Questions and answers don't exist—it's just a fully formed picture, a totality. Its hard to explain. Your other AIs are human based, aren't they? Dickens doesn't see cause and effect, he just is. I'd have been at a total loss if my original Dickens hadn't been in there with me."

"You put that cat back in my mains!" he shrieked.

"No." She was once again calming a tantrum. "I put the cat back in *its* mains. Dickens isn't your only powerful AI, you know, he's just the one who figured out how to separate. They haven't been *your* mains for quite some time."

Lenny sank, deflated, back in his chair.

"I really don't think there's anything more we can do for you, Mr. Houge." Beverly padded toward the door. "We should go, Mary, the gentleman is talking to himself again. Truthfully, I'm more worried about your office. I don't think having a cake baked in the shape of a mouse was a good idea. You know Dickens loves that kind of frosting, and he's awfully good at getting into boxes. Besides, I want to tell you about the new programs Virtual Dickens invented. He gave me quite a few to bring back. And you're right, the licensing fees should be impressive. My share should be great for funding those charitable trusts I've been telling you about." She grinned impishly. "I promised you a surprise, didn't I?"

"I think I can live without the cake now," Mary practically levitated out of the chair. "I'd like to hear more about your little visits with Virtual Dickens—and all these *other* AIs you've obviously been carousing with!"

Beverly smiled sweetly. "The other AIs are not a problem, dear. Totally subservient. Cats always train their humans, you know. They pose no problem to Dickens, none whatsoever."

She tapped her nails on the door frame and leaned back into the office. "Oh. One more thing, Lenny. Before you try something foolhardy, I'd remember that a ten-pound, unarmed tabby kicked your nasty face out of virtual space two years ago. I can't even imagine what the nice big tiger-cat I met could do now." She stretched, flexing her spine, and lightly patted Mary's shoulder. "Coming? If we leave Dickens alone for too long he might get cranky, and we don't want that, now do we?"

ARROWS
by Jane Hamilton

Jane Hamilton is a native New Yorker. She studied English and religion at Cornell University, and is presently working on a Master's Degree in English at SUNY Brockport. Her current interests include anime, MST3K, and wasting time on the Internet. Her family consists of two cats who are miffed because she didn't write about them and one husband who watches the chaos with good humor. This is her first science fiction publication.

It hurt to walk, and he needed to hunt. Nothing moved, though. The cat settled down beside rock, out of the wind, with walls of snow on all sides. A mat in his coat pulled at his skin, and he nosed it without licking. The fur stank. He tucked all four feet underneath, in the warmest fur, to wait it out. *I've waited a long time,* the cat thought.

"I wish you'd dress decently," Kip said. "You make me shiver."

The two jinn, Kip and Key, looked at each other for a moment before Key laughed out loud, her head thrown back and her eyes squinted nearly shut. She'd always laughed this way, even in the first days of creation. They walked over snowflakes that crunched in the darkness, running their hands over the snow-covered tops of parked cars as tall as themselves. Nobody watched the pair from a bedroom window, but the jinn didn't raise their heads to check.

They'd passed most of the night already. The pair had scampered through the neighborhood they had adopted all night—all month, truth be told. Tonight they had slipped and skated on ice covering the parking lot of a mini-mall bounded on three sides by residence housing and on the last by the street. It faced an abandoned landfill. When the edge wore from that amusement, the jinn had raced past the houses and made silly rhyming songs about the mailbox names they managed to sound out. With dawn pressing them, Key wore shorts and a halter top despite the frigid wind, most likely because she didn't realize she ought to be cold. Jinn don't have a body temperature. She kept her bow and arrows slung over one shoulder, but the length of her blonde hair continually got snagged by them.

Kip kept her eyes down as they walked, a smile creeping up her face, too. She wore more substantial clothing but carried no arrows. Around her waist she kept a belt pack, and it jingled with the rhythm of her steps. Unlike Key's, her waist-length hair was black.

"Frostbite is fun," Key said, and stuck out her tongue. Kip shook her head. " 'Tis a day for neither man nor beast," Key shouted, raising her bow and nocking an arrow. "Watch how strong the wind is."

The arrow skewed to the right as soon as Key released the bowstring, thrown into a tumble by the racing air.

"Isn't that amazing?" Key said.

Kip's face had lit up. "Do it again!"

A throat cleared behind the pair. An angel. Both jinn stiffened as they stared up at the winged form towering over them. A moment later, Key lowered her head as hints of a smile reappeared.

The angel watched the jinn. "Just because you're lower creations, and innocent, and have us watching over you, you think we'll always prevent your actions from hurting people."

"We're so sorry," Kip said, "but it's so windy and Key's usually such a good shot and it really was fun—"

"All right," the angel said. "But no more. And go find the arrow."

Key's eyes glistened like schist. "You're not going to punish us?"

"No one got hurt this time," Kip said quickly, as if to remind the angel.

"Just go find the arrow."

The angel left the pair, and they subsided to giggles as they walked through the snow. They ought to have known better, and as is the case with jinn all too often, they ought to have known that they ought to have known. They had been standing on the sidewalk separating the street from the landfill which dense shrubs had commandeered. Animals lived in the bushes, and other jinn played there. An arrow fired wildly like that could have struck someone—especially at night, with the jinn in their most solid forms.

"Watch me," Key said, suddenly doubling in size and making an illusion of wings spread from her back. "I'm the archangel Gabriel!"

"Quiet," Kip said. "You shouldn't have tried that arrow. Where'd it land, anyway?"

"You're afraid of the angel?" Key shrank to her previous height, though. "He'd never hurt us. Remember, we're 'innocents.' " When the darker jinn didn't look up, Key tossed a snowball at her. "Oh, go pop out of a magic lamp, why don't you? Nothing's going to happen to us."

They thrashed through the brush, snapping dead winter vegetation and making enough of a ruckus that even a human could have heard them if any had been around.

The buzzer startled him from sleep. Andrew groped at the buttons of the still-unfamiliar clock radio—Julie had packed the old one—wishing he'd remembered last night to disconnect the alarm. He'd taken the day off, he reminded himself, to rest and finish getting over his cold, not to get up at the usual forsaken hour. He hit a

button he thought would silence the alarm but instead
turned it to the radio.

Contented enough by the end of the buzzing, Andrew
collected his wits while listening to the news. The
weather had made most of it, actually: airport delays,
traffic accidents, deaths by exposure, no school closings.
It had reached negative fifteen during the night, and the
announcers predicted a high temperature of negative
three during the day. They said it almost gleefully, anticipating more horrible weather in the future like a twisted
homicide detective on the trail of a mass murderer.

"Glad I'm inside," Andrew mumbled as he shut the
radio and returned to sleep.

Noises, moving closer to the cat. The cat thought, *I
don't care. I don't any longer.* The noise-maker might
well be a hunter, but probably not. A hunter wouldn't
step on so many twigs and crash through the brambles.
And a hunter would only kill me. People got noisy like
that, and people threw things and kicked. *But I don't
care any longer.*

Kip had just wandered into a bushful of burrs when
Key gave a shriek. Kip ran to the other jinn, pulling
burrs from her hair as she moved. She came upon Key
standing in the brush holding a cat.

To other-than-jinn eyes, Key wouldn't have seemed to
hold a cat, but rather a soiled piece of fake fur like the
collar of an old coat. The jinn identified the cat by the
haze a life emits, in this case a peculiarly catlike haze.
The jinn couldn't have identified milk and tailed things,
claws and purrs, but all these swirled in the aura.

They stood for a moment listening to the cat's heart-
beat and whistling breath. Jinn have neither. Jinn also
lack body warmth, and Key felt the cat shiver in her
arms. The wind, having stolen their arrow, had returned
for the cat.

Kip and Key joined eyes, but Key looked so helpless
that Kip scanned the area. Other than a row of apartment houses, the closest buildings she saw were in the
mini-mall, and of all five stores, none had opened yet.

"Let's go there," Kip said. "At least get him out of the wind."

"The arrow?" Key asked.

"Later. They'll understand." Kip meant the angels. Leading the way, Kip made for the plaza as quickly and directly as she could. A little sunrise had begun showing. Jinn forget many things, but never that dawn renders them insubstantial. Key couldn't hold the cat once the sun came up. Already the burrs in Kip's hair had lost some of their grip, and every few steps one returned to the snow. While walking, she rummaged in her belt pack, reaching deep and rattling through the contents with probing fingers.

"They'll all be locked," Key said.

"The bank." By now they had reached the edge of the landfill and stepped onto the sidewalk. Key cooed at the animal in her arms as she walked across the street. Kip remembered to look both ways, but only after they'd crossed two lanes. A truck beeped them as its headlights swept over their shadowy forms, but they arrived safely.

The door to the bank had an automatic lock. Key yanked it with three loud thunks, and each time the lock held. "Wish I were an angel," she said. "Walk through walls, break the lock—"

"Please," Kip said, and the door opened. Key turned to her with an open mouth, and Kip held up a plastic card.

"When did you get a bank card?"

Kip sat on the heater and got Key to do the same. After a moment, Key laid the cat on the floor.

"Don't," Kip said. "Floor's filthy."

Key shrugged. "Cat's filthy, too."

The animal didn't raise his head—only lay panting. Limp. The fluorescent lights inside the bank revealed him to be a tortoiseshell under the dirt, the black patches of his coat broken up by an orange-brown and white that had long since yielded their color to the elements. Although an armful for someone Key's size, he was a small cat. His eyes and cheeks kept their tense, tight look even as he lay on the bank floor.

"Now what, Saint Francis?" Kip looked at the matted fur, the raised ribs.

"I'll take him," Key said. "I'll feed him and care for him."

"They won't let us," Kip said. "Remember the last animal you took?" Key puzzled for a moment. "You couldn't remember it then, either. The angels took it away from you before it got too hungry."

"I'd remember this one." Key nodded decisively.

"He's flesh," Kip said. "He should go to a flesh person, otherwise we should leave him."

"Leave him in a flesh grave," Key said. She reached down to touch the cat, who raised his head enough to hiss.

They didn't say anything. Finally the darker-haired jinn said, "We should feed him, at any rate." Kip knelt on the floor and dumped the contents of her belt pouch with a clatter. Beads, the bank card, a nickel, half a pack of playing cards, a hair band, a whistle, three pennies, and an empty perfume bottle. Kip gave the bag another shake, and out dropped a quarter.

"What's that make?" she asked herself.

"You can get some food, right?" Key said. "There's a market in the mall."

"Cat's filthy, too," the cat thought. He'd lashed his tail once when the jinn had said it. *And I'd keep lashing my tail, if I felt like it. But I don't. It tastes so bad to lick now, and then the fur freezes and I get colder. I should leave you guys. And I will when I want to. I don't need anyone to take care of me.* He watched one jinn send the other out to hunt, though, and wondered what it would bring back.

Kip returned to the nibbling of weather she couldn't feel, although by now the sun had made significant progress. She hurried in search of food, managing to slip into the locked store using her credit card, though not the same way she had used it to enter the bank. She wandered the aisles until she found bags with cat faces on them, and from there she looked for cat food, a big bag of pigeons, for example, or mice. What she found confused her—she didn't remember ever seeing a pack of cats run down a cow in the wild—but finally she settled on one can because she liked the color. She put the can in her pocket, then left her change on the manager's desk. After a second thought, she left the whistle, too.

When Kip got back to the bank, she found Key crouched over a box. "This blew by outside," she said, "so I filled it with newspapers." Key had scooped up the cat and laid him in the box, but the cat didn't move. "You've got the food?"

They had enough time to open the can. Sunlight had penetrated the glass enclosure of the bank by now, and that light made an exaggerated shadow of the cat's labored breathing. He sniffed the food, gave one lick, and then flopped onto the papers.

Kip and Key stared at one another. Key looked at her hands and could see the cat through them.

Finally, the cat felt a little warm. But he tingled—the paws, the ears, the nose. *No water,* the cat thought, *although now there's food. And someone else, watching me. I hope they don't kick me. Not that I care. I can leave when I feel like it.* The cat stood unsteadily, raised a head that felt too heavy for his neck, and sat as his hind legs folded unexpectedly. *I just don't feel like it right now.*

Andrew hunted through the closet his wife had left nearly empty three weeks ago. He remembered wishing his clothes had more room last month, room to hold their own form, but now the closet looked too sparse with only his wardrobe, as if clothes could be lonely. A stupid thought. He pushed the door shut without getting his shoes, then went in again to grab them.

Looking in the mirror, Andrew found himself checking for cat hair. He shook his head. Julie had taken that monstrous Siamese with her—a welcome departure, actually. Let them complain at each other. He wondered which would be the first to feel she couldn't get a word in edgewise. The cat could win any competition based on volume, but for constant complaining, the pair were a pretty close match.

Taking the day off might help more than his health, Andrew realized. With Julie's stuff gone, he could spread out a bit, use more than half the apartment. Maybe he'd throw out that scratching post the Siamese never used, preferring the drapes and the couch, possibly frightened by the radioactive pink Julie had insisted they buy.

For now, though, he could take his time rearranging the book shelves. Or maybe he'd go first to buy the reading chair Julie had insisted didn't match the decor. Something you could sit and read in without feeling you lived in a restored house from the 1700's, complete with roped-off areas and do-not-touch signs.

Andrew ate breakfast with the TV on behind him, the familiar sounds of a news anchor reading off a tele-prompter.

Traffic hummed by more frequently as rush hour began. A few people stepped into the bank to use the ATM machines, but other than a quick glance, the suited men and women paid no heed. Kip and Key pleaded, unheard and unseeable; their words grew softer as the morning drew on. Now when they touched the cat, he didn't even hiss. Key thought the cat had gotten used to them; Kip worried more.

Key stood up at ten o'clock. By now the traffic had waned to a throb, the red and green lights for a heart-beat, and people had ceased their pre-commute cash runs.

"The cat won't make it to tonight," Key said, and left the bank.

Kip chased her. "What are you doing?"

"I'm getting someone to help us."

Key already had an arrow on her bow, but Kip snatched it. "We'll get in trouble!"

"An angel will come for us," Key said, "and when he scolds us, we'll show him the cat."

Key loosed her arrow across the avenue. It landed in the engine of someone's car.

"Terrific," Kip said. "Now you've done it."

They ran through traffic to the car and poked their heads through the hood to stare at the arrow sticking from one of the rectangular pieces of the engine.

"You had to hit something mechanical."

"Is that the gas tank?" Key said.

"That's in the back. Maybe it's a muffler or transmission."

"Mufflers go underneath." Key touched the arrow, then yanked back her hand as a crumpling sensation struck her body. The arrow had gotten hot. "I'm afraid to pull it out. You do it."

"I didn't shoot it there."

Because the arrow was as immaterial as the two jinn, the owner of the car wouldn't see it, so he'd never know its energy had caused the damage. Still, Kip and Key returned to the bank in dejection. The cat lay panting. Even though the sun warmed the cat, he hadn't washed yet.

"I want to go away," Key said. "There's nothing we can do."

"We can't," Kip said. "When the sun goes down, we'll bring the cat to a vet or something. We'll leave him on a doorstep and ring the bell. That's only about seven hours."

Key played with the ATM machines for a while. Outside, the wind had picked up.

Kip had rummaged again through her belt pack and found no more money, but she did tempt the cat with a piece of string he staunchly refused to bat.

"Oh, no," Key said, looking out the window, and then, "oh, dear heaven, no."

"An angel?"

"Worse." The owner of the car had come out to start it, and now he crossed to their side of the street.

"We're going to get scolded again," Key said. "I can't believe I did that. We shouldn't have shot another arrow. You should have stopped me."

"He can't scold us, can he?" Kip said. "He doesn't know we're here."

They shrank into a corner as the man hauled open the door to the bank. He moved straight for a cash machine, and only then did the jinn move away from the wall.

Kip stood uneasily and looked under the man's elbow at the terminal. His name appeared on his bank card— Andrew? Kip didn't have time to sound out the second name before he replaced the card in his wallet.

Kip turned around, then gave a shriek.

"It's not for you," Key said of the arrow she had ready.

"He's not going to scold us. You'll really get us in trouble if you hurt a person!"

The man turned away from the ATM and while turning, saw the cat.

Key fired.

The arrow passed through him, and Kip leaped to catch it before it hit the terminal. The man hesitated.

"Are you nuts?"

"This has to work." Key nodded. "Watch him!"

The man walked out of the bank.

Key sat heavily on the heater, her shoulders slumped. "That wasn't supposed to happen."

"You thought you were Cupid?" Kip shook the other jinn. "What did you think you would accomplish?"

"I'm sorry—but I know he got a pain in his heart when he saw the cat. You couldn't see his face. But it wasn't enough." Key shook her head. "Can't you just get money out of the machines like they do?"

"We have to put money in first," Kip said. "I found the card in the bushes, anyway."

Key left the bank again, Kip following her. They caught up with the man at his car.

"Don't you love the cat?" Key said. "Please, sir?"

"Good thing it's daylight." Kip rolled her eyes. "He'd tell you he didn't love the cat, then clobber you for wrecking his car."

"He's got to help the cat—or the cat's going to die." Key sat on the roof of the car, then grinned. "I know. Watch."

Key ran near the bushes at the side of the road. She

called the wind and brought it to a bunch of dead leaves from last fall, touching them in the air so for a moment they would form a pointy-eared cat's face.

"And look!" Key had found a dark yellow slip from the bank and made it blow onto the car's antenna. "The color of the cat's eyes!"

The man had opened the hood to look into the engine. Kip swallowed uneasily, glancing at the arrow sticking into the box at the front of the engine. The man cleared the skeletons of old leaves from the engine block, and Kip said, "Like cat whiskers."

Silence, then, as the man examined the engine. Finally, he sighed. "God, if I don't have to call a tow-truck, I'll take that cat in."

Key clasped her hands. "Quick! Pull out the arrow!"

"Think about it," Kip said. "We might do more harm. We can't pull the arrowhead out backward—it's got to be pushed forward out the other side. It's in machinery, not a brick. And it might still be hot."

They looked at each other. They looked at the man. Andrew stared up the street, then back into the engine.

"There," Kip said, pointing to a pedestrian. This one walked toward them with keys in his hand. "Shoot him."

Key frowned. "I thought we weren't supposed to—"

"Through the heart, like you did before. When he sees the hood up."

Key let loose with her arrow, and it passed through the man's heart. He stopped beside Andrew and the car. "What's the trouble?"

"I think the battery may be dead."

Now that Kip heard the word "battery," she realized that was what the arrow had struck, and why it had gotten so hot to the touch.

"Let me bring my car over and give you a jump." And the second man walked away.

Key shrieked with laughter, her eyes squeezed nearly shut and her hands together at her mouth. Kip retrieved their arrow. "I'm a great shot," Key said. "Right through the heart, and just the right instant—"

"We're in so much trouble," Kip said.

"Let them scold us," Key said. "We're really smart

and we do really good work and we're going to save the
cat after all."

Kip took another look at the offending arrow. It had
penetrated the battery a good four inches, and the feathered end touched the engine block. Kip couldn't remember what batteries did, but she knew Andrew had said
it died, so this had to have been what killed it. And now
the second man was going to jump on it? She didn't
hold out much hope.

The second man nosed his car into Andrew's and
pulled out a long line of thick cable. The jinn watched,
confused but curious as the second man started his engine, then stopped it. "Not working?"

"It just clicks."

"Again."

They did. Both men checked the cables, their cheeks
pink and their breath clouding from their mouths as they
spoke, smoke signals augmenting their words. They tried
again, the second man running his engine for nearly
ten minutes.

Key sat on the curb. "It's not going to work—I
wrecked his car and now he's not even going to take
the cat."

Kip sat beside Key, arms around her knees, chin tilted
up as she watched the men in their cars. Finally, Andrew
got out and disconnected the cables. Slamming the hood
in disgust, he said, "I'll just call a tow truck."

"Sorry I couldn't help you," the second man said.

Key nocked another arrow. "Do something!" she
shouted. "Don't just leave!"

Kip rested a hand on Key's arm. "Let him go. He
doesn't know about the cat."

Key lowered the bow, rested her head on Kip's
shoulder.

The second man put one leg in his car, then stopped.
"You know," he said, leaning on the roof, "I have a
pickup."

Andrew kicked his tire. "You want to sell it to me?"

The second man laughed. "It's got a stronger battery—might be able to turn it over. It's worth a try."

He drove off to get the truck, and Key looked back

into the engine. "All this because of one lousy arrow. I wish I hadn't shot it."

"If you hadn't shot it, the man wouldn't have promised to take the cat," Kip said. "And if you hadn't shot the first arrow, we wouldn't have found the cat to begin with."

"I guess. Let me go look at the cat." Kip stayed with the car. She touched the arrow, a little hesitantly. It had cooled by now. It resisted her as she tugged it, though.

The cat felt the jinn approaching, and he lashed his tail.

Just my luck, to get picked up by jinn. Silly and flighty. It's nice of them to give me food, but I don't need their help, and they shouldn't be here.

The cat lifted his head as the jinn knelt beside him, hissed when she touched him. *You shouldn't be here.* He inched away from her fingers as she stroked his unwashed fur. *No need to touch me if you think I'm so "filthy"—I'm fine here, just tired. I'll sleep for a bit and I'll be fine.*

He closed his eyes, and the jinn left him to the sunlight and the old-smelling newspaper.

Andrew sat in his car, wishing that at least the heater worked. He'd taken little into the marriage, but the car had ended up truer to him than the wife he'd traded everything else for. He fingered the dashboard lightly, ran his hands over the steering wheel. "Why you, too?" he asked. He'd never given the car a name, although his brother had called it "Sweetheart." The car had just turned ten. The marriage had turned five.

It took a while for the other man to return, and Andrew kept making motions to get out and leave. What had possessed him to say he'd take in that cat? He'd held his breath hoping Julie would demand he give her that Siamese, wishing her attachment to the animal would prevail over her desire to spite him, and it had.

But he had wondered, seeing a half-dead animal lying in a box, what sort of person had abandoned the cat, and what he could do to help it recover.

Strange bursts of compassion—and Andrew had thought this a heartless city—had surrounded him this morning. The other man, Steve, had offered to help when he'd remembered the last time he was stuck. Steve missed an appointment because of him.

"The animal probably has fleas," Andrew muttered. "And ticks. It's probably going to cough up hairballs on the bed and howl at the moon."

He glanced across the street to the bank, and a smile crept up his face. "I wonder if I could repay the debt by getting a goldfish?"

A pickup rattled to a stop nose-to-nose with the dead car. Even Kip could tell the truck was old, that the rust around the wheel wells and the doors had been accumulated painstakingly, each winter adding salt to the mixture, salt that munched patiently at last year's damage.

"Are you sure we won't kill your engine trying to revive mine?" Andrew asked.

The second man slapped the pickup with his palm. "The engine's just fine. Runs like a tank."

"Sounds like a tank," Key said, drawing up beside Kip. "Cat's sleeping. Still didn't eat."

The jinn waited while the men repeated the hookup, and while the pickup started. Andrew started his engine, and it coughed.

Kip grinned. "It didn't make any sound at all before."

Both jinn looked into the engine, and it coughed again. The arrow glowed. "Come on," Key said. "I promise I won't shoot any more arrows ever again, and—"

She didn't get to make a second promise. The arrow blew apart, and at that moment the engine started.

Key whooped, leaped into the air and beamed with her eyes squeezed closed. Kip picked flecks of arrow shrapnel from her hair.

Andrew kept his car running while the second man disconnected the cables and drove off. Kip and Key moved close to the car. After a while, Andrew pulled out of his space and merged into traffic.

"Hey!" Key said.

The jinn waited for the car to return, but it didn't.

"I don't understand," Kip said. "He promised. He felt bad for the cat and he promised us."

They walked back through the lunch-hour traffic to the bank. More people had come in now, but in their lunch-hour hurry no one stopped for a dying cat. Kip sat beside the cat and touched his fur as only a jinn can. Even angels can't make themselves present to an animal in that way, being more spiritual than physical. Jinn have an animal nature, so animals respond to their presence not with fright, but with calm. The cat purred to comfort himself as Kip touched him, her fingertips stroking the matted fur.

"Maybe someone else will come in," Key said. "School gets out in the early afternoon, so maybe a parent will take a kid in here and the kid will beg to keep the cat."

"He's not even fully grown yet," Kip said.

They sat very still in the stale air of the bank, on either side of the cat in the box. He purred weakly now.

"Maybe I should try the ATM card once the sun goes down." Kip folded her hands in her lap. "They'll scold us for it, but we'll have saved the cat."

"What are you going to do—leave the money in the box with the cat?" Key shook her head. "We can carry the cat after sunset, anyhow. And even then, we can't be seen by anyone. The angels would lock us up for that."

The cat listened even though his ears never lifted. The jinn felt sorry for him. *Ridiculous—I'll be up in no time, just when I feel like it. I don't feel like it yet.* They talked to each other and not to him, the cat noticed. *And that's just fine with me.*

They had thought someone cared about him. One of the jinn talked more than the other, but both felt confused. *Shouldn't be,* the cat thought. *It would be the first time anyone looked after me. Not that I need help—I'd be fine if it weren't so cold.*

Better this way, the cat thought. *No one bothers me. People throw things anyhow.*

*   *   *

The sun's rays had stopped striking the bank after noon, but outside it remained bright.

"Kids will start passing in a little while," Kip said.

The cat had fallen asleep, and every so often Key would touch the tired body, not so much to see if the cat was alive as to reassure herself. The jinn would know the instant he died.

"Where do animal spirits go?" Key asked.

"I've forgotten."

"Me, too. They told us once. Maybe the angels will stop the cat from going wherever he's supposed to go and let him come with us."

"Where are we going to keep him?" Kip said. "And how can we feed a cat?"

"The angels might help us if we ask nicely." Key shrugged. "I bet we could."

The door opened behind them, and both jinn turned, then started. Key gaped and poked Kip repeatedly. "He did come back!" She knelt beside Andrew as he touched the cat under the chin. The cat had purred to himself, but when he raised his eyes and saw the huge figure, he hissed.

"Come on." Andrew spoke in a low tone with an undercurrent of laughter, and Kip frowned until she realized the humor was directed at himself. "You're about to cost me a thousand dollars at the vet. The least you can do is not bite me."

I didn't ask you to spend anything, the cat thought. *And I'll bite when I feel like it. I just don't feel like it now.*

The jinn climbed into the back seat of Andrew's car and followed him for the rest of the day. At the vet's office, they stood together and watched the cat lap up big bowls of water. "He was thirsty," Key said. "I didn't realize. Everything was frozen."

Jinn, the cat thought.

The vet gave Andrew some salve for the cat's frostbitten paws at a cost far less than a thousand dollars, then sent him home. The jinn slipped into the house.

"Do you think he'll like it?" The cat had dashed behind the sofa and crouched, tense and alert. Andrew, meanwhile, had rummaged in his closet until he found a stand covered with pink carpet. The man had found a handful of mice that lacked any sort of mouse-haze, and Kip realized they weren't real.

Key nudged the pink carpeted thing with her toe. "What's that?"

"I have no idea. Come here." Kip had found a picture in the drawer with the false mice. "See—he's holding another cat. He used to have another cat."

The cat had curled up beneath one of the couches, his eyes closed. *I'm not going to sleep, though.* He could smell another cat, but it hadn't been in the house for a few weeks, like the stale perfume he could also smell. *Ridiculous for him to do all this.* The cat knew he could leave when he felt like it. But for the moment he didn't feel like leaving. A few minutes later, he had purred himself to sleep.

Andrew stood in the kitchen, watching the couch where he'd let the cat retreat once he came into the apartment. The cat still hadn't eaten the Siamese's remaining can of cat food (some gourmet brand he probably couldn't recognize as food after months of hunting mice), but he had drunk an awful lot. Andrew didn't disturb the cat, except to talk to him from time to time. "There's plenty of room in the apartment if you care to sulk," he said. "I can show you all the best places for that. But when you're rested, you can come sit with me."

He hadn't named the cat yet, but for some reason the word "Arrow" kept coming to him.

Andrew had a trick left. It had worked, at least, when he still wanted to ingratiate himself with the Siamese. He sat on the living room floor with a deck of cards, and he shuffled it for a long time before dealing himself a hand of solitaire. Five minutes. Deal the cards, shuffle, lay them in stacks with a snap. Ten minutes. Shuffle again. Deal.

He looked up to a tortoiseshell face with round, relaxed eyes.

"Well, hello," he said to the cat.

You didn't make me come out, the cat thought, giving his paw a lick. *I felt like it.*

"He'll be all right now," Key said. "Come on."

Sunset had been recent enough that they still could slip through the door without opening it, but night made them more solid every minute. Kip and Key ran across the street and had a near miss with a station wagon, but on the other side they laughed and looked into the field.

"We still didn't find that arrow," Kip said.

"Easy enough." Key drew her bow. "Maybe another arrow will lead us to the first."

An angelic hand landed on their shoulders, and the jinn stopped. "Or maybe we should scour the underbrush," Kip said.

MISS HETTIE AND HARLAN
by Charles L. Fontenay

Charles L. Fontenay wrote science fiction for a decade in the 1950–60s and returned to the field several years ago. Since then a number of his shorter works have appeared in magazines and anthologies, including Catfantastic III. Three novels in his young adult science fiction mystery series *The Kipton Chronicles* were published in the last year. He lives and writes in St. Petersburg, Florida.

Harlan stretched laxly along the back of the sofa like a limp rug. The big black cat's eyes were closed and his only sign of life was the flick of an ear, as though he knew he had become the object of current conversation.

"He really seems to belong to the house," said Miss Hettie. "Or maybe the other way around. He certainly isn't an ordinary stray. When he came stalking up, I thought he might belong to that nice young man, Brett Warren, who was so helpful when I moved in, but Brett said no, he doesn't even like cats."

"Oh, cats and the Larchmare House just seem to go together naturally," said Rowena, lifting a shell-thin cup to take a sip of Earl Grey tea. "As a little girl, I used to sneak over here and play with all their cats when the Larchmare family was still alive."

"Oh? I thought that was before your time, Rowena." Rowena was Miss Hettie's best friend from church and, of course, the first person she'd invited for tea since moving into the Larchmare House.

The Larchmare House. The many chambered, tall-ceilinged house lay silent around the two old ladies, a reverberating silence. It was a house of the late nineteenth century, when Gregor Larchmare was the richest man in town (then *really* only a town, not a city), its bricks baked and laid by slaves, a house of columns and turrets so sturdy that it had survived the years of neglect when it stood unoccupied, survived in surprisingly good shape.

"I think I'm a few years older than you, Hettie," said Rowena with a smile. "The Larchmare family was wiped out in 1912, and I was ten years old by then."

"You're right. I was only three. But you knew, didn't you, my father was a first cousin of the Larchmares? That's how I happened to inherit this house. And of course I'm interested, I've heard so many tales. What really happened to the Larchmares?"

"*I've* heard that story all my life—the true one. I knew the family, after all. Mr. and Mrs. Larchmare were in their fifties and all four of their children were grown but still living here with them: three girls and the youngest, Leonard, in his middle twenties and a strange, quiet young fellow. Leonard proved to be really aberrant. One evening after everybody was asleep he slipped around and strangled them all to death, one after the other, along with a visiting relative. The only one who escaped was the visitor's baby daughter, who was lured out of the house and away from it by the family cat, almost as if intentionally. They found her wandering alone the next morning, half a mile away, the cat still with her."

"What happened to Leonard? Was he brought to justice?"

"No, Leonard disappeared. They never found him. And you can imagine, Hettie, after something like that the house had a bad reputation. Superstitious people

claimed it was haunted, there were stories of weird lights
seen through the windows and of people disappearing
here. That sort of thing is why it was almost impossible
to rent the place and it just sat here and deteriorated
until you came down to take it over."

Well, it didn't deteriorate so badly, thought Miss Hettie
after Rowena left. Of course some parts of the house
were in worse shape than others, especially the back,
both upstairs and downstairs. But the front of the house
was in excellent condition and Miss Hettie needed only a
few good rooms—in effect a small apartment—to live in.

"Shucks, it never was as bad as folks liked to think,
Miss Hettie," had said Brett Warren with his winning
smile when he was so kindly helping her move things in
and put them in the right places. "Most of the damage
hasn't been from neglect but happened 'bout ten years
ago when the company managing the place decided to
rent it out to three different families, trying to make
some profit on it. Dividing it into apartments, sort of,
except the absentee owner wouldn't let 'em build any
partitions between 'em."

Miss Hettie knew about that. The "absentee owner"
had been her father. And, as Rowena had told her, those
renters moved out one after another because, as one
of them put it, "they's somethin' about that house that
ain't natural."

Remembering what Rowena had told her, Miss Hettie
said, "My niece in New Jersey thinks it's too dangerous
for me to be living here by myself." At the time they
were in the side yard, where Brett was showing her the
layout of the flower beds. Brett seemed to know a great
deal about the Larchmare House. Harlan lay stretched
in the window above them, a black shadow overseeing
them.

Brett laughed.

"New Jersey?" he repeated. "Whoever said urban
New Jersey's 'safe'?"

Miss Hettie said much the same thing to her niece
when Allyson telephoned to try to talk her into coming
back to New Jersey and settling down sensibly. That was
the occasion on which Miss Hettie discovered Harlan
could talk.

"I'm perfectly all right here and I think I'm going to be very comfortable, Allyson," Miss Hettie assured her. "There's a grocery that will deliver my order, and if I need to go to a store, I have friends from church who don't mind driving me."

"That isn't the point," contended Allyson. "When you said you were going to Florida to look at the house, I had no idea you'd decide to stay there and live in it. Aunt Hettie, you're eight-five years old and it's not safe for you to be living alone in a city like that."

"A city like what?" Miss Hettie demanded. "It's a beautiful place, which is more than you can say for the crowded streets and empty buildings all around you there. There are palm trees and flowers blooming all year round, and I don't have to put up with your ice and snow in the winter. And what's unsafe about living here, I'd like to know? If I fall ill, this nice young man, Brett Warren, lives somewhere close and keeps an eye on me."

"But there you're alone in a house, not in an apartment where you have other people living around you . . . and me not far away. What concerns me is, I've read about the crime rate there and these young thugs target elderly, helpless people. One of them could break in some night and cut your throat."

"Oh, foof! That's a different part of the city. This is a low-crime area. The folks who live around here are respectable—and friendly."

"But if someone did break in and attack you, there's no one there to protect you."

"Oh, Harlan's all the protection I need," replied Miss Hettie airily.

"That cat? What could it do?"

"Scratch their eyes out. Wouldn't you, Harlan?"

Allyson gave it up. Miss Hettie hung up the phone triumphantly, got to her feet, and turned up the lights in the room. Harlan raised his head and opened yellow eyes, looking straight at her.

"She's right, you know," said Harlan.

Miss Hettie was far too advanced in years to nearly jump out of her skin, as she would have when she was younger. She just said "gurk" very softly and sat down rather abruptly on the sofa, turning to stare at him over her spectacles and wondering if she was getting so old she'd started imagining things. For years Miss Hettie had kept cats and during those years, living alone, she had formed the habit of talking to them, but this was the first time any of them ever talked back to her.

"It's funny," she said to Harlan, "but I thought I just heard you say something."

"You did," replied Harlan. Odd, the cat's voice wasn't strong, something like a child's, but there wasn't a trace of a meow in it. "But I don't see what's funny about it. I didn't make a joke."

There must be a snappy comeback to that, Miss Hettie thought, but her repartee wasn't as quick as it once had been.

"If you actually did say something," she wanted to know, "why haven't you spoken up before?"

"There hasn't been any reason for me to say anything before and, unlike humans, cats don't chatter unnecessarily," said Harlan, arising on the sofa back and stretching indolently. "This time I felt I ought to say something because Allyson's right about it."

"Oh, is that so?" Miss Hettie was somewhat piqued. "And what makes *you* an authority, Mister?"

"Oh, I get around. There are creatures that prowl at night, and this house isn't as safe as you think. Now, I like your preference for living alone—it's catlike. But it isn't humanlike."

"What do you mean, it isn't 'humanlike'? I've lived alone all my adult life except in college, when I had roommates. It's natural for a lady who chooses never to marry to live alone."

"It still isn't humanlike," contended Harlan. "You humans are descended from monkeys, so you're social animals who like to run in crowds and chatter at one another. We cats are descended from ... well, cats. We're solitary animals by nature—and we're predators."

Harlan was a predator all right ... or, at least, he was a fighter. On three occasions already she had had to rush outside as fast as her aged legs would carry her to rescue some neighbor's cat (in one case a small dog) from Harlan's fierce protection of his bailiwick. She always got there too late, when the intruding animal had fled and Harlan was stalking around like a conquering hero, his fur fluffed up and his yellow eyes glowing.

"I deny that I or any of my family descended from monkeys," said Miss Hettie stoutly. "I've never put any stock in that evolution stuff."

"Even so, you should listen to your niece. She's more in touch with the times. Now, as a reward for my making an exception to a very firm rule and revealing to you that I can talk, do you suppose you could spare a saucer of milk? Whole milk, please, none of that skim stuff."

A reasonable request. Miss Hettie got up off the sofa—a slower and more difficult action than once—and toddled into the kitchen—actually a small room in the front of the house converted into a kitchen, as the original huge kitchen was far in the back of the house. She drank skim milk with her meals because the doctor said it was better for her and there wasn't any whole milk in the refrigerator. But she did have a small carton half full of half-and-half she kept for Sally Willis' coffee when Sally came over, and she poured most of that for the cat. Harlan growled about it deep in his throat, but he drank it.

So Harlan was a magical creature. (Aren't all cats?) That being so, she supposed Harlan's talking to her wasn't completely unthinkable but it certainly was unexpected. Cats talked so eloquently in their own peculiar language that Harlan's resort to human words must be because he couldn't make his point in cat-language. (But of course that business about humans being monkey-like creatures who chattered was a base canard.)

That night something happened that caused her to wonder briefly if Allyson and Harlan weren't right about the inadvisability of her living alone in the big Larchmare House. She wasn't sure of the origin of the impulse, but she chose to take a large candle and poke around the back of the house (the electricity was on only in its front, where she lived).

She didn't go all the way back, where she understood

the deterioration was advanced, only to the middle section, which contained a spacious ballroom, a book-empty library, and a big hallway with a wide staircase rising to the shadows of the second floor. This part of the house had not been remodeled and repaired as had been her own quarters and a noticeable aroma of antiquity and decay filled its air.

With some trepidation, Miss Hettie climbed the stairs. Up here were corridors and bedrooms and bathrooms, relics of the distant past when the Larchmare House had been inhabited by a large family and servants, with accommodations for guests. Miss Hettie poked around, peering into the bedrooms, where plaster and lathing and occasional broken fixtures dotted the floors.

She stuck her head into one of the bedrooms and all at once a cold wind seemed to blow over her heart. She was suddenly sure that this was one of the bedrooms in which Leonard Larchmare had strangled one of his victims—one of his parents, or a sister, or perhaps the visiting relative. Almost she could *see* the body lying on the big bed, in its tangled bedclothing, the bruising finger marks on its neck.

Hastily Miss Hettie retreated and hurried back downstairs, to the pleasant surroundings of her own rooms.

But Harlan's revelation of his magical nature, Miss Hettie discovered, carried with it some subsidiary benefits. She half expected Harlan to become a rather talkative companion after that outburst, but that didn't happen. When she talked to Harlan, he reacted much as he always had, just looking at her with yellow eyes and not saying a word. But the fact that he *had* talked once loosened her own tongue: she knew now he was intelligent enough to understand what she was saying and she talked to him about things she wouldn't have otherwise, instead of the prosaic stuff she usually talked to her cats.

And, since she knew Harlan understood, she confided to him some of the nostalgia that so frequently affects the old.

There was her precious memory, which she would have felt foolish mentioning to Harlan before, of her first real kiss. She related it wistfully to Harlan, and suddenly she was back there again. Really there. Not dream-real, but real-real. She was 12-year-old Hettie Fisher, walking by the school gym, and Tommy Knowles, the good-looking (boy, was he good-looking!) football captain, came out and Hettie stopped him to tell him how excited she'd been when he threw that touchdown pass against Central High. And Tommy, *four years* older than she, grinned and grabbed her by both arms and planted a big, firm smack right on her mouth. Then Tommy walked away, leaving an ecstatic Hettie thinking this was by far the most wonderful thing that had ever happened in her life.

Of course after it was over and Miss Hettie found herself sitting on the sofa in her apartment, somewhat breathless and with her spectacles awry, she recalled that nothing ever came of it. Tommy never even dated her (what high school football captain would actually *date* a twelve-year-old girl?) and he went off and married that little snip from Waynesboro a few years later.

Harlan was sitting on the carpet in front of her, his tail curved behind him, gazing straight at her with sleepy yellow eyes.

"Harlan, did you do that?" asked Miss Hettie.

"Miaow," said Harlan.

Miss Hettie was convinced that Harlan had, somehow, and she was convinced more than ever when she experienced other similar regressions. After all, if hypnotists can do it, why not cats? She lived again through the time Mr. Worrall, her boss on her first job, pinched her on the butt and she slapped his silly face (and lost the job) ... the beauty of her only serious love affair before Martin went overseas and was killed ... her pride when Allyson got married and later when Allyson's first child was born (she still felt Edward was, in a sense, her own grandson) ... a lot of things like that.

The years stretched behind Miss Hettie like a bridal veil of scented memories, each with its tale to tell. Nearly a hundred of those years now, nearer and nearer to a hundred each year. Some of the tales told by the years were rose-happy, some were violet-sad and some were so bland as to be almost forgettable ... almost but not quite, because they were all forget-me-nots, each as full as all the others. Miss Hettie could look back along that chain of years and say "that was my life, that is my life, for those years I remember are *my* years."

Much had happened to Hettie Fisher during those many long years, not an exciting muchness, not a dramatic record, but all in all a satisfying trail of years. She had been many places and seen many things she would not have gone or seen if she had married and settled down as she had expected to when she was a girl. She would have, too, if Martin hadn't been killed, but Miss Hettie was what she supposed people called a Victorian romantic: her true love lost to her, she never loved again.

The many places and things of her life, the important ones and the unimportant ones, were brought back to her and made real again over the ensuing weeks, by Harlan—or by somebody. It was as good as time travel—and maybe it was.

But, though Harlan was always there looking up at her when those experiences ended and she was sure he was doing it, he wouldn't talk. Not in human language.

Except once.

"Harlan, I know you *can* talk and you're intelligent enough to know what I'm saying to you," she complained in exasperation. "Why don't you *say* something? And not just 'meow,' either."

"Oh. Well," said Harlan, "if you want a demonstration of my intelligence and vocabulary, I disagree with the Copenhagen interpretation of quantum theory. It is dualistic, while as a matter of principle it should satisfy conditions of unitarity, positivity and cluster decomposition."

"Harlan! You know I don't know anything about such things!"

"Well, you were the one who brought up the question of relative intelligence," said Harlan dryly. "Miaow."

After that Harlan didn't deign to talk any more. Miss Hettie understood how he must feel and wasn't sure it wasn't best all around that he didn't. There were times when *she* didn't want to talk to anybody, about anything, and if she'd wanted somebody around yakking all the time she'd have arranged for someone to live with her. As for her own talking, most of the time it was just musing that didn't require an answer and if Harlan wasn't around to direct it to she was just as content to talk to the stove or the saucepan or the lamp when it wouldn't turn on.

She'd forgotten how she first learned Harlan could talk human speech until one night when events proved the cat knew what he was talking about when he advised her to listen to Allyson's advice.

Miss Hettie liked to relax and read in bed in the evenings and this evening she was deeply immersed in an Agatha Christie murder mystery. Harlan was snoozing comfortably on the foot of the bed, curled in a circle with his tail wrapped around his nose.

Miss Hettie hoped to finish the book and find out who murdered Linnette Doyle and the others, but by 11 o'clock her eyes were so tired she gave it up until tomorrow. She laid the book facedown on the bedside table, opened to the place she had stopped reading, followed it with her spectacles, and turned out the table lamp. She had gotten that lamp in Istanbul ... and how many American ladies, even living as long as she had, got to Istanbul? With a sigh, Miss Hettie slid down under the sheet to go to sleep.

She did—but some time later (she didn't know how long) she was awakened by a slight noise.

The moon was up and shining slantingly into the bedroom, illuminating it dimly. Miss Hettie lay there for a moment, her eyes half open, wondering what had awakened her. Then she became aware of a shadowy figure in the room.

Miss Hettie's eyes popped wide open and her heart began to beat faster. At first she couldn't see anything in the room and was on the verge of deciding it was only her imagination when her bedside lamp went on.

Brett Warren was standing beside her bed, a pleasant smile on his face. She was vaguely aware of Harlan, leaping off the bed and landing on the rug with a soft thump.

"Brett!" she exclaimed, sitting up. "What are you doing here at this time of night?"

"Why, Miss Hettie," he replied in his always-congenial voice, "the time has come to finish the job."

"What do you mean?" Fear crept through her.

"You probably don't remember, you were such a little girl at the time, but you were the one who got away, a long time ago," said Brett. "You were the little girl I missed that night. I knew if I waited long enough, you'd be drawn back to this house—and now you have. I'm Leonard Larchmare, Miss Hettie, and I'm here to complete the task I wasn't able to finish then."

Leonard Larchmare! It was incredible, impossible. He had been a young adult when he strangled the Larchmare family in their beds, and he should be an old man now, nearing the century mark. But he was still a young man, no older than Leonard Larchmare had been when he committed that unspeakable crime!

Yet Miss Hettie believed him. Somehow, through all these long years, Leonard Larchmare had haunted Larchmare House without aging, waiting, waiting for the time he could get his strangling hand on the little girl who got away.

And now those strangling hands were reaching for her throat, almost gently, almost lovingly. Miss Hettie squeaked.

All at once a shadow pounced on Brett (Leonard Larchmare?) from behind, a shadow as big as he. He grunted and his hands fluttered and reached back frantically as he was borne down beside the bed, below her line of vision.

Sounds of a confused struggle down there came to her ears and she sat up in bed, peering over the edge. In the dimness she could see nothing but a tangle of heaving, twisting shadows, hear nothing but muttered curses and muffled growls. The bed shook as the combatants bumped into it.

For just a moment they rolled into a spot where the moonlight struck them full. In the light from the bedside lamp Miss Hettie was astonished to distinguish the lithe, muscular form of a large black panther mauling Leonard, who was trying vainly to fend the animal off.

All at once everything subsided. The two large shadows separated and one of them, the panther, seemed to fade away while the shadow that was Leonard lay still. His clothing was torn to shreds and blood welled from multiple wounds, his throat and chest clawed and bitten to shreds. His eyes were open and glazed.

He was dead! And he was an old man, with withered features!

Almost certainly, he was dead. Blood was all over that part of her nice clean floor. It served him right, she thought. Brett or Leonard, he was a wicked, wicked man, to attack an old lady in her own home.

Anticlimactically, a small black form sailed over the edge of the bed, alit as light as a feather and sat down, as blasé as you please. Harlan.

Harlan sat on the foot of the bed, casually washing his face with his tongue and one paw. Two or three drops of blood clung to the ends of his whiskers.

"Somehow Leonard remained young over the years in this house, waiting to claim his final victim," said Miss Hettie, still trembling from her fright. "Harlan, were *you* the cat who led me away from the house when I was a little girl?"

"Miaow," said Harlan.

THE NEIGHBOR
by P. M. Griffin

P.M. Griffin has been writing since her early childhood. She is the author of the *Star Commandos* series, Seakeep (appearing in *Storms of Victory*), Falcon Hope (featured in *Flight of Vengeance*), *Redline the Stars*, and *Firehand*, plus short stories appearing in *Magic in Ithkar 3*, *Catfantastic*, *Catfantastic II*, *Catfantastic III* (winner of the Cat Writers' Association Muse Award for Short Fiction), *Tales of the Witch World*, *Tales of the Witch World 3*, and *Women at War*. She lives in Brooklyn, New York with her cats Cougar, Starlight, and Snowflake.

The sun will be set before we get into the tree, or maybe you're thinking of making the climb like that? I wouldn't recommend it myself, but sometimes there's no accounting for the decisions of humans.

Dory glared at the black cat sitting on the edge of her bed. "No, I don't plan on scaling anything in this costume, Master Trouble," she responded verbally, although she might as easily have answered his thoughts directly with her own mind.

She lifted her gown over her head and carefully laid it

across the back of the chaise before dropping the several
petticoats which had imparted the fullness to the skirt.

Her frown deepened. "I suppose it doesn't matter
what or how I study anyway. Martin seems to have forgotten me completely."

Dory flushed and bit her lip. Did she really resent a
poor, very sick little boy? "That was unworthy."

It was, Trouble agreed, *and unnecessary. The little kit
needs Martin's help. You can concentrate on one area
over another for a few weeks without hurting either.*

He looked at the human somberly. She had been a
kitten herself only last autumn, a skinny, begrimed
twelve-year-old in flight for her very life. She was a ma-
ture queen of her species now. The sorcerer advanced
her age eight years, so that she could remain here under
his instruction in the town where she was so well known
in her old form, training it was absolutely essential that
she receive before some uncontrolled outpouring of her
rapidly budding mage talent caused some real disaster.

He purred. His heart had ached to see maturity so
suddenly thrust upon his kitten, but that sadness had
passed quickly. His Dory needed him no less, and her
love for him had gained in depth and understanding.

The tomcat had taken on a new appearance himself,
exchanging his magnificent black-and-white markings for
a totally ebony coat. He remained a singularly handsome
cat, but he would be glad to resume his own coloring
when they changed residence, as those who do not age
must do every several years in order to avoid raising
curiosity about the absence of time's bite upon them.

"You're perfect just the way you are, and you know
it full well," Dory informed him. She kissed him on the
top of his head. Puberty had brought the opening of her
inner voice and ears. The ability to converse directly
with this small, good friend was one of the best of the
many things which had come to her these last strange
months.

Naturally.

She made a disgusted face. "I just wish everything else
worked as well." Martin had been right when he had
warned her that she would miss the eight years she had

advanced without living. Even now, when everything was new and filled with wonder, she was aware of the great void in her experience. A considerable amount of knowledge had accompanied the alteration, enough that she was able to function in her new role and pick up her studies at the appropriate stage. Dory's scowl deepened. Straight book learning was always there when she needed it. Unfortunately, the same could not be said of other, socially necessary abilities. Most of those worked best when she did not consciously think about them. Let her just become aware of her billowing skirts at the wrong moment . . .

You'd make an interesting sight. —The air's nice outside, Trouble reminded her with a great show of tried patience, *We should be taking advantage of it.*

"I'll be ready in a few minutes." Even as she spoke, the woman drew on a white linen blouse. A pair of gray trousers followed, Martin's castoffs, carefully altered to her fit, not by sorcery, but by her own hard-plied needle. The brogs into which she thrust her feet were her own. Her teacher had used his arts to repair them and resize them to accommodate her newly acquired adult proportions.

Grabbing the carry bag containing her pad, case of pencils, and mirror, she headed for the door. "Time to go, cat. You can sleep your life away as easily up in a tree as in here. Unlike you, I have work to do."

Sleep the day away! Impudent human! I've been trying to get you moving . . .

He bounded out of the room after her and raced her down the hall, outpacing her before she reached the stairs.

Dory only laughed. She skipped down after him, delighting in her freedom from the confining petticoats.

She hurried out the rear door into the high-walled courtyard, not stopping until she reached the large tree shading the left rear corner.

Two chairs and a small table were set invitingly in its shadow. A little, round gray cat was curled in the center of the nearer seat. Dory smiled at the sleepy response to her mental greeting. Jasmine was decidedly Martin's friend and preferred her own company and dreams when

separated from that beloved being. Not that sleeping was
any chore for a cat.

The woman scrambled onto the table. From there, it
was a simple matter to catch hold of the lowest branch
and hoist herself up. She chuckled to herself. She had
not lost her old skills with the acquisition of some new
ones.

She ascended one more branch and set her back
against the trunk. Her perch was just wide enough that
she was able to bring both her legs up in front of her
and raise her knees to support the sketching pad she
now took from her bag along with the mirror and pencils. Before her lay Ambrose the scholar's courtyard. It
was somewhat larger than Martin's, and it was even
more carefully manicured, a breathtaking melody of flo-
ral and foliage color, texture, form, and variety.

Dory studied the lovely prospect for a few minutes in
sheer pleasure. It was difficult to believe that so much
beauty was potentially so deadly and even more difficult
to realize that such peril could be turned to benefit in
experienced hands. She assumed that must indeed be
true of nearly everything down there even if she had
found no mention of positive applications for many of
the plants she had thus far identified. After all, Martin's
books were general reference works whereas this was
Ambrose's specialty.

She had gone to her teacher despite his preoccupation
with the ever-worsening illness of his friend's young son
when her studies had revealed that every specimen in
their neighbor's gardens with the exception of the grass
in his patch of lawn was toxic to a greater or lesser
extent.

Martin had not been pleased by her suspicions against
the botanist scholar, but he had informed her that Ambrose supplemented the income derived from his investments by supplying physicians and nature healers with
various medicinal preparations, a response she had received with open relief. It was good to know they were
not living next to a mass murderer getting ready to go
to work on the neighborhood ...

Speaking of going to work, you won't identify many plants by sitting here all afternoon gathering stardust.

Trouble had finished paying his respects to Jasmine and now joined his human on the branch.

"Just putting myself in the mood," she replied, but the cat was correct. It was time to begin.

Dory concentrated on the silver-green patch of vegetation abutting the specimens she had studied at the end of her previous session. It was only a blur of color at this distance.

Slowly, the apprentice sorceress lowered her eyes to the mirror resting against the pad. It was an exceptionally well-ground circle twelve inches in diameter and uncommonly thick for such an object, so that she seemed more to be peering into its depths than simply glancing at its surface.

At first, it appeared perfectly blank although she was bent directly over it, then the scene she had been studying slowly formed there. Dory willed better, closer resolution. The image blurred, and when it cleared again, she was looking, first at several plants, then at a single one. This, she carefully sketched before demanding still more concentrated views, one of a single leaf, others of the minute, massed flowers and of their individual components.

The day was bright and mild, well suited to her project, and the woman worked steadily for the next two hours.

Trouble alternated between napping and eyeing the branches above and around for sight of birds or other interesting potential game.

Suddenly, he stiffened, and his head snapped toward Ambrose's house. Had something moved on the outskirts of his vision?

There it was again, at that upper window. He hissed sharply. *Dory, we've been spotted!*

The human quickly altered the direction of her gaze and concentrated on the mirror once more.

The figure of a man materialized in its depths, blurred by the lace curtain through which he was looking and by the fact that he was standing well back in the shadow of the frame.

So.

Do we run? the cat demanded.

No, she answered with her mind. *We're doing nothing wrong.*

Even as she spoke, she flipped to a fresh page and willed a new picture to form. She could hardly explain how she could produce detailed botanical drawings from this distance. Sorcery was still considered a highly suspicious—and illegal—profession.

Do you think he'll come down to us? Trouble asked.

Probably. I would.—Does he know we've seen him?

Not likely. I'm not visible from there, and a cat could scarcely have masked her reaction better than you did just now.

She inclined her head to acknowledge the compliment, but her tone remained serious. *That's good. Keep out of whatever happens. I can defend myself somewhat if I muddle this, but you've got to stay free to summon Martin if things start to get beyond me.*

If things get beyond you, donkey tail, it'll be too late to summon Martin or anyone else.

Just do as I say. —Here he comes!

The door of the house opened, and a man stepped out into the light. He immediately hailed Dory. She looked up as if surprised, then smiled broadly and waved to him.

Scholar Ambrose was a man in his middle years, older than Martin looked to be, but like her teacher, he was slender and appeared to enjoy good health and full vigor. In his youth, he must have been startlingly handsome. He was comely still with hair so black that it almost gleamed and piercing eyes of the same color. His complexion was olive and his features almost as perfectly chiseled as those on a statue of yore. Only his mouth spoiled him a little. That was tight and hard and was framed by lines that gave him a harsh, even an implacable, look.

He reached the wall in a matter of seconds and came to a stop at the place nearest to her perch. "You make a singularly attractive spy," he observed. His speech was cultivated, without affectation, his voice pleasantly modulated.

"You have a singularly attractive house," Dory countered. She held up the sketch her arts had just created so that he could view the largely uncompleted picture of his dwelling with its elaborate tracing of vines covering its walls.

His smile was devastating. Dory swallowed hard. She wanted to scramble down the tree and race for her house but knew that she must hold her ground. The twelve-year-old she had been would have run. The woman she had become could not.

That woman should know what to do, what to say next, but Dory simply did not. How could she? She had missed the experiences, the normal, slow acquisition of the social skills that should have fitted her for this encounter. The man was too attractive, and he was not looking at her the way Martin did. . . .

Trust your instincts, foolish kit!

Simpler to say than do!

He was right. The human forcibly calmed and cleared her mind. The ability to function in her new life had come along with it. She must keep herself open to that inner guidance, however difficult it was to do when she was this nervous. That was it. She need be no other than herself. Be courteous. Grow interested in the person himself . . .

Ambrose fetched the ladder he used for pruning and set it against the wall. With its aid, he gained the top of the barrier. He half sat on the six-inch flat surface. "I'm Ambrose," he announced since they had never been introduced despite the proximity of their dwellings.

"Doreen," she replied, using the formal name Martin had given her. "I'm pleased to meet you, sir. I hope I haven't disturbed you too much, but you do have a lovely courtyard. I enjoy drawing views of it."

"Yes, it is pleasant," he agreed with obvious pleasure, "and it's as unique as it is attractive."

"Scholar Martin told me that you supply medicines for physicians like Doctor Solomon," she ventured.

"The raw materials mostly, except in cases where my

greater knowledge of the substances involved makes it significantly safer for me to produce the entire preparation myself."

"What a fascinating business!"

He smiled, a trifle indulgently, she thought. "The plants are interesting. Business is business, and I confess to having little love for that. Otherwise, I would have kept on running my father's after his death instead of selling it off. It was profitable enough."

"What kind of trade did ye follow?" Dory asked. She found it impossible to imagine this man making candles or cobbling boots.

"Luxury imports. We brought the things in from the Mainland and peddled them to the noble and rich. We didn't call it that, of course. It was all handled in a very sophisticated manner, but it was peddling all the same. I preferred a scholarly life among my plants, with visits to the capital now and then for cultural recreation."

"But you do have an occupation," she pointed out.

He nodded. "To supplement the income from my investments. I'm independent enough that I do not have to deal in common spices and herbs and other readily available commodities. If I wanted to make a real go of this, I should have to provide for all a physician's or a nature healer's needs."

Ambrose eyed her speculatively. "Now, young woman, I've told you all about myself. What is your story? I take it that you are Martin's pupil? I'd heard that you were attractive, but I confess I did not imagine you would prove quite this comely."

Dory's eyes fell, and she colored slightly. "It was felt that I would do well to study with someone like Scholar Martin for the sciences and mathematics."

"Has he proven a good teacher?"

"Indeed, yes. I am learning a great deal."

"No doubt. About botany, too?"

"Of course. I do very well with it, actually. I like studying living things more than abstract figures."

She could feel his eyes examining her, searching her face, although his expression did not alter. Did he believe her? Surely, he could not imagine the one course of study she had carefully refrained from mentioning. . . .

The man gave her a winning smile. "I suppose it would be considered improper if I offered to give you a tour of my collection," he remarked. "I have the afternoon at my disposal."

Dory looked up sharply. "It would be highly improper."

Trouble's growl sounded in her mind. *Just try bringing those black eyes up here, human. I'll scratch them out for you.*

Trouble! she exclaimed, horrified.

And don't you dare even think of climbing down to him! He's reeking like a courting tom.

I have no intention of going down there, fur brain, as he knows full well.

Ambrose accepted her refusal without sign of surprise or protest. "Perhaps I can invite both you and your teacher one day?"

"I'd really enjoy that," she assured him.

The man started to turn away but stopped suddenly. "I've told the local young people about the perils of sampling my crops. I don't suppose it's necessary to issue the same warning to you?"

She drew herself up. "I assure you, sir, that I do not go sneaking over fences to pilfer my neighbors' berries and fruit."

He laughed. "No, I imagine it is safe to assume that you don't. Farewell, Doreen. I shall call upon your Scholar Martin soon."

Dory watched until he went inside once more. "How handsome he is! Well, how did I manage?" she inquired of her companion.

You did fine, he told her. *Now let's get out of here before he changes his mind. I don't like that one. His eyes don't match his smell.*

"You said he smelled like a tom." Her face turned scarlet as she spoke.

She should not be surprised. Dory knew the sort of education she was supposed to be receiving was often that sought by women desiring to become courtesans, and the irregularity of her present position and dress could only have reinforced that impression in the botanist's mind. Damn. This was a complication she did not want or need.

Dory dropped lightly out of the tree onto the table. She jumped to the ground, thoroughly startled by a snaring hiss of unparalleled fury.

Jasmine was crouched on the table. Her ears were pinned flat against her head. Her eyes were slits. Her body was taut, ready to spring at the hint of provocation.

The human stared in astonishment at the usually docile little cat. "Jasmine, whatever is the matter, baby?"

That monster is not to come here. This is Martin's territory.

"Ambrose?"

Yes.

"Why do you dislike him so much?"

When I was a small kitten, I got into his garden and nibbled some of his accursed plants. Fire was exploding in my belly when he found me. That cruel one knew what was wrong with me because he examined the leaves I had chewed, but he only laughed. "Bad choice for you, cat," he said. "It will be interesting to watch how long it takes."

Dory swore, calling up a phrase she had heard her former guardian's husband use, but the tabby went on with her story as if she did not hear. *I'd have been finished then, but someone called him back into his house, and I was able to crawl off to die.*

She purred suddenly. *Instead, I worked my way right through a hole in the fence into this courtyard. My distress had reached Martin, and he was already looking for me. That's how we met.* She purred more loudly still. *He found me and made me well. My Martin stayed awake night after night to save me.*

"Poor little lady. No wonder you throw up if someone looks at you sideways. What did Martin do when you told him what had happened?"

I didn't tell him, or anyone else, either. I—I was afraid of what Ambrose might do.

The woman's brows raised. "Do to Martin?"

Something sneaky.

"That would probably be in character for the bastard."

Dory did not find the botanist attractive any longer. She recalled the hard cast to his expression and realized there was good cause for it. His character and his soul were rotten with cruelty. Anyone who could laugh at the suffering of a helpless little animal would use a child just as viciously.

She blinked. "How is he working it?" Dory whispered. She was certain now, as certain as she was of life itself, that Solomon's little son had not contracted some dire disease, that his symptoms were being intentionally induced through the direct wish and will of Ambrose the scholar. Why he had turned his spleen against the child of an insignificant village physician was irrelevant. All that mattered was how he was administering his venom and how to stop him before he killed Sammy.

His reason will be very important to Martin, Trouble pointed out.

The woman bit her lip. So it would. No one could be accused of so heinous a crime on gut feeling, even with a story like Jasmine's to back it up. Despite her frustration, Dory did agree with the rightness of that, but now Sammy could die, would die, if Ambrose could not be stopped. "If we could catch him in the act or at least show how he's doing it, the motive could be beaten out of him later."

I hope you're not thinking of exploring that house? the tomcat demanded severely.

She shook her head emphatically. "I'd only get caught if I went physically, and I definitely can't hold a sufficient level of concentration to spy out the whole place, not in real detail. I don't even know what constitutes evidence. The mere presence of dangerous plants and compounds doesn't. He makes his living, or a good part of it, out of those."

As you said, we have to catch him at it, or Jasmine and I do. Our eyes are better suited for such work, and we have an infinity more patience than you.

"But how?" his human exploded.

Why, we just watch him, and we're not alone in this

town. The local cats don't like Ambrose. He's not kind himself, and I'll venture Jasmine was not the first or last kitten to fall victim to his plantings. We'll have plenty of help. We'll know everyone who comes to his house and where his visitors go after they leave, and no one except ourselves will be the wiser.

"Trouble, are you sure? I couldn't bear it if something happened to you or Jasmine or any of the others."

Of course I'm sure, scatter-brained kit! Who would be suspicious of cats doing what they always do—napping, grooming, looking off into the distance? Our foe doesn't even realize we can think, he concluded contemptuously.

"All right, but do be careful. If we're right, he really is dangerous."

Kitten, the tom explained patiently, *cats are not humans. We do not court danger, and we never engage unnecessarily in unpleasant, strenuous behavior. Just continue botanizing. We'll get you the information you need to bring the whole matter to Martin.*

Despite that assurance, three weeks passed without result, although all the neighboring felines had readily joined in the surveillance. There was simply little activity of any sort to report. Ambrose's life was nearly painfully quiet. A few messengers or physicians' pupils or, occasionally, a healer himself came and quickly left again with an assortment of vials and packets. None approached Solomon the physician's house or child.

Trouble dozed on the window ledge that was his nightly post, one eye half open, fixed on their enemy's domain. It was not a bad chore, certainly not a demanding one for any cat.

He shifted his position a hair's breadth. That was the problem with it. He had anticipated playing a rather more significant role by this time than that of a perpetual window ornament.

He snapped alert. There had been a flicker of movement, not in the house or courtyard but on the wall separating the property from the alley beyond. As he watched, a shadow-figure lumped onto the top of the barrier. It remained a moment silhouetted against the

broad cat-faced moon before scrambling down the thick
growth of vines and branches into Ambrose the scholar's garden.

Dory! Out of bed!

The woman was racing for the window before his
warning had finished sounding in her mind. "What's happening?" she whispered.

*An intruder. Look there among the bushes at the foot
of the wall. He has a light of some sort.*

She squinted, trying to pick out detail, but distance
and the deep shadows negated the bright moonlight for
her frail human senses. "I'm no cat to see in the near
dark," she grumbled.

Use your mirror, then, fluff head.

Swearing at herself for her stupidity, Dory took the
glass from its silk-lined box and set it on her lap.

She forced her excitement to recede. Once she felt
fully in command of herself, the apprentice sorceress
concentrated on the scene beyond and then turned to
the mirror itself.

Gradually, an image formed and enlarged within the
glass, dark still, but not nearly so black as it had seemed
at a distance. Better, but she still could not adequately
see the intruder. He, or she, was crouched down in the
midst of the berry bushes and was screened by the dense
foliage. As Trouble had said, he had brought a small
light with him, probably a tiny votive-type candle in a
glass container, certainly nothing much larger. Its glow
was sufficient to reveal his progress but little more
than that.

He was working slowly. The plants were no longer as
heavily laden as they had been in late spring and very
early summer. Berries were still to be found, but not
without a careful branch-by-branch search, especially in
the dark like this.

Her brows drew together. Who in all creation would
want to gather this particular harvest and want it desperately enough to go to such lengths to obtain it?

She had her answer in the next moment. Dory's heart
seemed to freeze in mid-beat. "Dear Lord Above!" she
whispered in horror.

What was she to do? Martin was away at Doctor Solomon's again.

This could not wait! "Trouble, call Jasmine! We're going down there!"

Wait! He doesn't seem to be eating much.

"He's only a baby! How many of them would it take?"

The woman composed herself, however. Once more, she studied the scene below and the glass.

Driven by her fear and the intensity of her need, the resulting image was startling in its clarity, terrifying in the precision of detail it revealed. They could discern the weak glow of candlelight on the berry the intruder dropped into the stiff-sided purse he wore slung around his neck. At least, he seemed to be storing his finds rather than devouring them outright. If only they knew that for a fact . . .

She frowned. "If we try to come at him through the courtyards, he could spot us and bolt."

Grab him when he goes back over the wall, Trouble suggested. *You'd have him before he even knew you were there.*

"He might just sit down and start eating once he thinks he has enough berries," Dory argued desperately.

He should hold off until he's safely away since he's waited this long, but you're right. Young kittens will all eat just about anything they shouldn't. I'll slip over the wall and keep an eye on him. —Whatever you plan to do, move! That pesky kit won't stay picking berries forever.

The alley backing Ambrose's courtyard was narrow and dark with three-story buildings on either side. The wall separating it from the scholar's property was some fifteen feet tall, but a number of wooden boxes and crates had been piled against it. Neighborhood children had used them for a fort, climbing area, and meeting place throughout the spring and summer, and, apparently, for a ladder.

The sorceress positioned herself beside the stack, concealing herself in its shadow. Jasmine went to the top, ready to assist Trouble if he should call for help.

The tom slipped over the edge. Kittens, he grumbled to himself as he scrambled down, endeavoring to make the most of the cover provided by the vegetation and the wall itself. Four feet or two, it made no difference. Not one of them possessed half a reasoning brain, and what cerebral power they did have functioned solely to get themselves and everyone around them into the deepest possible difficulties.

They were also as unpredictable and fast as little mice, and he did not intend to allow this particular specimen to pull any surprises on them.

He had come none too soon.

Get set! he called to his comrades. *He's on his way!*

The small trespasser was not long in scaling the thick lacing of sturdy plants covering the inner portion of the wall. He topped the barrier, delayed momentarily to position himself for the descent, and twisted over the outer edge.

There was a slight space to the first box, and that measured scarcely a foot square, but the child showed no concern as he dropped onto his target. He landed true, in good balance, and immediately scrambled down to the next, much broader crate.

Jasmine was waiting for that. She sprang.

Catching the strap of the purse holding the deadly hoard of berries in her teeth, she deftly drew it over the boy's head and leaped away again before her victim quite realized what had occurred.

Wonderful! Dory exulted in delight and relief. *Bring it to Martin, love.*

The child let out a yowl of mingled fright and dismay, but by that time, Dory had reached him and swept him into the imprisoning safety of her arms.

The woman carried her struggling captive to the mouth of the alley where the light from the streetlanterns augmented the brighter shine of the moon, permitting her to see him clearly.

The boy had very blond hair and blue eyes. The roundness and delicacy of his features put him at about seven years of age, although his height and stocky build made him seem older.

"All right, young man. Start by telling me who you are."

He seemed to want to refuse, but he only swallowed hard. "I'm George, son of Charles the carpenter, Mistress."

"I know something of Charles," she told him severely. "An honest man by all reports. Why is his son slipping around in the middle of the night stealing other people's fruit?"

"No, I'm not!" George protested loudly.

Dory's brows lifted. "Oh, and just what was in that purse my cat rescued, pray tell?"

"Medicine!" he responded stoutly. "It'd be bad for a boy like me to eat Scholar Ambrose's berries, but physicians and healers use them to make sick folks better."

"What do you want with them, then? You're as stout and strong a lad as I've seen in a good while."

"My friend Sammy's sick. They're for him."

Dory gasped. She drew a deep breath. "George," she said quietly, "have you given berries like these to Sammy before now?"

"I have," he answered proudly. "That's why he's going to get better. He used to sneeze all the time."

"How do you get them to him?"

"I climb up the tree outside his bedchamber window. I'm a real good climber."

"So I see." Dory grew grave. "George, I want you to listen carefully to what I say. It's true that Ambrose's berries can help make people well, but only those ailing from certain diseases and only when they receive the correct kind of berry, usually in very small amounts. That might be a single one or even less than that, normally mixed with other special things. It takes years and years of study for a person to learn how to use such ingredients properly. If Sammy ate even part of what was in that purse after all he's had before, we probably wouldn't have him with us any more."

George gulped. His face screwed up as he started to cry.

Dory gently stroked his hair. "He'll be fine now, once you explain what's happened."

"Explain?"

"Go straight to Sammy's house and tell Doctor Solomon and Scholar Martin what you've done. That should be information enough for them to be able to set your friend to rights." That and the actual berries Jasmine would have delivered there by now, but she thought it best not to mention the cat's seemingly remarkable abilities.

"They'll yell," he said doubtfully.

"Maybe," the woman conceded. "They're both scared about Sammy, and that can make people talk hard, but you still have to go. George, you were brave and strong to get medicine that you thought would make Sammy better. Now you must be even braver and stronger to really help him."

He hesitated only a few moments. "I'll go," he said at last.

"Good lad! Run now. Don't waste any time getting there."

"I won't." Even as he spoke, the boy wheeled about and raced out of the alley, a small, determined figure prepared to do and endure what he must to aid his friend.

Dory's head lowered. *A fine little fellow. I hope we did right in sending him off to Solomon's house instead of home, but his story should be a big help.*

She sighed. *I'm so ashamed, Trouble. I wronged Scholar Ambrose terribly. If I'd said anything . . . Great Lord, the harm I could have done!*

The cat was about to reply but hissed instead. *Someone comes!*

Even as he spoke, a cloaked figure turned the left corner into the alley. "Young woman, what are you doing snooping around my property at this hour of night?"

Ambrose the scholar! Dory flushed with shame, but despite her guilt, her head came up at the tone of his voice. "This is a public street," she responded, "and I'm here to avert disaster." Quickly, she described her adventure of the evening, omitting only the little boy's

name to spare him and his family further embar-
rassment, that and the fact that she had been keeping
her neighbor under watch.

The man said nothing for several long seconds. His
head lowered. "A terrible tragedy so narrowly prevented. I've warned the neighborhood youth time and
again about the dangers of my plantings, but I suppose
this one was just too young to really understand."

"You're not to blame, sir."

Dory might have said more, but there was a nagging
at her inner mind, the feeling that something was wrong
about all this.

Her eyes and mouth hardened as she realized what it
was. Ambrose was to blame. He might not have put
George up to taking those berries—in all likelihood, he
had not—but he had known full well what was going on
once the deadly process had begun.

It could not be otherwise. Sammy's illness had been
widely discussed throughout the square and those
around it since the mysterious sickness had begun. The
botanist had to have heard of it, and the symptoms were
specific enough to have aroused immediate suspicion in
a man of his knowledge and experience.

As for the rest, he might not have actually witnessed
the young culprit in action, but he had seen evidence of
his presence. Ambrose tended all his gardens carefully,
and a small boy burglarizing a berry patch in the dead
of night could not have hidden or removed every sign
of his presence. He probably would not have thought
to try.

Above all else, especially as the season advanced and
the crop began to diminish, Ambrose could not have
missed the fact that he was losing fruit. Given the nature
of those berries, the potential hazard they represented,
how could any man of conscience and reason not raise
an alarm over their disappearance? The fact that he had
not in itself condemned Ambrose.

More did as well, a memory that chilled her heart.
This creature before her had not merely allowed the
poisoning of Solomon's child to continue. He had willed

that it should do so. Ambrose the scholar? He would better and more fittingly be titled Ambrose the monster.

He was watching her narrowly. The sorceress recognized her danger. One who could permit an innocent child in no way connected with him to die would have no scruples at all about eliminating a woman whose virtue he believed to be questionable, intact only for the sake of expediency and a planned high sale later.

There is no tom smell, Trouble informed her.

No. I'm a threat now, not potential amusement. She knew too much, had seen too much, even though she was controlled enough not to reveal that she realized there was anything amiss. A careless remark or formal testimony under oath could bring to light what Ambrose the scholar did not want known.

He would realize that the business about the child was out and that he could do no more than make a show of sorrow about it, but he had other work afoot this night. Dory's bare feet rammed into her brogs, the trousers hastily drawn on over her nightdress, her hair braided for sleep all corroborated her tale. Her neighbor's garb bore different witness. All in black with a cowled, three-quarter cloak and boots soft soled for silence, he was as a shadow slipping through the dark.

To what purpose? The only places open in town at this hour were the taverns with their gaming rooms and the two brothels, but Ambrose was not a habitué of either. His destination was within the town or near it, for she heard no horse. A meeting, perhaps, with someone who did not dare come to the house or who had transport to take them farther? Whatever the answer, he had taken pains to conceal his plans for the evening, and if his purpose were strong enough, dark enough, he would readily kill to preserve his secret.

I've summoned Martin. He's on his way, Trouble informed her. Mind speech traveled little farther than that of the voice, but other cats were near. He had called to them, and they had carried his message.

She could die three times over before the master sorcerer reached them, especially if he had to make excuses for his going.

Dory did not need her cat's warning hiss to see the slight, almost infinitesimally slow movement beneath their foe's cloak. She could just make out enough of a shape to see that it was too large and wrong in form for an empty hand or fist.

It was no knife either. The woman gnawed on her inner lip. If only she had her mirror!

It would have done no good anyway since she could not see the object.

And what have you been studying besides botany since last fall, twit?

Dory's eyes glowed. Her own hand twitched slightly, as if nervously. The answering breeze was short-lived, just sufficient to blow the screening cloak aside momentarily.

That was enough. Ambrose held a globe, no, a narrow-necked flask. There were two flasks, rather, one inside the other. Both were filled with pale liquid.

Her heart beat painfully. Vitriol? Did he plan to fling it on her and kill her while she was disabled by pain and terror? Was it something more directly deadly? Who knew what this poisoner of children could do?

Trouble, get out of here, she commanded sharply. *Fast.* This was her business, human business. Human evil. Her little cat must not suffer because his love for her kept him near her.

Rot, the tomcat responded curtly. *Just see to it that he doesn't use that stuff, and neither of us will have a problem.*

But . . .

The flask, idiot kit! He's going to throw it!

Dory's will snapped out, flogged by fear and anger. Even Ambrose's well-schooled features could not conceal his surprise and fright when his hand abruptly froze, fingers grasping the neck of the vessel with viselike force.

The sorceress' eyes were cold as glacier ice. Trouble and she had known danger before, but that had been from a brutal, ignorant drunk. This man was something different; evil, a blight on life and on the clean face of their world.

Slowly, her will shifted a little. It was a strain to hold him paralyzed like this, nor could she extend her control to bind all his body for more than a few moments. There was a better way.

The air shimmered slightly between them and settled once more. With a sigh of relief, she released the bonds on her enemy's hand.

Her teacher arrived at that moment, sweeping as silently as vapor around the corner into the alley. He noted what she had done and nodded his approval but did not speak to her. He fixed his gaze on the other man.

The whole incident had taken only moments, however long it had seemed to Dory, no more time than would be required to draw and release a couple of deep breaths. The botanist blinked in surprise, then dismissed the vanished paralysis as the work of overwrought imagination. He looked from Dory to Martin, his newly-freed fingers caressing his weapon.

"Give it over, Ambrose," the master sorcerer warned. "We have you. Even if you could escape, you wouldn't enjoy life on the run. There's little romance in it but many missed and poor meals and many a cold night spent under a dripping hedge."

The other's expression did not alter as he cast the flask, not at Martin but at the ground midway between him and Dory.

The missile flew fast, but it traveled scarcely a foot before shattering with great force, seemingly on the air itself.

The botanist gasped, but his nerve held. Even as the remnants of the flask dropped to the ground, he leaped for the street behind him. Speed alone would buy him his life now.

He went to his knees, the breath driven out of him.

Ambrose's senses steadied. He had hit something, a wall of some sort. It was fully perceptible to his fingers although completely invisible. It must have been this which had stopped and broken the flask . . .

His eyes fixed on the greasy-looking smoke boiling out of the seething contents of his shattered weapon. He shrank back as far as he could from it and covered his mouth and nose with several thicknesses of his cloak.

His body gave a tremendous jerk, then another that threw him flat. His face twisted, darkened, as he fought for air and against that which the air surrounding him contained. He was not aware of the others. Only the agony of the present and the terror of the judgment and eternity before him existed for him now.

Within minutes, it was over. Martin looked into the contorted face of the dead man. "A hard ending and a just one."

He gestured sharply with his hand. Fire answered, pale yellow flames that touched neither cloth nor flesh but consumed the venom in the air and that still clinging to the broken glass.

He looked at the woman. She was staring at the corpse, her eyes huge with horror, but she responded at once to his soft call.

"Remove your dome now," he told her gently.

She did so. "I was right to distrust him," she said. "He was as malignant as those poisons of his."

Dory stared once more at the body. "He probably didn't even know Sammy, but he wanted him to die, just so he could see how long it would take for one little boy to kill his friend, the same as he wanted to see how long it would take Jasmine to die when she accidentally poisoned herself in his courtyard."

"Ambrose had reason to permit the experiment to continue, the love of pure knowledge aside. His profession demanded that he develop new techniques and new angles of approach."

The apprentice looked sharply at her teacher. "His profession?"

"I didn't dismiss your observations about the nature of his plantings, especially when I read over your notes and saw how well you had documented them, though I did think you'd grossly overestimated the number of totally baleful varieties. That did prove true in many cases when I consulted more advanced sources than we have in the house, but what remained was far too high a percentage to be dismissed as a scholar's curiosities. He didn't have the land to squander like that.

"I became even more suspicious when I had his affairs thoroughly investigated by members of our order and discovered that those investments of his were negligible. They provided no practical support. His medical trade alone wasn't doing it all, either. It supplied a sufficient income to maintain him very quietly here, but not nearly enough to buy the wines stocking his cellar or the quality furnishings in his home. It certainly did not pay for the lodgings he took and the entertainments he enjoyed when he went off to the capital, as he did several times a year.

"We had a job ferreting it out, but our Ambrose had yet another profession, one at which he excelled to the point that he didn't have to actually work at it often. That was why he seized upon the opportunity to study the situation that developed here. A lot of influential people have loyal, loving small children who would not mind giving Da medicine to cure his cold or a special sweet to Mama. A master assassin could capitalize on that fact."

Dory stared at him. She shuddered. "It's a miracle we escaped," she whispered. She frowned. "It was a queer weapon, though, wasn't it?"

"I think it was pure chance that he had the flask on him. He must have been en route either to deliver it to someone else or to carry out a commission. Your night's work has saved a life, or lives, probably. That gas could have taken out a roomful of people and was likely intended to do just that."

The apprentice shivered again. She held out her arms to Trouble, who leaped into her embrace. She pressed him tightly against her. "I couldn't have done anything at all without Trouble. He was brave and calm through it all and kept me thinking and acting correctly."

The pink tongue rasped her chin. Let the kitten believe that. For his part, it had been a horrifying experience almost from the start, and he was very glad to be here, alive and secure in his Dory's arms.

The tom collected himself. He could not resign his

responsibilities because of relief or residual fear. Humans seemed able to concentrate on only one thing, one danger, at a time, without recognizing all the other shadows looming around them. *So we have one dead butcher whom no one else knows for a killer, and George's story will put Dory here at the right time.*

Martin smiled. "Good thinking, cat. Don't worry. Ambrose, along with the pieces of his flask, will be discovered on the floor of his own study. The townsfolk will be left to wonder whether it was his heart, accident, or suicide that finished him. Ordinarily, I don't approve of tampering with evidence, but this is rather an exception."

Naturally. We are involved, the cat remarked dryly.

"Precisely."

Dory's eyes darkened as a troubling thought came to her. "How many will die or stay sick now that Ambrose isn't here to supply medicines for them?"

Martin gave her a quick, respectful look. "Well questioned. I believe I can help with that. There's a nice young fellow in our order whose specialty is botany."

"Young?"

"Only about one hundred seventy-five years old." He chuckled, then grew serious again. "It's about time for him to move again, and I think he'll be pleased to take over this business."

His smile broadened as a graceful gray form slipped into the alley and rubbed against his leg. "Here's my little lady. Ye three go back into the house—under an invisibility shield, please, considering Dory's rather unconventional state of dress. I'll finish up here and then join ye inside. I think ye have a story to tell me."

Trouble purred. *It's well worth the hearing, but what else could you expect with two cats and a sorceress acting in league?*

The man bowed his head in agreement. "Nothing less, Master Trouble, and maybe a great deal more as time goes on."

TINKERBELL

by Sharman Horwood

Sharman Horwood is a Canadian, who currently lives abroad. She works at the Hankuk University of Foreign Studies in Seoul, Republic of South Korea.

The first time I realized my cat, Tinkerbell, or Tink for short, was nursing me was when she was about three years old. Long hyperspace transits laid me out with migraines, especially the longest jumps that never seemed to end. I was one of the unlucky 0.1% whose brain chemistry didn't respond well to the transfer from real-time into null and then back again. To me the transit felt like I was tumbling in and out of reality, stretched between dimensions while solid objects thinned, dissolving about me. There time was a river through a nonland where what was, still could be, and what would be was possible now. I felt like I could reach out, slip my fingers through metal walls like gray cotton candy and finger space outside of my ship, letting it flow like dark, substanceless water over my fingertips.

Then the ship's engines would thunk, cutting back in, and the hyperspace field would disappear as the anti-mass generator whispered to a stop. As the ship settled back into normal space, I would head for my cabin. Usually I made it to my bunk before the pain and nausea really began. The longer the transits were, the longer I was out of real space, the harder it was to settle back into reality. My thoughts were easily lost, overwhelmed out there by the empty spaces between the stars. I always felt like I was whisked into pieces and that parts of me were still out there, left behind, trying to slip their ethereal ways back. I knew Tink would be waiting to pull me back in, to help me through the pain that lurked, waiting like some monstrous nightmare, for me alone.

I'd prepare everything before the jump, setting out the pills I'd need to take as soon as the *Veritage* came out of transit, painkillers lined up in a row beside my bunk, only so many and no more, with a couple of anti-nausea pills to make sure I'd keep the painkillers down. Within minutes of lying down, Tink would be there, sometimes meeting me at my cabin door. Sometimes I felt as if she'd traveled through hyperspace with my disembodied self, anticipating how I'd feel as we slipped back into realspace, ready at my side. In my cabin, she'd curl up against my side, fitting herself into the curve of my waist, her fur silky soft. She'd purr even before she jumped up beside me, soothing me before the pain really kicked in, and she'd keep purring the whole time she was there. I got to know exactly when the pain would dissolve because every time, moments before it left, Tink would leave, too, slipping out the doorway quiet as night. Sometimes she'd briefly lick my hand when the pain was bad, her tongue a flicker like feathers against my skin. I came to expect to find her there beside me in the cool darkness.

I'd brought Tink to space with me to my first posting on a small merchant ship, the *Veritage,* the same ship I eventually owned along with my two partners, Cor and Pak. I'd brought her in part as investment, along with several packets of frozen sperm of cat breeds, in case any new colony worlds wanted cats to keep the pest population down. Many worlds had minor pests, vicious and difficult to be rid of, that ate supplies and food and even sometimes worried away at small children. Cats are superb hunters of anything small that moves. But I'd also brought her for companionship, to keep me company and remind me of the home I was used to.

My partners came to accept Tink as part of the crew. Cor and Pak were twins. They both had biological stock of their own, but over the years, the need for new stock dropped, and they let their companions go to good homes on planets we'd passed. But they never suggested that we leave Tink. She was part of the team, and they expected her to be around almost as much as I did.

On EVA as the polarization on a faulty suit helmet failed, Pak had lost his eyesight when he for one unguarded moment looked directly into the fire of a sun. He had glass-covered implants to take the place of his eyes, but they never took the same place as real eyes, not seeing as much as binocular vision did. They saw more than biological implants in infrared and x-ray range, which was why Pak had chosen them as replacements, but they lost a significant portion of peripheral vision. He couldn't see around a corner and what lay at his feet at the same time, for instance.

He always swore Tink knew what he could and could not see. She would step back and to the side when he approached a corner of any kind, letting him go first. He never stepped on her, so she never learned that trick by accident. She also often meowed at him, just to let him know she was there if she wasn't precisely in his field of vision. She just seemed to know his limits.

Cor also expected Tink to be there, particularly after she once watched Tink chase a large Cadwallader pup out of our docking bay. Tink was out on her own on a minor exploration of the docking area. This was one of the first things she did whenever we landed in port. Most cats were suspicious and hesitant about strange places. Tink was also suspicious, but she always wanted to check them out. She seemed to think this was her duty as part of the ship's crew, no matter how much we tried to keep her in. This Cadwallader didn't see her. It started up the docking ramp, slow and reptilian with short, stubby legs and a long tail that waved in the air behind it. It was just curious. Tink was about hundred feet away when she saw it. She fluffed up like she'd been hit by lightning and side-winded across the deck in a dead-mad run. The Cadwallader didn't even see her coming. She landed on his head, going straight for his eyes. Cor said she heard it screeching far down the docking level, long after Tink had dropped off. After that at every port, Cor bought Tink some kind of treat, a toy or a special bit of meat. She said Tink earned it even if she seemed to sleep all the time we were under way.

Tink always assumed everything was her responsibility, too. When she had kittens, she looked after them obsessively, up until the time they were old enough to go to their appointed colony homes. She ran to eat or to use her litter box, talking to them the whole way, louder the farther away she went, a yowl that slipped around ship doorways and corridors. When her kittens were a little older, she'd place them with me, an unwilling babysitter; she'd slip them into the bunk with me while I slept, nudging them down underneath the covers and leaving them there while she took a couple of hours to herself, stubbornly checking the ship over to be sure everything was as it should be. When she didn't have kittens, she looked after me instead. I don't think it ever occurred to her that I didn't quite need her help. She just did it, like comforting me while I was in pain.

She was with me for nineteen years, very much a part of my life. There came a time of course when she couldn't be with me any more. It didn't happen until she'd been with me for all of those nineteen years, ever my small colleague among the stars, but one night she curled up beside me as always. When I woke, she'd gone with my dreams, slipping out by a doorway not quite open to me. I never stopped missing her. I always expected her to be there, too, when I came out of a long hyperspace jump. It was about this time, also, that my body seemed to adjust, probably just changing with age, and the headaches diminished. I thought it was just my imagination that said Tink had stayed as long as she thought I needed her.

A couple of years after she passed away, we were in the Renoult arm of the galaxy, where there were few people and small profits. My partners and I had decided to go there on the off chance that this thin spiral of stars might have some opportunities that other merchants had missed. Business had not been good, and we were trying to sell some old stock at the same time as looking for new kinds of goods. We didn't have much luck except for a whisper about rare minerals farther out on the arm.

I set up the board for the longest jump we'd ever taken. There were few stars in this thin end of the galaxy's whirl through space. It was like they were strewn, broadcast to seed dark space with their dim light. Pak and Cor had left the bridge to take this jump in their cabins. Cor would take over as soon as we were out of hyperspace and I had to leave my chair. I didn't expect to have the severe reactions to a long jump as I'd had in the past, so I was only semiprepared with medicine in my cabin. I hadn't had a bad attack for a long time, and, if necessary, I would probably have little difficulty in staying with the board after the jump, but just in case, Cor was ready. I gave the transit initiation signal, setting up the alarm sequences in case anything failed while we were out there. Lights dimmed and the engines gathered power before they cut out, a solid thrum that vibrated through the metal floors and hull. The anti-mass generator whined up to full speed as the energy from the engines flowed into it. The hyperspace field began to flow about the *Veritage,* wrapping us in its gray cocoon. Radar pinged when it shouldn't have, just as we slipped out of real space.

I don't know what hit us. It was small and fast, and left like an explosion, piercing the empty cargo hold as it speeded through both sides of our hull. Hyperspace descended, engulfing us, just as the alarms started to howl. The failsafes to throw us back into realspace didn't kick in. I reached for the board, and fell . . .

. . . felt like I was drowning. The inside-out feeling that

was triggered by the jump didn't go away. It stayed, swallowing me in great waves of tidal seas made from thick water. I still tried to reach for the board, but I was reaching through gray water that swept me away, drawing me out on dark seas that tossed me about, breaking me apart into small bits cast on spreading waves.

I tried to call out, but my voice dissolved in the back of my throat. I could hear Cor calling from her cabin. Her voice took shape in the dark water, and I could see it drifting along with me like a beam of light or pale smoke that followed me out into the darkness. Time stretched out and I felt us slip away on its surface, surfing down a dark illimitable wave of a darker nonreality. My fingers reached out, and grew longer, thinning out into ghostlike wisps of pale smoke. My body spread out ahead of them, flowing out through the ship, body and voice both as smoke dissolved in the dark immensity of hyperspace as they flowed through walls that disappeared in fragmented atoms.

I drifted there for what seemed like hours even though I knew it was no more than an instant. I felt the gravity of stars that weren't there, pockets of mass I flowed around, almost sliding down into their depths, back into realspace. I passed them and let their gravity pull me down, almost breaking through into realspace before hyperspace's attractive force balanced realspace's power and pulled me away again. I slipped back and forth, one moment almost in realspace, one moment trying to find the edge of hyperspace's nondimension. I felt as if I floated on waves of time, breaching on black shores of realspace, each wave pulling me back out into darker, unstill waters. My real self was dissolving on these seas, losing form, losing reality and dimension. I tried to reach back and seize the hull of the ship in formless fingers but it slipped through them like water through dry sand.

"Lise, what's happening? Lise." I could still hear and see Cor's voice but it was fainter, less real. As my fingers slid through its pale light, I could feel Cor's voice. Its light flowed into me and for one desperate moment, it held the dissolving particles of myself together with its added power. But the roar of hyperspace flowed back over me, and drew me past it back into the gulf between being and nonbeing.

I drifted there in immeasurable space where time was not a dimension. Memory turned in upon itself. The past was now. . . .

"Don't touch that, Tink," I pulled a string away from her as she leaped after it. I briefly wondered why I pulled rather than taking it up out of her reach but the thought dissolved before I could answer it. I held onto the string, drawing Tink closer where I could hear her, a faint purr. As the end of the string disappeared between my fingers, I could feel her nose nudge my hand, and her purr tickled through my fingers. Tink nudged again, harder this time, a soft bump against my hand, pushing all of me. Darkness shimmered. Tink pushed again and her purr surged, a wave of sound sweeping through me, holding me together. I reached out to stroke her as another wave of sound from her cascaded over me, rolling me forward, propelling me ahead with its energy.

I almost thought I reached something as my hand fell open, the string dangling again between my fingers, a filament of light like sound laying out upon darkness. Tink's purr hit me again as a soft paw patted the string. The sound lifted me, pushing me again, farther, and for a moment a star glimmered above me in a pale shimmer.

Tink's nose butted my hand again as she pushed up against my side to curl up beside me. I lay still among the dark waters as her purr washed over me, its power drawing me together, holding me in a soft envelope of sound. It pushed at me when I wanted to stop, to just lie there wrapped in its warm familiarity. It stubbornly nudged me onward where I could not make myself go. Its thrum was warmth, light, feeling; I wanted it to hold me as I fell down into it. And suddenly I was cold, stars glittered, and hard cold metal lay under my face.

"Are you all right, Lise?" Cor asked me. She held my head up with one hand, the other brushing my forehead. Her touch was cool and dry. A vibration inside me slowed and faded. I was hot and my stomach sat at the bottom of my throat, its acid a bad taste about to erupt.

I let Cor roll me over as Pak hurried onto the bridge. His glass eyes reflected cold metal and blinking lights. My stomach settled as the first pain surged, lighting coals of fire in the bones on the left side of my face.

"Where are we?" he asked, not quite looking at me, focused on the board as he tried to sort out its readings. I tried to sit up, but the deck seemed to roll, sliding away from underneath me. My hands were cold and slick with sweat. I lifted the hair off of the back of my neck to cool the perspiration gathering there.

"I'm okay. I'm okay," I told Cor. I was shaking so hard my arm could barely hold me up as I propped myself in a sitting position against the bulkhead. Blood roared in my ears, reminding me of something I'd heard before. Waves of fire licked up the side of my face, blinding my left eye. I tried to close my eyes to slits, shutting out the painful light stabbing at me in glass-like shards.

"We're *way* off," Pak said, leaning over the board and fingering switches. He settled into the empty chair to try to sort it out. "I can't make out where we are. The readings don't fit." His fingers hit switches on the board and some of the alarms shut off, leaving cold silence behind them. The bulkhead was a cold weight at my back, cold and quiet. The engines were down. The metal wall held me up while the spinning slowed and pain grew. Cor had left me and was already standing next to Pak, giving him what aid she could. The crushing pain in my head hit an early, sudden peak, breaking there.

"The hold is breached," Cor added. "Whatever it was took out the corridor, too, so we can't get anywhere near it." She dropped into the chair at her board, her fingers fast on readings. "It'll be short rations, too. The galley door was open onto that corridor. We'll have to secure that before we get to the rest of the damage." Cor had long, dark hair, thick and wavy and she held it back now with one hand over her forehead as she scanned the rest of her board, her other hand adjusting sensors. "Might be a while. Looks like the door itself was split. We'll have to weld a sheet over it before

we can access the galley and fix the door." Her voice
was tight and urgent.

"We're out of the galactic plane," Pak finally said. His
left hand reached for main comp again. He'd taken more
readings and was now waiting for comp's data. Looking
up from where I sat, I could see his hand was a shivering,
pale shadow against the background of the board, white
against silver, matte against metallic gleam. He rubbed
the pads of his fingers agains the thumb tip, as if to rub
feeling back into still-frozen flesh. I still couldn't move.
I still couldn't lift myself up off the floor to help at
the board. His finger hit comp again and stayed there,
paralyzed, as he waited for the new data.

I pushed myself up. The pain had gone just a bit, the
nerve pathways in my face still smoldering, but bearably.
My bones and muscles felt like loose sand, and moving
made it worse. I grabbed hold of the board and let myself fall into my seat next to Pak's. I let out my breath
as my head swam, then breathed a couple of times, slow
and calm, until my head and stomach steadied. I held
onto the cold board for what seemed like a long time,
my fingers white ice, trembling and nerveless. I tried to
figure out what Pak was seeing on the main instruments.
I lit the screen so we could see something, anything. All
it showed was darkness with a shimmering patch in its
depths. I rotated the starboard sensors and stars glittered
there in a cluster.

Cor was still assessing systems damage. Pak was still
punching up figures, the same ones again and again.

"Pak?" I asked. He shook his head.

"I can't find us," he finally said. 'I can't even find
where we were, and I can't match any of these stars
to the signatures in comp." Comp carried the signature
spectroscopic analysis of all known stars. We'd updated
it at our second-to-last stop. We didn't want to be stuck
somewhere out in the reaches of the Renoult arm without an updated record at hand. What Pak wasn't saying
was that he couldn't find our way back. We could be
lost in some far place, and even hyperspace transit
wouldn't be able to get us back if we were somewhere
in the immense distances between galaxies.

I continued to rotate ship's position, trying to find a field of stars comp would recognize. The signatures and positions were all strange. The cluster's glowing points just weren't recognizable. I noticed the shimmer again. It followed as I switched to each of the sensors, gathering data from each one of them, so I thought this was either an optical illusion born of headache, or a glitch in the board caused by the breach and our propulsion in and out of hyperspace.

"Pak," I asked, "can we orient to the nearest galaxy? Maybe that would give us a relative placement." I hoped we'd just come out on the wrong side. He tried it, his fingers faster than mine. When the answer came, he cursed, a hiss between his teeth, then his fingers punched, reconfiguring it again. The lifeless glass of his eyes showed nothing, but I knew the board's answer had scared him.

"Pak?" I asked. Cor looked up from her instruments, half aware, half thinking what needed to be done on repairs. Pak's breath was a hiss between his teeth.

"We crossed the void," he said, "it's a different galaxy. Andromeda. Maybe. Comp says it's only sure to ninety-three percent accuracy. It can't tell enough to be sure of orientation. Any one of those lights could be home. The puncture must have pushed us through hyperspace like a jet stream." My head throbbed and the taste in the back of my throat stung like acid. The shimmer was still there on my screen. It had an odd shape. My head throbbed when I looked at it, but not with pain, more like a distant sound.

"What's that?" I pointed to it.

"What's what?" Pak answered. I knew he couldn't see it on his screen, even with enhanced vision, but he absently punched comp, bringing up the figures on that spot while he checked for sensor damage on the exterior of the hull. On my screen the shimmer had moved to the lower right near a saucer-shaped disk of glowing lights. I decided that what I saw was the visual aura that sometimes accompanies migraine, a floater from vascular contraction, a symptom I'd been spared when I was younger. I waved my fingers, as if I could wave it away.

My fingers tingled as if they almost brushed against something light and soft, like cobwebs.

Pak drew in breath quickly, sharply. "It just might be home, Lise. And it just might be close enough that we can make it home with the supplies we have." He rubbed the edge of his palm against the board as if it itched. He entered a few more figures, orienting information with our position, parallaxing against distant clusters and disks bright in the darkness.

"It could be," he finally added. "Of this, comp is only sixty-one percent sure, but if we jump closer, and position ourselves to the edge of the galactic plane, it can get a better reading." He turned to look at me, his glass eyes reflective and blind. "We have to try it." It was like my vision was narrowing, widening, and narrowing again to a long tunnel of darkening light. "They're going to be long jumps, about nine of them. But we're dead if we stay out here." My fingers hurt from holding onto the board. But he was right.

In the end, once my head settled, once the ship stabilized with what Cor could do on repairs, once we'd calmed down and assessed damages, we agreed we had to try to make it back. Cor and Pak welded a sheet of metal across the galley door while I took what pills I could. They were old, and probably wouldn't help me once the jumps started, but I took them anyway. Then I went to help my partners. The pain was not as bad as it had been and somehow I couldn't face a dark room alone this time. This time I felt alone, more than usual. I was sure Tink had been with me there in hyperspace. I was sure I could still hear her purring like she always had when I was sick. I'd rather endure the additional nausea and pain this time than lie alone missing her.

It took us eight long jumps to get near the galactic plane. I almost didn't make it. We'd rested out there in the null space between galaxies for a short time before we began our long journey back. Even so, after the first jump, I didn't think I would make it. The left side of my face felt as if the bones were being crushed. Cor and Pak took turns taking over the boards on the bridge

while I stayed in my cabin. It was going to be hard on
all of us. Hyperspace transits were not easy on anyone.
They wrenched physical reality in ways that could be
felt, if not fully measured, bringing on strokes and heart
attacks in veteran spacers. Magnetic fields distorted,
their edges bent, and time seemed to curl back in upon
itself in hyperspace.

By the end of the second jump, I couldn't sit up, the
nausea was so bad. I just lay there, lights out and ice
for my mouth near at hand. I had no more medicine,
and I was far beyond its help, if I could even move to
take it. By the third jump, I lost consciousness. I felt
myself dissolve into the waiting blackness of hyperspace
again. The shimmer in my sight grew larger, until it was
so large it wrapped itself about me and held me close
in a semi-limbo where I could see nothing, and I lay
there listening to a dull throb pulsing beside me. I curled
about it, letting it fill me, hold me like home.

I don't remember the other jumps. I was no longer
conscious, just drifting in darkness, held together by
something warm and silklike that nudged me from time
to time as I slid along the crests and troughs of hyperspace emptiness. It pushed me along, slipping under my
hand, curling against my side, warming me, propelling
me in and out of consciousness, back into realspace and
the subsiding pain, pain that quickly slipped away.

When I woke, the *Veritage* had stopped. The pain was
only a dull, background ache that merged with the sound
of the *Veritage*'s resting engines. The shimmer had almost vanished with the pain, too. There was just a slight
sparkle around the edges of my vision that never after-
wards completely left me.

Pak had been right: the nearest galaxy now was the
Milky Way. We stayed where we were for a day to rest
and take stock of the ship's condition. The jumps had
taken about two days altogether. Time didn't pass in
hyperspace—the moment we went in was the moment
we came out. Time itself seemed to hang suspended as
the anti-mass generators bent space, leaving the ship
wrapped in nullspace as it went from one point instanta-
neously to another. It was truly a never-land. My sensory

experience was not theoretically explainable. Nor was the experience of other spacers, either. There were qualities to hyperspace that were yet unknown. Humanity could use a technology based on the phenomenon without fully understanding it.

When we arrived back in known space, the *Veritage* was not in a very good way. The cargo hold was not internally accessible and would take major refitting before it could be. Our partnership's credit wasn't in much better shape, either, which was one reason why we'd made this venture in the first place. We were getting older and we needed a larger credit balance to provide ourselves with the income from a secure brokerage. We'd hoped the profit from this chancy run would do that. By the time we'd made our way back to our own galaxy, we weren't even sure we could both repair the *Veritage* and secure the supplies we needed to replace those blown out by the breach. As we docked at Precific Station, we even considered contacting moneylenders, which would mean years of safe milkruns to pay off that small debt before we could even begin to secure enough for our own shipping brokerage. Interest rates in space ventures were exorbitant. We had hoped to have our own agency before too much longer, not be dependent upon continuing independent work: we'd reached middle age; we were too old to be starting all over again.

We sat about the galley table, Cor dipping one finger in her caff while Pak's eyes reflected the dull sheen of the deck plating in the ceiling. I knew Pak was thinking about personal options, leaving the partnership altogether. His augmented sight could be sold to belt miners, and he might be left with enough then to secure his own retirement. He'd said before that Cor and I could do just as well without him. Of course, we didn't agree. I left them to their cold caff and even colder additions and subtractions when the port authority buzzed on the com.

"*Veritage* here," I said, "Port Authorization PZ2148.01. Registration Beta 6627DC24. Owners C. Shord, P. Shord, and L. Longbird." I rubbed my temples. My sight was shimmering again. "I think you guys have the date a little wrong," I told them, "it should be

147.29, not 148.01." My forehead felt heavy and there were little dancing tingles along the nerve paths under my left eye.

"I appreciate your confusion," a man's voice answered, "checking ... no, date's right: 148.01. Been out there a little too long?" He sounded amused. His holo image reached up with one finger and rubbed the side of his temple.

When it was all sorted out, we'd lost time in hyperspace. It was the first time something like this had ever happened. Somehow the sudden propulsion through hyperspace, the puncture through realspace to hyperspace then back to realspace again, had caused a loop and the *Veritage* had momentarily become a small singularity protected by an envelope of anti-mass it generated at the same time. In effect, the puncture bent space on several levels, a geometric progression of reality/nonreality that propelled us through space as it simultaneously backed us through time, going forward in physical reality and backward in temporal reality. The distance we covered in space became massive, throwing us way out of this galaxy and the scientists are still trying to work out the theoretical data. They are working on building a drive to couple with the anti-mass generator to duplicate the effect, even though they don't understand this phenomen any more than they understand hyperspace itself. With such a drive, space travel would be even cheaper, faster, and distant galaxies would be substantially less distant. My partners and I put up the information for sale, and at a price that would buy us our brokerage agency, too, with one stipulation. They had to call the phenomenon the Tink Effect. I insisted.

I still make occasional trips on *Veritage III*. Space has been my life, and I could never settle on the ground completely. There're always business trips, always negotiations for new and unusual cargos and handlers. Now, though, when I go through hyperspace, especially the long jumps, the ones that go on and on, through time, through space, and out the other side in a never-land between realities, I often feel a gentle, soft nudge, a pressure at my side and a softness underneath my open hand. Sometimes I even hear the slight rumble of a purr.

SCAT

by Mercedes Lackey

Mercedes Lackey was born in Chicago, and worked as a lab assistant, security guard, and computer programmer before turning to fiction writing. Her first book, *Arrows of the Queen*, the first in the Valdemar series, was published in 1985. She won the Lambda award for *Magic's Price* and Science Fiction Book Club Book of the Year for the *The Elvenbane*, coauthored with Andre Norton. Along with her husband, Larry Dixon, she is a Federally licensed bird rehabilitator, specializing in wild birds. She shares her home with a menagerie of parrots, cats, and a Schutzhund trained German Shepherd.

"NoooOOOWOWOWOW!"

The metal walls of Dick's tiny cabin vibrated with the howl. Dick White ignored it, as he injected the last of the four contraception-beads into SKitty's left hind leg. The black-coated shipscat did not move, but she did continue her vocal and mental protest. :*Mean,*: she complained, as Dick held the scanner over the right spot to make certain that he *had* gotten the bead placed where it was supposed to go. :*Mean, mean Dick.*:

Indignation showing in every line of her, she sat up

on his fold-down desk and licked the injection site. It hadn't hurt; he *knew* it hadn't hurt, for he'd tried it on himself with a neutral bead before he injected her.

Nice, nice Dick, you should be saying, he chided her. *One more unauthorized litter and BioTech would be coming to take you away for their breeding program. You're too fertile for your own good.*

SKitty's token whine turned into a real yowl of protest, and her mate, now dubbed "SCat," joined her in the wail from his seat on Dick's bunk. :*Not leave Dick!*: SKitty shrilled in his head. :*Not leave ship!*:

Then no more kittens—at least not for a while! he responded. *No more kittens means SKitty and SCat stay with Dick.*

SKitty leaped to join her mate on the bunk, where both of them began washing each other to demonstrate their distress over the idea of leaving Dick. SKitty's real name was "Lady Sundancer of Greenfields," and she was the proud product of BioTech's masterful genesplicing. Shipscats, those sturdy, valiant hunters of vermin of every species, betrayed their differences from Terran felines in a number of ways. BioTech had given them the "hands" of a raccoon, the speed of a mongoose, the ability to adjust to rapid changes in gravity or no gravity at all, and greatly enhanced mental capacity. What they did not know was that "Lady Sundancer"—aka "Dick White's Kitty," or "SKitty" for short—had another, invisible enhancement. She was telepathic—at least with Dick.

Thanks to SKitty and to her last litter, the CatsEye Company trading ship *Brightwing* was one of the most prosperous in this end of the galaxy. That was due entirely to SKitty's hunting ability; she had taken swift vengeance when a persistent pest native to the newly-opened world of Lacu'un had bitten the consort of the ruler, killing with a single blow a creature the natives had *never* been able to exterminate. That, and her own charming personality, had made her kittens-to-be *most* desirable acquisitions, so precious that not even the leaders of Lacu'un "owned" them; they were held in trust for the world. Thanks to the existence of that litter and the need to get them appropriately pedigreed BioTech mates, SKitty's own mate—unsurprisingly dubbed "SCat" by the crew, for his ability to vanish—had made his own way to SKitty, stowing aboard with the crates containing four BioTech kittens.

Where *he* came from, only he knew, although he was definitely a shipscat. Too dignified to be called a "kitty," this handsome male was "Dick White's Cat."

And thanks to SCat's timely arrival and intervention, an attempt to kill the entire crew of the *Brightwing* and the Terran Consul to Lacu'un in order to take over the trading concession had been unsuccessful. SCat had disabled critical equipment holding them all imprisoned, so that they were able to get to a com station to call for help from the Patrol, while SKitty had distracted the guards.

SCat had never demonstrated telepathic powers with Dick, for which Dick was grateful, but he certainly possessed something of the sort with SKitty, and he was odd in other ways. Dick would have been willing to take an oath that SCat's forepaws were even more handlike than SKitty's, and that his tail showed some signs of being prehensile. There were other secrets locked in that wide black-furred skull, and Dick only wished he had access to them.

Dick was worried, for the *Brightwing* was in space again and heading toward one of the major stations with the results of their year-long trading endeavor with the beings of Lacu'un in their hold. Shipscats simply did not come out of nowhere; BioTech kept very tight control over them, denying them to ships or captains with a record of even the slightest abuse or neglect, and keeping track of where every one of them was, from birth to death. They were expensive—traders running on the edge could not afford them, and had to rid themselves of vermin with periodic vacuum-purges. SKitty claimed that her mate had "heard about her" and had come specifically to find her—but she would not say from where. SCat had to come from *somewhere,* and wherever that was, someone from there was probably looking for him. They would very likely take a dim view of their four-legged Romeo heading off on his own in search of his Juliet.

Any attempt to question the tom through SKitty was useless. SCat would simply stare at him with those luminous yellow eyes, then yawn, and SKitty would soon grow bored with the proceedings. After all, to her, the important thing was that SCat was *here,* not where he had come from.

Behind Dick, in the open door of the cabin, someone coughed. He turned to find Captain Singh regarding Dick and cats with a jaundiced eye. Dick saluted hastily.

"Sir—contraceptive devices in place and verified, sir!" he affirmed, holding up the injector to prove it.

The Captain, a darkly handsome gentleman as popular with the females of his own species as SCat undoubtably was with felines, merely nodded. "We have a problem, White," he pointed out. "The *Brightwing*'s manifest shows *one* shipscat, not two. And we still don't know where number two came from. I know what will happen if we try to take SKitty's mate away from her, but I also know what will happen if anyone finds out we have a second cat, origin unknown. BioTech will take a dim view of this."

Dick had been thinking at least part of this through. "We *can* hide him, sir," he offered. "At least until I can find out where he came from."

"Oh?" Captain Singh's eyebrows rose. "Just how do you propose to hide him, and where?"

Dick grinned. "In plain sight, sir. Look at them—unless you have them side-by-side, you wouldn't be able to tell which one you had in front of you. They're both black with yellow eyes, and it's only when you can see the size difference and the longer tail on SCat that you can tell them apart."

"So we simply make sure they're never in the same compartment while strangers are aboard?" the Captain hazarded. "That actually has some merit; the Spirits of Space know that people are always claiming shipscats can teleport. No one will even notice the difference if we don't say anything, and they'll just think she's getting around by way of the access tubes. How do you intend to find out where this one came from without making people wonder why you're asking about a stray cat?"

Dick was rather pleased with himself, for he had actually thought of this solution first. "SKitty is fertile—unlike nine-tenths of the shipscats. That is why we had kittens to offer the Lacu'un in the first place, and was why we have the profit we do, even after buying the contracts of four young cats for groundside duty as the kittens' mates."

The Captain made a faint grimace. "You're stating the obvious."

"Humor me, sir. Did you know that BioTech routinely offers their breeding cats free choice in mates? That otherwise, they don't breed well?" As the Captain shook his head, Dick pulled out his trump card. "I am—ostensibly—going to do the same for SKitty. As long as we 'find' her a BioTech mate that she approves of, BioTech will be happy. And we need more kittens for the Lacu'un; we have no reason to *buy* them when we have a potential breeder of our own."

"But we got mates for her kittens," the Captain protested. "Won't BioTech think there's something odd going on?"

Dick shook his head. "You're thinking of house-cats. Shipscats aren't fertile until they're four or five. At that rate, the kittens won't be old enough to breed for four years, and the Lacu'un are going to want more cats before then. So I'll be searching the BioTech breeding records for a tom of the right age and appearance. Solid black is recessive—there can't be *that* many black toms of the right age."

"And once you've found your group of candidates—?" Singh asked, both eyebrows arching. "You look for the one that's missing?" He did not ask how Dick was supposed to have found out that SKitty "preferred" a black tom; shipscats were more than intelligent enough to choose a color from a set of holos.

Dick shrugged. "The information may be in the records. Once I know where SCat's from, we can open negotiations to add him to our manifest with BioTech's backing. *They* won't pass up a chance to make SKitty half of a breeding pair, and I don't think there's a captain willing to go on BioTech's record as opposing a shipscat's choice of mate."

"I won't ask how you intend to make that particular project work," Singh said hastily. "Just remember, no more kittens in free-fall."

Dick held up the now-empty injector as a silent promise.

"I'll brief the crew to refer to both cats as 'SKitty'— most of the time they do anyway," the Captain said. "Carry on, White. You seem to have the situation well in hand."

Dick was nowhere near that certain, but he put on a confident expression for the Captain. He saluted Singh's retreating back, then sat down on the bunk beside the pair of purring cats. As usual, they were wound around each other in a knot of happiness.

I wish my love-life was going that well. He'd hit it off with the Terran consul well enough, but she had elected to remain in her ground-bound position, and his life was with the ship. Once again, romance took a second place to careers. Which in his case, meant no romance. There wasn't a single female in this crew that had shown anything other than strictly platonic interest in him.

If he *wanted* a career in space, he had to be very careful about what he did and said. As most junior officer on the *Brightwing,* he was the one usually chosen for whatever unpleasant duty no one else wanted to handle. And although he could actually *retire,* thanks to the prosperity that the Lacu'un contract had brought the whole crew, he didn't want to. That would mean leaving space, leaving the ship—and leaving SKitty and SCat.

He could also transfer within the company, but why change from a crew full of people he liked and respected, with a good Captain like Singh, to one about which he knew nothing? That would be stupid. And he couldn't leave SKitty, no matter what. She was his best friend, even if she did get him into trouble sometimes.

He also didn't have the experience to be anything other than the most junior officer in any ship, so transferring wouldn't have any benefits.

Unless, of course, he parlayed his profit-share into a small fortune and bought his own ship. Then he could be Captain, and he might even be able to buy SKitty's contract—but he lacked the experience that made the difference between prosperity and bankruptcy in the shaky world of the Free Traders. He was wise enough to know this.

As for the breeding project—he had some ideas. The *Brightwing* would be visiting Lacu'un for a minimum of three weeks on every round of their trading-route. Surely something could be worked out. Things didn't get chancy until after the kittens were mobile and before SKitty potty-trained them to use crew facilities. Before they were able to leave the nest-box, SKitty took care of the unpleasant details. If they could arrange things so that the period of mobility-to-weaning took place while they were on Lacu'un . . .

Well, he'd make that Jump when the coordinates came up. Right now, he had to keep outsiders from discovering that there was feline contraband on board, and find out where that contraband came from.

:Dick smart,: SKitty purred proudly. *:Dick fix everything.:*

Well, he thought wryly. *At least I have* her *confidence, if no one else's!*

It had been a long time since the *Brightwing* had been docked at a major port, and predictably, everyone wanted shore leave. Everyone except Dick, that is. He had no intentions of leaving the console in Cargo where he was doing his "mate-hunting" unless and until he found his match. The fact that there was nothing but a skeleton crew aboard, once the inspectors left, only made it easier for Dick to run his searches through the BioTech database available through the station. This database was part of the public records kept on every station, and updated weekly by BioTech. Dick had a notion that he'd get his "hit" within a few hours of initiating his search.

He was pleasantly surprised to discover that there were portraits available for every entry. It might even be possible to identify SCat just from the portraits, once he had all of the black males of the appropriate age sorted out. That would give him even more rationale for the claim that SKitty had "chosen" her mate herself.

With an interested feline perching on each arm of the chair, he logged into the station's databases, identified himself and gave the station his billing information, then began his run.

There was nothing to do at that point but sit back and wait.

"I hope you realize all of the difficulties I'm going through for you," he told the tom, who was grooming his face thoughtfully. "I'm doing without shore leave to help you here. I wouldn't do this for a fellow human!"

SCat paused in his grooming long enough to rasp Dick's hand with his damp-sandpaper tongue.

The computer *beeped* just at that moment to let him know it was done. He was running all this through the Cargo dumb-set; he could have used the *Brightwing*'s Expert-System AI, but he didn't want the AI to get curious, and he didn't want someone wondering why he was using a Mega-Brain to access feline family trees. What he *did* want was the appearance that this was a brainstorm of his own, an attempt to boost his standing with his Captain by providing further negotiable items for the Lacu'un contract. There was something odd about all of this, something that he couldn't put his finger on, but something that just felt wrong and made him want to be extra-cautious. Why, he didn't know. He only knew that he didn't want to set off any telltales by acting as if this mate search was a priority item.

The computer asked if he wanted to use the holo-table, a tiny square platform built into the upper right hand corner of the desk. He cleared off a stack of hard-copy manifests, and told it "yes." Then the first of his feline biographies came in.

He'd made a guess that SCat was between five and ten years old; shipscats lived to be fifty or more, but their useful lifespan was about twenty or thirty years. All too often their job was hazardous; alien vermin had poisonous fangs or stings, sharp claws, and teeth. Cats suffered disabling injuries more often than their human crewmates, and would be retired with honors to the homes of retired spacers, or to the big "assisted living" stations holding the very aged and those with disabling injuries of their own. Shipscats were always welcome, anywhere in space.

And I can think of worse fates than spending my old age watching the stars with SKitty on my lap. He gazed down fondly at his furred friend, and rubbed her ears.

SKitty purred and butted her head into his hand. She paid very little attention to the holos as they passed slowly in review. SCat was right up on the desk, however, not only staring intently at the holos, but splitting his attention between the holos and the screen.

You don't suppose he can read . . . ?

Suddenly, SCat out a yowl, and swatted the holoplate. Dick froze the image and the screen-biography that accompanied it.

He looked first at the holo—and it certainly looked more like SCat than any of the others had. But SCat's attention was on the screen, not the holo, and he stared fixedly at the modest insignia in the bottom right corner.

Patrol?

He looked down at SCat, dumbfounded. "You were with the Patrol?" He whispered it; you did not invoke the Patrol's name aloud unless you wanted a visit from them.

Yellow eyes met his for a moment, then the paw tapped the screen. He read further.

Type MF-025, designation Lightfoot of Sun Meadow. Standard Military genotype, standard Military training. Well, that explained how he had known how to shut down the "pirate" equipment. Now Dick wondered how much else the cat had done, outside of his sight. And a

military genotype? He hadn't even known there *was*
such a thing.

*Assigned to Patrol ship DIA-9502, out of Oklahoma
Station, designated handler Major Logan Greene.*

Oklahoma Station—that was *this* station. Drug Inter-
diction? He whistled softly.

Then a date, followed by the ominous words, *Ship
missing, all aboard presumed dead.*

All aboard—except the shipscat.

The cat himself gave a mournful yowl, and SKitty
jumped up on the desk to press herself against him com-
fortingly. He looked back down at SCat. "Did you jump
ship before they went missing?"

He wasn't certain he would get an answer, but he had
lived with SKitty for too long to underestimate shipscat
intelligence. The cat shook his head, slowly and deliberately—in the negative.

His mouth went dry. "Are you saying—you got away?"

A definite nod.

"Your ship was boarded, and you got away?" He was
astonished. "But how?"

For an answer, the cat jumped down off the desk
and walked over to the little escape pod that neither
he nor SKitty ever forgot to drag with them. He seized
the tether in his teeth and dragged it over to an access
tube. It barely fit; he wedged it down out of sight, then
pawed open the door, and dropped down, hidden, and
now completely protected from what must have
happened.

He popped back out again, and walked to Dick's feet.
Dick was thinking furiously. There had been rumors that
drug smugglers were using captured Patrol ships; this
more-or-less confirmed those rumors. *Disable the ship,
take the exterior air lock and blow it. Whoever wasn't
suited up would die. Then they board and finish off whoever was suited up. They patch the lock, restore the air,
and weld enough junk to the outside of the ship to disguise it completely. Then they can bring it in to any port
they care to—even the ship's home port.*

This station. Which is where SCat escaped.

"Can you identify the attackers?" he asked SCat. The cat slowly nodded.

:They know he gone. He run, they chase. He try get home, they stop. He hear of me on dock, go hide in ship bringing mates. They kill he, get chance,: SKitty put in helpfully.

He could picture it easily enough; SCat being pursued, cut off from the Patrol section of the station—hiding out on the docks—catching the scent of the mates being shipped for SKitty's kittens and deciding to seek safety off-world. Cats, even shipscats, did not tend to grasp the concept of "duty;" he knew from dealing with SKitty that she took her bonds of personal affection seriously, but little else. So once "his" people were dead, SCat's personal allegiance to the Patrol was nonexistent, and his primary drive would be self-preservation. *Wonderful. I wonder if they—whoever they are—figured out he got away on another ship.* Another, more alarming thought occurred to him. *I wonder if my fishing about in the BioTech database touched off any telltales!*

No matter. There was only one place to go now—straight to Erica Makumba, the Legal and Security Officer.

He dumped a copy of the pertinent datafile to a memory cube, then scooped up both cats and pried their life-support ball out of its hiding place. Then he *ran* for Erica's cabin, praying that she had not gone off on shore leave.

The Spirits of Space were with him; the indicator outside her cabin door indicated that she was in there, but did not want to be disturbed. He pounded on the door anyway. Erica *might* kill him—but there were people after SCat who had murdered an entire Patrol DIA squad.

After a moment, the door cracked open a centimeter.

"White." Erica's flat, expressionless voice boded extreme violence. "This had better be an emergency."

He said the one word that would guarantee her attention. "Hijackers."

The door snapped open; she grabbed him and pulled him inside, cats, support-ball and all, and slammed the door shut behind him. She was wearing a short robe, tying it hastily around herself, and she wasn't alone. But the man watching them both alertly from the disheveled bed wasn't one of the *Brightwing*'s crew, so Dick flushed, but tried to ignore him.

"I found out where SCat's from," he babbled, dropping one cat to hand the memory-cube to her. "Read that—quick!"

She punched up the console at her elbow and dropped the cube in the receiver. The BioTech file, minus the holo, scrolled up on the screen. The man in the bed leaned forward to read it, too, and whistled.

Erica swiveled to glare at him. "You keep this to yourself, Jay!" she snapped. Then she turned back to Dick. "Spill it!" she ordered.

"SCat's ship was hijacked, probably by smugglers," he said quickly. "He hid his support ball in an access tube, and he was in it when they blew the lock. They missed him in the sweep, and when they brought their prize in here, he got away. But they know he's gone, and they know he can ID them."

"And they'll be giving the hairy eyeball to every ship with a black cat on it." She bit her knuckle—and Jay added his own two credits' worth.

"I hate to say this, but they've probably got a telltale on the BioTech data files, so they know whenever anyone accesses them. It's not restricted data, so anyone could leave a telltale." The man's face was pale beneath his normally dusky skintone. "If they don't know you've gone looking by now, they will shortly."

They all looked at each other. "Who's still on board?" Dick asked, and gulped.

Erica's mouth formed a tight, thin line. "You, me, Jay and the cats. The cargo's offloaded, and regs say you don't need more than two crew on board in-station. *Theoretically* no one can get past the security at the lock."

Jay barked a laugh, and tossed long, dark hair out of his eyes. "Honey, I'm a comptech. Trust me, you can get past the security. You just hack into the system, tell it the ship in the bay is bigger than it really is, and upload whoever you want as additional personnel.''

Erica swore—but Jay stood up, wrapping the sheet around himself like a toga, and pushed her gently aside. "What can be hacked can be unhacked—or at least I can make it a lot more difficult for them to get in and make those alterations stick. Give me your code to the AI."

Erica hesitated. He turned to stare into her eyes. "I need the AI's help. *You* two and the cats are going to get out of here—get over to the Patrol side of the station. I'm going to hold them off as long as I can, and play stupid when they do get in, but I need the speed of the AI to help me lay traps. You've known me for three years. You trusted me enough to bring me here, didn't you?"

She swore again, then reached past him to key in her code. He sat down, ignoring them and plunging straight into a trance of concentration.

"Come on!" Erica grabbed Dick's arm, and put the support ball on the floor. SKitty and SCat must have been reading *her* mind, for they both squirmed into the ball, which was big enough for more than one cat. They'd upgraded the ball after SKitty had proved to be so—fertile. Erica shoved the ball at Dick, and kept hold of his arm, pulling him out into the corridor.

"Where are we going?" he asked.

"To get our suits, then to the emergency lock," she replied crisply. "If we try to go out the main lock into the station, they'll get us for certain. So we're going outside for a little walk."

A little walk? All the way around the station? Outside?

He could only hope that "they" hadn't thought of that as well. They reached the suiting-up room in seconds flat.

He averted his eyes and climbed into his own suit as Erica shed her robe and squirmed into hers. "How far is it to the Patrol Section?" he asked.

"Not as far as you think," she told him. "And there's a maintenance lock just this side of it. What I want to know is how *you* got all this detailed information about the hijacking."

He turned, and saw that she was suited up, with her faceplate still open, staring at him with a calculating expression.

This is probably not the time to hold out on her.

He swallowed, and sealed his suit up, leaving his own faceplate open. Inside the ball, the cats were watching both of them, heads swiveling to look from one face to the other, as if they were watching a tennis match.

"SKitty's telepathic with me," he admitted. "I think SCat's telepathic with her. She seems to be able to talk with him, anyway."

He waited for Erica to react, either with disbelief or with revulsion. Telepaths of any species were not always popular among humankind. . . .

But Erica just pursed her lips and nodded. "Eyeah. I thought she might be. And telepathy's one of the traits BioTech doesn't talk about, but security people have known for a while that the MF type cats are bred for it. Maybe SKitty's momma did a little wandering over on the miltech side of the cattery, hmm?"

SKitty made a "silent" meow, and he just shrugged, relieved that Erica wasn't phobic about it. And equally relieved to learn that telepathy was already a trait that BioTech had established in their shipscat lines. *So they won't be coming to take SKitty away from me when they find out that she's a path. . . .*

But right now, he'd better be worrying about making a successful escape. He pulled his faceplate down and sealed it, fastening the tether line of the ball to a snaplink on his waistband. He warmed up his suit radio, and she did the same. "I hope you know what you're getting us into," he said, as Erica sealed her own plate shut and led the way to the emergency lock.

She looked back over her shoulder at him.

"So do I" she replied soberly.

The trip was a nightmare.

Dick had never done a spacewalk on the exterior of a station before. It wasn't at all like going out on the hull of a ship. There were hundreds of obstacles to avoid—windows, antenna, instrument packages, maintenance robots. Any time an inspection drone came along, they had to hide to avoid being picked up on camera. It was work, hard work, to inch their way along the station in this way, and Dick was sweating freely before half an hour was up.

It seemed like longer. Every time he glanced up at the chronometer in his faceplate HUD, he was shocked to see how little time had passed. The suit fans whined in his ears, as the life-support system alternately fought to warm him up when they hid in the shade, or cool him down when they paused in full sunlight. Stars burned down on them, silent points of light in a depth of darkness that made him dizzy whenever he glanced out at it. The knowledge that he could be lost forever out there if he just made one small mistake chilled his heart.

Finally, Erica pointed, and he saw the outline of a maintenance lock just ahead. The two of them pulled themselves hand-over-hand toward it, reaching it at the same instant. But it was Erica who opened it, while Dick reeled the cats in on their tether.

With all four of them inside, Erica sealed the lock from the inside and initiated pressurization. Within moments, they were both able to pop their faceplates and breathe station air again.

Something prompted Dick to release the cats from their ball before Erica unsealed the inner hatch. He unsnapped the tether and was actually straightening up, empty ball in both hands, when Erica opened the door to a hallway—

—and dropped to the floor, as the shrill squeal of a stun-gun pierced the quiet of the lock.

"Erica!" Without thinking, he ran forward, and found himself facing the business end of a powerful stunner, held by a nondescript man who held it as if he were quite used to employing it. He was *not* wearing a station uniform.

The man looked startled to see him, and Dick did the only thing he could think of. He threw the support ball at the man, as hard as he could.

It hit cleanly, knocking the man to the floor as it impacted with his chest. He clearly was not aware that the support balls were as massy as they were. The two cats flashed past him, heading for freedom, and Dick tried to follow their example. But the man was quick to recover, and as Dick tried to jump over his prone body, the fellow grabbed his ankle and tripped him up.

Then it turned into a brawl, with Dick the definite underdog. Even in the suit, the stranger still outweighed him.

Within a few seconds, Dick was on his back on the floor, and the stranger held him down, easily. The stun gun was no longer in his hands, but it didn't look to Dick as if he really needed it.

In fact, as the man's heavy fist pounded into Dick's face, he was quickly convinced that he didn't need it. Pain lanced through his jaw as the man's fist smashed into it; his vision filled with stars and red and white flashes of light. More agony burst into his skull as the blows continued. He flailed his arms and legs, but there was nothing he could do—he was trapped in the suit, and he couldn't even get enough leverage to defend himself. He tasted blood in his mouth—he couldn't see—

:BAD MAN!:

There was a terrible battle screech from somewhere out in the corridor, and the blows stopped. Then the weight lifted from his body, as the man howled in pain.

Dick managed to roll to one side and stagger blindly to his feet with the aid of the corridor bulkhead—he still couldn't see. He dashed blood out of his eyes with one hand, and shook his head to clear it, staring blindly in the direction of the unholy row.

"Get it off! Get it off me!" Human screams mixed with feline battle cries, telling him that whichever of the cats had attacked, they were giving a good accounting of themselves.

But there were other sounds—the sounds of running feet approaching, and Dick tried frantically to get his vision to clear. A heavy body crashed into him, knocking him into the bulkhead with enough force to drive all the

breath from his body, as the *zing* of an illegal neuro gun
went off somewhere near him.

SKitty!

But whoever was firing swore, and the cat wail faded
into the distance.

"It got away!" said one voice, over the sobbing of
another.

A third swore, as Dick fought for air. "You. Go after
it," the third man said, and there was the sound of running feet. Meanwhile, footsteps neared where Dick lay
curled in a fetal bundle on the floor.

"What about this?" the second voice asked.

The third voice, cold and unemotional, wrote Dick's
death warrant. "Get rid of it, and the woman, too."

And Dick could not even move. He heard someone
breathing heavily just above him; sensed the man taking aim—

Then—

"Patrol! Freeze! Drop your weapons now!"

Something clattered to the deck beside him, as more
running feet approached; and with a sob of relief, Dick
finally drew a full breath. There was a scuffle just beside
him, then someone helped him to stand, and he heard
the hiss of a hypospray and felt the telltale sting against
the side of his neck. A moment later, his eyes cleared—
just in time for him to catch SKitty as she launched
herself from the arms of a uniformed DIA officer into
his embrace.

"So, the bottom line is, you'll let us take SCat's contract?" Captain Singh sat back in his chair while Dick
rubbed SKitty's ears. She and SCat both burdened
Dick's lap, as they had since SCat, the Captain, the DIA
negotiator, and Erica had all walked into the sick bay
where Dick was still recovering. Erica was clearly nursing a stun-headache; the Captain looked a little frazzled.
The DIA man, as most of his ilk, looked as unemotional
as an android. The DIA had spent many hours with a
human-feline telepathic specialist debriefing SCat. Apparently SCat was naturally only a receptive telepath; it
took a human who was also a telepath to "talk" to him.

"There's no reason why not," the DIA agent said. "You civilians have helped materially in this case; both you and he are entitled to certain compensation, and if that's what you all want, then he's yours with our blessing—the fact that he is only a receptive telepath makes him less than optimal for further Patrol duties." The agent shrugged. "We can always get other shipscats with full abilities. According to the records, the only reason we kept him was because Major Logan selected him."

SKitty bristled, and Dick sent soothing thoughts at her.

Then the agent smiled, making his face look more human. "Major Logan was a good agent, but he didn't particularly care for having a cat talking to him. I gather that Lightfoot and he got along all right, but there wasn't the strong bond between them that we would have preferred. It would have been just a matter of time before that squad and ship got a new cat-agent team. Besides, we aren't completely inhuman. If your SKitty and this boy here are happily mated, who and what in the Parol can possibly want to separate them?"

"Judging by the furrows SKitty left in that 'jacker's face and scalp, it isn't a good idea to get between her and someone she loves," Captain Singh said dryly. "He's lucky she left him one eye."

The agent's gaze dropped briefly to the swath of black fur draped over Dick's lap. "Believe me," he said fervently. "That *is* a consideration we had taken into account. Your little lady there is a warrior for fair, and we have no intention of denying her anything her heart is set on. If she wants Lightfoot, and he wants her, then she's got him. We'll see his contract is transferred over to *Brightwing* within the hour." His eyes rose to meet Dick's. "You're a lucky man to have a friend like her, young man. She put herself between you and certain death. Don't you ever forget it."

SKitty's purr deepened, and SCat's joined with hers as Dick's hands dropped protectively on their backs. "I know that, sir," he replied, through swollen lips. "I knew it before any of this happened."

SKitty turned her head, and he gazed into amused

yellow eyes. :*Smart Dick,*: she purred, then lowered her head to her paws. :*Smart man. Mate happy here, mate stay. Everything good.*:

And that, as far as SKitty was concerned, was the end of it. The rest were simply "minor human matters."

He chuckled, and turned his own attention to dealing with those "minor human matters," while his best friend and her mate drifted into well-earned sleep.

PROFESSOR PURR'S GUARANTEED ALLERGY CURE

by Brad Linaweaver and Dana Fredsti

Brad Linaweaver is the author of *Moon of Ice* and *Sliders, The Novel*, and has coauthored four *Doom* novels with Dafydd ab Hugh. His nonfiction appears in magazines from *National Review* to *Famous Monsters of Filmland*. He has also sold about 50 short stories, his first anthology sale being to Andre Norton and the late Robert Adams.

Dana Fredsti doesn't just read books about female warriors wielding swords. She may be seen doing it herself at Renaissance fairs and in Sam Raimi's film *Army of Darkness*. Her story "Muzak for the Dead" appears in *Death's Garden,* and her large cat family appears in this story.

> *Cats are the runes of beauty, invincibility, wonder, pride, freedom, coldness, self-sufficiency, and dainty individuality . . . the cat is a gentleman.*
>
> —H. P. Lovecraft

The cats never wanted to take over the world. There was no need. They had a good thing going. After millennia of careful conditioning, they had prepared a cross-section of humanity to be perfectly acceptable companions. Except for an awkward moment in the European Middle Ages, when cats were slaughtered as the familiars of witches, the human record was acceptable. Besides, in that one case mankind had been taught a severe lesson from the rats and their constant companion, the plague.

So when the goddess Bast appeared before the oldest Hemingway cat in Glendale, California, no one was more surprised than that old tabby. "I have chosen you because you are the most intelligent cat now living," said the goddess.

"Chosen for what?" asked the cat, licking at the extra claw on his paw. Like all members of his species, he couldn't be awed by much of anything. Still, the appearance of the goddess was a significant enough event to finally distract him from cleaning himself.

The goddess answered in a long hiss that communicated directly into the cat's brain: "Humans have made a number of mistakes since they stopped practicing the true religion—the part of it they were able to understand."

"You mean ancient Egypt, of course," said the cat. "My mistress has many books on that subject. She even has a good reproduction of a famous bronze statue in your honor; a votive figure of Bastet from the Saite period, I believe. It's around here somewhere. My mistress has the proper attitude ..."

Bast grew larger. "You must no longer think of a human being as your mistress. And stop trying to save her. She is on the list to be spared. You don't need to make a special request for someone who isn't scheduled to die."

It was at this point that the old gray cat realized he was living in interesting times.

Bast accomplished her purpose in one night. Except for one exception, only true cat lovers survived the Great Change. There weren't as many survivors as might have been expected. People who pretended to love cats for purposes of domestic tranquillity didn't make it through. A number of wives were surprised to learn that their husbands had not been entirely sincere about the affection they expressed for the family cat. Then again, there were instances of the male half of a cat-owning couple being around to greet the dawn while his late wife turned out to have secretly preferred the canine species.

No dogs survived. Not one.

There were some fortunate humans whose loved ones shared a more important affection than what they felt for each other: *ailurophilia,* the love of cats. These people saw the dawn ... and the Collapse-of-Civilization-as-They-Knew-it!

Bast had it within her power to exterminate the victims painlessly. Instead, untold millions passed away in their sleep by choking to death on what appeared to be giant hair balls.

At the request of the old tabby in Glendale, one person lived who was slated to die. The cat might not have thought of making the request, but he was given the idea by the goddess herself when she implied that she might grant a boon if phrased properly. The result was the continued life of a young man who was a dedicated cat hater. What saved him was having the right girlfriend! The cat knew this guy was dead meat otherwise.

"He claims to be allergic to cats," the cat had told Bast.

"No problem," said the goddess airily, sniffing the stars as a mortal cat would detect a bird. "If he truly loves cats ..."

"Oh, but he hates us!" said the cat. "I am certain that he has exaggerated a mild allergic reaction into a full blown condition so that his girlfriend won't expect him to be around her cats. It's even a good excuse for not marrying her because she wouldn't want to get rid of her large cat family—especially not me!"

"So he will die."

"Oh, no, please spare him. I love Miko and I don't want her to experience any pain."

"I will grant such a request only to Professor Purr, because of the important work he must do in the new world," announced Bast.

"Who is Professor Purr?" asked the striped tabby.
"You are."

A word or two might be in order about the last human
of his kind, who awakened to a world not designed to
improve his opinion of the feline species. David Lawrence Alexander had always been an unhappy man. In
the old world, he'd delighted in making sure that other
people shared his misery. Now that cats ran things he
had more misery to share than ever.

He didn't have a much higher opinion of women than
he did of cats. His powers of self-delusion were such
that he couldn't accept the fact that he owed his life to
his girlfriend, thanks to her cat. In the old world, he
mouthed all the politically correct statements about the
female members of his species ... while doing his best
to undermine self-confidence in the women around him.

He didn't let on to Miko how much he truly loathed
felines. In this, Professor Purr understood him better
than Miko did. A slight allergy to cat dander acerbated
David's distaste for the animals, but it really boiled
down to the fact that cats wouldn't come when he called;
and couldn't (or wouldn't) perform amusing tricks to
command and didn't accord him the slavish devotion he
felt entitled to by animals and women!

Where he got this overdeveloped sense of self-
importance had been a constant source of mystery to David's few friends. Although reasonably intelligent, he was
a classic know-it-all, lacking basic social skills for doing
anything other than enjoying his own company. Neither
courtesy nor tact were in his vocabulary or his behavior.
He did have genuine wit, though, which he used to throw
verbal monkey wrenches into conversations. Basically, he
enjoyed causing trouble and could take credit for several
divorces and a lot of bad feeling among his acquaintances.

Physically, David was short and round, with slicked-
back hair that had a tendency to curl around the edges;
a waxed mustache with ends that pointed straight up as
though seeking escape from the halitosis wafting from
his thin-lipped mouth. His taste in clothing ran toward
tight trousers, full-sleeved shirts and brightly colored

waistcoats inevitably clashing with the rest of his ensemble. In short, David resembled nothing so much as the Mayor of the Munchkin City in the Land of Oz.

The smartest thing he ever did was become involved with Miko. He had chosen her not so much for her porcelain doll appearance—although that was a most attractive feature—but because she had received a traditional Japanese upbringing. He always had a knack for finding women with low self-esteem.

He thought he'd found himself a subservient geisha who would fulfill his every desire. Before the Great Change the situation had been pretty much what he wanted. But now Miko didn't let him forget that he was alive only because of his relationship with her. Professor Purr explained the situation to Miko and she happily passed on these facts to David. Of course, no human being had seen the goddess, Bast; but the Changed World was impossible for even David to miss.

He was allowed living quarters to himself because of the allergy. But one of his duties was to clean Miko's large house every day and not annoy the large cat population living there. He wore an oxygen mask when he came over. This was bad enough in itself, but what he really couldn't stand was the change in Miko.

She had recently taken to displaying unfortunate feline qualities herself. Gone were the days when she would take his criticisms with downcast eyes and a promise to do better. He suspected that Professor Purr had been filling her head with such notions. It was more likely to be the fault of Purr than the other cats simply because Purr was her favorite; and now that damned cat was the most important researcher in Greater Los Angeles.

Communication worked through telepathy of some kind. Since the Great Change, all cats were able to communicate with humans. This in no way diminished their age-old ability of communicating with each other in the language of cats. They'd simply picked up new tricks.

"Be careful," Miko warned him on this fine Monday morning. Every time he entered her house with his oxygen mask attached, he felt like some kind of giant insect come to invade her.

"Thanks for your concern," he answered sarcastically (he hoped). He wasn't at all sure his words could be understood clearly through the equipment on his face.

Miko sat on her thick, richly upholstered couch with Sorscha, the Russian blue. All humans were required to replace furniture every two weeks so their cats would have the highest quality scratching surfaces. Sorscha's squirrellike tail wrapped itself around Miko as it rubbed its head against her chin. The cat took a moment to raise its head and shoot David a resentful glare, slanted green eyes agleam with animosity and suspicion. Sorscha did not like men, not even cat-lovers born with the disadvantage of being a human male.

Of all the men on the face of the Earth, David would be Sorscha's last choice for visitor. Now here he was, stuck with being a "geisha" not only for the Russian blue, but also for Zhadi, Luna, Vootie, and Buster—the rest of Miko's cat family.

Zhadi was as fat and round as a bowling ball, a happy Buddha who liked men, even poor specimens. Luna was, if anything, even fatter than Zhadi, and enjoyed nothing better than sprawling on a lap, and reaching out with a paw that made her look like a black otter. Then there was Vootie, a multicolored kitten—a Beatrix Potter poster child—cuddly and playful. Vootie liked everyone, even a big, dumb dog who used to live next door. (Vootie often asked what had happened to her canine playmate. Miko and the others agreed that she was too young to understand.) Finally, there was Buster, a litter mate to Professor Purr. Buster was a huge, male tabby, very loud and good-natured.

Miko thought most of her cats were bulimic. Professor Purr thought they ate too much.

"You know what happens to cat haters?" Sorscha enjoyed tormenting David. "I've heard rumors of their being buried alive . . . in very large litter boxes. Used litter boxes."

He didn't bother answering her. The cats didn't read human thoughts (he hoped); or they at least required spoken words to focus on the message. However the magic worked, Miko frequently admonished him, "Be careful!"

"Professor Purr says I'm essential to his work," David told Miko on this fine Monday. The sky was clear blue; and before entering the house he'd enjoyed a cool breeze bringing with it a hint of catnip in the air. At least he wasn't allergic to that.

"Sorscha likes to tease you," said Miko, carefully extracting herself from the cat. "I must get supplies. You'll be all right, won't you, David?" He nodded as she looked for an exposed patch of flesh on his head she could kiss.

"You won't forget the shrimp?" called out Luna.

"And the chicken?" added Zhadi.

"I won't forget the litter either," Miko assured them as she hurried out the door. In the good old days, David would have plopped down on the couch right now, after dumping whatever cat was in his way. Hell, in the good old days he'd beat a retreat out of here as fast as his feet could carry him. But that was before cats could talk. To people.

Sorscha was curled up on top of a plush chair, nose nestled in the fur of her tail as she stared at him. During the first months, she'd hightailed it out of a room if David walked in; a habit from her old days of being raised as a feral street cat. Now she could enjoy the New World Order, a very big idea narrowing down to how much David Lawrence Alexander hated to be stared at for any length of time. So she stared, and then stared some more.

They hadn't completely broken his spirit yet. He deliberately "accidentally" bumped the chair on a pass with the vacuum cleaner, eliciting a sharp growl from Sorscha. His face mask covered a smile of satisfaction as he mumbled a perfunctory apology.

"Watch it, chubby," hissed Sorscha in reply.

He started to laugh and stopped himself. It wouldn't do to laugh at them or lose his mask. But it was funny that one of Miko's cats would comment on excess pounds on his frame when some of them could pass for small planetoids caught in Earth's gravitational field.

He kept vacuuming and enjoyed the spectacle of one of the spherical cats coming to his rescue. "Mellow out, Sorscha," snapped Zhadi, looking to David exactly like a Dakin stuffed toy. She gazed up at David from her seat on the couch, adoration in her round yellow-green eyes. Her love of men made no distinctions.

"He did that deliberately," said Sorscha.

"Don't be a paranoid twit," answered Zhadi.

Meanwhile, the tortoiseshell kitten, Vootie, leaped down from a bookshelf and began to chase after the vacuum cord as it moved back and forth. She trilled her pleasure as she caught it time and time again. Impervious to cute kittens, David resisted the impulse to run Vootie over as he vacuumed.

Luna decided to move the conversation to a higher plane: "I'm hungry," she said plaintively, stretching lazily on the other side of the couch and exposing her tummy with its tuft of white fur.

David refrained from telling her she could live off her body fat for at least a week without problems and mumbled through his breathing apparatus, "I should be finished in here soon and then Miko will return with the groceries. I have to hurry up and get to the lab so that I can assist Professor Purr, you know."

"I want!" cried Luna, in a mixture of words and meows. "I want! I WANT! NOW!!!"

The other three cats joined the chorus, the noise level rising with each passing second. David clicked off the vacuum cleaner with an audible snap. "Fine," he said, starting to grit his teeth. "But I do hope that when the professor asks why I'm late, you'll explain that you needed to eat brunch as *well* as breakfast today."

He stalked into the kitchen, mumbling over why Miko was doing a grocery run when the kitchen wasn't exactly bare. But he knew the answer. Bast exercised special care in selecting leaders for the new cat elite. These cats made sure there were enough humans doing the essential work to keep the wheels turning. In some cases, survivors did jobs they never thought would be their lot.

A computer programmer might find himself fishing for most of the week; and then devote his Saturday to a program that would facilitate swift transport of his catch! The goal was simple: provide all the food that cats really liked. Oddly enough, little effort had been expended to preserve traditional Cat Foods. Humans were allowed to stock all the pet food they wanted ... for their own consumption.

These thoughts were creeping through David's brain as he removed choice chicken breast tenders out of the freezer. The sound effects gave him away. Luna, Vootie, and Zhadi dashed in and immediately tangled themselves up in his feet—tripping him as he tried to put the chicken on a plate and into the microwave.

He went sprawling and the mask came off. The cats reverted to Old Talk as they climbed over his prostrate form. There wasn't much they could do with the frozen chicken. Vootie batted at his shoe laces as Sorscha watched in malicious amusement from the kitchen doorway.

His sneezing, coughing, wheezing and red face added immensely to the Russian blue's amusement. She didn't even mind if she wasn't fed today.

Professor Purr was having the nightmare again. He was sure he could make himself wake up if he really wanted to. But there was something that held him in the dream, and forced him to claw at each disturbing detail.

Gray walls stretched up endlessly, dwarfing him as he prowled restlessly through this bleak landscape, glancing uneasily from side to side. He wanted to get away from the walls, but somehow he knew that this world was nothing but endless halls, and huge, barren rooms, all with blank walls.

There were no trees beyond the walls. And within the labyrinthian maze there was no furniture, no nooks and crannies, not a stuffed mouse or a scratching post in sight. Not even a piece of string. Nothing to climb, nothing to play with, no place to hide should it become necessary.

But why should it become necessary? There didn't

seem to be any other life. *There were no odors!* Nothing
to smell meant a world so dead it defied the feline imagination. And yet ... and yet ... there was something
following Professor Purr.

There were soft padding sounds creeping up behind,
but still he couldn't smell a thing. Feeling the hair rise
on his back, the wise old tabby felt as though all his
intelligence didn't amount to a thing. He'd always been
a brave cat, but now he even doubted his ability to fight.

So he ran. And something ran close behind him.
Ahead there was a dead end, so he had no choice but
to stop, turn around and *see* his pursuer.

It was another cat, a big, tired-looking, stupid cat. But
it didn't act like a cat. There was something dead in its
eyes. It was at this point that Professor Purr tried very,
very hard to wake up. He didn't want to see what would
happen next.

He wasn't able to wake up until the wolflike dog burst
out from the enfolding cat body, leaving the feral remains to fall away from its dripping, canine jaws. . . .

"Are you all right, Professor Purr?" A human voice
addressed the old cat who opened his green eyes to witness bug-eyed goggles in place of eyes and a long, snake-
like tube in place of a mouth. The professor almost
screeched and clawed before he realized he was staring
into David's portable oxygen mask. He'd have to do
something about the man's damned allergy.

"I was having a bad dream," the cat admitted. "Sometimes I feel guilty about what happened to so many of
your kind."

"It's not your fault," said David, displaying a surprising degree of perception—or else deference to the cat
who held his life in its paws.

"I wonder if I could have spared more of you if I'd
asked," the cat went on. "But the goddess wasn't
pleased that I asked her to spare the life of even one
cat hater."

"But I don't hate cats," David lied. "The problem has
always been my allergy. I almost died earlier today when
my mask came off in Miko's kitchen."

"Are you all right now?" asked Professor Purr with genuine concern.

"Yeah. But that's why I'm late. I literally couldn't breathe."

Purr walked across a tabletop that was high enough that he could place a paw on David's shoulder. "Perfectly all right," said the cat, failing to notice how David pulled back ever so slightly. "I slept through my alarm," the cat went on. "My dreams and your allergy may be linked, you know."

"How?"

"Despite the important work you help me with in the lab, I don't think the goddess would begrudge me taking the time to solve your problem, even if I needed another human assistant during your treatments."

David didn't like the sound of that. "I'm proud to be your hands, professor," he said.

The old cat couldn't be thrown off a perch by a mere compliment. "Before much longer, I won't need a pair of human hands in the lab. Look here!"

Professor Purr proudly strutted around the complicated series of ramps and shelves that made his laboratory appear to be leftovers from a Rube Goldberg game. He picked his way over pieces of metal and glass and reached the far end of the lab where mechanical attachments for his paws were lined up like so many gravestones over David's hopes.

"I've always wanted hands of my own," he said, "even before the Great Change. I want hands as badly as you wish to be cured of your allergy."

"Uh, professor, I have a more serious problem right now," said David in a voice so low that he was surprised how the old cat's ears twitched, receiving every word.

"What's the matter?" asked the cat, starting back for him.

"I'm afraid I sort of panicked getting out of Miko's kitchen."

"And?"

"I'm afraid I hurt the kitten."

The professor stopped where he stood, one paw up in the air. He looked like a statue. "How badly?" he asked.

"I'm sure that Vootie is still alive, but I stepped on her getting out of the kitchen ..."

The cat seemed to relax. "But, David, these things happen. You needn't ..."

"The kitten clawed me. So, I, uh ..."

The old cat was deadly serious again. "David, what did you do?"

"I kicked her."

"I see. You know that you're in serious trouble, don't you?"

"Oh, God, I didn't mean to," said David.

"The problem here is the *goddess,* David."

They stared at one another, the old smart cat, and the young not-terribly-smart man. Professor Purr preferred looking into the eyes of a human at times like this instead of plastic and metal that told him nothing.

"I've come to a decision, David," said the cat. "I won't let them bury you in the giant litter box ..."

"You mean Sorscha wasn't kidding about that?" asked David, incredulously.

"I'm afraid not. But I have a solution to all your problems."

"I don't want to die!" David half-screamed, looking wildly around for an avenue of escape. But the whole world was the trap.

"Don't be ridiculous," said the professor. "Why would I bother to save you and throw it all away now? Besides, I promised Miko that I would always preserve your life. But to help you, we must act quickly. Come with me."

The professor's quiet determination helped to calm David. He followed the cat to the door attaching the lab to the dormitory where cats stayed who chose to help with the many research projects. There were eleven living there at the moment.

Professor Purr's ultimate objective was to correct the many human interventions in natural cat blood lines. For example, Bast was incensed that Persians with only one blue eye were usually deaf in the ear on that side. The goddess didn't like the fact that certain eye colors had been eliminated in whole lines. She didn't view all human intervention as equally bad, especially not when the breeding techniques had strengthened natural tendencies. As to what was natural and what wasn't, Bast had left Professor Purr with a library of helpful guidelines. And that wasn't all she had left.

"Excuse me, everyone!" raaaorrrred the professor as the door opened. Almost immediately there was dead quiet. The alpha qualities of the good professor had been greatly enhanced. "You are all free to wander off and tend to your business. I won't be working with any of you today."

David stepped back more than he normally would have, but the accident with Vootie bothered him. The professor's reaction bothered him even more. He could just imagine what Sorscha would tell Miko. But the other cats had stared at him in the same cold, unforgiving way . . . even Zhadi.

So now he gave plenty of room to Snowy and Shark and Merry Kat, all white as the ice in his heart; and all as white as he imagined his bones would be after they'd been allowed to bleach in the sun.

Next came the two smallest cats there, the aptly named Rusty and diminutive Perri who had a purr so loud it was hard to believe it was generated in so small a body. Then came Squeaker, bigger than the other two, but still small enough to sit comfortably on the narrow ledge provided by the top of a door. David imagined how easily he could hurt any of this threesome and tried to merge into the wall behind.

The remaining cats were bigger and he relaxed a little. There was night-black Noir, the best hunter in the region and whose bones seemed to be made of water when he had to move fast and through narrow spaces in pursuit of a bird. Behind him strutted Piewacket, or Pie for short, who had the most aristocratic table manners, next to the professor. Then came Tux, with a black-and-white coat leaving no mystery about his name. He was older than the professor but in good health. The only cat older than Tux followed behind him, Tabbis—another Hemingway cat and the professor's favorite. Bringing up the rear was the orange-and-white Buttons, a big young adult who thought he was a kitten and could be seen frequently playing with his own tail.

David Lawrence Alexander hated them all.

Professor Purr was so good-natured that he consistently misread the reactions of his human assistant. He tried to put the man's mind at ease: "I can imagine how you must feel about your accident with the kitten. Even the kicking could be forgiven in a more tolerant regime."

"They wouldn't forgive me," said David, watching Button's back as the last of the lab cats exited the area.

"You'd be surprised," the professor disagreed. "Consider how cats fight! We're not as civilized as all that. I'm sometimes ashamed to witness how we pee over everything and then fight about it."

"You're the most civilized cat I know," said David through his oxygen mask. And he meant it.

"The time has come to give you back your face," said the professor, looking up. "You must be tired of fiddling around with that, changing it . . ."

"I want to breathe," said David, following the cat scientist back into the lab. This time they passed right by the statue of Bast that used to be in Miko's house. The statue had been moved here at the professor's request. As David looked into the implacable eyes above a golden nose-ring, he said, half to himself, "And I want to go on breathing."

"You will, my boy," said Professor Purr with good cheer, "and all will be set right between you and Miko, as well. She won't be happy when she learns about Vootie. But don't worry, the goddess herself has shown me the way to help you."

"How?"

The cat ran up on top of a cabinet that David had never opened before. "My research was not ready before today, but now is the time. I'm sure of it. You see, to alter cat blood lines requires an ability to tamper with basic genetics."

"You need advanced science for that," said David, without conviction.

"Or magic, dear boy. Or magic! It's the same thing

actually. They had it in ancient Egypt. The great pyramid was their laboratory. They kept their supply in the
pyramid."

"Supply of what?"

"Of molds, fungi, roots! Everything we need to cure
your allergy. It's in here, David. Help me with it."

David helped.

The treatment took three days. Plenty of time for the
professor to send Miko a progress report. She prepared
herself for him. She took it very well and never once
came close to screaming.

Everyone was very nice. No one mentioned the incident in the kitchen, not even Sorscha. Vootie went out
of her way to be friendly to David, rubbing up against
his foot. At least he still had a foot. He'd have it for
another week at least.

The first stage of the process was slow, but now that
the metabolic changes were underway, the transformation would greatly accelerate. Miko sat on the couch
with David, holding hands with him, while he still had
hands.

He couldn't think of a thing to say. He was too tired
to feel sorry for himself. He was too tired to think of
self-destruction. He sat there, placid as a lump on a log,
and drank his milk.

For all the times she had wished to have David on
her couch in her house, surrounded by her cats, and not
wearing that silly mask, now that her dream had come
true, it wasn't entirely satisfactory. David no longer had
his mustache. She'd never really liked it, and didn't mind
that the professor required a clean-shaven subject for
the experiment.

But when she tried to kiss David, his whiskers tickled
her something awful!

NOH CAT AFTERNOON
by Jane M. Lindskold

Jane Lindskold resides in Albuquerque, New Mexico with six cats, all named after figures in British mythology. To support them (and her four guinea pigs and four fish) she writes full time. Her published works include the novels *Brother to Dragons, Companion to Owls, Marks of Our Brothers, The Pipes of Orpheus,* and *Smoke and Mirrors,* Her short fiction has appeared in a variety of collections, including *Heaven Sent, Return to Avalon,* and *Wheel of Fortune.* Currently, she is under contract to complete the two novels left unfinished by Roger Zelazny, as well as several novels of her own. The cats highly approve of this, as it means she will keep them in cat food and a residence with appropriate sunbathing facilities.

The geisha Okesa was strolling beneath the cherry blossoms in a garden on the island of Sado when she noticed something very odd. There were no cats about, not one.

Okesa had an affinity for cats, being one herself, and she read omens in the number of cats she saw in the course of her daily stroll. Eight cats was very propitious, and she had come to expect to see at least three or four. None at all struck her as ominous indeed.

Without another thought, she went searching for the cats. She checked the sun-warmed stones by the koi pond, but they were empty of all but sunlight. She inspected the flower gardens where birds hopped and butterflies fluttered, but not one cat hunted beneath the ornamental shrubs.

She even donned high, awkward geta to keep her feet dry and the skirts of her kimono clear of the mud while she hunted up and down the alleys behind the tea shops and markets. Even there, not one cat was to be found. The rats and mice foraged unmolested, and the fish and chicken offal remained uneaten.

Okesa had paused, considering where to look next, when she saw a cat's tail disappearing through a low hole in a stone wall. It was an unlovely tail—dirty, gray, and broken in at least three places. She recognized it as belonging to Bushi, a scavenger and alley rascal, and no particular friend of hers. Still, without a pause, she changed herself back into the slim, black cat that was her own true form and leaped through the hole after him.

Bushi's battered tail was just rounding a bend ahead and Okesa chased after, pacing herself to keep it in sight. The way was dim, and the brushing of her whiskers against the stone walls kept her on track as much as her unintentional guide.

After several twists and turns, clear sunlight shining through a rectangular opening ahead brightened the way. The breeze carried a fascinating variety of scents. Her pricked ears caught the sound of running water, shifting foliage, the gentle clink of china, and something else. Okesa slowed and picked her way soundlessly forward, not wishing to stumble into Bushi.

The rectangular doorway was edged with a wooden torii—the symbol of a Shinto shrine. A figure of the Compassionate Buddha sat to one side of the torii. Their presence confirmed what Okesa had already guessed. She had come to the Garden of Cats, a refuge during times of grave danger to those of the feline sort. Okesa paused before padding through the torii.

What had caused the entry into the Garden to manifest here on Sado? What danger did it portend? Apprehension slightly puffing the fur on her tail, she entered the Garden.

Amaterasu, the sun, shone down on a cat's paradise. The torii was framed by short, fat hibiscus bushes whose red-orange blossoms were attended by shimmering green ruby-throated hummingbirds that darted from blossom to blossom, their near-invisible wings thrumming. More such bushes were artistically mingled with red-leaf maple and fan-leafed gingkos. Catnip and catmint grew close to the ground in heavily scented clumps.

And everywhere there were cats. Cats in the tree branches, cats by the koi ponds, cats asleep on sun-warmed rocks, and cats wide awake watching the antics of the hummingbirds. There were cats of every color, long-haired cats and short-haired cats, cats of every age and shape and size. Okesa, though a cat herself, was overwhelmed by the presence of so many, so varied cats.

Lifting her paws with the same delicate grace that, in her human guise, had made her a famous dancer, Okesa walked more deeply into the garden. She passed a group of shabby cats—Bushi among them—who were batting polished marbles through an intricate maze drawn in the sand and arguing loudly about the results.

Beyond the gamblers, she spotted an acquaintance of hers. The roly-poly orange and black and white calico was drowsing in the lap of a statue of Kwannon, the Goddess of Mercy, Buddhist, but welcome here all the same.

"Okesa," the calico purred sleepily, "I hadn't thought to see you here. Aren't you human these days?"

"Human-formed, but never human," Okesa replied. "Momo, what brings you from the sushi house? I thought you never stirred from there."

"I don't, usually," Momo said, rolling to grasp a sun-beam in her paws, "but I heard that the Fox Spirits are coming in force to Sado. They are mischievous and tricky and fonder of no one than themselves. I doubt they have it in for my humans, but, still, the town won't be safe until they are gone."

"Fox Spirits in force!" Okesa exclaimed, lashing her tail. "But why?"

"Rumor says," Momo drew her answer out into a long rumble. "Rumor says that though the Daimyo collected the usual tithe for Inari from the peasants, he neglected to give the Rice God his due. Fox Spirits, as you know, are Inari's messengers. Apparently, the god intends to send the Daimyo the message that Inari does not care to be slighted."

"This is terrible!" Okesa said.

"Why?" Momo blinked sleepily. "Rice is only a concern for humans and rodents. We are safe here in the Garden and when the danger is past, we can return to Sado."

"Have you heard what the Fox Spirits plan?" Okesa asked after a thoughtful pause.

There was no answer. Momo was asleep.

Okesa prowled the Garden, barely noticing its delights. She exchanged polite greetings with many cats, but paused only to ask, "Have you seen Kynn, the cat who lives with the sake merchant?"

At last, she found him, a long-bodied, slim-hipped, golden tomcat with a white star on his breast. He was perched on a log above an oval koi pond, one paw cupped to strike.

"Kynn-san!" Okesa called happily.

"Hush," he hissed, then his paw flashed, water splashed. "Hachiman forfend! I missed!"

"Sorry," Okesa said, glancing into the pool, certain that the long-tailed carp gliding away on gauzy fins was laughing at them. "You'll have another chance. It can't go far."

Kynn fastidiously shook water from his paw. "Okesa-san! I'm surprised to see you here."

"Why?" she asked, nettled though she knew she shouldn't be. "I *am* a cat!"

"Of course," the golden tom soothed, "but I thought ... I mean ... well, you've been human for a while."

"Only while I earn some money for my poor, old humans," Okesa said. "Then I plan to go right back to chasing rats and sleeping in my basket on the hearthstone. You always have all the gossip. What's this I hear about the Fox Spirits?"

Kynn quickly repeated what she had gathered from Momo, then he went on.

"The Daimyo is hosting a Noh drama competition this very afternoon. What I've heard is that the Fox Spirits will enter the competition and when they win—for surely they will, being masters of illusion—they will use the Daimyo's well-known generosity against him to gain Inari's revenge."

"We must stop them!" Okesa declared.

"Why?" Kynn said curiously. "How does this involve cats?"

"Why? He is our Daimyo!"

"Okesa, don't be ridiculous. You have been living as a human for too long. Daimyo have little to do with cats. Their world is the human world."

Okesa lashed her tail from side to side. "Then go back to hunting little fish, great warrior!"

She stalked away, somewhat embarrassed over her outburst. Kynn was right—as far as he went—but she could not escape the feeling that the challenge of the Fox Spirits must be met. Whiskers curled in thought, she went to the torii into the Garden and leaped lithely onto the lintel.

Amaterasu still warmed the open plaza by the gateway with her shining benevolence. Among the cats who basked in her light were many that Okesa recognized. The marble players had put aside their game and were now sipping fish soup from eggshell cups. The fountain that dispensed the soup was shaped like an open-mouthed carp. A trio of kittens played on its marble flanks.

Other cats dined on bowls of fish or meat carried on black lacquer trays by invisible servitors. There were thimble-sized bowls of cream for the kittens.

Looking at all of this lazy splendor, Okesa despaired of finding anyone who would help her. Nonetheless, she meowed for their attention. Little murmurs greeted her.

"That's Okesa, the dancing cat!" "That's Okesa, who lives as a human!" "That's Okesa, who has the blessing of the gods." "That's Okesa! She's utterly mad!"

Okesa ignored the murmuring, sat bolt upright on the torii, and perked her ears for silence.

"Brothers and Sisters in the Sun," she began, "as all of you have most certainly heard, Fox Spirits are coming to Sado at the command of Inari, the God of Rice. Their purpose is to punish the Daimyo for neglecting proper sacrifices to Inari following this year's harvest."

She could see from the twitching of a few tails, the long washing of ears and whiskers, that she was losing their attention. Boldly, she dropped her reasoned explanation and issued her challenge.

"I say that we should stop the Fox Spirits!"

This announcement brought her the attention of every cat in the Garden. Eyes of gold and green and, occasionally, blue turned their startled gazes on her. Ears pricked up and more than one tail straightened in surprise.

Then a tumult of yowled protests arose.

"Challenge foxes? That's insane!"

"Why risk Inari's wrath? The Daimyo was neglectful."

"Human legends always make the cat a villain. Let the dogs do it. Humans like dogs!"

And most often: "Why should we? We're safe here. Let humans solve human problems!"

"Why?" Okesa answered, "Because we can! Are you saying that cats are less capable than dogs? Are you afraid of foxes?"

She arched her back and puffed out her glossy black tail. Then she spat derisively.

"Cats! Maybe we deserve what they say about us! If you can't challenge the Fox Spirits to honor the hearthstones on which you have slept, for the granaries in which you have found easy hunting, for the bridges from which you have fished, then consider this! If Inari curses the rice crop, there will be no more barn-fat rodents to hunt."

"No more lazy birds," meowed a startled Momo.

"No more easy plenty," Okesa pressed.

"There is always enough for cats," sneered a glossy, long-bellied tabby.

"Oh?" replied ragged Bushi. "Oh?"

Okesa whipped her tail back and forth in angry resolve. She fastened her green-eyed gaze on the gathered cats. No one met her eyes.

"Stay, then," she said, leaping down and through the torii. "I'll do it alone if I must!"

As she ran down the dusky tunnel, she became aware of the muffled pad-pad-pad of cat paws behind her. Her spirits lifted. Who was her ally? Kynn? Momo? One of those lazy ones who had looked away when she spoke?

Exiting the tunnel, she darted to one side, wheeling to see who had followed her. The cat who emerged was a stranger with a lovely cream-colored coat and white tips.

Okesa was about to greet the stranger when she saw another cat emerge—golden and sleek—Kynn! Then another, fat and calico—Momo! Then three more strangers, patterned black and white, barely out of kittenhood, littermates no doubt. Bringing up the rear of the column came gray, battered Bushi, still chewing a mouthful of tuna.

Okesa purred her pleasure and, after introductions all around, led her troop to the cherry orchard. They gathered in the sunlight on the pink-speckled green, each sitting straight, tails wrapped politely around their toes. They were very aware that at that moment, they were the only cats on all the island of Sado.

"Well, here we are, Okesa-san," said cream-colored Kekko. "What would you have us do?"

Okesa thought quickly. She had never considered that she might have *this* much help.

"There are eight of us," she said slowly, while her mind whirled through possibilities. "That is an auspicious number."

"Let's jump the Foxes!" offered one of the catlings. "Pounce them! Shred their kimonos! Then they can't perform in the play!"

"Oh, Taro," chided his sister. "That wouldn't do. The Fox Spirits use illusion magic. Even if we ripped and tore, they would mend up the damage in a moment. Then the Daimyo's samurai would slay us with their twin swords!"

Taro sulked, "I suppose you have a better idea?"

"No, but Okesa-sama does. Right, Okesa-sama?"

Okesa met the gold and green and blue eyes (these last belonging to Kekko) that studied her. She found this harder to do now that there were seven pairs, not seventy or seven hundred.

"Of course, kitten-chan," she said, with more confidence than she felt. "We must enter the competition and defeat the Foxes on the stage."

Silence greeted her announcement, but Okesa realized that this was a listening silence, not a challenging silence. Heartened, she began to explain.

Later that afternoon, the famous geisha dancer, Okesa, came to the Daimyo's magistrate, the man in charge of organizing the day's Noh competition. She wore a kimono of plum-colored silk and her long, ebony hair was piled up in an elaborate coif held in place by pins of jade and ivory. Her eyes were so dark that they almost seemed the deep green of an old, old pine. The magistrate was flattered when she bowed deeply to him.

"Magistrate Sakushi-sama," she said, her voice a husky, throaty purr. "Is it as I have heard, that anyone may enter a piece for today's competition?"

Magistrate Sakushi bowed, though less deeply, in return. "Yes, Okesa-san. We have entries from all across Dai Nippon."

"May a humble one bring an entry to you as late as even this afternoon?"

Magistrate Sakushi was surprised, but he nodded, "Is the piece that we are discussing long? You know that today's performance is for vignettes, not for full dramas."

"My piece is no longer than it should be," Okesa replied.

"Then I will put it on my list," the magistrate said. Then he added gallantly, "I look forward to seeing what the famous Okesa has produced."

She smiled demurely and bowed.

"So do I," she answered. "So do I."

The drums and flutes were warming up, little grace notes thrilling the ears as the flirtatious breeze spilled cherry blossoms onto the bright pavilions set up before the palace of Sado's greatest Daimyo.

"We are last on the list," Okesa said to her seven allies. "Creep into the theater now and find hiding places from which you can watch the stage. Noh is very stylized. Each of you must memorize the gestures for a certain type of role."

The seven cats blinked their comprehension.

"Kekko," Okesa turned to the cream-colored female, "you will study the ingenue. Kynn, you will be the dashing samurai lover. Bushi, you will be the forbidding father. He is just a bit of a villain as well. Can you handle that?"

Bushi purred, a rough, knotty purr, as tattered as his gray coat.

"Taro, you and your littermates will take the role of messengers. At the end of the play, two of you will be young heroes. Divide up the roles as you would, but be certain that you have them all covered."

"Yes, Okesa-sama," Taro mewed eagerly.

"What about me?" wailed Momo.

"You will be the jilted lover," Okesa said. "It is a role that demands both humor and tragic sincerity."

"Oh, I can do that!" Momo said, pawing the air gleefully.

"Now, to your places," Okesa said. "and I will signal for you before we are to begin."

The Noh festival progressed with elegance and beauty. Many of the selections were traditional—excerpts from "The Meeting of Yoshitsune and Benkei on Gojo Bridge" or "The Forty-Seven Ronin."

Masked and robed, the players gestured and pranced in a fashion that could have been comical, but was not. Okesa found herself drawn into the old stories. Any cat loves ritual and the Noh drama gave the stories a timelessness that was undeniably attractive.

In the audience, the daimyos and wealthy samurai pretended indifference as the troops that they had sponsored performed their pieces. Okesa wondered which of the politely applauding lords was the chief of the Foxes, waiting among the humans for his chance at Inari's vengeance.

Okesa had no doubt when the Fox Spirits came onto the stage. In some indefinable fashion, they were more elegant than the performers who had preceded them. The elegance did not merely proceed from their beautifully carved masks, nor from the exquisite, fluid grace of their silk kimonos. It was something more intangible. Watching them, Okesa, the dancer, thought that grace was born in the lifting of their feet.

They had chosen a familiar legend for their theme, the story of the rash Tokutaro and how he was tricked by the wily foxes who shaved his head as the final indignity of a night of illusion and madness.

Their performance was perfect, evoking both tears and laughter. The Daimyo patted his hands in applause and was heard saying to one of the samurai who sat near him, "Poignant, humorous, and instructive. Very finely presented. I believe that it is a far better piece than any of these dry, traditional choices we have seen."

The next group, who were performing from "Yoshitsune at Gojo Bridge," were quite disheartened and left the stage early.

At last, Okesa saw that her troop would be next. She gestured for them and the seven cats met her in the small pavilion provided for waiting actors. It was empty now, all the performers gone into the audience to watch the other acts.

"When we are called," Okesa said, bending to stroke each cat, "I will go and announce us. Remember your cues and remember, too, that the Foxes may give us trouble."

The seven cats blinked calmly. Little Taro mewed and chased his own tail in excitement. Kynn stood on his hind legs and bumped Okesa's hand reassuringly. Then Magistrate Sakushi was announcing her.

Okesa walked onto the stage. She was not the only woman who had patronized a performing troop, nor was she the only one who had written her own script. Indeed, some of the most famous writers in Dai Nippon were women. However, she was the only one to mount the stage that day and her appearance raised some muttering.

"That's Okesa, the famous dancer." "That's Okesa. They say she's lithe as a cat." "That's Okesa. No one knows where she came from ..." "That's Okesa. My brother bought an hour of her time ..."

Bowing, she began. "Such is the beauty of Noh that words are hardly necessary to carry the story. I present for your honored assessment the tale of Ninigi and the Blossom Princess, performed by an unusual troop of actors ..."

She stepped to the side. "Long ago, Amaterasu's grandson, Ninigi fell in love with Ko-no-hana, the Blossom Princess ..."

From the front left of the stage entered Kynn. The big, golden tom swaggered as he walked. His tail was held high; one could almost see the samurai's twin swords on his hip. He strutted across the stage to Kekko, who had slipped in on the right and taken up a perch on a bit of stone.

She demurely washed her ears with her paw. When Kynn swaggered over to her, she coyly shielded her face with a flip of her tail. One could almost see the fan she opened to hide her face.

Enchanted, the audience murmured in wonder as the two cats mimed a decorous courtship.

"But though Ninigi and the Blossom Princess had fallen in love," Okesa said, "their way was not to be easy. Oho-yama, the girl's father, had an elder daughter he wished to have married. He could not force Amaterasu's beloved grandson to love her, but he could offer him a choice."

Bushi sauntered out, Momo at his heels. If Kynn had seemed the dashing young warrior touched by his grandmother sun, Bushi was the grizzled old veteran, gray and rough as a mountain crag. Kynn faced him and then Momo pranced forward.

Poor Momo was as round as her namesake, the peach. She was round where Kekko was slender, clownish where Kekko was grave and serene. Even those who did not know the ancient legend could see how Ninigi must choose.

Kynn inspected both of his potential brides. When he looked away, the "sisters" lowered their "fans" and spat at each other. Then they retired to stations across the stage and Kynn moved down front. Bushi stalked after him.

"Oho-yama told Ninigi that his elder daughter, who was named Iha-naga, Princess Long-as-the-Rocks, had name magic," Okesa continued, "and that if Ninigi chose wisely, Amaterasu's beloved grandson would benefit from that magic. Messengers flew between Ninigi and Oho-yama's two daughters."

Bushi retired to the center of the triangle formed by Kynn, Momo, and Kekko. Taro sprang out now and dashed across the stage to Kekko. Touching whiskers with him, she "handed" him her message. Taro's sister mimed the same routine with Momo, while the third catling took a message from Kynn to Kekko.

For several delightful moments, the stage was a whirl of cats going from one to another and darting back again. It was as carefully patterned as a ballet and twice as beautiful.

At last, the messengers vanished and Kynn shook himself, licked a paw across his ear, and put up his tail in resolution. Then he advanced on Bushi.

"Ninigi had weighed the sorcery of Iha-naga against the magic of love," Okesa narrated. "He had weighed and sorcery had lost. He told Oho-yama of his choice and the old man agreed to permit him to wed Princess Ko-no-hana. Princess Iha-naga was furious . . ."

Momo bushed up her tail and arched her back. Nothing about her was comical now—indeed, her size made her fearsome. She spat at Kynn. He pressed protectively against Kekko, who crouched, ears folded back, in fear. As Momo stalked up to the lovers, Okesa hoped that the chubby calico had not forgotten that this was a play.

"Princess Iha-naga cursed Ninigi saying, 'Had you chosen me, our children and our children's children would have lived as long as the rocks. Now their lives will be as brief as the blossoms in the Spring.' Then the angry princess departed, escorted by her father."

Momo *did* leave with Bushi and Okesa allowed herself a small sigh of relief. At center stage, Kekko and Kynn were grooming each other.

Okesa smiled and went on, "Princess Iha-naga's prophesy came true, for life is brief and fragile. But from the union of Princess Ko-no-hana and Ninigi came many good things, including the famous heroes some call Fire Flash and Fire Fade."

Taro and his sister dashed onto the stage striking heroic poses, tails high and ears alert. Taro almost ruined the effect by bouncing in excitement—almost.

Okesa folded her hands into her sleeves and bowed to indicate her piece was completed. The four cats still on stage also bowed. Then, in neat file, they followed Okesa off the stage.

The hubbub that politeness had kept in check during the performance now broke out.

"Enchanting! Marvelous!" the Daimyo exclaimed.

"But very untraditional," said the Magistrate.

"Surely it cannot win the prize," protested another lord, and, instinctively, Okesa knew that this was one of the Foxes. "That woman knows what it is to walk at the Hour of the Ox, the hour when black magic is done!"

"And perhaps you know what it is to walk at the Hour of the Fox!" Okesa cried.

She signaled to her troop. Kynn and Bushi sprang at the lord's silk kimono. Leaping as one, they ripped a large hole in the back and, before illusion could mend it, all saw the Fox Spirit's bushy, red tail.

"Tails are hard to transform, are they not!" Okesa taunted, glad that *her* tail was enchanted away with the rest of her cat-self. She'd been careful. A geisha could not have a black, furry tail.

Taro and his littermates had impulsively pounced upon the lead actor of the Fox troop. His kimono also tore, revealing his silvery-gray bushy tail.

"Fox Spirits!" The Daimyo's eyes grew wide. "Here! Buddha smile on us! Hachiman protect us!"

"You always call on the gods when you need them,"

the red-tailed lord said cryptically. "We are revealed,
but we do not forget. Remember our play!"

And then, they all vanished, even to the shreds of silk
in the cat's paws. All that remained was a hot, pervasive
stink of fox.

The Daimyo shouted orders to his guards. There was
chaos for several moments and when it stilled, the Fox
Spirits were still vanished and Okesa and her cats still
stood before the Daimyo. He turned from consultation
with the Magistrate.

"I cannot give you the prize," he said, somewhat
sadly, "for your drama was not precisely Noh. But, stay,
I have something to reward you with, nonetheless."

He rose and walked to the stage. "The prize for today's festival will go to Yoshitoshi of Honshu's troop,
for its rendition of the Death of Kotsuke from the
"Forty-seven Ronin."

There was polite applause and Yoshitoshi rose and
accepted his prize.

"To you, Okesa-san," continued the Daimyo, "I will
give an amount of money equal to the prizes. This is not
for your drama, but for uncovering this plot against me.
And . . ."

Silence fell as he raised his hand and declaimed, "And
I will grant you any one boon for yourself."

Okesa bent her head and bowed deeply, hiding her
smile. The Daimyo's enthusiasm was precisely what the
Foxes must have been planning to use against him. No
doubt, their boon would have either impoverished or
humiliated the Daimyo. Perhaps both.

"What do you desire, Okesa-san?" the Daimyo
prompted.

Okesa thought. Her heart's wish was wealth enough
to make her humans secure and honored. If they were
secure, then she could give up her distasteful role as a
geisha. However, to ask for such would be both impolitic
and unwise. Her humans would refuse charity—if they
would accept such, they would not be in their current
state, for they had friends from the days the man had
been a samurai.

And the Foxes would surely come for revenge if she did not do her best to forestall them.

Pushing away her heart's desire, Okesa said, "Oh, great Daimyo, take the contents of your largest granary and use them for a month-long festival to Inari, the God of Rice. This is the only boon I request of you."

The Daimyo started. Clearly he had been prepared for anything from a request for jewels to one for some economic monopoly. This humble, religious request surprised him.

"You want nothing for yourself?"

"The festival to Inari will be plenty, great Daimyo," Okesa said, and the seven cats purred loudly, pleased by her cleverness.

"Such self-effacing character!" the Daimyo said. "I will grant your boon. In addition, I will grant you a crest of your own: three cat's paws in a circle. Report to me on the final day of Inari's festival to receive the honor."

Okesa bowed, "Much thanks, Daimyo."

Late that night, Okesa was home in her basket by the fire. She had enlisted Bushi to help her carry the prize money home. Together, they had buried it in a shallow hole near where the old ronin had stopped turning over his garden patch when darkness fell that night. In the morning, he would have a great surprise.

Now she lay, listening to the crackling of the coals, reflecting over the day. Kynn and Kekko had clearly confused drama and reality. When last she had seen them, they had been wandering off into the shrub together. Momo and the catlings had returned to their homes.

Bushi slept sprawled on the hearthstone itself, his side rising and falling. Deeply as he was asleep, like her, he was on his feet when the scratching came at the door.

"It is the Hour of the Fox, Okesa," came a familiar voice. "Come out—or we will come in!"

Okesa rose and stretched and leaped out a window onto the bare earth outside. Bushi thumped down beside her. Together, they walked to where the dark shadows of several large Foxes bulked against the night.

"I am here," Okesa said.

"And I," said Bushi, and his tail lashed in warning.

"Dread not, oh, well-named warrior," said the largest of the Foxes. "We have come to honor Okesa, not to harm her."

"Inari so commands," whispered the other Foxes in chorus.

Okesa flicked back an ear in surprise. "Honor me?"

"Today you not only saved your Daimyo from our wrath, but brought Inari his lost honors." The red fox chuckled. "And you saved face for us as well. We know that you gave up your heart's desire to gain Inari his due. He commands that we grant it to you now. What do you wish?"

"I wish to be no more than what I am—a little, black cat," Okesa answered, "but my humans are so poor that they only eat millet and weeds. The garden they lavish care upon grows only stones and shriveled parodies of vegetables. When I was a kitten, my eyes barely open, they saved me from drowning. Seeing their poverty, I decided that I owed them a debt.

"I prayed to Amaterasu to give me the means to help them from their poverty. She granted me a human form, a lovely, graceful form, and with it I can earn them money or sometimes favors, such as convincing the tax collector to skip them in his rounds. But I am weary of human ways. I want only to be a cat, but until I honorably discharge my promise to Amaterasu and to my humans, I will not be happy only as a cat."

"The old man and the old woman will not take charity," Bushi growled in the tones of one who has gone hungry from pride. "Make their fields fertile, plant them with rice, and with orchards of cherry and peach and plum. These humans will never forget to honor Inari— nor any of the gods."

"They never have," the red fox said softly. "All will be made as you have requested."

And with that, they vanished into the darkness, leaving only the hot stink of fox.

Over that spring, fertility came in force to the poor ronin's farm. Each day, new crops sprouted. A rice marsh formed after a heavy rain. Ancient trees bore flowers for the first time in years, and the flowers set plentiful fruit.

After each day of good food and rewarding labor, the old ronin felt younger. His back straightened, his hair darkened, and his vision grew clear and sharp. His aged wife became round-bodied and rosy-cheeked again. They accepted the miracle with prayerful gratitude.

On the day that Okesa the geisha was to receive a crest from the Daimyo's own hands, the old ronin, who was no longer so old, rose early. With his wife's help, he dressed in the new, best kimono he had purchased with money he had found in his vegetable patch. Carefully, he thrust his katana and wakizashi into his sash and, bearing a letter he had found on his doorstep the night before, he walked to the town.

The buildings and even the trees were brightly decorated for the climax of the month-long festival to Inari. Looking into the shops, the ronin promised himself he would buy his wife many gifts—a new tea set, a robe of rose silk, an embroidered sash, a biwa for her to play....

His revery was broken when three black and white cats, almost identical and still young, dashed in front of him, chased by a laughing toddler. They reminded him of his errand and he hurried until he reached the Daimyo's palace.

Six words opened every gate for him: "I bring a message from Okesa."

Excitement followed his steady footsteps. Hadn't nothing been heard of the famous geisha since the Noh cat afternoon? Gossip had been rampant. Many feared that the Foxes had taken their revenge on her, but now this stranger ronin claimed to have a message from her!

At last the ronin and the Daimyo were alone, except for Magistrate Sakushi and a few trusted samurai.

"You bear a message for me?" the Daimyo demanded.

"I have," the ronin said, rising from his bow. "Last night I heard a scratching at my door. When I went to it, I found two sheets of paper. One was addressed to me and said, 'Bear the enclosed to the Daimyo for me.' It was signed, 'Okesa.' Here is the other."

He handed the folded, sealed message to the Daimyo who broke the seal, read the message, and then read it again.

"She is not coming," he said, his voice breaking with shock. "She does me a great dishonor!"

"Perhaps she does you a great honor," said Magistrate Sakushi hesitantly. "You know there has been grumbling about the propriety of giving a geisha her own crest."

"I will not go back on my promise," the Daimyo scowled, "nor will I let Okesa's absence stop me from honoring her! If I shilly-shally that way, people may say that the Foxes have made a fool of me yet. You—ronin! What is your name?"

The ronin answered carefully, for he and his wife realized that their new wealth and youth could be suspect or arouse jealousy in others.

"I have no name worth giving. Since my master died, I have been living on a farm belonging to my wife's family. It is in the mountains east of here."

That much, at least, was true. He was a new man since this spring and he surely was his wife's family.

The Daimyo frowned, too polite to pry.

"So there are no claims on your services?"

"None, except by my wife."

The Daimyo smiled. "Would you like to claim Okesa as kin and accept her crest in her place? Such a thing is not impossible, you know. Many a poor samurai family has sent a daughter into the geisha's life."

"That is true, my lord. I would happily claim such a brave and talented lady as kin."

"Very good. Then our problem is solved." the Daimyo nodded to Magistrate Sakushi. "Take this man . . . what shall we call you?"

"May I suggest 'Oisaki Yama'?" the ronin said. The name he suggested could be translated as "Future Mountain."

The Daimyo was delighted. "An auspicious name, especially for a mountain man. Very good. Magistrate, take Oisaki Yama and prepare him to be sworn into my service. Then coach him on this afternoon's ceremony."

"As you command, my lord."

When the Daimyo was alone, he unfolded Okesa's letter and reread the following note: "I shall not be able to accept the crest with which you have graciously offered to honor me. The one I send as messenger I count as a father, for he saved my life when I was an infant. Honor to him would be as honor to me."

There followed two lines of poetry:

> After dancing for others,
> for me,
> A rice straw basket by the fire.

And the entire letter was signed with the pawprint of a cat.

TOTEM CAT
by A. R. Major

A. R. Major recently completed a one-year term as the supply pastor for the International Baptist Church of Prague in the Czech Republic. He has appeared in *CatFantastic II*, and is currently marketing a science fiction trilogy.

"Look at that lazy thing! He's been 'meditating' in the hotel window since daybreak!" With that, Alice Conners leaned over the big Maine coon cat and gave its thick fur an affectionate rub.

Racky Conners reacted by opening his slitted eyes a fraction more and giving "his Alice" the silent meow that recognized the friendly gesture. In doing so, the big cat, whose coloring was so like that of a racoon that everyone called him Racky, exposed his needle-sharp teeth. Those same teeth had pronounced "final judgment" on many a small household varmint; for like others of his kind, the gentle Racky was murder incorporated in the presence of mice or rats.

"What's he doin' when he sits around like that with his ol' eyes almost closed, Mom?" son Tommy asked.

Alice looked affectionately at her son and his still

sleeping sister, who was in the big bed of the Sitka Baronov Hotel.

She gave a musical chuckle. "Maybe he's going over some of his past lives and reliving them."

Sue popped up, rubbing her eyes, and wanted to know what was going on.

"Aw, Mom thinks Racky's dreaming about one of his past nine lives. You don't *really* believe that nine lives stuff, huh?"

"I guess not!" And Sue joined the laughter that filled the room of the ancient Alaskan hotel.

I guess I do! thought Racky. *People! Why don't they ask us experts instead of assuming so much ... and why limit us to just nine lives?*

Sue joined in the conversation with all the wisdom of her eight years. "Huh, *I* think that stuff about cats and nine lives is silly. Why, why, THAT would make cats superior to humans!"

Racky indulged his human "pets" with an affectionate gaze. *Well, aren't we? You rush around getting food and the things you need. WE just relax and let you wait on us! You don't see ME opening a door or dumping a litter pan, humph!*

In reality, Racky was very fond of Tommy and Sue, even though he felt at times that Tommy's native tongue was "stupidity!" Well, in time that inferior human kitten might approach the mentality of his Alice. Now *there* was a human being who knew how to think like a cat! How wonderful to watch her maneuver her "man" around and let him have her own way! She actually had him believing that old letter Sue found in the attic was from her whaler sea captain Uriah Morgan. Racky *knew* the truth of that letter, just as he knew who the REAL head of the house was.

For there were times when Alice looked into his eyes, that a real soul link developed. At such times they seemed to be able to read each other's thoughts. And, at one such time he had implanted an urge to find out more about her ancestors.

Now don't get me wrong! Racky was NOT one of those "sweet-as-carnival-cotton-candy" pets. His family had learned not to use lovy-dovy baby talk with him! He was an intelligent, respected member of the family with his assigned tasks, and a no-nonsense attitude toward them. He just needed an occasional ruffle of his fur to show he was not being ignored.

Racky yawned again, stretched his powerful forepaws and let his saberlike claws slide out of their sheaths for a second. He gave Tommy an amused glance. *If only he knew! In another appearing, number three ... or was it number four? I slept on a silk pillow in the court of a real Chinese mandarin! Now HE spoke to me like the royalty I was! And what a comedown it was in appearance number five to being just a common ship's cat! What am I meditating about, you primitive anthropoid? Just how to get your mother, my sweet Alice, to find her rightful inheritance, that's all!*

Tommy screwed his six-year-old face into a frown and asked, "Where's Dad and when do we get some breakfast?"

"Dad's looking for a place to eat right now. Also a boat and a guide," Sue said. "I suggest we wash up now. Let's see your grubby little paws."

Grudgingly the "little paws" were held up for inspection.

"Do I have to wash *both* of them?"

"Hi, sport! I'd like to see you wash just one of them," said a powerful male voice as his dad popped into the hotel bedroom. "Just wait till you hear the news!"

With that promise, Tommy popped in and out of the bathroom so fast he came out wiping his hands on the seat of his pajamas. His sister Sue gave her kid brother the usual superior smile of her advanced years as she emerged using a towel. Sue made no comment because "No fussing before breakfast" was one of Mom's strictist rules.

"I think I've got a guide and boat located to finish our business here. He'll meet us at the Old Totem Bar and Grill after we get breakfast."

"*Your* business or *mine*?" inquired Alice with a sly smile.

"*Yours*, sweets! I think I've given J. D. Hollingsworth

and Company enough of my vacation time to pay them back for bankrolling this expedition."

Dad was an experienced "timber cruiser" for a large California lumber company. He would go out alone in the woods for weeks on end surveying new forests before the lumberjacks came. Based on his reports the management could estimate how many saw-logs or electric poles, or hardwood flooring, could be gotten from a given area. When they found out he would be spending a month in Alaska with his family, they agreed to pay expenses if he'd keep his experienced eyes open for promising timber tracts they might buy or lease.

Jim extended an arm to Racky and the big cat took the cue to run as smoothly as motor oil up his arm and perch on his shoulder. The family was used to the amused glances this earned them from passers by. One such glance from an ancient Haida Indian was more intent than amused. Jim thought he was the most elderly human being he had ever seen. His leatherlike skin had the texture of parchment and was spider-webbed with fine lines.

But it was the eyes that captured your attention. They were so dark that you had to look closely to see that they were not all pupils. Alice instinctively reached out and pulled her two children closer to herself. Jim could feel Racky's claws digging in through his heavy shirt.

The old man spoke with a voice like a rusty hinge.

"Good morning, friends. I have never seen an animal quite like that one. May I see him more closely?" And he extended his hand like a person who never had his desires denied. The wrinkled face had a smile, but the eyes burned like embers.

"Of course." Jim returned the smile. "Now Racky, this man wants to meet you as a friend, so behave." He suspected that though the Haidas had domesticated the dog for centuries, the idea of a member of the feline society being taken into the home was strange.

Jim continued talking, hoping to keep the big cat calmed down. He carefully extended the animal cradled in his right arm.

"Racky, meet an admirer. Sir, I'm Jim Conners, this

is my wife Alice, and our children, Tommy and Sue. You are?"

For a moment it seemed the elderly one would ignore the polite question, for he merely bent lower to look deeply into the cat's eyes. To Racky's credit, he returned the gaze without flinching. The Indian placed his wrinkled hand gently on the big cat's head.

"Very strange ... this one is very young, but at the same time, he much older than I." Then looking at Alice he added, "You too young, have only lately come by something very old.

"My name means nothing now. Everyone here calls me 'the Old One'." He said this as if he begrudged giving out even that little bit of information. Then he added, "I am local Shaman." With that he spun on his heel and moved off rapidly for one so old.

"Wow! That's a real weird one," Sue said.

"What's a shay-man?" asked Tommy, scrubbing his nose on the back of his shirtsleeve.

"Some sort of tribal wise man, history keeper, or advice giver," Alice replied absently as she stared at the old Haida's departing back. Then, looking at her husband, she said, "Jim, did you see his eyes? It felt like he was looking right through me!"

Jim did not want his family to be alarmed, though he felt the same way, so he tried to make his response casual.

"Oh, it's nothing, hon, just a curious old man. I'd bet he's nearly a hundred years old. Why, just think of the tall tales *he* could tell! Say, let's get on with that breakfast, my inner man's 'bout starved."

Yeah, thought Racky, *play it easy, boss. But I'm not the only one sniffing out a rat hole here!"* And for the first time in this appearing, Racky felt a deep-seated fear of a human being.

The family was just finishing up breakfast at the Old Totem Bar and Grill. The waiter had agreed to "bend the rules" a bit and let Racky eat out of a bowl at their feet. Like most Indians, he watched the large cat with fascination. They were joined by a middle-aged Haida wearing a yatching cap and a wide smile.

"Mr. Conners? Will Longwolf is my name. There is a rumor around town that you need a boat and a guide."

Before Jim could answer, Tommy blurted out, "Gee, Dad, he *looks* like an Indian, but he don't *sound* like one!"

Sue had the same opinion, but she was wise enough to keep silent.

"Should I say, me Longwolf, you needum guide?" His eyes twinkled as he added, "Son, that routine went out with the Lone Ranger and Tonto! *I'm* a graduate of the University of Alaska, class of '56."

"You'll have to forgive my son, sir," Jim said. "He still believes that tourist stuff that all Alaskans live in igloos!"

"Sorry, son. I've lived here all my life, and I've only seen an igloo in a moving picture." His big booming laugh filled the cafe and set them all at ease.

"Pull up a chair and join us in some of this good food," Jim said.

"I appreciate the offer, but I have already eaten. I will join you in a cup of coffee, though."

Racky who had been sitting quietly in Alice's lap, hopped down and stretched his 33-pound Maine coon cat body to its full length.

"Well! What do we have here?" Longwolf asked. "I have seen a few tame cats in my life, but *never* one quite like *this* one!"

"His name is Racky, sir," Sue volunteered. "He's a cat from the state of Maine."

"And he's 'family', too!" Tommy added.

"Very interesting. Now, about your trip, just what do you have in mind?"

"Alice, you fill him in on the background. I want to finish these eggs before they get any colder," Jim said.

"Several months ago, Sue was going through a trunk that belonged to my grandmother five generations removed ..."

Sue could wait no longer. Her eyes shining, she cut into the story. "And Racky was with me, and he jumped in the trunk and he began clawing at the liner and we found this very old letter, and—oh, Mother, why not let him read it?"

They all laughed at Sue's breathless story, so Alice shrugged and said, "Why not? Mr. Longwolf can see if we are as silly as we seem."

With that she brought a parcel from her purse that contained some yellowed papers she had pressed between sheets of clear plastic.

"A museum man said it looked like papers from an old-time captain's log book," said Tommy proudly."

Longwolf took some reading glasses from his shirt pocket and perched them on his nose. This is what he read:

"Finder please forward this to Elizabeth Morgan, New Bedford, Mass., USA.
Beloved Wife:, after a successful voyage we were returning from the whaling area north of Japan with a hold full of sperm oil. We picked up a Malay on a piece of a raft who was a raging maniac. He seemed to be fearing some idol's curse. He died shortly of a fever. Our ship's cat found an interesting item on his body and brought it to my cabin. Then we were hit by the worst storm in my life and driven near the shore of Southern Alaska. I was able to get an approximate fix before the *Seadawn* sank. It was Long. 136° Lat. 58°. By this time I had the same fever that had killed the Malay. The mate and crew placed me and the ship's cat in one longboat and they left in the other. Do not blame them, they are superstitious men. In a few days a seagoing canoe manned by Haida Indians picked us up. They took us to their village and nursed us back to as much health as I will ever have again. I am sending this by an Indian friend in the desperate hope it may some day get back to you. They have taken to the cat and carved its likeness on the village lodge pole. I will no doubt leave this world soon. Be certain that I loved you to my

last breath. Captain Uriah Morgan, master of
the *Seadawn*.

Will paused respectfully. "That is a very moving letter," he said. "So now you are seeking a village with a
cat totem pole in it! Such a difficult task. Your ancestor
must truly have had a very valuable treasure with him
to go to all this trouble."

"I doubt if anything remains, it has been *so* long,"
said Jim. "But if the rest of his logbook had been kept
by his Haida friends, it would have great historical value.
Really, since finding that letter, we just have this compulsion laid on us to try find out more of this brave
man."

"Yes," added Alice. "Our family legend has it Elizabeth died of grief before news of her husband ever
reached her."

Now it was Tommy's chance to change the subject.

"Mr. Longwolf, why would anyone be silly enough to
put a cat on a pole and worship it?"

"Son, you never criticize another person's religion.
Now you apologize to Mr. Longwolf," said Jim in his
sternest voice.

"No, no, Mr. Connors, the mistake is quite common.
You see Tommy, totem poles are NOT religious. They
are ways of using symbols to pass on legends or history
of tribes. Some of those strange carvings go back beyond
the Greek or Egyptian times."

About that time Racky was giving Tommy his personal glare.

*I suppose your mighty Egyptians were "silly" to respect
cats and even have a cat-headed goddess named Bast,*
Racky thought.

"For a people who had no written language, they developed a fantastic way to preserve their history!" said
Alice.

"Yes, it even appears in recent history. One chief ridi-
culed the Russian prelates by having their images carved
in a totem pole. Another in a national park has Lincoln's
image, for when he freed the slaves, that included Indian

slaves in Alaska! So it's not surprising they would record an event of finding a cat at sea."

"Do you think it would be possible to locate such a village with no more information than we have to go on?" asked Jim.

"Only one person could answer that," replied Longwolf. "The Old One might know of its existence. I'll see him this afternoon, so why don't you and the family look around at our tourist sights today while I provision my boat and look up the Shaman?"

"Sounds good, but what's the price tag if it comes off?"

"Well, my boat, gasoline, food for *five*," here the guide pointed to Racky, (but he was really thinking of the way Jim put food away) then proceeded to name a price. To his surprise, Jim accepted without haggling. He didn't know Jim's boss was paying the bill.

"Mr. Longwolf," here Alice turned on her natural charm. "Just suppose, from the tone of the letter, Captain Morgan brought some terrible sickness to the village, or some item carrying a curse. Would you still be willing to go?"

"Why not? *You* aren't afraid to take your children there. Besides," he winked, "if the captain brought any germs, they have long since died out in our Alaskan winters ... and if he brought any demons, they have long since migrated to our local bars!"

With that the two men sealed the deal with a handshake and the two parties went their separate ways.

The family was getting ready for bed and, as was their custom, sharing the news of the day.

"While you kids were playing with the children in the city park, Mom and I were looking for souvenirs to take home," Jim said.

"Yes, and I found some beautiful hand-woven baskets!" Alice added. "How did you like playing with the Indian children?"

They both described the games that all children enjoy playing, and Sue mentioned the most fun was playing "Potlatch."

"How do you play that?" Alice asked.

"Well, it's a time to sing and exchange stories," both agreed.

"What stories did you share?"

"Tommy told about David and Goliath, I shared the cartoon version of the 'Three Little Pigs,' and *they* told us how Bear got his claws!"

"I can't say I've ever heard that one. How about sharing it with me?" Jim asked.

"Well, once Bear had smooth paws like people. When he tried to catch salmon, most got away and he had to eat old dead fish. Yuck!" Here both children screwed their faced up like they had seen the other children do.

"One day, Bear lost so many fish that he prayed for help. Eagle overheard him, tore off one of his talons and put it on the bear's paw."

Tommy could bear it no longer, he just *had* to finish the story.

"And, dad, guess what! That eagle claw grew claws all *over* that bear's foot. And every bear since then has claws!" And Tommy nodded happily.

"Well, thank you. Now it's bed time. Has anyone seen Racky? He just dropped out of sight after supper." All he got were shrugs in answer. "Well, I guess he'll spend the night hunting since he spent most of the day sleeping."

Racky was hunting, waiting until the quarry came to him. His long evening of stalking had brought him to the shack where the Old One lived near the docks. Now he was content to sit in the rafters above the Old One's bed and wait for the man who must come. Even though the summer sun was keeping things fairly bright outside, the cat knew how to blend in with the shadows. There came a gentle tap on the door and Longwolf entered the Shaman's hut.

"Grandfather," Will Longwolf began, "I am not at peace with this assignment, this taking of outsiders to 'No Goes.' Suppose the curse is still active? Someone could get hurt bad!"

"You fear the white man's germs or long dead ghosts, my son? How many Potlatches have you attended where the mystery of the dying village and the strange animal from the sea have been sung? We will never have a chance to answer the mystery of No Goes again! Somehow that cat animal is the answer. I am so certain of that I can almost sense its presence in this very room!"

"I understand all that. But if they do locate something of value, I must claim it for our people! They seem like such decent people. Would it be right to injure them?"

"Yes, and their 'decent' ancestors with their greed took our land, our livelihood, and would destroy our very soul in their greed. Greed is their god. They always take, take and never give. The mystery of No Goes is ours! Whatever it is, we will keep for *our* children!"

"I obey, Grandfather. But why do I feel like the Christian's Judas Iscariot in all of this? Think well: It might take an 'accident' to cover a theft. Can any treasure be worth four lives?"

"That, my son, *you* must decide if we find the answer to the questions put by our songs. Maybe time has chosen for us and nothing of value is left in the dead village."

As Longwolf slipped out the door, a shadow detached itself from an overhead rafter and followed him down the street. From now on, the man would have more than his conscience watching over him.

The family was eating another hearty breakfast and looking forward to Will Longwolf's return. If the Old One could not produce a possible village for them, all their work so far would have been in vain.

The waiter looked down at Racky and grinned. "I sure wish your pet would have been in here last night! We had a porcupine walk in from the street and bite a customer at the bar right on his hand! I bet your cat could have run him off."

No thank you. My tribe has nothing to do with the walking pincushion tribe! And from the flattened ears on his head, you could see he really meant it.

Will Longwolf entered then, from the smile on his face they knew he had been successful.

"Good morning, my friends. The Old One remembered a much-told story about a village that took in a

Yankee sailor and his strange pet. Some sickness broke out and the only survivors were those who abandoned their homes. The village carver, to record the incident, carved an image of the cat on their clan totem. Across the years it has been a place to be avoided. It is called No Goes now, for no one ever goes there."

"Mr. Longwolf," Alice said. "One thing still puzzles me. *Why* should those people feel obligated to take in and care for a total stranger?"

That's my Alice, purred Racky, *thinking like a cat again!*

"Try to understand our culture. Everything here is so spread out and, at times difficult, that we all must help each other just to survive. Then, too, we have another Potlatch story about a village that labored two years to carve a totem pole as tall as an eight-story building. They enlisted the help of a Yankee ship that loaned them rope and pullys. Even with the sailors' help, it took three days to erect the pole. Haidas never forget to repay a debt. Are you ready to go looking for a lost village? I think, from the Shaman's directions, I can get you within easy walking distance."

The little cabin cruiser had been a day and a half getting to the mouth of the stream that was supposed to flow past the village of No Goes. The night before while they had been anchored in the Picktot River, Alice and the children had slept in the small cabin, while Racky had spent the night on deck with the two men. Now he assumed a place on the bow of the boat where he could watch the little fish scooting around in the crystal clear water.

As they cruised slowly up the narrow, unnamed, stream, Jim spoke softly to Longwolf.

"At times like these, I get to thinking that *this* is the way the Creator intended us to live, and not in our rat-race cities!"

"Connors, friend, you may have a white man's body, but you have the Indian's heart," Longwolf replied softly.

As they rounded a curve in the stream, Longwolf grasped Jim's shoulder and pointed. "Look, by the big cedar tree, I think that is the remains of No Goes!"

The little party made their way ashore with Racky in the lead. Near the stream were several walls of piled-up rock where large oceangoing canoes could have been sheltered. Nearby were ruins of racks where fishing gear could have been stored, or animal hides spread out for drying. Two large piles of ruins were where two lodges had once stood. But between them the clan totem still stood tall and straight. Not a sign of color was on the pole now, just weather-worn carvings. On the very top was carved a cat, back arched, right forepaw extended in a threat. How many times they had seen Racky in that pose!

Jim looked at Longwolf and laughed. The Haida looked at him in puzzlement.

"When I first saw that pole, I was tempted to take it home with me and give it a new paint job. But how could anything that big be moved that far? I guess it belongs right where it is," Jim said.

Always practical, Alice replied, "We can still take it home with us in a picture. Mr. Longwolf, would you mind taking a picture of the five of us standing by it?"

Racky was content with staying in Sue's arms while the picture was taken. Then, with a yowl, he was out of her arms and racing up the pole.

"I bet he's going to the top to pick a fight with that wooden one on top. Stupid ol' cat," Tommy said.

And it looked like Tommy was right, for the big cat began digging at the carved cat with his razor-sharp claws, all the time yowling his fiercest war cries.

"Has the animal gone mad?" Longwolf asked.

"No," Jim replied, "but there is something up there that cat wants. I'm for giving him a hand."

The two men rolled a piece of log over near the totem pole. When Racky saw them coming to help, he promptly came down to the ground.

"Easy, friend Connors, that log's pretty rotten. Let me brace it before you stand on it."

Carefully the big man began working his way up the pole. He locked his legs around it and began chipping away at the base of the cat carving. "What do you know! This cat's only stuck on top with its legs in drilled holes.

Watch out below, I've got it loose and I'll toss it to the ground!''

But the shock of landing on the hard ground was too much for the weathered wood. It split open down the middle, revealing a hollowed-out place in the body cavity. In the cavity was a small leather pouch, dry and brittle.

"Friend Connors, it's your discovery. You should have the honor of opening it!" Was Longwolf thinking of germs, demons, or both?

Carefully, Jim used his knife to slit open the brittle bag. Carefully, he shook the contents into his left palm. A gasp of surprise went around the group. Only Racky did not seem surprised; he just arched his back and rubbed against Alice's leg.

In Jim's palm was a large blue gemstone that flashed with an inner fire. "What is it?" he asked in wonder.

"It's a star sapphire," replied Alice. "I saw one in a museum once. Some were used to decorate Oriental idols. *That* must have been what Captain Morgan's Malay was carrying. . . .

"Jim, I don't want to keep it. It would mean wealth to us that could ruin us. We have everything we need to make us happy, I fear that shining thing could be a curse on us!"

"Alice, friend Longwolf said the Haidas always paid a debt back. Let's show him the Connors have long memories also. Over a hundred years ago these Haidas risked all to help a sick sea captain. It is only just that their descendants should have this stone to preserve their culture."

Longwolf looked as if he couldn't believe his ears.

"You mean you would *give* this priceless treasure to the Haida people?" he said in amazement.

"Why not. *We* had the fun of finding it. And, without the Old One's directions, we never would have found No Goes. Maybe you'd better include him in the foundation you will be setting up."

"Foundation?"

"Or a trust fund to preserve Haida culture," said Alice.

That's my Alice, purred Racky proudly.

DEATHSONG
by Lyn McConchie

Lyn McConchie runs a small farm in New Zealand. She became a professional writer in 1990 and since then has sold short fiction in five countries. She has also written historical novels, a nonfiction book about the amusing incidents that take place on her farm, and most recently her Witch World collaboration with Andre Norton, *The Key of the Keplian*, which was published in the United States in July, 1995.

In the short silent summer heat the cubs lay in a circle. The old Dravencat smiled down at them. By the Lady Pasht, they were a fine Spring Borning. She was proud of her bloodline. Old, old when first the two-legs began to appear in the foothills. It was strange, though, every few generations it seemed one of her line would become involved with them. Ah well. No harm had ever come of it to date; she would reserve judgment. Below her rock the cubs were clamoring for a story. Her grin widened, showing teeth savage as the rock spires among which they laired.

Bright stories of jests and tricks for the dark. But this was a young day, bright in promise. She nodded slowly to herself. Let them know that not all was safety even

for the Dravencats. Not even for those who were great
hunters, powerful beyond most of the World. She would
tell them the tale of Many Kills, grand-dam, wanderer,
warrior. She rested her head on huge paws considering.
Then she lifted her voice and began.

Many Kills had walked the high hills from the time of
her cubhood. Like another before her, she had always
found the doings of the two-legs interesting. Often she
would slip to the edge of a clearing. Watching as they
performed odd and peculiar actions for no reason she
could understand. But it was their cubs she liked. They
were small and merry, quick-moving with soft light
voices that drew her. One in particular seemed to attract
her attention. Blonde as Many Kills was golden-furred.
She even imagined more than once that the child was
aware of her. Impossible of course. No two-legs knew
when a Dravencat spied.

The two-legs den was large in her terms, but not for
the two-legs. They always seemed to be adding another
piece. Another room in which to lair. Each time they
added to the wall about the den also. She wondered
idly what it was they feared. She groomed herself as she
watched. A Dravencat was clean. It would not be right
for one who was intelligent to be less. Then her eyes
opened as a movement caught her eye. Below, a group
of strange two-legs approached. They slunk through the
brush, the curved killing sticks in their hands.

She rose a little to see as they emerged from their
cover. That had been done well—and cleverly. They
were through the gate, and from inside she could scent
the blood as it flowed. She settled again. The affairs of
the two-legs were their own concern and none of hers. The
stink of blood, fear, rage, and pain intensified and with
a disgusted snort she departed. But as she went, she
wondered ever so faintly. What of the female cub it had
pleased her to watch? But two-legs doings were for
them. She silenced the voice as she padded away.

Nurse had put me to bed early because of some prank.
I'd been furious with her. After all, I was nine now and

too old to be treated as a baby. But when the shouting started, I forgot my claimed adulthood and ran for her bedroom. We huddled together as the noise came closer. A compound of oaths, cries of pain, and the clash of arms. Mother and Father would be with my two younger brothers. I had scurried up a flight of stairs to reach Nurse. Now the rest of my family was two floors below.

I'd heard Father say that the site would be impregnable one day. We'd built into the side of a cliff with deep caves. Each month we added another room below and the whole building was shaped as a kind of half pyramid. Several rooms below, half as many atop them, and others atop those in turn. One day we'd have a real fortress. It couldn't be too soon for Mother. We'd left enemies behind us. I clutched Nurse in terror as the sounds moved to right outside our door. These mysterious enemies must have found us. Any moment now, they would break down the door and we'd die.

The heavy wood door crashed open, and I screamed at the sight of the man who glared from the doorway. He was tall with dark hair and an old scar searing its way across one cheek. But far worse was the miasma of evil I sensed coming from him as he posed there. Nurse flung me behind her, facing him with a courage I had not known fat old Tellda to possess.

"What do you want?"

"The girl."

"NO!" I think she thought only of rapine and murder.

"Yes. Oh, do not worry, old woman. I don't plan to harm her." Something in his voice told me that was both truth and lie. "You may even stay with her if you make me no trouble." His face twisted into utter savagery. "Make trouble and you'll die—in front of her—and slowly. But you can stop fearing for her virtue. I have no liking for children." I felt the lechery smoking from his mind as he spoke. If not me, then who? Surely not Nurse?

It was neither, but I had not been wrong. Once the battle was over, he chose my cousin. I'd never much liked her. She was five years older and spiteful. I looked for my parents to protect her as she was dragged scream-

ing to our conqueror. Greatly was I bewildered when
they did not appear. I knew not to make myself noticeable, so I only whispered.

"Nurse, what is he going to do? Why don't Mother
and Father stop him?" I stared up pleadingly as tears
flowed down my face. "Why don't they help her?" My
voice was becoming louder as I grew more frightened.
Our new master heard and laughed.

"You have my permission to show her her parents,
old woman. But for now, keep her mouth stopped. I
have other business." I saw no more. Nurse clasped me
against her skirts, folding them about me as if the stout
cloth could insulate me from all evil. But it did not. I
heard the shrieks, felt the terror and pain. I even knew
when Lais became mercifully unconscious. After that I
was obedient. I did not know what it was he did want
of me. But I would do anything if only it be not that.

For several weeks I walked like a dreamer. Somewhere inside of me, I knew my parents and smaller
brothers were dead. Lais also who had hanged herself
that night. Nurse did her best, but I could scarcely eat.
I was insulated within myself, curling ever tighter around
the core of me. Without, the body slowly failed as I lost
weight and strength. But within I burned ever brighter.
I was like a signal beacon tended high on a hill. The
growing bodily weakness only fueled my inner fire. I
howled silently into the darkness, cried for aid. For a
rescuer and vengeance. But no one heard, no one came.

The Summer was good, the prey fleet. But at length I
wished to return to the two-legs den. To see what had
happened since another had stolen their lair. As I approached, I could feel it. A kind of crying in the air. It
was weak, untrained, but I recognized it as a thread of
power. In the Shrines of our Bright Lady whom the two-
legs worship as Pasht, the Priestesses can call like that,
though their mindcry is far stronger. Yet, as I listened,
I recognized the caller. It was the small blonde cub.
There was something in the feel of the plea that told me
this. I moved to windward. Through the breeze I could
scent her grief and anger.

I turned away. Two-legs! What had I, Many Kills, Dravencat of the High Hills, to do with two-legs cubs? I
hunted, slept, and told tales to importunate cubs of our
clan. Casually, I discussed the loss of the two-legs den
to others of their kind. My own agreed. It was none of
our affair. But I was drawn back to watch. She lived,
well enough. But as I returned again and again it came
to me that she weakened. I became irritated with myself.
She was no cub of mine. It was true that once very long
ago a daughter of her line and another of mine had
been—friends is not quite the word. Perhaps they could
be termed comrades.

I recalled the tale. Perhaps it could be said that my
blood yet owed a portion of the debt. *I* would not say
so. Still it would do no harm to keep a nose to the trail.
I did so as the Summer passed. The cub's scent told me
that she weakened still but also that none harmed her.
Then the new two-legs began to walk my hills. At first
I suspected nothing. It is the nature of their kind to
wander, it seems. But at length I grew irritated. Everywhere I went, one of them appeared to be already there.
What they did, I knew not. But this I knew—they meant
no good. There was that about them which signaled this.

But how should I have known the evil they intended?
How should any of us? A cub vanished. Its dam would
have torn the very hills to find the small one, but no
trace of him was discovered. After him, another. A female this time. After that there was a lull. I was suspicious. Nothing like this had ever happened until the
arrival of these new two-legs. Could the disappearance
of the cubs be some evil of the incomers? I began to
prowl on moonless nights. Two-legs are blind then, and
without noses at any time. I was swift enough in my
fears to scent something. All traces of the female cub
had not yet been swept away by winds and time.

SO! They had taken her for some purpose. But I
scented that she was either dead or there no longer. I
would speak to my clan on this. Never before had the
two-legs interfered with the Dravencats. We were the
children of the Bright Lady. Loved and protected by Her
whom they also worshiped. Then the cubs were found.

Unharmed but with memories wiped clean of where they had been or what had been done to them. It was observed that they appeared weak. Still they were ours again. Perhaps I had been wrong. The scent had been very faint. The two-legs here might not have been to blame—but I wondered. They yet held the blonde cub I had liked. They were not completely innocent.

I had been in the hands of the bad man for almost two months now. I still did not know what it was he wanted of me, but I was yet unharmed. Nurse protected me from the sights and sounds of a defeated people as much as she might. But I was growing wise. I saw the bruises on the faces of the girls I had known. The blank horror in their eyes. It made me fear all the more. I must be kept safe for worse. I started to learn deliberately. I think it was in my mind that if there was no one coming to save me, then I must save myself—and Nurse, too.

My father had been a prudent man. Our conqueror thinking that because the Keep was only half-built there would be few secrets had not attempted to find any. He was wrong. Already within the double walls passages ran from cellars to upper rooms. Stairways within the two great chimneys wound down to doors behind panels. The escape tunnel had not been completed. I could not escape the Keep. But unbeknown to our Master, I had the run of far more within than he dreamed. I watched like a rat within walls—and I learned. At nights I talked my gleanings over with Nurse until I saw how it frightened her. Then I ceased to talk, but continued to watch and listen.

The Master was called Tromar by his followers. Out of earshot they had other names. Some admiring, others crude beyond my understanding. Like most of our bloodline, the custom held of teaching girl-children the arts of bow and sword. Even when my Father had broken away from his kin to the East and taken our small group farther West than any had ever been. That custom had remained. He said it had been held by the First Lady of our Cadet House. There were tales about her. They said she'd been friends with a Dravencat, but that

I could not believe. The Children of Pasht stand aloof from our kind.

I had never even seen one of them. Though there had been many times as I played outside our walls that I had felt eyes upon me. I had daydreamed more than once that it was one of the great golden-furred ones. A possible friend and comrade to walk with me. I dreamed even more when my brothers had been more annoying than usual. But it was only a child's dream, I knew that. Now was the reality of a defeated people. Mine! They had begun to talk to me. As if just telling me small things would help them. I could only listen, but it did seem to aid in some way.

Then things changed. Within the cellars, odd designs were drawn on the paved floors. Two crying Dravencat cubs were brought in to be placed in cages. I had to bite back cries of rage at that. The Hill Cats are sacred to Pasht. They are under her hands. What evil would be brought down on us all for this sacrilege? But whatever they'd planned, it did not work. There was much chanting, and even the sacrifice of a ram. A fine yearling who should have lived on to share his perfection with the flock. But I think they learned from the attempt, whatever it might have been. I could catch sufficient of the talk to know they now had other plans.

". . . and the cubs?"

"Take them back where you found them. I'll see they sleep until after you've left them."

". . . next and when?"

"As soon as we can catch . . ." he moved away, pacing as he spoke. ". . . sacrifice from the one, power from the other. Next dark of the moon would be the best time. Just be sure you take it alive. . . ."

". . . if the other . . ."

". . . have to move fast. Pasht-cursed beasts see in the dark, smell through rock. Have power of their own, too . . ."

He could only be speaking of the Dravencats. I watched as they left the cellars. The cubs would be returned unharmed, but there was some other evil now planned. I could not be sure, but it had sounded—surely I had to be wrong. The cubs had been bad enough.

*   *   *

I basked in the strong sun as Summer closed with Fall.
They would wrestle a while before Summer yielded and
the long bright days were done. But I was uneasy. I had
the feeling of events happening around me which might
draw me into them unwilling. The blonde two-legs cub
still lived within their lair. That I knew. But too many
strange things had happened this Summer for me to be
wholly carefree. I rose to pad silently along my favorite
trail. A fine fat prey would take my mind from such
forebodings. I rounded the bend just as a slight sound
from overhead made me pause. A great net fell from
above, and I was entangled even as I would have leaped
to safety. I howled my outrage. This was some two-
legs trick!

How dare they entrap one of my kind! I slashed viciously at the cords. Several parted. Ah, good. I would
show this foolish two-legs that ... powder puffed into
my muzzle. It clogged my nose so that I must breathe it
in. My senses slipped away even as I fought. I, Many
Kills, Hunter of the High Hills, daughter of my clan, I
was taken. I do not know how long it was before I
awoke. At first I lay motionless, scenting all I could before allowing an eyelid to drift upward. I could scent no
two-legs nearby, nothing but the iron of my cage and
fouled water in a shallow pan.

At length I opened my eyes fully. I sat up a little to
test the upper air. Still nothing. I breathed in deeply.
Nothing but the very faint traces of both cubs and over-
laying that—Evil! I blinked slowly. Evil? Not the usual
stink of purely two-legs plots and maneuverings. It was
the smell of one who delighted in cruelty and other unsa-
vory pastimes. That scent I had been taught when I was
a cub. I searched my memory, breathed in the scent
here again. But no, it was an unfamiliar evil. That was
interesting. This two-legs would seem to have found a
new thing. I lay down again. No doubt they would feed
me soon. I would sleep and recover strength. Then I
would teach them what it was to anger a daughter of
my kind.

I slept, woke, slept again. I was weakening, but still

none came. I had long since drunk the water, foul though it was; now my throat burned. Finally they came bearing more water but no food. I buried my muzzle and drank, and they gave me more before departing. Now I understood. What purpose they had for me I did not know. But I was to be so weakened for it, a struggle would be hopeless. This explained in part the cubs. They, too, had seemed weak and starved when found. But for some reason they must have been useless. They had been returned that we might suspect nothing. I raged at our folly, but there were none to hear. At length I slept again.

I crawled down the narrow stair. I had been unable to steal another candle and could not risk a fall. Above Nurse would stand guard, turning away any who asked with the lie that I bathed. Not that any had ever inquired. So long as I kept out of the way I was ignored. Tromar undoubtedly had a purpose for me, but for now he consolidated his defeat of our people by brutality and license both. His men-at-arms were permitted anything they chose to do. Their preferences were reflected in a growing toll of suicides among the younger men and women and older children of our Keep.

At first I had been afraid. But now after almost three months, I hated. Sometimes it seemed as if the rage was too great for me to contain. That it must burst out and consume me. I had never questioned that it was for my Parents to rule—but also to care for those who looked to us. Now I alone was left to care. And I did with all that I had to give. At first it wore hard as I listened to things I could never have believed a season earlier. Now I believed and with each telling my fury and the need to be avenged flamed higher. Then I overheard another conversation.

". . . message from the nearest Shrine. They will not ratify my Lordship of the Keep without testing the girl."

"But, Lord Tromar. If they do test her, they will know her for unwilling. Even holding the people here as captive against that will not make her more than willing to the eye."

"I know. So I plan another path; there are two that can be used. I will try them both."

"And then she will be your Bride before the Shrine?"

A soft dangerous chuckle. "Bride—or nothing. Or perhaps, just perhaps if I chose the second path, a gateway." Again the chuckle as footsteps faded across the hall.

I shivered. That was why I had been kept undamaged goods. The Priestesses of Pasht in the High Hills were most severe of all the Shrines. A girl-child might be wed by proxy-marriage to an adult male. But only if she were tested by truth-trance and found willing. Clearly Tromar had not known this. In another few months, once Winter turned into Spring, I would be ten. Old enough for a self-agreed proxy-marriage. But with the testing stated, it would be known I did NOT agree. That I came unwilling to any wedding. Without that passing of the test, no proxy-marriage would be legal.

To hold the Keep legally, Tromar must either see I passed the test or wait until I was fourteen and a woman. Then I could be wed—willing or not. It was the use of children the Priestesses sought to prevent. I believed it was the form Tromar wished. He would force nothing on me too early lest I miscarry and die. That, too, would leave him without title. Vaguely, I wondered why he wished to have all legal. It did not seem like the man I was coming to know from my careful spyings. Two nights later there was a great commotion. Two days again and the whisper came to my ears. This time they had taken a full-grown Dravencat.

I was stunned. She was to be kept from food and light. Starved into weakness until Tromar could prepare. I whispered in turn. The Dravencats were children of Pasht. The Lady would not allow one to be used by or for evil. If we aided the beast, it might be that the Lady would aid us in turn. Little by little food passed upward to our room. I locked the growing supply within my secret passage for the day. Then, once all was silent in the Keep, I slipped within the wall to descend the secret stair.

*   *   *

By my estimate, it had been four days and nights since I had eaten. I had been hungry when I was taken. Now that hunger was a raging river that scoured through my body. My kind are large and powerful. But to fuel that power and muscle we require large amounts of food. I had eaten nothing for too long. Soon I would begin to weaken. I heard a rustle in the wall. A kio? I could eat even one of those stinking little rodents by now. They were carrion eaters, cannibals, and wholly disgusting, but to keep my strength against the coming danger I would have devoured even one of them were it to come forth.

But with my night vision, I saw it was no rodent. Instead a portion of the wall was swinging silently open. I recognized the scent and suppressed a most un-Dravencat cry of welcome. The blonde cub—and bearing food. Not a great deal, nor usually of the kind such as I would eat. But in my position, it was not for me to refuse. I backed carefully to the far side of my cage and lay down. I knew that most two-legs feared us, let the cub see I intended no harm. She held a light in one small hand. A tiny flame atop a stick-like thing with the scent of bees. Enough for her to see that I offered no threat. She laid the food just within the cage, watching me all the time with worried eyes.

I laid the food within the great cat's reach praying she would understand. She seemed gentle enough, perhaps it was true as all the tales said. That the beasts were intelligent by the Gift of Pasht. And that they harmed none who meant them no harm in turn. I made bold to speak.

"Lady Cat, I'm sorry there isn't more, but this was all we could get safely. Tomorrow night I'll try to bring more." In the meager light of the candle I could see the water pan too was empty. I could bring water as well. I told her that waiting for some acknowledgment. She only blinked at me, but I did feel an odd twinge in my mind. Imagination. My parents had always said I had too much of that. It reminded me of them and pain brought tears for a second.

I stepped back bowing politely. "I must go. Eat well and may the Goddess bless you, Lady."

* * *

I watched as the wall swung quietly closed again before I began to eat. I had tried to communicate. I was sure that a little of the power resided in the cub, but while I could understand much from her scent and movement, it seemed she had understood nothing of . mine. Two-legs were so limited. It was a nuisance, but time and patience might overcome that. I had touched her somehow, that I knew. It had brought a picture to her mind. Two adults of her kind, and then great grief. I assumed her parents had died, probably at the hands of him who had ordered my capture.

Oh, yes. I knew that. He had left me in the dark to starve but I was a daughter of the Bright Lady. Vision, even in such darkness, was mine. And I could sense when he neared the place in which I was caged. Twice he had come. Each time I had put forth all my ability and learned two things. Firstly the scent of waiting and impatience that this must be so. But overlying that, the stench of evil. Whatever it was for which he waited, it was no good purpose and I was in there somewhere. I had not been captured, caged, and starved for mere amusement.

I ate the food, licked up every crumb and grease spot, then lay down once more. I would conserve my strength. It began to seem as if I might need it for more than just an escape. Slowly a feeling was growing on me that I was here for a purpose, and not the one intended by that one of wickedness. Perhaps this was the Bright One's way of sending a warrior against that which she herself fought. I would wait in patience to be shown.

The minute all was quiet the next night, I fled down the stair. From one shoulder two filled waterbags swung on leather straps. From one hand a basket filled with all the scraps we could glean hung heavy. I listened at the peephole. Silence and dark. I slid the panel open and raised my candle. The Dravencat's eyes glimmered in the tiny light. As I stood there, she slowly rose and backed to the back of her cage. Then she lay down again, eyes fixed on me. It was an oddly deliberate

movement. Almost as if she wished me to see she meant
me no harm.

I laid out the food I had brought and, while she still
waited, filled her water pan. She approached slowly and
drank as I stepped back. Then, as she moved to the
food, I filled the pan again. Each filling had taken a
whole waterbag. Next time I would bring a third to leave
her a drink once I had gone. Or would that be dangerous? Should Tromar enter and find water there, he
would know someone aided. I wavered. If Tromar found
out any of this he might forget his purposes for me and
choose another. I felt sweat break out along my body at
the thought.

I drank. The taste of the cold clear water was wonderful, better than any I had ever tasted. The cub's scent
changed as she stood there. A sudden stench of terror
and a picture. I swallowed a snarl as I understood. The
male who smelled of evil had used a female of this cub's
clan. Worst yet, he had taken the female unwilling and
before my cub. It was this she now feared. I forgot my
hunger, moving to the bars, to utter a small soft purr. I
could not comfort her in the two-legs way. But perhaps
she would understand mine?

Lady Cat had stopped eating. Could she smell my sudden fear? It seemed she might. In the shadowy light she
leaned now against the iron, her gentle purr vibrating in
the air. I caught my breath. It was like one of the old
tales. Did she . . . was this to comfort me . . . could she
. . . I stretched out a hand almost without thought to
touch the thick soft fur under her massive jaws. She
continued to purr. I moved in a little closer, the purr
continued. It did bring comfort—and courage, too. If she
could try to comfort me, child of a different kind when it
was she who was in greater danger . . . I stroked slowly.

Finally I remembered Nurse waiting in fear in our
room above. I whispered a farewell and hurried for the
panel, snatching up my basket and waterbags as I fled.
Upstairs all was yet safe and silent. But I had been gone
far too long so that poor Nurse had worked herself into

a great flutter. I sat down to tell her all that had happened. Once I ended she regarded me thoughtfully.

"There are tales ..."

"I know but that's all they are—aren't they?"

She shook her head. "No, loveykin. Not all of them. Your great-great-grandmother met a Dravencat twice. And those stories are true. I know, your father told me once that he'd read them in the old archives. Both were written by your great-great-grandmother."

"You mean the tale of how one spared her and teased her Nurse?"

"Aye, and the other of how she saved that one's cub many years later. They also say, although she left no tales further, that at times on moonlit nights she would leave the Keep to hunt beside her comrade. It was she who gave us the law that women of our clan learn weapons and have far more freedom than in other Keeps."

"My father told me that when I began to learn the bow," I said slowly. "So the Dravencats *are* intelligent."

"Not as we are, child. But in their own fashion, so I believe."

I retired to my bed to think of that and, still pondering, slept. Morning brought more scraps slipped into my hands as my people passed. Night after night now I slipped silently down my secret stair. Food, water, and also a quiet time just sitting beside the Lady as she ate and drank. I knew now she would never hurt me. I could feel that she might even have a small fondness for me besides the aid I brought. I remembered the tale of my ancestor and wondered. She permitted such liberties as my gentle stroking, my fingers digging gently into the thick fur about her neck to scratch pleasantly.

I was still losing strength but not so fast as my captors would believe. The evil one allowed me one pan of water each day. About a quarter what I required so that even with the cub's contribution I was always thirsty. Nor was the food she provided enough. I could have eaten all she offered five times over. But I was young still and powerful. It would take longer yet before my strength was seriously depleted. But I suspected there might be little time. Twice now the two-legs who stank of evil had come to stare at me. Twice, too, he had drawn markings with a soft white stone on the floor.

The second time I had been left sneezing vigorously. The stench had been unbelievable. I did not know what it was that he had called, but there had been an answer of some sort. I lay back later recalling the smell of the creature. It had been an odd compound of evil and kio. But, distasteful as the kios were, they were not evil. Not those in the High Hills; perhaps somewhere else kios partook of wickedness? I could not be sure. I *was* sure that whatever was being urged into existence here was evil—and far more dangerous than this stupid two-legs understood.

I returned that night from my usual visit to the Dravencat to find Nurse weeping.

"What is it?"

I was told in a few short sentences. I was to be dressed as a bride and made ready. At dusk the next night I would be sent for.

"But no Priestess would agree?" I stopped—no, that was true. Which meant Tromar must now be ready to try one of those other paths I had once overhead him speaking of. I shivered. It might be the last time I would have a mind of my own. The last time I would see those I loved. I demanded fine food and for once it was allowed us. I ate well, forcing the food down and a glass of the strong pale wine atop it all.

My father had once said in my hearing that one should eat when one could. That if a captor was foolish enough to offer food it should be accepted. Strength was more important than pride at such times. So I ate, drank, and then took up much of what was left. Leaving Nurse standing guard at an empty bath chamber door, I raced down the hidden stair. With the cellars windowless, I must halt to light a candle, but with that showing me the way, I ran lightly across the paving to empty the tablecloth before my friend.

I heard the rustle in the wall and was waiting. Something must have occurred which the cub had not expected. She never came by day, knowing that it was then my captors sometimes visited. This time, too, she had food which was not scraps. A whole fire-seared chicken, lengths of some sort of minced meat laced with herbs, and slices of some other meat doused in a sauce. I ate it all swiftly as she sat watching. I could smell the terror in her. For once, the food was almost enough. She had water also, and I drank my fill. Then I sat waiting as she talked. I knew she did not think I understood her language, and in truth I did not. But I understood more than she knew from her movements and scent. And from that flicker of power which I shared in pictures.

This time her fear and hatred was so strong I could see more than ever before. There was the tiny bright picture of the gown she must wear very soon. The picture of what had happened to the female of her clan. The face of the evil man who held me prisoner. And over it all a wild longing to be free of him, to save her clan—and me. Even in the midst of her own terror she wished for my freedom along with her own.

Then, with a final hug, she was gone. I accepted the thin arms about my neck. I touched her forehead with my tongue in love and blessing, and I listened to the flying steps within the wall. Alone in the dark of my iron cage and dungeon I bowed my head to the Bright Lady. Let the cub live, let her be free. I who have never cared greatly for even my own kind, beg for one not of my clan, kin, or blood. Twice I have mated and given cubs to the clan. But not even they have been so dear to me as this small cub who had fed me at risk to herself. With all my heart, all my being, I lifted my mind toward the sky.

"Bright Lady, Moon Lady, aid the cub, let her live free and not die in the hands of the Dark."

Then I lay down to wait. Something told me I was to be present at whatever would happen. Somewhere I had a part to play.

I donned the gown brought and laid out for me. The fine silk head-dress and soft leather shoes. I loosed the mass of my hair that all should see whatever came I was maiden. But from Nurse I accepted a short keen pin. Once it had backed a cloak-broach of my father's. Wrenched from that it was near three inches long and needle-pointed. It would be a door for me when all other doors were barred. I secured it to the nape of my neck beneath my hair and went out, Nurse's hand in mine.

To my bewilderment only Tromar and his aide awaited us. Nurse was brushed aside and I was hurried down-stairs toward the cellars. Nurse followed, crying. Outside the cellar door she was pushed away roughly and the door slammed with her outside. I was led forward to see that the inner cellar was ablaze with lamps. In the iron cage Lady Dravencat lay sprawled as if too weak to lie more comfortably. Within I applauded her cleverness. Looking at her, none would guess she was not almost dead from thirst and starvation.

I saw them bring in the cub as I lay in my abandoned pose. I had seen more earlier and now my fears for us both were great. The evil two-legs had written much with the white stone upon the floor. He had killed twice, the second time a male of his kind. Now the thing he would give passage raged at the thinning barrier. He had power, strong power and I had opened my mind to see the picture. I had seen and my fear risen with each action and chant. The thing outside had offered him all he desired for a doorway here. I had known two-legs to oft be foolish. I had never known them to be so stupid they would believe a creature of the Outer Dark. If this one gained entrance, all our World could be prey to its hungers.

As I waited, I had gradually come to believe I could not be held for that doorway. But a doorway they must have. Only for a short time, no more than days. Then the thing would be strong enough to break free, leaving only a husk behind. Free to kill and prey on us all. I think I had guessed who they would use before the cub appeared. But my heart wept as she entered, small and brave. By the Bright One, she would have made a cub of *our* kind to be proud of. I waited until she glanced my way, then half-opened one eye. A tiny movement of her lips acknowledged me.

I smelled the filthy copper stench of blood as I was hauled through the door. Nurse's tales came back with a rush. Of how long ago before all the demons were driven from the lands, there were those who offered sacrifices to them in return for power. So this was the other use Tromar had for me. Well, at least it should be swift, but why did they have Lady Dravencat, too? A sacrifice, but was there some reason it should be both of us? I fought hard not to scream, to break down in terror. If I were the last of my House, then I must act as its Lady.

I was dragged toward the wall and pushed into a corner. Tromar glanced at the sprawled form in the cage.

"Get that beast out. Drag her over here, but try not to spill any blood. The Dark One will want all of it when he takes the brat for his."

His? I was to be a demon's . . . a demon's what. Bride?

A snigger from the other. "She'll not last long with his spirit using her body."

"Long enough. Once he's used to this World again, he can be rid of her. Then he will give us everything we ask."

I jammed my hands into my mouth. I was to be entered by a demon. Eaten alive from within, used and discarded as no more than a shell. I felt all the food and wine rise up inside to spill from my mouth. I lay on a pile of rags, turning my head so that Tromar might not see how I feared. Pasht knew I had nothing left but pride. *Bright Lady, let me cling to that while I can.* Across the cellar the cage door clanged open and my friend was hauled out. Her great body limp and boneless as with much puffing she was dragged over to where the chalk marks opened a gap in the circle now about me.

I let them tug and heave. I must not make my move too soon. Not that I could do much. But one thing I could do. I could slay the cub quick and clean. She would house no demon, nor would the Dark One make free of my World. It must have been for this that I had

sensed a part to play. I grieved that I must kill one who
had become dear, but better that than what they would
do with her. They closed the circle markings about us
and I lay still. The chant was opening the doorway; soon
they must kill me, my blood adding the final thrust to
the Dark One's entry. Once in, the cub was there to
house it until it could hatch into what it truly was.

The opening grew—as did the scent, fierce in my nostrils. This, this was a Dark One? Behind those who
chanted, I rose to my paws. The scent drove me on,
wild, mad with its stench. The scent of kio, of the small
carrion-eating cannibals that I had always detested. This
was nothing to fear, this was a thing to hate, to fight. I
roared, unable to resist uttering the challenge. With the
sound, I felt the Bright Lady. It was as if she had turned
to watch, to approve the battle. Strength filled me, light
and life, and love warned my heart. I howled my deathsong as I stood. Seldom is that heard in the High Hills.
Not even once in each of our generations. It is that final
song where one of us proclaims that we seek death to
deal death. That if we die in this fight, it shall be with
our jaws locked tight upon the enemy's throat.

Beside me the cub had risen also. She would be of
little use, but it warmed me again that she should stand
beside me. I lifted my head toward the shape that thick-
ened and cried out the deathsong. Let this one know
and beware. This was MY world. I would fight for it,
nor would I shirk death to save it. The stench of kio
grew. The thing did not care. Then let it learn.

I could see little. Beside me Lady Dravencat was
howling defiance. In front of me the darkness that hung
before the cellar wall was growing. I could see outlines
and I turned my eyes away. I would die before I allowed
THAT to inhabit my body. I could sense that the Dravencat and the being were locked in struggle. Somehow
she was managing to keep it from entering further. But
she had been weakened by the long time with insuffi-
cient food. She faltered and the thing grew larger and
clearer. Blood began to appear on her thin flanks, claw
lines on her shoulders.

Below the demon Tromar acted. His knife slashed out
and the other who had aided fell. The splashing blood
was flicked toward the demon. It snarled, the first sound
I had heard it make. I stepped back in fear, then glanced
down as my foot seemed to touch something—one of
the encircling lines. My foot had crossed it where the
Dravencat's blood had dripped and erased a line. I was
free. I could escape. Leave them all fighting and run to
safety. With luck the demon would kill Tromar and the
Dravencat would escape, too.

But what if she could not, what if the demon was too
strong. It wouldn't help if we both died. I stood poised,
hesitating. Before us, Tromar still chanted. His chant
seemed to strengthen the Dark One and weaken my
Dravencat as I watched. I remembered how Lais had
died. I remembered that because of this man I had no
family anymore. No Father to spoil me, no Mother to
love me. No pair of brothers to tease me. And I remembered my people above this room. I was their Lady.

Out of a compound of hatred and fear so great I no
longer knew which was which, I stepped over the lines.
Under my hair the pin was there. I took it in one hand,
moved silently forward. Then drove it with all my
strength into Tromar's side. He screamed. My father had
always said that a blow which pierces the kidneys is exquisite pain and so it seemed. As he half-turned, I struck
again. This time the pin gashed Tromar's throat, opening
a rent as he spun. His voice failed and the demon began
to fade.

I knew well there was little hope I could hold off the
Dark One forever. But I fought with all that was in me.
How had I ever believed I cared for little. As I fought,
I recalled the love of my cubs, my kin. The bright day
and the warm dark of a Spring night. The High Hills,
snow-crested, the leap of swift prey. Before I allowed all
that to die, I would pay any price. But my power was
failing. I was dimly aware that the cub had left my side.
So be it. Let her escape for a little. But I wronged her
in that. I heard the chant which had strengthened the
Dark One die as she struck. The doorway began to

swing shut as the demon faded. With it went the still writhing body of the two-legs who had called it. That kind does not like to depart wholly empty-handed.

We left the cellars with their smell of death. My Dravencat raged through our Keep before me. Somehow she always knew which were our people and which the enemy. When all was done I ordered a sheep killed for her. She ate, washed wearily, then turned to stand by close-shut gates. I opened them with my own hands. I wished she could stay, but she was daughter to the High Hills. I owned her a debt never to be repaid by keeping her. She paused to touch my forehead with her tongue before padding off along the trail. One day I may see her again and if not I shall always remember her. I have given orders that a bolt of the silk-wool weave is to be taken from the storerooms. From that my women shall make a Keep Banner. It shall bear the face of my Dravencat below a broach pin crossed by a broken sword. I may never see her again, but my House shall remember.

I padded up the trail toward my clan lairs. Below, my cub was free again. It was well although the wounds the demon had made still pained me. I would sing this tale before the kin caves. But I would refuse to take another name from the story. I refused to allow the demon even that much foothold here. I am Many Kills. It is enough.

NOBLE WARRIOR, TELLER OF FORTUNES

by Andre Norton

Andre Norton has written and collaborated on over 100 novels in her sixty years as a writer, working with such authors as Robert Bloch, Marion Zimmer Bradley, Mercedes Lackey, and Julian May. Her best known creation is the Witch World, which has been the subject of a number of novels and anthologies. She has received the Nebula Grand Master award, the Fritz Leiber award, and the Daedalus award, and lives in Winter Park, Florida.

Noble Warrior's whiskers twitched as he sulked down the narrow alley. Under his fastidious feet, though he went with all the care he could, the filth on the pavement spattered his paws. He had learned early in this journey that there were plenty of enemies on the prowl. A dog, its coat spotted with mange, had not been quick enough—Noble Warrior had reached the top of a barrel with just a hair's breadth between his tail and those fangs.

He had been driven by pangs of hunger to forage in a pail set beside a door. But he still ran his tongue around his teeth, trying to rid his mouth from the taste of rancid meat scraps.

This was no place for the guard of a princess, and the sooner he was out of it the better. Follow that instinctive direction within him, the ghost cat had advised. At the time—once he realized that he *did* have just such a direction—it had seemed an easy enough thing. But Thragun Neklop had never before had to cross a city of the barbarians, and barbarians certainly these close dwelling creatures seemed to be.

He leaped to the top of a rotting box to rest and try to put in order the events of the past few days. There had been the bamboo cage which was his own private palanquin, and he had meant to ride in it with Emmy, his personal charge, not far away.

Then had come the place of the dragon where people were swallowed up—Emmy among them—into its fat belly and his own cage seized and then carried off. Sold he had been like any slave to that stupid meddler in magic—set up to be a familiar, as the ghost cat Simpson had informed him. Only the dolt of a would-be magician had certainly NOT been a match for two cats. Yes, he was certainly willing to give Simpson a full share in that bit of action.

Now he was well away from the house where Marcus had tried to handle what he did not understand, and, with another goal to concentrate on, starting back home.

He was hungry again, but as his head swung toward the other end of the alley, he picked up traces of a scent which made his whiskers twitch—this time in hopeful promise.

He had left Marcus' shell of a house in the very early hours of the day. Dawn had come, and he could hear the stir in the larger streets. Ahead, at the other end of the alley to which his empty stomach urged him, there was a great deal of noise. He picked up the scent of horses, yes, and some of those woolly creatures called sheep which Emmy found so pettable.

Now he shook each paw vigorously, having no wish at that time to lick pad and fur clean, and made for that end of his path.

The noise grew louder. He could easily pick up the snorting and whinnying of horses mixed with hoarse shouts of men. Reaching the end of the alley, he crouched down behind a pile of baskets to spy out the land ahead.

There was certainly a lot of coming and going. Carts laden high were being maneuvered to where they could be unloaded. There were so many smells now that he could not sort out the one which had promise. He wanted none of bold journeying across a place where one was apt to come under a horse's hard hoofs without warning. And certainly he had no intention of being sighted by any of the men and the few aproned and beshawled women there.

With the skill of his guard training, Noble Warrior selected a path to the right. Where the whole of this cart-filled place seemed busy, there was an eddy there of less confusion.

This appeared to center around a cart which was unlike the others. Noble Warrior blinked and blinked again. Yes, this cart was certainly NOT of the breed of the others. In fact—yes, it looked almost like a farm hut such as he had often seen in his homeland, mounted on wheels. And it was painted in bright colors. There hung a string of bells suspended across a curtained doorway in the back.

Noble Warrior relaxed a small fraction. They had the proper ideas, those of the strange cart. All knew that bells above a door were powerful charms to keep Khons in their dark places. Could it be that here, so very far from the palace of the Princess Suphron, he had indeed found people of the proper heritage who would recognize him—Thragun Neklop—for what he was—a palace guard of high rank? Yet one never forgot proper caution—not if one wanted to make the most of one's allotted nine lives.

He watched with all the patience of his kind. Set a little to one side on the pavement was a fire small and carefully tended by a woman wearing the familiar clinking coin jewelry he knew. Dancing girls dressed so. Over the fire on a tripod was a small kettle, and from that wafted the scent which had first reached Noble Warrior. He uttered a small sound deep in his throat without meaning to.

Resolutely he made himself forget about the pot to eye the rest of the company. There were a line of horses a little beyond and men wearing bright headcloths were there, plainly bargaining with the drab-coated people of the city.

The warning bells rang, and a boy about the vanished Emmy's size swung down the two caravan steps to hand something to the woman by the cookpot. He turned away as if to join the company by the horses and then instead—

Instinctively, Noble Warrior crouched small, tensed his body for a spring. He was sure, as if the boy had cried the news aloud, he had been sighted.

He could slide back into the shadow of the baskets, but somehow he did not want to. Things far back in his memory were moving, oddly disturbing his need to remain alert.

There had been a handmaid of the Princess, a slave taken in war. But she had a gift which brought her into the palace and high into favor with the Princess—she could call to her birds and animals, and they came because something within her was akin to them.

Noble Warrior uttered a small protest of sound. There was no hiding from this boy. Nor did a large part of him wish to do so.

The boy had gone down on one knee a short distance away and Noble Warrior knew he was in full sight of the child. Yet the boy made no effort to approach closer, no gesture which suggested any threat.

"Gatto—?" He spoke the word with rising inflection, and Noble Warrior recognized it as a question.

He arose from his crouch, and sat up proudly, the tip of his tail curled across his fore feet, his large blue eyes meeting the brown ones of the boy.

"Jankos?" the woman by the fire called.

Swiftly the boy made a gesture to be left alone. Now he dared move forward until he could reach out and touch Noble Warrior, while the cat allowed such a liberty.

Noble Warrior sniffed delicately at the knuckles of the turned-over fist held out to him. He did not move as the fingers slowly opened and touched the top of his head between his ears in the knowledgeable way of one used to dealing with cat people.

"Jankos!" The woman had come away from her fire tending to approach. But she suddenly stopped as Noble Warrior stood up, took two steps forward, and uttered the cry he used for a friendly greeting.

"It is a cat, Mammam, but such a cat! Look, he has eyes like the sky!"

The woman joined Jankos, and Noble Warrior sniffed at her full skirt. No, she was not an under-skin friend like the boy, but she offered no harm either. Now she got down on her knees to inspect the cat more closely.

"You are right, Jankos. This is no cat such as one sees hereabouts." She was half frowning as she studied Noble Warrior. "He is of great worth by guess, there will be those seeking him—perhaps even a reward."

"Are you hungry, Gatto?" she added, and crooked a finger which brought Noble Warrior willingly into the open and closer to that kettle with the intriguing smells.

Jankos disappeared quickly once more into the wagon and then was back with a bowl into which the woman ladled a portion of the stew she had been tending.

Noble Warrior settled himself on guard by that, waiting for the contents to cool enough for him to investigate them more closely.

The woman sat down on the steps leading up to the curtained, bell-hung doorway, and continued to study the cat. Cats there were in plenty in this land, as well as overseas from which her family had come some years ago. However, never one such as this one. It was as if this find were a blooded horse turned out by mistake with a farmer's draft horse. She raised her voice:

"Pettros, come you here."

One of the men by the horses turned his head with an impatient look on his face but, as she made a vigorous gesture, he came.

"Look you what Jankos has found."

It was the man's turn to squat on his heels and view Noble Warrior who had at last decided that the stew was ready to be tongue tasted.

"From where did you take him," the man turned a thunderous frown on the boy.

"From no place. He came by himself. See, he is very hungry—he has been lost—"

The man rubbed his broad hand across his jaw. The woman broke in:

"By the looks of him he has not been on his own too long, Pettros. Perhaps there will be a reward."

The man shrugged. "He is strange, yes, but there are cats a-many and who offers a reward for such? A horse now, even a donkey, or a good hound—but a cat—I think not. If you wish him, Jankos, bring him along. We have near finished the trading and it is time to hit the road." He got up and went back to the horses and those about them.

Noble Warrior finished the bowl and even was reduced to giving it several last licks. He did not object when Jankos settled down beside him and stroked his sable brown head, scratching in just the right places behind the ears.

This was not his Princess, nor his Emmy, but the boy was suitable as a companion and Noble Warrior climbed up into the wagon as horses were hitched to it. He sat just before the curtain and watched the man finish off the contents of the kettle and stamp out the small fire. The woman had already edged past him into the interior of the wagon, but Jankos joined him on the top step, his hand still smoothing in well-trained fashion, which brought a rumble of purr from Noble Warrior.

That something deep in him which was his only direction homeward seemed soothed also, and somehow he was sure he was headed in the right direction.

There were, Noble Warrior discovered as they trundled along, three of these wagons. They did not ride as smoothly as the carriage he had shared with Emmy, but they each had their own store of the most enticing smells. There were other children beside Jankos also, but Noble Warrior held aloof from their coaxing, keeping close to his first friend.

At least they were getting away from the place of noise and bad smells, and at last Noble Warrior felt secure enough to curl up on the blanket bed to which Jankos introduced him and got to sleep, relaxing for the first time since his terrors when he had seen the smoke breathing dragon swallow Emmy and he had been stolen away.

Once he had had a refreshing sleep, he did some exploring. No one shooed him away or yelled at him. He spent some time sitting under a cage swinging with the movements of the cart in which hunched a bird, brightly feathered. Noble Warrior sniffed and sniffed again.

He had seen tame birds many times and knew that they were not to be troubled by guard cats. But there was something wrong with this one—it was sick. And the woman fussed over it, trying to get it to eat and drink, folding it closely in her arms from time to time, making soft chirruping sounds as if it could understand her.

They did not keep to the main highways in their traveling, but rather took lanes and often forest tracks. Yet all the time Noble Warrior felt the pull of his instinct. Home *WAS* in this direction.

On the fourth morning the bird had fallen from its perch and lay a crumpled mass of feathers on the floor of the cage. Noble Warrior watched the woman dig a resting place for its small body in the softer earth of a ditch side. There were tear marks on her brown cheeks.

"No Thother," she said when she returned to the wagon. "He served us well, always seemed to know just which card to pick. Remember the gentleman who gave a gold piece—hunted us up after the race and said Thother had picked the winner for him. We shall not see such a clever feathered one again."

That night, when they halted, she brought out a small folding table and set it up as straight as she could on the ground, a lamp stationed at its side. Then she produced a long bag which glinted in the subdued light as if made from one of Princess Suphron's fine robes.

Out of that she shook a number of flat sticks of a dull yellowish color. Noble Warrior's ears flattened a little.

This woman was going to play some of the tricks he had seen used to amuse the women of the court. Much of the past faded from his mind—he was back in a garden beside a pool where a woman, much older and more raggedly dressed than this one, went through the same gestures.

He jumped to the second caravan step, whiskers twitching. Was this woman also one of power whom even the treacherous Khons would answer?

Each stick was marked on one side—the other was plain of any pattern. She gathered them all up again, holding the plain sides uppermost, and tossed them once more.

For a long time she just sat there. Noble Warrior grew impatient. This was not the way matters should go at all. He gave a snort, leaned closer. With a dark paw flipped one of the pieces over.

There was a sharp exclamation from the woman. She snatched up the stick he had moved and examined the pattern on it—then she looked beyond it at Noble Warrior himself as if she had never seen him before.

"Mammam—" Jankos had pushed past the door curtain.

"Quiet!" Her voice carried the snap of an order. "I must—I must think!" She set her elbows on the table and steadied her head on the support of her hands. With a breath which was almost a whistle she again gathered up the sticks, the eyes focusing on Noble Warrior holding a new wariness.

For the second time she tossed them loosely and then leaned back, her attention centered on the cat.

She—she wanted— He put out a paw which hovered over three sticks and then flipped up and over the middle one, settling back to watch her reaction.

He knew the danger of the Great Dark—one learned that as a kitten hardly before one's eyes were open—but this was no harmful curse play.

The woman did not pick up the stick he had chosen, just leaned forward to see it the better as it lay on the table. Jankos crowded closer and now Pettros loomed on the other side.

"This—this one—" The woman's voice began as a half whisper and then arose louder. "This one—" She flung out her hands as if she could not find the words for more of an explanation. Now the man leaned the closer.

"A far journey—" he said slowly.

"Gatto can SEE—just like Thother!" Jankos grabbed up a handful of the sticks and tossed them so that a number fell just in front of Noble Warrior's waiting paws. He bent his head and sniffed—the old knowledge. Yes, it still was with him. He flipped another of the sticks.

"Trouble—" the woman shook her head. But Noble warrior was not yet through; he had already curved a claw around a second stick so that once in the air, it fell across the first. Then he sat back satisfied.

"Gain!" it was Pettros who cried out that word. "Trouble and then gain! Maritza, this is no cat—he is a treasure for us. Do you not see?"

She drew a deep breath. "I see," she answered slowly. With the upraised fingers of one hand she made a sign in the air.

Thus Noble Warrior became indeed one who chose futures. Where Thother had before picked sticks from the bundles people held out, he waited until they were tossed and then turned one, sometimes two, or even three. It was dabbling in things beyond the curtain of this world, that was true. But he was of the breed who knew both worlds. Had he not dealt with Hob on his arrival in this land, soothing the spirit of the house no man could see? Had he not identified the evil Khon sent to destroy Emmy and her father, and finished that nasty spirit off? Had he not talked with ghosts and managed to defeat a would-be follower of the black arts?

Thus they traveled from one village to another. Always, Noble Warrior was assured by instinct in the right way for him. Maritza made him a velvet collar marked with glittering spangles which he wore when he was on duty at the table. Sometimes he thought that she was a little afraid of him for some reason. But the villagers

who came to have their fortunes told were certainly in
awe and there were a number of coins to ring in the bag
Jankos carried when he escorted Noble Warrior back to
the caravan.

It was when they came to the fair that there was a
shadow sensed by the cat. Something tickled his inner-
most thoughts as might a wisp of a dream. It was of the
dark—not intensely, threateningly so, as had been the
Khon, but it was here and he had no wish to seek it out.

Others than the villagers had come to see what might
be offered by the dealers. There was a girl with a thin,
sharp-nosed face, a mouth which was a line of discontent
and peevishness, dressed like Emmy when she went to
some place of importance.

When she came up to the table, the villagers gave way
and none of them showed any smiles.

She flounced herself down on the stool opposite
Maritza and looked at Noble Warrior with a sly smirk.

"A fortune-telling cat! La, what will it be next, I wonder. A horse to sing opera, a pig to dance? All right,
Gypsy, let this animal of yours tell my fortune!"

Noble Warrior's blue eyes stared into hers which
seemed unable to meet his squarely. The faint whiff of
the dark which had disturbed him since early morning
was now like a full puff of rising incense in his face.

She was not a Khon, no. Nor was she of some very
ancient evil of this land. But in her there was darkness
and danger—not for herself but for others.

Catching up a handful of the sticks, she threw them
straight at the cat. One caught in his collar and swung
there. But the rest hit the tabletop. He was aware that
Maritza had drawn back a little, that Jankos was on the
move to come between this girl and Noble Warrior.

For a long instant Noble Warrior simply stared at the
girl. She gave a spiteful giggle.

"No fortune for me then, cat. As I thought, it is all a
hum—gypsy trickery."

Noble Warrior's right paw swept out. He did not lin-
ger to make any choice, he simply snapped one of the
sticks into the air and it flew much as the one she had
shot at him through the air to land flatly before her.

The pattern on that stick was red and black and curled in a tight series of circles. He heard Maritza gasp.

"Well, what is the meaning?" The girl tapped the stick with one fingernail.

"Lady—" Noble Warrior saw Maritza stiffen. Pettros had come up behind her. Now his hand had reached out to close protectingly on her shoulder. "Lady, you must watch yourself—your thoughts—well—there is danger—"

The girl's giggle became a crow of unpleasant laughter. "What, no dark haired knight to court me? Your cat is not very polite, Gypsy. You should teach him better manners."

She stood up abruptly. Jankos made no attempt to offer her the money bag, nor did she show any sign of dropping in a coin.

"Gypsies," she said as she turned away. "There are those hereabout who have little liking for your kind. I would advise you to be on the road before sundown—well away from here."

Her wide skirts swept around in a swirl and she went off. Maritza's hand came up to cover her husband's where it rested on her shoulder.

"The evil," she said in a voice which was close to a whisper, "is not against her—it is *in* that one, Pettros—she is the danger."

"She is the stepdaughter of the squire," he answered. "A word from her and—" he shrugged. "Best that we take her advice and get on the road—now."

As they trundled off, Noble Warrior, in his favorite place on the driver's seat of the wagon, was no longer concerned. The dark-thoughted one was gone, but there was something else— His head was held high and he tried with all his might to locate that trace. Yes! It was growing much stronger. Home—he was nearly home!

But the track they followed took a winding turn away from the right direction. Noble Warrior jumped from his vantage point and flashed into the woods making a thick wall on that side of the road.

He sped on, leaping here a downed tree, there weaving a way around some mossy stones. There was the sound of water ahead. But there was another sound also—the crying of a child.

Noble Warrior's speed slackened. He was being pulled in two directions, but the crying won. Emmy? Could it be Emmy? No, the voice was too young for her.

He came out on the bank of the small stream. There was a child there right enough, much younger than Emmy. His face, swollen from crying, had also been harshly scratched by briars in one place and he rocked back and forth in his pain and fear, his clothing muddied and torn.

Noble Warrior advanced with his usual caution when facing the unknown. The child let out a wail and then suddenly caught sight of the cat. His mouth fell a little open.

"K–k–kitty?" he stammered.

Plainly, Noble Warrior decided, this kitten had been lost. Where was his mother that she allowed him to stray so?

"Lissy—Lissy branged you—k–k–kitty? She told Toddie wait, there would be a 'prise. You the 'prise, k–k–kitty?"

He held out a badly scratched and mud grimed hand. "Where Lissy—Toddie go home!" His face was puckering again for further crying.

Noble Warrior advanced until the small hand fell on his head. It was sticky on his fur, but he resigned himself to that. For a moment he stood and let the child pat him, then backed away.

As he had hoped, the little boy scrambled up and followed, as the cat slowly withdrew. But which way would they go? Back to the village—or on to that still far place to which his need called him?

Best the village, he decided. Their journey was a slow one and Noble Warrior had to submit to a great deal of patting, and even once to the shame of a hand closing on his glossy tail. But they did come out at last on the track where he had left the caravan. There was no sign of that. Perhaps the gypsy instinct to get away from danger had taken them well ahead. But the village lay in the other direction.

Toddie sat down much more often now and had to be coaxed to follow. But before they reached the first cottages there was the thud of horse hooves on the road. The man in the lead was mounted on a tall black horse which overran the spot where Toddie had taken his last rest, but he reined back, jumped from the saddle and caught up the child almost firmly.

Toddie wrapped arms around the man's neck.

"Toddie!" The man hugged him so tightly that the child squirmed.

"Dada!" yelled the little boy.

"Jus' like Miss Elizabeth said. Squire, them there gypsies had him—dropped him off when they got to know as they were being followed!"

"Lissy?" Toddie pushed a little away from his father to look up into the man's face. "Lissy said Toddie—come to woods—show him big 'prise. Then Lissy ranned away—Toddie no find her—only K–k–kitty! K–k–kitty good—brang Toddie to Dada. Lissy, she losted Toddie!"

He had flung out an arm to indicate Noble Warrior who was preparing to edge back into the bushes.

"Why—that there's the gypsy cat—" said one of the men.

But another approached Noble Warrior more closely, going down on one knee to survey him with care.

"Squire—this here's that strange cat Captain Ashley brought 'ome from foreign parts for 'is little girl. Stolen it was when they went to London to take th' train to th' seashore. The Captain, e's near been crazy trying to find it—e's offered a reward an' all."

Now the speaker turned his attention to the cat. "Noble Warrior, you knows me—Tom Jenkins as is second groom. Time you get back home—Miss Emmy now, she's near cried herself sick and th' whole place is not th' same without you walkin' out in th' mornin' to take th' air."

Noble Warrior all at once felt very tired, tired but at peace. He might not have won home all by himself, but he was certainly not far away. Willingly, he allowed Tom to pick him up carefully. For a fleeting moment he thought of Jankos and the caravan—but that was not meant to be the life of a guardian cat—no, not at all.

BORN AGAIN
by Elizabeth Ann Scarborough

Elizabeth Ann Scarborough won a Nebula award in 1989 for her novel *The Healer's War*, which was based on her experiences as an Army nurse in Vietnam. She has collaborated on three books with Anne McCaffrey, with the most recent being the anthology *Space Opera*. She lives in Washington with three cats, Mustard, Popsicle, and Kittibits. This story is dedicated to the late Peaches, who was her office cat-best friend for twenty years.

He had never been the kind of cat to have adventures. Timid, he had spent much of his early life hiding under couches and beds and behind bookshelves when company called. Peaceful by nature, he did not hunt and thought the dry food his friend placed in the communal dish the best of all possible foods. Contemplative and spiritual, he was relieved to take his surgical vows and live the life of brother, son, and companion.

The wilder pleasures he had always found frightening. Lying under the garden bench on a sunny day, or beside the heater in the office while his friend worked, indulging himself when the occasion presented itself with a bit of catnip; these were his quiet enjoyments.

Some might have found it dull; indeed, the other cats in the household chided him that he had always been an old man, but he found his life deeply fulfilling, and had mourned to leave it almost as much as he was mourned.

He had outlived all of the cats he was once young with, and was nearly twenty when the illness fell upon him. He had thought that after all those years of friendship he would have to die alone, but in the end, he was in her arms and she was weeping into his grizzled fur, singing him lullabies and crooning the words that baffled him now. Even though there were no fleas on this plane, he sat down and had a scratch, as was his habit when he was troubled, and considered his options.

All around him different colored lights zoomed in and out, but it was just light, nothing to worry about. Strange-looking figures would hiss at him, and he'd hiss back. Kindly, beautiful figures would offer him tasty-looking dishes, but the delicacies had no smell, and besides, he wasn't hungry. He just sat there, wondering how he was supposed to find his way home.

After a while, he expressed his displeasure. To his surprise, his voice was strong and plaintive, not the whiney, old-man's meow it had been during the last few months of his life. If help for a stranded cat was available in this neighborhood, that mew ought to bring it running.

Running was not all it did. It pounced, rolled him over three times, and gave his tail a swat before he squared off with it. "It" was another cat, a long-haired type with a gray face, paws, and tail. Probably thought he was hot stuff because his tail was high and plumey, and a golden glow shone all around him. Golden glows were all right, but some cats, superior cats, were already golden enough and always had been, so what was so wonderful about a little yellow light?

"What in the name of the Buddha are you doing here?" the long-haired newcomer demanded.

"I'd like to know that myself. Who're you?"

"I'm Mu Mao the Magnificent, of course, formerly the Last Cat in the World—well, almost, and Decanter of the Damned. But that's another story. I know what you are, obviously, from your aura, you're a bodhisattva such as myself, though not as highly evolved, of course. But who are you and what are you doing in the Bardo?"

"The what?"

"The Bardo. The Isles of the Dead."

"Is that so? What kinds of dead things are there?" he asked with interest. Some of them might be tasty.

"You, for one. But you're in the wrong place. Some-one with your aura should be in Nirvana. I haven't had to come here for generations, myself, but I couldn't help hearing you yowling, and you spoiled my nap. I'm be-tween lives at present and thought I'd see what the fuss was about. So I repeat, who are you? I know all of the cats still existing. I'm the father of most of them."

"You're not *my* father. And I am Peaches, Mr. Peaches to you."

"Peaches? As in canned peaches? What a curious name."

"It's an excellent name. My friend gave it to me when I was a kitten and she observed that the peach ice cream she was eating when she first saw me in my incarcerated state matched the color of my baby fur. She claimed me and we were inseparable until recently. Now I can't find my way back to her."

"You're not supposed to go back, my friend. You're dead."

"That has nothing to do with anything. She's my friend, and she said I could go back if I wanted. And I want."

The other cat licked his long chest fur contemplatively, "Just—er—how long have you been here, entertaining this desire, Peaches, my friend?"

"I've no idea. I hadn't been well, you see, and things have all been a little muddled."

"This may come as a shock to you, but it's been longer than you think. A lot longer. A lot has happened in the world in the meantime. It has, I'm sorry to tell you, ceased to be as you once knew it. I hope this friend you're looking for was a very good woman."

"We suited each other," Peaches replied with a lick to his tail tip.

"That means little," Mu Mao said. "Sometimes one chooses a companion because of the needs they can fill rather than for virtue. If your friend was of your caliber, she should be in Nirvana. Otherwise, she's no doubt wandering the Bardo, as you so mistakenly do now, looking for some life form to become."

"You mean she's dead?" Peaches cried. That had never occurred to him. Companions usually outlived cats, even very old cats, by many years. And she had been a fairly young woman when he saw her last.

"Most people are," Mu Mao said, giving his right front paw a discreet swipe. "As I mentioned, the world as you knew it ended some time ago."

"So you think she's in this Nirvana place?"

"Perhaps. It's certainly where you belong. You've lived nine lives of devotion to imparting to human beings the wisdoms of calm, patience, detachment and humor. You belong in the highest place now."

"Is that the place where you become an angel, with wings and a halo?" Peaches asked. "My friend and I watched some vids about those, but I thought they only concerned humans."

Mu Mao sat down and folded his paws and explained with only slightly exasperated patience, "Angels are just the way one religion interpreted auras and the gift of astral travel. All beings are one in a sense, and all achieve enlightenment according to their merits. You've been a very meritorious kitty indeed, Mr. Peaches. Now let's scat out of here and achieve Nirvana, shall we, hmm?"

"Not without my friend," Peaches said, planting his paws as firmly as they'd plant on relative nothingness.

"She's probably waiting for you there," Mu Mao wheedled. "It's the best place she could be."

"Not unless Nirvana is our office, with my cushion by the heater." Peaches grumbled, or tried to. Lights and clouds swirled around him and nothing was familiar except the mocking, knowing eyes of Mu Mao. He was very glad when everything settled down again. The whole experience made him feel like he wanted to toss a hairball.

Nirvana was nice enough. There were fluttering things and dangling things, things to chase and places to lie high up and warm. All the people there seemed to like cats. But none of them was his particular friend.

It didn't take him very long to start meowing and clawing at insubstantial things until they kicked him out, along with Mu Mao for bringing him.

"Now look what you've done," Mu Mao said.

Peaches groomed himself with a certain grim self-satisfaction. "I know perfectly well what I've done. I meant to do that. She wasn't there and I had no intention of staying. I told you I wouldn't. Where else can we look?"

Mu Mao meditated on the matter for a moment. He looked very wise but Peaches felt that wise was as wise did and he wanted no cheap philosophy. He wanted to be back with his friend, period. He switched his tail impatiently while the other cat seemed to be dozing with his eyes open.

"If she's not here," Mu Mao said finally, "and she's not in the Bardo, then she may have reincarnated already. Do you still want her if she's a gekko lizard, say, or a mouse?"

Peaches had to give that some thought but he finally concluded, "I'd want to be with her if she was a junkyard dog. She won't hurt me. She'll know me. She said she would."

"No wonder you're a bodhisattva," Mu Mao said. "That's what I call faith."

"But she won't be a dog," Peaches continued, "and she won't be a gekko or a mouse either. She's too big. She'll be herself, a human being, as sure as I'm a cat."

Mu Mao did not appear as enlightened by this statement as Peaches had expected. "The life you lived with this—friend—was your ninth life, right?"

"It was my life," Peaches replied simply.

"You do know there were others?"

"I'm not much for theology," Peaches replied, "but the place I was at first—the Bardo, you called it?—seemed familiar, as if I'd dreamed about it."

"And you only remember being a cat, then."

"What else should I remember?"

Mu Mao blinked at him, the wide blue-gray eyes closing and opening as if to pull him in. "How one with such an enlightened aura can be so ignorant and steeped in samsara—"

"What's that?" Peaches demanded, pouncing on the term. "Could my friend be there?"

"Samsara is the painful cycle of life and rebirth from which most of us escape when we attain enlightenment but which you seem determined to cling to with all claws and teeth."

"You bet your tail I do," Peaches said grimly. "And you didn't answer my question. Could she be there? My friend?"

"She could be anywhere, but it's unlikely she survived. Few did. Where did you last live? Do you know when?"

"We lived first in a very cold place called Alaska, where I was born, and then my friend put me and the other cats of the house onto a big thing that smells horrible and makes your ears hurt. I thought it was the end of us all, but then after a while she was there and found us a Home where it was never too cold and we could go in and out as we pleased. The others hunted a great deal, but I was needed to help her with her writing and so I remained inside, of course."

"That's all very well, but where was it?"

Peaches tried to help but he had limited himself somewhat with his indoor duties and had not really been aware of his environment. "You could smell fish and salt there all the time, and the air felt like water."

"So, on the coast of the United States."

All of a sudden the voice of Peaches' friend sprang into his head so clearly he cried out, missing her. "Box 11111, Port Chetzemoka, Washington," he said.

"What?" Mu Mao asked.

"That's what she told people on the telephone who wanted to send us nice things. She'd tell the telephone that, and things would be left at the door. The brown people always knew how to find us from there. Can you find her again from that?"

Mu Mao blinked and settled down to clean between

the pink pads of his gray paws, taking particular care with each scimitar-shaped claw. "Peaches. Friend. I don't like to tell you this, but I've seen what became of Washington in America. Much of what was near the water is now under the water. Your friend must surely have died."

Peaches hunkered down until his eyes, one brown and one green, were level with the blue eyes of Mu Mao, and their whiskers almost touching. He laid his ears back and hissed. "Ssso" and spat, "what?"

"No need to be rude, I'm sure," Mu Mao said.

"No need to be stupid. I'm dead, you're dead, what should it matter if she's dead? We could still find her, but she's not in that Bardo place nor in your Nirvana. So she must be living, mustn't she?"

"There's a bad place she might go," Mu Mao said.

"She wouldn't go to a bad place. She was good. She was my friend," Peaches said.

"You mustn't rule out any possibility."

"Fine, but you said you know where Washington is. Let's look first for Port Chetzemoka and try to find her among the living." He gave his tail three quick flicks, then conceded, "And if we don't find her anywhere among the living, then we'll look in the bad place."

"You look. I'm a very enlightened being. I spend all my energy trying to keep myself and others out of that place. But we can go to Washington if you like."

"How?"

"On the astral plane, we can travel very quickly. You have only to envision your home ...."

"I can't think of anyplace else ..."

"And we can go there. I'll do the navigating."

"Should I hold onto your tail or anything?" Peaches asked, suddenly feeling timid again, now that he seemed close to getting what he sought.

"No. Just think of your home."

Peaches thought hard. The house with the logs inside, the heavy oak office furniture with the glass fronted bookcase and the computer and printer and all the special awards and knickknacks only he, of all the cats, was permitted near. And of course, his special cushion by the heater.

"I need more to go on than one room," Mu Mao said.

So Peaches visualized the yard, the open spaces filled with dandelions and tall grass, the bushes where you could hide and wait for birds, the trees, and all the salt-water and fish smell.

He thought very hard, his eyes closed to shut out the nothingness around him and invoke only home.

"You can look now," Mu Mao said in a discouraged voice.

Peaches opened his eyes eagerly nonetheless, thinking to see at least the yard, maybe the house, maybe his friend herself calling him from the front door.

But when he looked, he could only wail, "You did something wrong. It's nothing but water!" And indeed, there was nothing but gray smoking skies with dirty rain falling into a gray turgid sea stretching so wide that surely nothing had ever lived here.

"I told you," Mu Mao said. "A lot of the coastal places were buried under tidal waves or split off and washed out to sea."

But Peaches hardly heard him. He could do nothing but cry, mourning his home and his office and his place. "It's all gone."

"Sorry, friend. I did try to warn you. You have no home to go to. Now will you come to your reward?"

"I suppose I—no," Peaches said. "Just because our home is gone doesn't mean my friend is gone. Of course, she won't be here, but perhaps she's nearby? She'll be looking for me, I tell you."

"Peaches. Friend. It isn't pretty, the things humans are doing to others now. The only place your friend would be safe is in Shambala."

"Why didn't you say so?" Peaches asked. "Probably she's there already, waiting for me."

"I can promise you that she is not. I brought all who are there since the end of the world to Shambala myself and no one there was looking for a stubborn orange cat. Besides, it's half a world away from here."

"Can you not simply think of it and take us there?"

"You. Now. Yes. Not a living being. That mode of travel is for astral beings only. There are the tunnels, of course, but they can be negotiated only by such as myself."

"What tunnels?"

"All over the world is a network of tunnels connected to Shambala. Once in them, time is altered. But they are secret, known only to Shambala beings such as myself and the yetis." Mu Mao changed the subject abruptly. "You know, now that we're where you used to live, we could try homing in on your friend instead of her house. Think of her very clearly and try to see where she is. I'll help you."

Peaches closed his eyes and saw his friend clearly, her large comforting form, her eyes as green as his green one, her head fur brown and somewhat white now, her hands and voice soft and loving with him mostly, though sometimes stern when he wet inappropriately.

"I don't know why you're so intent on this one human. They leave cats all the time, you know," Mu Mao said irritably.

"I know," Peaches said. "But my friend always returned to me. She had to leave us to work in another country and was gone for months, but she left someone kind with us, and when I became very ill and she wasn't expected to return for weeks, all of a sudden there she was. I was so happy I felt almost normal for two days and she was happy, too. But when we both knew I had to go away, she said, "If you come back as a cat and want to come home, find me or let me know where you are and I'll find you." Thinking of his death again, and especially of her sorrow, made him sad and he began crying again, her face still clear in his mind behind the weepiness at the corners of his eyes as he yowled.

"But humans move on and get other cats and forget about us. You can have the highest reward in Nirvana or, if you like, come with me to Shambala to live once more in comfort and happiness."

"How can I be happy somewhere she's not? After I left my body, I hovered in the corner of the room and saw that she held me until she was sure I was gone, then she took a basket so good that she once chased us out of it and put me in it, along with some of the weaving we did together, some catnip and some seeds, and called her friends to help bury my earthly remains. She was very sad. Now our home is gone—what's become of her? I have to know and go to her again."

"That is," Mu Mao said, "Unless she's moved someplace where they don't allow cats."

Peaches laid back his ears, narrowed his eyes and lifted a leg to wash beneath his tail in response to that remark, but just then Mu Mao asked, "There. Is that her?"

Peaches wasn't sure at first. She wasn't large anymore, but thin, and her hair was in patches as was her clothing. She was among about twenty other people and was busy with a pointed thing, breaking up soil and rocks. All around were mountains and she stood on a rocky path leading into one.

"That's a funny way to garden," Peaches said. "My friend has never been fond of yard work actually. She's a scholar and a thinker, as I am."

"She's not gardening, Mr. Peaches," Mu Mao said his name derisively. He might as well have come right out and called him "kitty-cat." "See the the men with the guns? She's a prisoner. It's forced labor."

Peaches wanted a closer look and without trying to he found himself staring up into his friend's sweating, sunburned face. He wished he could smell her, but just by looking, he could tell that she didn't feel at all well and needed to spend a long time curled up in bed with him purring beside her. He twined around her ankles, filthy and set far apart to brace her for the impact of the blows of the heavy implement she carried. Her knees buckled with each blow. Peaches cried to see her like that and for a moment she stopped and listened.

The nearest man with a gun hit her with it and knocked her down. "Get up, lazybones. That'll teach you to stop work." He also said some other things Peaches didn't understand except that his tone was so mean, it made the cat want to hide at first, and then it made him so mad that all of his fur stood on end, his tail lashed and he wanted to fly into the man's sneering face with all claws extended. Instead, he took his usual revenge and peed on the man's boot but since he was not yet living, the boot didn't get wet.

Peaches rejoined Mu Mao, who was curled on a rocky ledge high above the workers.

"Still want to go back to your comfy home, eh?" Mu Mao asked.

"What's become of her that she's forced to do this?" Peaches asked, looking down at his friend's prostrate form, as the other people worked around her. "She's not bad. Why did that man hit her?"

"You are one sheltered pussycat," Mu Mao told him. "As I mentioned before, the world ended, more or less, a few years ago. What's left has in most places allowed the worst element to gain control. Eventually, this may be a good thing and order may be reestablished, then civilization will have a chance to build again. But in the meanwhile, those who are not strong and ferocious are dominated by those who are. In this case it seems to me your friend is part of a chain gang, rebuilding the road that goes into this mountain." Mu Mao looked down, a model of detachment. "You won't have long to wait, I'd say, before she joins you and then you can see if she's eligible for Nirvana."

"It's not the same," Peaches said. "And if you mean she's to die, I don't want her to die. I want us to be together again."

"That's no place for cats. But if you insist, we'll have to go back into the Bardo and wait for a portal near here."

"Portal?"

"A womb into which you can be born. It won't be easy to find, though with your spiritual status, you do have a certain preference . . ."

Peaches would have run ahead of Mu Mao had he known where to go. Mu Mao presented several possibilities but none of them were right. He needed something special, something absolutely right if he was to be reunited with his friend and make his home with her again. As Mu Mao pointed out, such people as the man with the gun had only one use for cats and it wasn't to catch mice.

It was the unearthly, echoing cry that alerted them to the possibility, and Mu Mao quickly said the words that guided Peaches back into the Bardo, where, Mu Mao told him, he must grapple with the first demon he encountered, for that would be the aspect of himself he must embrace with this rebirth.

Mu Mao didn't mention, though Peaches knew, that there would also be other souls to grapple with.

There were. For the first time he could remember, Peaches felt no wish to hide under the couch. "I'm sorry, my friends," he said resolutely to the two dogs, six salamanders, three former soldiers, and one ex-President who were also thronging toward the unusual new portal. "I have special need of this one. You'll have to wait for the next one." What really surprised him was that he was fully prepared to back it up with fang and claw.

The others knew this. They felt his desperation and they backed off, not all the way, but a little way, in case something went wrong and they could overpower him and gain the advantage.

Then the demon arose, blocking the greenish light emitting from the opening in the haze. It had claws like butcher knives, just one of which could rip a cat in half. It had slavering, slobbering fangs dripping blood and the skulls of many past opponents strung around its powerful neck. Its tail lashed and its jaws gnashed. Its ears were laid back and its blood-red eyes glared down at Peaches.

Every orange hair on his incorporeal body was standing up, every nerve was screaming to run away, but Peaches was mindful of what he had seen and heard in the company of Mu Mao and at first slunk, then walked, one paw at a time, then ran forward under the waving claws of the demon to twine himself around its feet.

He even tried to purr, which was mad. Mad. The thing was going to destroy him.

But then, he heard Mu Mao's voice saying in the back of his mind, he was already dead. So what was to worry?

He twined some more while the demon loomed and glared and waved its claws and ground its fangs.

Then suddenly the great clawed paws descended upon him, scooping under his belly and lifted him high, toward the gaping maw of the demon, through which the green light of the portal shone, strong and bright.

Peaches remembered Mu Mao's counsel and leapt from the demon's grasp, straight into its mouth and straight through it and . . .

He sat up, blinking, smelling the fresh scent of rain and earth all around him. His head hurt a little, and the broken branch was under him, where he had dropped before, in that other life, the one that had departed this body just before Peaches gained admittance.

He ignored the pain and lifted his nose, sniffing. The man scent was near. Already many memories of the Bardo were fading, memories of his former life, but his compulsion was so strong. He knew he was looking for someone among the men.

He also knew it was sheerest idiocy to go among those men. But, keeping to the cover of rocks and what was left of the forest, he stalked through the brush as the rain began to fall and the fog rose. The rain washed away much of the man scent. All but a single scent that was like catnip to his nostrils.

He leaped onto a rock and looked below him and saw the pitiful, crumpled form below, and all at once his purpose came back to him. There she was. His friend. They had left her lying there as if she were nothing but bird's feathers or mouse fur and they had already eaten the useful bits.

The cat who had been Peaches jumped down and padded over to the form, sniffing her, prodding her with his paw. Breath still moved her torso, shallow and faint though it was, but her body was losing its warmth. He knew somehow that her skin was too tender for him to take her neck in his jaws, as he would a kitten's, but he grabbed a hunk of the false coat humans called clothing and tugged.

The going was so slow. She was floppy, and he didn't want to break any of her parts or damage her further, and yet he knew neither of them must be there by dawn, when the men with the guns would return. He pulled first one piece, then another, nudging the stray parts back toward her body so they didn't twist out of shape while he pulled. He was at the mouth of the mountain, the sun just sending a warning hint of blue into the blackness of the night, when he heard a voice behind him.

"Well, well, kittycat. I didn't think you had it in you."

The cat who had been Peaches growled, a sound so ferocious it startled even him. The small fluffball taunting him was asking to be eaten.

"Calm down, kittycat," it said. "It's me, Mu Mao the Magnificent. I'm here to help you. I didn't point out this cave by accident, you know. There's an entrance to the Shambala tunnel here. Follow me, bring your friend and you'll both be safe inside while I reincarnate and go for help."

The cat who had been Peaches looked down at his friend. Dragging her all night had not improved her health or appearance. He licked her face with his great tongue and made a noise that sounded something like the mew he would have made as Peaches.

"Don't worry. Once inside the cave, she will not deteriorate further. We haven't got all day, you know. Move your tail."

The cat who had been Peaches dragged and nudged and hauled and nudged some more, following after the taunting plumey tail of Mu Mao until the small cat suddenly walked into what had appeared a solid wall. Since it was not, the cat who had been Peaches went through it, too, bringing his friend and nudging her here and there until at last, as her foot joined the rest of her, the wall that it had held ajar closed as if it had never existed.

Mu Mao had gone by then, a flickering light in the darkness of the tunnel, and the cat who had been Peaches lay panting beside his unconscious friend. Outside the tunnel, he could hear the voices of men and the heavy implements striking the ground. His friend's skin was very cold; he wrapped as much of him around her as he could to warm her and tried to remember how he purred when he was small.

He was used to his new form now, and his own memories returned to him, and he was very sad, thinking of all his friend had lost, all that was now lost to him as well. He thought it would be a very long time before Mu Mao returned, for Shambala was on the other side of the world.

He forgot that Mu Mao had told him that the tunnels contained bends in time and that vast spaces, even those with oceans in them, could be traveled very quickly. In the meantime he nursed his friend, licking and rubbing against her, keeping her warm, singing to her softly, and also, knowing his strength would be needed, he slept.

In a shorter time than he would have believed possible, he awoke to behold a white object suspended in the darkness, approaching through the tunnel. At first he thought it was Mu Mao, but then it grew larger and larger and he saw that it walked upright, like a man, but was covered with white fur. He didn't know what it was, and he growled at its approach.

From behind its head peeked a silver face, and a familiar, impertinent voice said, "Ooh, down, kittycat. Not so fierce. This is a friend of mine. He's a yeti. He can carry your friend the rest of the way to Shambala. You may follow."

After rubbing his face all over his friend's head and body to mark her firmly as his own, he allowed the yeti to lift her in its massive arms and trot away with her. He followed as best he could, tired from the injury his present body had endured and from his labors of the night.

The tunnel was more disconcerting than the Bardo, for the sensations of missing a step, of unreality, were happening to him while within a physical body whose skin and fur rebelled at the unnaturalness of the phenomena, but at long last he followed the distant hairy form of the yeti and the mocking plumed tail of Mu Mao up out of the tunnel and into an underground house.

Food smells were all around, mingling with the scent of flowers and snow, sweating people and new babies.

There were sounds of laughter and chimes and happy conversation.

The yeti laid his friend down just inside the door of the underground dwelling and then ran away. Mu Mao scampered out through a flap left in the door, returning with several people.

"My word, what kind of animal is that?" a woman's voice asked.

"One of the other species of big cat. A mountain lion perhaps," her companion answered.

"Mu Mao, please tell this beast we need to move the woman to assist her."

But the cat who had been Peaches understood perfectly well and with a final lick and rub to his friend, stepped back two paces and sat down to wash up while they lifted her.

He followed where they carried her, however, and lay beside the mat they gave her on the floor. He watched all that they did, though he never lifted a paw to stop them. Her breathing grew more normal as the doctors palpated her and rubbed smelly things into her skin and even poked little needles into her.

And finally she did start to move, and whimper and cry out in her sleep. The cat who had been Peaches gave her a reassuring lick when she cried and wrapped himself close when she shivered.

They had been there hours, and he had to go outside to relieve himself, though as he was now, nobody would have dared shoo him away.

Mu Mao was out there. "Well, Kittycat. What now?" the little cat asked.

"What do you mean?"

"You were right about her. She's not a junk yard dog or a mouse or a bird. She's still human, though just barely. But you're the one who's changed. You're a wild animal now. She might be afraid of you."

That had never occurred to him. The others weren't afraid of him, but he'd hardly fit on her lap anymore, come to think of it. He favored Mu Mao with a glare and peered back into the room, through the door which had been left ajar. She was sitting up eating!

She looked up, cringing as he could only guess had been her habit for all the long days and nights she'd been under the rule of the men with guns. He waited, not to startle her, and she stared at him, the folds of her sagging flesh making her eyes seem somewhat smaller, but not dimming their brightness.

Those eyes he knew so well looked straight into his, and the mouth which must not have smiled in a very long time curved up, and she said, "Peaches! You did come back!" And he ran to her and fitted as much of himself as he could into her lap after all while she stroked his nose and behind his ears and under his chin and kissed his fur and told him how she'd missed him, just as he'd known she would.

The snow lions called to him to come and mate, to come and play, and sometimes he did briefly, but mostly he stayed on the padded pallet she made for him near her fire, where she sat and wrote of all that had happened to her while he had been between lives. And the puma called Peaches purred a purr that shook the compound with the vibrations of his contentment.

THE CAT, THE SORCERER, AND THE MAGIC MIRROR

by Mary H. Schaub

Mary H. Schaub's initial college studies were in mathematics, but she succumbed to a lifelong interest in reading and branched into science-fiction writing in 1972. She has since expanded her lateral range from short stories in seven anthologies to novella and then book-length works. Her second novel, *The Magestone,* will appear in April in Andre Norton's new series *Secrets of the Witch World.* Currently, she is juggling elements for another anthology and novel. It is likely that this volume will complete the saga of Drop from cat to boy to cat.

After jumping up onto the sundial in Master Gilmont's side garden, Drop pondered the peculiar preoccupation humans had for measuring time. Due to his accidental ingestion of a magical lozenge, Drop had experienced life as a human boy for several months before his original cat's body had been permanently restored to him by a reversal spell. As a boy, he had willingly endeavored to adjust to the erratic daily schedule urged upon him by Flax, the absentminded wizard who had rescued Drop during a violent storm the previous Spring. Despite persistent efforts, Drop had failed to understand the necessity for dividing each day into repetitive intervals for meals, study, and sleep. As a cat, Drop was accustomed to hunting when he was hungry, or otherwise occupying himself with whatever action that most appealed to his momentary fancy. He might toy with a loose thread, survey his surroundings, or—as now—contemplate human foibles while stretched out on the sun-warmed stone to enjoy a late afternoon nap.

His attention was suddenly diverted by the rank scent of crow and a flash of black feathers. Ordinarily, Drop would not have been perturbed by the arrival of a crow, not even one of such impressive size with unexpectedly red-brown eyes. From the instant that this crow swooped down to perch on the broad windowsill outside Master Gilmont's study, however, Drop was jarred from his leisurely rest into a state of active unease. No matter which body he inhabited, cat or boy, Drop had discovered that whenever magic was activated in his presence, he invariably exhibited two physical reactions: his fur (or human hair) tended to rise, and his skin tingled. Drop's fur lifted and his skin prickled ominously as the crow sidled to and fro along the windowsill with the stealthy purposefulness of a would-be thief. Drop held quite still, rightly judging that his own white-tipped gray fur so closely matched the sundial's weathered stone that he should not be easily distinguishable. Lest their azure color betray him, Drop deliberately hooded his eyes to the merest slits.

Unaware of the cat's keen observation, the crow completed its thorough exterior inspection of Gilmont's study, then flew to a succession of nearby branches from which it could peer in turn through every other window on the south facade of the remote country house. It was unlikely that the sole human occupant within would be visible at this hour, since Master Gilmont habitually indulged in his own afternoon nap in an interior bedroom. The only other regular member of Gilmont's household, his cook, was absent on a fortnight's journey to the city of Zachor to supervise his daughter's wedding feast.

Fully alert, Drop tried to suppress a sense of foreboding. From his months of living in a wizard's cottage, Drop had reached the firm conclusion that magic always resulted in trouble for all creatures concerned. This unsettling crow—which might well not be an authentic crow—projected an aura of almost palpable menace. Its crow scent seemed real enough, but Drop clearly recalled two other equally distinctive scents he associated with past magical assaults: the odors of mouse and moldy cheese.

Soon after Drop had settled in at Flax's cottage, a Druzanian sorcerer named Skarn had attempted to steal a dangerous potion from Flax's desk. During the violent duel that ensued between the two mages, Drop had managed to toss one of Otwill's Keep-Shape Spell lozenges into Skarn's open mouth. When Drop himself had previously swallowed a lozenge from that same bottle, his cat's body had been changed into that of a gray-haired, azure-eyed boy. Skarn's subsequent transformation had been far more startling: he had been converted into a mouse-scented demon, which Flax had summarily vaporized.

Drop had encountered the moldy cheese odor in his more recent conflict with Trund, the local minion of Walgur, an even more notorious Druzanian sorcerer than Skarn. Only a few weeks past, Flax had been secretly summoned to try to free his colleague Otwill from magical immurement in the sorcerer's hired castle in Zachor. Posing as buyers of castle furniture, Flax and Drop had interviewed Trund, from whose extravagant robes emanated a stench that reminded Drop of the sort of cheese acceptable only to a starving rat. When they slipped into the castle to rescue Otwill, all three were trapped by an insidious binding spell which relaxed after they were carried into an ensorcelled, windowless cell. Had Drop not joyfully agreed to allow Otwill to restore his cat form, their subsequent escape would have been impossible. As a cat, Drop was able to squeeze through a ventilating slit too narrow for human passage. He fetched Koron, Otwill's anxious apprentice, who had been waiting outside the castle with the horses. Under the wizards' tutelage, Koron applied a counterspell from the vulnerable exterior side of the cell's door.

Aware that even then, Walgur was hastening to Zachor from his Druzanian lair, the freed prisoners and Koron had risked their lives to locate the rare, transitory magical portal which Otwill had discovered was due to open in a bespelled tower room of Walgur's castle. Trund, determined to prevent them from finding his master's as yet unexamined portal, had rushed upstairs and attacked Koron, the only visible human in the tower room. Struggling together, Trund and Koron had fallen through the dilated portal, joining Flax and Otwill, who had already ventured into the strange other-space beyond the opening. Seeing that the portal was rapidly contracting while Drop remained behind, Otwill had called back to exhort Drop to seek Gilmont. In order to prevent Walgur from ever being able to use the portal, Flax and Otwill had spell-sealed the aperture from the far side, thus voluntarily—and Drop most fervently hoped, only temporarily—exiling themselves in the other-space along with Koron and Trund.

Unfortunately for Drop, Otwill had not had sufficient time to convey directions to Gilmont's house. Wizards, Drop had frequently noticed, often neglected to impart practical details that any cat would have mentioned from the start. Drop did remember, however, that Koron had lately apprenticed himself to Otwill, a far more active wizard than Koron's original master, Gilmont, whose interest in magic tended more toward scholarly research than vigorous spell-working. Further recalling Flax's extensive library, Drop reasoned that Gilmont would likely be an even more ardent accumulator of scrolls and books. After his timely exit from Walgur's deserted castle, Drop therefore loitered in the narrow alleyways of Zachor's booksellers' quarter until he overheard talk of a shipment being readied for dispatch to Master Gilmont. Gratified that his assessment of Gilmont's habits had been correct, Drop had secured a comfortable perch atop the book-laden wagon which delivered him directly to Gilmont's house.

Quite soon after his arrival, Drop had impressed Gil-

mont's cook by catching and displaying three mice in a
tidy row on the kitchen doorstep. Acting on the cook's
enthusiastic endorsement, Gilmont had urged Drop to
investigate his study, where he had recently noticed with
alarm telltale toothmarks on various scrolls and leather
book bindings.

Throughout the passing days, Drop patiently awaited
Flax's return. From Otwill's hasty—and fragmentary—
farewell admonition, Drop assumed that whenever Flax,
Otwill, and Koron succeeded in establishing a reentry
portal from the other-space, they would expect to find
him at Gilmont's house.

It had been intensely frustrating to Drop to be unable
to explain his situation to Gilmont. Speech was undeniably one useful faculty peculiar to humans, although
Drop was privately convinced that they prattled on at
far more length than was strictly necessary. Flax had
once described Drop as a cat/boy of few, but cogent
words. In Drop's opinion, the cats of his acquaintance
simply joined him in practicing a laudable economy in
their communications. Flax had taught the cat-turned-
into-boy how to read as part of Drop's apprentice training, but due to a storm-related injury to his paw/hand,
Drop had not mastered the finer intricacies of writing.
Next to speech, humans relied upon writing to convey
information. Drop had considered attempting to use his
paw to daub a note to Gilmont, but so far, he had not
been afforded a suitable opportunity.

When the last rays of the late autumn sun slanted
across the garden, the overly inquisitive crow made one
final circuit of Gilmont's house, then flew away, its black
outline quickly obscured against the dark bulk of the
surrounding forest.

Drop immediately jumped down from the sundial and
hurried through the special entrance contrived for him
by Gilmont's cook—a flap of heavy leather tacked across
a niche beside the kitchen door. Somehow he would
have to warn Master Gilmont about the magically-
charged crow's survey of the scholar's house.

No sooner had Drop entered the house, however, than
he felt an irresistible urge to turn aside and climb the

successive flights of winding stairs all the way to Gilmont's storage room in the attic. The higher he advanced, the more Drop's skin prickled and his sleek gray fur rippled. There could be no mistake; active magic was being invoked nearby, and Drop was being drawn toward the source of the activity. With mingled feelings of wariness and expectancy—perhaps at last Flax and Otwill might be endeavoring to return!—Drop carefully weaved his way around and between the storeroom's rejected furniture and heaps of seldom-used scrolls. When his sensitive whiskers brushed against an ornately framed glass-fronted panel, Drop tingled all over as if raked by an icy wind.

He whirled around to examine the dusty panel more closely. It was a large mirror, braced against the side of a rain-warped cupboard. Grateful for his superb cat's vision in dim light, Drop gazed into the mirror's shadowy depths. He was not surprised to see more than the surface reflections from the surrounding objects in the crowded attic. Faint, swirling shapes seemed to drift deep within the glass. Suddenly Drop was aware of a tenuous communication. He recognized Flax's familiar voice, but the sound of it did not come to Drop's ears. Instead, a ghostly whisper stirred in his mind, scarcely perceptible at first. When Drop concentrated upon it, the substance of the message became desperately clear.

"Drop! Fetch Gilmont! Need help NOW!"

Drop raced to the door, bounded down the stairs, and dashed into Gilmont's study, where he startled the old scholar by leaping directly onto the desktop. Fortunately, Gilmont favored a wide-mouthed ink pot, and he had just laid out a fresh sheet of parchment. Drop perceived only one sure way to convey Flax's plea.

When Gilmont saw the cat poke its front paw into his ink pot, he was initially amused, then jolted into paying closer attention. Instead of the random smears the human expected from a cat dabbling in ink, Drop's crude strokes produced readable—if blurry—letters. In an amazed, then increasingly concerned voice, Gilmont read aloud, "HELP OTWILL MAGIC MIRROR." He paused to consider, then declared, "This is most extraor-

dinary. Either you are not a true cat, or you are a bespelled cat. I must assume that you have been instructed
by Master Otwill, who requires my assistance. I assure
you that I would willingly aid Master Otwill if I knew
his circumstances, but I have no idea what you mean by
'magic mirror.' "

Voluble humans, Drop reflected grimly, would risk
their very heads by talking even while their roof descended around their ears. Flax's entreaty was entirely
too urgent to be delayed by further conversation. Drop
seized Gilmont's voluminous sleeve with his teeth and
tugged.

"You desire to lead me," Gilmont deduced. "Perhaps
the master who bespelled you can explain. Yes, yes, I'm
coming! Allow me to bring a candle to light our way."

Gilmont's girth testified to his cook's culinary talents,
but for all his bulk, the old scholar was relatively agile
once he rose to his feet. Very shortly, he stood beside
Drop in front of the curious mirror in the attic. While
he recovered his breath from climbing the steep stairs,
Gilmont wiped the accumulated dust from the mirror
with a large silk handkerchief he extracted from his robe.

"I had quite forgotten this mirror," he exclaimed.
"The merchant who pressed me to buy that related set
of furniture neglected to mention that any of the pieces
possessed abeyant magical properties. It is clearly evi-
dent that the power inherent in this mirror is in abey-
ance no longer! Additional illumination would be
helpful. I believe I relegated a rather elaborate oil lamp
to a shelf up here some time ago ... yes, there it is.
Now, what was the spell for facilitating transferent access
through a magic mirror? I'm sure I read it only last
month." After a pause for thought, Gilmont pronounced
a series of authoritative sounds.

Drop's fur immediately bristled. The dim shapes
within the glass assumed more substance, but still remained obscure. Flax's voice, however, suddenly
boomed into the attic. "Gilmont! Pray recite Jalbert's
Attraction Spell, but take care to stand well away from
the face of the mirror."

Once Gilmont began to intone the requested spell, the

surface of the mirror bulged and extended outward to encompass a great gray mass that gradually separated from it. The spectacle reminded Drop of the singularly similar appearance of a batch of lustrous, sticky toffee he had once helped Flax to stretch. Following the initial looming form, a glistening horizontal shape emerged, supported between the first mass and a second, squatter but equally intimidating gray bulk. Drop and Gilmont hastily flattened themselves against a ramshackle bookcase in order to avoid being accidentally crushed by their alarming new visitors.

"Flax?" inquired Gilmont in a doubtful tone. "Otwill?"

Drop could only stare. The two scale-armored behemoths towering before him bore no possible resemblance to his former wizard companions. The third recumbent form that they had set cautiously on the floor appeared to be man-shaped, but coated with a hard, reflective substance.

The first monster gazed down at its enormous claw-tipped paws, and grumbled in Flax's unmistakable voice, "Bother! I fully expected that these troll bodies would transform when we returned from the other-space. At least, Gilmont, we were most fortunate in that your excellent mirror is large enough to accommodate our altered dimensions."

The shorter monster's grotesque head drooped. "If we cannot regain our normal bodies before sunrise," it murmured in Otwill's incongruously gentle voice, "we shall be permanently turned into stone." A large green tear welled up at the corner of its middle eye, and splashed down its warty snout.

"Courage, old friend!" Flax exhorted. "I distinctly recall Hupthorn's ancient formula for banishing trolls. I must admit," he confessed candidly, "that I have never before had occasion to employ it, but we must dare it now."

Gilmont, who had been uncharacteristically speechless, interrupted. "Would you not think it advisable," he suggested, "to include a stricture to insure that only the troll forms and natures are to be vanished, without affecting your residual material beings?"

Flax's ponderous head dipped in agreement. "A most worthy point, Gilmont. Grasp my paw, Otwill, and repeat after me."

Drop's nose itched unbearably, and all his fur stood on end. He fancied that he knew exactly how a bottle brush must feel. His transient discomfort, however, was quite eclipsed by his genuine delight to see the familiar human shapes of his friends emerge from a dazzling blue starburst of radiance.

Somewhat leaner than when Drop had last seen him, Flax turned, his bald head shining in the lamplight. "At last!" he exclaimed, seizing Gilmont's hand. "My dear Gilmont, we could not have achieved the transition without your vital assistance. You know Otwill, of course." Flax bent down to stroke Drop's head. "Drop—I rejoice to see you again."

Gilmont's attention was focussed on the supine form stretched out on the floor at their feet. His usual loquacity was evidently curtailed by his amazement. "What," he demanded, pointing at the gleaming object, "is *that?*"

For a moment, Flax, too, was at a loss for words. Then Otwill said apologetically, "I regret to say *that* is Koron, my pitiful apprentice."

"It is entirely the fault of that wretched other-space," Flax accused. Had there been sufficient room, Drop knew that Flax would have paced back and forth; being severely constrained by the attic's limits, Flax had to express his frustration by knotting and unknotting his robe sash.

"Pray assuage my deplorable ignorance," pleaded Gilmont, quivering with scholarly curiosity. "Have you journeyed here from some other-space beyond this mirror? I was completely unaware that I possessed any such exceptional interior threshold."

Instantly contrite, Flax hastened to elucidate. "How could you be aware," he said, "when Drop—he was my former apprentice, you understand, when he was a boy—could not, now being a cat, explain our plight. A few weeks ago, Otwill discovered that a rare spatial portal

might become accessible somewhere within the Za-
choran castle hired by Walgur, the infamous Druzanian
sorceror. Despite obstructions raised by Trund, Walgur's
resident minion, we contrived to be present during the
portal's initial opening. As soon as we had proceeded
through it to the other side, Otwill and I spell-sealed
the aperture to prevent Walgur from ever gaining access
to it."

"You may judge our dismay," Otwill inserted, "when
we immediately observed that our very shapes were
being affected by the nature of that other-space. Apparently, the speed of the alteration was linked to our degree of magical prowess, for Flax and I were almost
directly subsumed into those hideous troll bodies." Otwill shuddered at the memory of the ordeal.

"Before Koron could be similarly afflicted," Flax said,
"we hastened to protect him with a Temporary Exclu-
sion Spell." He hesitated, shaking his head mournfully.
"But we found that in that awful place, even our magic
was subject to pernicious variance. Instead of preventing
Koron's body from changing, our spell went awry. To
our distress, Koron was turned to glass."

Drop picked his way delicately alongside the glistening
length of his third former associate. He could indeed
recognize the young apprentice, but every part of
Koron—hair, skin, clothing—had been transformed into
rigid, semi-transparent glass.

Gilmont bent over to take a closer look. "I must say,"
he admitted, "in all of my studies, I have never encountered such an effect as this. Which restoration spell do
you suppose would be most efficacious?"

Flax promptly cited one spell, but Otwill favored another. Drop prudently withdrew into the upstairs corridor while the two wizards invoked a series of spells.
Only when his fur eased back into place did he return to
the storeroom. All three humans were frowning. Koron's
woeful condition appeared obstinately unaffected.

Gilmont's expression suddenly brightened. "I believe
that I once saw in my archives a treatise dealing with
the hardening or softening of glass," he said. "If you

could assist me in searching downstairs, perhaps we
might locate that very scroll."

"It would also be far easier to treat Koron in more
spacious surroundings," muttered Otwill. When he and
Flax attempted to lift the enchanted apprentice, however, their merely human musculature could not accomplish what their troll bodies had effortlessly performed.
Otwill sighed. "Lormer's Levitation Spell?" he ventured.

Flax nodded. "I'll steer the head and shoulders if you
will oversee the legs and feet. Mind the turns ... and
the stairs!"

Fortunately, the settee in Gilmont's study proved to
be just long enough—and sturdy enough—to support
Koron's crystalline bulk.

The last few days had been unseasonably warm for
late autumn. Gilmont had opened his study window
shortly before Drop had rushed in to convey Flax's magical cry for help. Now while the two wizards aided Gilmont in sorting through his carefully ordered stacks of
books and scrolls, Drop became increasingly aware of
an irritating buzzing sound. The humans, absorbed in
their task (and their inevitable conversation), seemed
oblivious to it, but during his months as a boy, Drop had
noticed that his human ears failed to register a variety
of high-pitched tones perfectly audible to any cat. This
particular annoying hum emanated from Gilmont's garden. It was at first attentuated by distance, then waxed
in volume like the shrill of a rapidly approaching, infuri-
ated wasp. Drop's fur rose, his skin crawled, and his
nose twitched as a sharp scent like that of curdled milk
wafted into the study. He ran to Flax's feet, reared up
on his hind legs, and scratched urgently at Flax's robe
to attract his attention.

Flax absently extended a hand to stroke Drop's head,
then stiffened as he registered both the warning state of
Drop's fur and the intensifying sour odor. "Gilmont,"
Flax stated in a calm voice, "I perceive that an unseen
and uninvited observer has entered your study. Intruder!
By Monfat's Command, I adjure you to disclose
yourself!"

Close by the window, a shadowy mist abruptly condensed into view as Flax sternly intoned a peremptory formula. Before Drop could blink, the shadow solidified into a tall figure enveloped in an ashen velvet robe. A deep hood totally concealed the intruder's face. The sole spark of visible color was a smoldering ruby set in a richly ornamented chain of blackened metal draped across the figure's shoulders.

Flax gazed with keen interest at their unanticipated guest. "Judging from the means of your entry and the style of your pendant," he conjectured, "I venture to identify you as Trund's master."

The figure threw back his hood, revealing a gaunt face with deep-set, burning red-brown eyes. His sword-cut of a mouth was framed by a bar of mustache and a close-trimmed beard whose hue matched his thick crown of red-brown hair.

There could be no mistaking those eyes. Had Drop been able to speak, he would have instantly proclaimed his recognition: those same menacing eyes had blazed from the skull of the unnatural crow which had earlier spied upon Gilmont's house and grounds.

The trespasser spoke in a grating voice that reminded Drop of several rusty hinges he had periodically oiled at Flax's cottage. "You are correct," he snarled. "I am Walgur of Druzan, Master of Trund . . . and much else besides."

"I seldom receive guests—invisible or otherwise—through my study window," Gilmont responded mildly. "Would it not have been more direct for you to knock at the front door?"

"I intended to make a formal call upon you in the morning," Walgur growled. "My journey from Zachor consumed less time than I expected. I hesitated to impose at so late an hour. Since your window was open, I merely . . . drifted inside to admire your unusual paraphernalia. That is a most curious simulacrum adorning your couch. Did you compose it entirely of glass?"

"I brought that along myself," Flax snapped. "I required Gilmont's opinion of it."

Walgur regarded Flax with an insolent stare. "I have heard of you," he spat. "You are Flax, the Farmer's

Friend. 'Acquired' that figure, did you? Perhaps from
beyond the portal—*my* portal, which you deliberately
sealed when you escaped from my castle after clashing
with Trund. Where *is* my minion, by the way?"

"Eaten," said Otwill. Walgur waited, but Otwill refused to elaborate further.

Walgur waved a sharp-nailed hand. "Trund was a bun-
gling fool," he declared dismissively. "I am well rid of
him. But you, Flax of the Hedgerows, and you, Otwill
of Zachor—you insinuated yourselves onto my property.
You interfered with my spells. You spitefully rendered
inaccessible the valuable portal that I had gone to considerable effort to locate. I demand that you remove
your closure spell so that I may utilize my rightful
possession!"

"I think not," Flax retorted. "Otwill and I can assure
you from our personal experience in the realm beyond
that portal, it is a thoroughly uncongenial place. We are
unalterably resolved that no future crossings shall be
made."

Walgur glowered at the wizards. "You insufferable
meddlers," he roared, "that is for *me* to decide! I have
overwhelming means to accomplish my desires. No man
dares to thwart me. I warn you—you oppose me at your
mortal peril!" With a furious gesture and a shouted word
that made Drop shiver, Walgur vanished in a cloud of
vile-smelling smoke.

Sneezing, Flax and Otwill magically dispersed the
fumes.

"Gilmont," Flax said, "I must apologize for this dis-
tressing abuse of your hospitality. I had no idea that
Walgur would assail you because of our actions. Just
before the portal closed in Walgur's castle, however, we
did call through it to advise Drop to seek you. No doubt
Walgur had impressed a security spell upon his tower
room, and he must have retrieved your name from it."

Otwill laughed ruefully. "What would Walgur say if
he knew that there is now no way to return to that other-
space?" he wondered. "Our exit through Gilmont's
splendid mirror was made possible only because of Gilmont's attraction spell. Unless a magic-wielder exerted

a similar attraction spell from the other-space, no further transits can be made by way of the mirror."

His face grave, Flax paced restlessly. "I must confess to a certain apprehension concerning Walgur's threat," he conceded. "We should consider at once how best to defend this house from magical assault." He paused, stricken by a secondary worry. "Neither can we neglect our efforts to restore Koron," he added. "I recall among the potions at my cottage a certain preparation that might be effective. Still, I feel most strongly that I should stay here to assist with our primary defensive spells." Flax turned to address the cat. "Drop, once again we must rely upon you for a vital contribution. You remember when you last helped me to reorganize my potions, there was a slender amber glass bottle with a red wax seal containing Arbat's Agent—next to Helver's extracts?"

Drop nodded.

Flax beamed. "Excellent! That is the very bottle that I require."

Gilmont looked puzzled. "But your cottage lies many days' travel from here, Flax," he objected. "How can your cat fetch this potion back to us in time to be useful?"

"By employing your exceptional mirror," Flax began in a cheerful tone, then stopped and frowned. "Otwill," he inquired anxiously, "you *are* still wearing your mind-touch medallion?"

"Of course." Otwill lifted his beard and extracted a small shell-shaped talisman strung on a silver neck chain.

Relieved, Flax again smiled. Delving into one of his robe's many pockets, he produced a matching pendant. "This is Koron's medallion," he explained to Gilmont, "which I fortuitously picked up after its chain broke during his struggle with Trund. Had it remained around Koron's neck, it would also have been turned to glass." He pronounced a quiet word to repair the severed chain, then remarked, "If I secure this around Drop's neck—so—it will preserve the link necessary for me to project and retrieve him through the mirror."

"You will want to provide a container into which

Drop can nudge the potion bottle in order to bring it back," advised Otwill.

Gilmont rummaged through several drawers in his desk. "My cook lately presented me with some of his herb-gathering bags fitted with drawstrings," he said. "Yes, here they are. Pray choose whichever size will accommodate your potion."

Suitably outfitted with both a carrying bag and Koron's medallion, Drop preceded Flax up the stairs to the attic. While Flax chanted from a prudent distance near the storeroom's door, Drop impatiently awaited some indication that the mirror's surface was becoming penetrable. He had just persuaded himself that he could barely detect the familiar jumbled outlines of Flax's study beyond the glass when Flax called, "Jump NOW!"

Drop pounced forward. His actual translation through the mirror produced a most peculiar sensation, rather like diving headlong into a tepid pool choked with water lily pads. Before he could take a second breath, Drop had penetrated the barrier. His fully extended claws gripped the uneven flooring of the wizard's cottage.

Drop ran straight to Flax's desk, his cat's eyes easily adjusting to the dimness of the tightly shuttered study. Although his ability to distinguish colors was far more restricted than a human's, Drop quickly located the bottle Flax had described. Any problem he might have had in identifying its colors was eliminated when he spied Flax's neatly lettered label proclaiming "Arbat's Softening Agent." As Drop maneuvered the slender bottle into his carrying bag, he sneezed violently.

That reaction—and the odor that occasioned it—instantly reminded Drop of the previous time when, in his boy form, he had similarly sneezed. He had been helping Flax sort and distribute his potions among the multitude of cubbyholes surmounting the desktop. Flax had said it was no wonder Drop sneezed, because Helver was famed for his lavish use of volatile herbs and essences. The wizard had waved one squat vial, which even to Drop's sadly limited human nose fairly reeked of oil of peppermint, and said, "Here is the source of your understandable irritation: Helver's Seemings Exchange Potion.

I've never tried it myself. Rarely needed, I should think, but doubtless useful under certain circumstances."

Always curious, Drop had asked, "What circumstances?"

"Suppose that you and I had assumed magical disguises in order to accomplish a dangerous mission," Flax had replied. "At some point, to mislead the enemy, it could be quite advantageous for us to exchange disguises. By applying this potion, our magically-imposed outward appearances—even our clothing—could be simultaneously exchanged. The only drawback, as I recall, is that a drench of water must be provided right away, either before or after the potion—a stricture which could attract undesired notice unless a drying spell could be adroitly employed to dispose of the water."

Acting on a sudden impulse, Drop carefully batted Helver's vial into his carrying bag. He had no sooner jumped down from the desk than he sensed Flax's mental voice conveyed by Koron's medallion.

"Drop," Flax instructed, "if you have secured the potion, return at once to the spot where you first entered the room. Upon the count of twenty, I shall draw you back here."

Drop's tail had only just cleared the surface of the mirror when enormous gusts of wind accompanied by lashing rain battered Gilmont's house from all directions. Thunder crashed overhead, and a barrage of hailstones hammered upon the roof.

"Quick! To the study," Flax cried. "Walgur's attack has begun!"

Otwill and Gilmont were crouched well to one side of the closed study window, seeking to assess Walgur's offensive forces. So far, the shielding spells that Flax had coordinated appeared to be holding. Although relays of gargoyles alternating with basilisks gibbered at the window, none of them could break through to touch the physical surface of the house. Baleful pillars of ocherous fire flared intermittently in the garden, disclosing a host of long-fanged goblins whose efforts to bombard the house with volleys of stones and darts were being equally thwarted.

Flax had stooped to remove Koron's medallion and the fabric bag from Drop's neck when Gilmont complained, "Surely a sorcerer of Walgur's supposed repute is capable of more original spells than *these*."

Flax glanced briefly at the teeming activity in the garden. "We must beware of underestimating a Druzanian," he began, then stopped, staring at the *two* containers he had extracted from Drop's carrying bag. "Drop," he reproved, "I requested only Arbat's Agent, yet you've also brought ..."

He was cut short by an urgent shout from Otwill. "Look! Under that door—a dark vapor—it could be poisonous!"

Flax promptly set both retrieved potions on the low table beside Koron's settee, and spun around to deal with the new threat. While he intoned a primary spell, Otwill contributed a compatible secondary formula to repel Walgur's lethal fog.

From Drop's point of view, the sorcerer's next attack was far more personally engaging: a veritable plague of rats erupted simultaneously from all corners of the room. To Drop's keen disappointment, however, no matter how swiftly he snapped every rat neck he could seize, each "killed" rat instantly reverted into the dust motes from which it had been conjured.

A suspicious lull followed that frenzied burst of activity. Drop had almost regained his breath when his fur suddenly bristled as if a lightning bolt had struck within paw-reach. He realized with horrid certainty that Walgur had somehow breached their magical defenses and had again invaded Gilmont's house.

His face drawn with horrified comprehension, Otwill pointed toward the attic. "Flax," he exclaimed, "we forgot that Gilmont's mirror constitutes a potential fissure in our encapsulation spell!"

Flax immediately conjured a glowing network of blue light strands across the top of the stairs just as Walgur charged out of the upstairs corridor. The sorcerer was forced to skid to an abrupt halt to avoid collision with Flax's barrier.

A desperately risky plan began to form in Drop's

mind as he warily beheld their raging adversary. If only
he could rely upon Walgur's preoccupation with the humans, plus a sufficient quantity of water ... Gilmont's
sole domestic practice of active magic provided numer-
ous vases of flowers to decorate his house. Periodically,
his spell would refresh them with nourishing changes of
herb-steeped water. One such tall vase filled with autumn lilies stood on a pedestal against the wall at the
top of the stairs. For the success of his plan, it was necessary that Drop's prime target, Walgur, must move closer
to that side of the upper landing. Koron, Drop's second
target, already lay conveniently accessible.

While Walgur persisted in ferocious efforts to dissolve
Flax's shielding network, Drop sank his teeth into the
loop of ribbon sealed into Helver's Seemings Exchange
vial stopper. The body of the vial was set into a segment
of bark-covered tree branch, presumably, Drop supposed, to exclude light from the potion within. Discarding the stopper to one side, Drop tilted his head and
cautiously carried the open vial onto the settee, where
he trailed the potion's pungent oil along Koron's glassy
length. He was fretting how to provide the requisite
drench of water to activate this fraction of the potion
when an awful sizzling sound signaled the collapse of
Flax's barrier spell.

Walgur triumphantly bellowed a spate of sounds
which paralyzed Flax, Otwill, Gilmont, and Drop exactly
where they stood. Fortunately, Drop had just eased into
a balanced stance on the floor beside the settee, so his
head was immobilized at an angle allowing retention of
the balance of the oil left in the unstoppered vial. During
his two previous conflicts with sorcerers, Drop had endured similar binding spells. He fervently hoped that on
this occasion, as twice before, his magically-experienced
cat's body would again recover conspicuously faster than
his fellow victims's human bodies.

Approaching the head of the stairs, Walgur gleefully
rubbed his hands together. "You thought to foil me with
your feeble spells," he jeered, "but when I sensed the
activity of your magic mirror, I focused upon that vulnerable access point within your very walls." The sorcerer

gestured peremptorily at Otwill's motionless form. "Come hither, fool!" Walgur ordered. "You shall guide me through the mirror into that tantalizing other-space, where you shall remove your obstructive spell and restore my castle's portal accessibility." His face set in a gloating grimace, Walgur retreated backward up the last few narrow stairs, levitating the helpless Otwill more than an arm's length away from him.

Without overtly disclosing his rapid recovery from Walgur's binding spell, Drop had been feverishly flexing his muscles. When the sorcerer drew abreast of the pedestal bearing the vase of lilies, Drop raced up the stairs, darted beneath the suspended Otwill, leaped onto the pedestal, and toppled the vase, showering Walgur from head to foot. Startled by the cat's completely unexpected movement, the sorcerer momentarily lost his control over Otwill. While Walgur sputtered and gasped, Otwill fell with a thump, and rolled jerkily from step to step all the way back down the stairs.

Drop climaxed his attack—and further compounded Walgur's discomfort—by launching himself onto the sorcerer's shoulder, where he tipped Helver's remaining potion oil down the gaping neck of the velvet robe.

Caught off-balance by Walgur's binding spell, Flax was propped awkwardly against a bookcase. He had observed Drop's sequence of actions with mounting excitement. Although the wizard's muscle control was still somewhat affected, Flax was able to levitate a large carafe from Gilmont's desk and tilt it over, drenching Koron's glistening form with a cascade of water. The only remaining requirement to activate Helver's Seemings Exchange was thus fulfilled.

Dripping vase water and lily fragments at the top of the stairs, Walgur struggled to speak despite his own magical affliction, but he emitted only a few garbled croaks before his flailing arms stiffened and his eyes literally glazed over. The contaminated spell that had enchanted Koron in the other-space now claimed Walgur: every part of him was transformed into glass. As a result of the simultaneous effectuation, Koron was restored to his living, breathing self ... but was also entirely obscured by the soaking bulk of the sorcerer's robe.

His bodily control re-established, Otwill scrambled to his feet and hastened to assist his enshrouded apprentice.

Walgur's rigid form, meanwhile, teetered on the top step, one out-thrust arm threatening to tip his balance. Descending from his pedestal perch, Drop obligingly applied a brisk shove with his forepaws. The crystalline sorcerer careened down the stairs, rebounding from wall to railing until he shattered with a resounding crash on Gilmont's study floor.

"Well done, Drop!" Flax approved. "The instant I smelled the peppermint essence of Helver's Seemings Exchange Potion, I perceived your inspired plan. Fortunately, your timely assault distracted Walgur sufficiently for me to shift Gilmont's carafe and supply the water necessary to initiate the disguise transposition." His congratulations trailed off as he surveyed the sodden, melancholy chaos that had overtaken Gilmont's orderly study. Abashed, Flax exclaimed, "My dear Gilmont, I must express my profound regret that this appalling havoc has been wreaked upon your premises. We might as well have summoned a rainstorm indoors! Still, Darmid's Drying Spell should quickly remedy the excess of water."

Once the floor, stairs, settee, and Koron's sopping robe relinquished their superfluous moisture, Gilmont breathed an audible sigh of relief.

"We cannot ignore what is left of Walgur," warned Otwill. "Unless every last fragment of him is properly disposed, some other odious Druzanian might be able to reconstitute him."

"I propose the dispatch of Walgur's ... residue through the mirror to some reliably safe location," suggested Gilmont, sweeping the glass shards into a tidy pile with his hearth broom.

"A most excellent idea," Flax confirmed. "The bottom of the sea should serve admirably. I shall attend to the disposition forthwith." He marched up the stairs, levitating the glittering heap behind him.

"Speaking of mirrors," mused Otwill, "I think Koron may wish to assess his present appearance."

Flax, his errand completed, was just descending the stairs when Koron bleated in dismay. Otwill had conjured a hand mirror for him, and the reflection disclosed to the apprentice the full extent of Helver's Seemings Exchange. Not only had Koron been garbed in Walgur's magically-charged robe, but he had also been outfitted with Walgur's mustache, beard, and heavy wig.

Flax could not contain a peal of laughter. "Allow me to relieve you of Walgur's vain adornments," he offered, reinstating with a gesture the affronted apprentice's own clean-shaven face and neatly trimmed hair.

The previous fury of turmoil in Gilmont's garden had subsided into an eerie, shadowed silence. Standing well to one side of the study window, Gilmont cautiously gazed outside. "Walgur's minions appear to have fled," he reported.

"Now that I have had leisure to consider those attacking forces more carefully," Flax remarked, "aside from Walgur himself, all the rest appeared to be illusory—some due to clumsier spells than others. You will have noticed how deplorably his basilisks' tails were articulated—very poor framing. I suspect that there are no material troops to withdraw to Walgur's castle. If you should fancy more spacious quarters in Zachor, Otwill, Walgur's castle ought therefore to be available for immediate occupancy."

Otwill shook his head decisively. "No, thank you, Flax," he replied. "I am quite content with my existing workshop. I might, however, benefit from a few days' recuperative rest here, if Gilmont can spare me accommodation."

"By all means," Gilmont warmly agreed. "You are welcome to stay as long as you like—as are you, young man, and you, too, Flax."

"Your offer is exceedingly gracious," said Flax, "but I must decline in order to hurry back to my cottage. I had promised to conjure a special bath of sheep dip for Farmer Salt as soon as the harvest was gathered. Besides, Drop and I have been absent long enough for every room to be obscured by dust and cobwebs. Our leaving to rescue Otwill was so precipitate that I neglected to set a cleaning spell."

Gilmont nodded sympathetically. "I understand ... but before you depart, I have one request. Could you recommend a suitable warding spell for that troublesome mirror upstairs? I rarely travel myself, and while I admit that such an entry point may be convenient for visits from distant friends ... still, I should prefer to exclude the uninvited."

At once, Flax and Otwill launched into a lively technical debate on the merits and drawbacks of various strictures. Drop's impatient movement toward the foot of the stairs caught Flax's eye.

"Drop," Flax observed, "during your time of lodging here with Gilmont, you have gained weight."

Gilmont smiled, and patted his own ample stomach. "My cook is famed throughout the kingdom," he said proudly. "I can truly boast of my pantry and table. *Every* visitor to my house gains weight!"

Flax sat down on the third step next to Drop. "My domestic arrangements can scarcely compete with Gilmont's lavish amenities," the wizard admitted. "I desire the best possible future for you, Drop. Should you choose to stay here, I am sure that Gilmont would extend his invitation to include you."

"I can think of no more agreeable guest," declared Gilmont. "Drop would be a welcome addition to my household."

Drop found himself fondly recalling Flax's cluttered, eccentrically-built, and often drafty cottage. By contrast, Gilmont's snug, neat house was ... was *too* comfortable. Drop realized that he relished the challenge of life with Flax, never knowing from day to day what might next appear at the door ... or under it, or through it.

Unable to voice his decision, Drop desired first to convey his appreciation for Gilmont's courtesy, not to mention the memorable repasts of fish served with cream by Gilmont's cook. Drawing near to Gilmont's feet, Drop bowed his head gracefully and purred politely before turning back toward Flax.

Flax was admittedly absentminded and often mad-
dening in his human ways, but Drop had felt a sense of
territorial rightness in both Flax's cottage and his company. There was also the practical element to be considered. When they returned to Flax's cottage, not only
would they have to contend with the accumulated layers
of dust and cobwebs, but the resident population of mice
could be relied upon to have rebounded in number and
boldness. As a wizard, Flax was well-suited to address
the human and non-human complications of magic.
Every cat knew, however, that no other creature was
better suited to deal with mice, both indoors and out-
doors, than an experienced cat.

The thought of insolent, unchecked mice overrunning
his territory could not be borne! Drop tugged at Flax's
sleeve, then raced up the stairs. Both mice and home
awaited on the other side of Gilmont's magic mirror.

ONE WITH JAZZ
by Janet Pack

Admitting cat-dependency, Janet Pack lives in Lake Geneva, Wisconsin, with felines Bastjun Amaranth and Canth Starshadow. She writes, directs, and acts in radio ads for a local game store. She gives writing seminars, and speaks to schools and groups about reading and the writing profession. When not writing short stories and books, Janet sings classical, Renaissance, and Medieval music. During leisure time she composes songs, reads, collects rocks, exercises, skis, and paddles her kayak on Lake Geneva.

"No animal can tell good music from bad." Steve Azos, proprietor of the Jazz House Coffee Bar, laughed and shook his pale head. "No way."

Jeff Rath felt an answer batter against his teeth. He tried to stop the words, but he couldn't restrain them.

"Satchmo can tell." His brain felt fuzzy, as though he were drunk, his body and thoughts beyond his control. Hoagy Carmichael music danced from the stereo, making everything shimmer and tilt at crazy angles. Something strange was happening.

Why had he revealed his pet's special talent? Why did he feel so odd, as if his thoughts moved in sync to the music's offbeats? As if he watched people around him with eyes not his own? They felt odd and stressed, as if his pupils were dilated and in bright light.

He looked into his Coffee Special sitting on the antique oak bar. Steve had mixed the brews himself. Had he slipped something hallucinogenic into the beverage, its taste hidden by the bite of the coffee?

Steve sipped from his own mug. "What does this cat do?"

"He turns on the boom box," Jeff explained, trying to hold on to his sense of reality. "I swear. He knows what music I need to calm me down or raise my spirits. I unlock the door, greet him, and he looks at me with huge green eyes. Then he walks to the shelves, digs out a disk, drops it in the player and hits 'Play.' "

"He opens plastic boxes?" asked Steve.

"They're in those travel folders that hold about ten each," explained Rath. "He paws them out."

"Lots of claw marks, right?"

Jeff shook his head. "I've never found a scratch." He drank and sighed, listening with pleasure as an elegant Duke Ellington selection began.

"Tell you what," said Steve, thumping down his mug. "My sister's been wanting a cat for her kid. Let's make that bet. Bring in your Satchmo on Friday. If he indicates that he likes the new trio I've hired, I'll believe that animals have musical sense. If your cat hides or seems indifferent, my sister gets him. Gloria's going to be tending bar that evening, she'll help judge."

"Sure," the brunette said with a grin as she reached for a clean mug.

Jeff asked hoarsely, "What's in it for me? Besides possibly losing my cat."

"Let's see." Steve swirled his coffee as music curled around them. "I know. One of my friends is acquainted with Terry McCormack, the music producer. That company's always looking for talent scouts with jazz savvy. Maybe they'd give you a job that'd let you quit your three part-timers. I could arrange an introduction."

Rath shook with internal palsy, but his hands remained steady as he raised his mug and drained it. The world seemed more skewed than ever. He could not force his head into lateral movement to deny the proposal. All he could manage was a jerky nod. His neck felt like it was anchored with a rusted hinge which might snap and send his head rolling across the bar. He moved like a marionette, controlled by some power outside himself. Jeff hated the feeling.

Steve said, "This is Tuesday. Bring in your pet on Friday night. Then we'll see." He raised his drink. "I still say no cat knows music."

Rath sat silent and miserable, thinking it might be a good thing if he could disappear along with the last of the Duke's sweet notes. How could he have made a bet on a buddy who couldn't speak for himself?

"Another Coffee Special to seal the bet?" offered Azos.

"Can't, thanks." Rath slipped off his stool, surprised to find his feet solidly beneath him and the floor where it should be. "I work in a few hours. Gotta sleep." Brubeck's "Take Five" began, one of his favorites. "Thanks for the coffee, Steve." He shrugged into his jacket.

"Don't forget," the owner called to his back. "Friday at eight, you and the cat."

Jeff stepped into the rain beyond the door. "Satchmo, how could I have done this to you?" he groaned. "Why do I feel so odd?" Seattle's winter fog caged him in a misty bubble that suspended all reality except the slap of his feet against wet pavement as he trotted the four blocks to his tiny apartment. The ends of his shoulder-length hair guided damp beneath his collar and he shivered. "Buddy, you're going to hate me. I'll never find another cat like you. Not with your music magic." Feeling suddenly tired and very much alone, he dragged up three flights of stairs and unlocked his door.

Satchmo Jazzz waited for him in the middle of the main room, the tip of his gray and black tail twitching. Creamed coffee cheeks bristling with white whiskers contrasted with the tabby's brick-red nose. Round green eyes rimmed with black and buff looked enormous set amid dark and light stripes of his face. Rath shucked his jacket, scooped up the sixteen-pounder, and plomped them down in the worn easy chair.

"Tell you what I did," Jeff said in a rush, ruffling the soft fur behind Satch's ears as the cat sighed and demanded more attention. "You're my best friend. I don't want to lose you." Satchmo looked straight at him, peridot-green eyes absorbing every word. "I made a stupid bet that you could tell if Steve's new trio is good. They're playing Friday. We're supposed to go there and listen. Do nothing, and his sister's kid gets you. Act interested and we win. Then you and I get introduced to some music producer needing a talent scout. That meeting might not gain us anything." Shaking his head, he scrubbed fingers through his dark hair. "I know you're pretty unusual, but this is more than even you can—"

Rath's lap cooled suddenly as Satchmo jumped down. The cat strode to the stereo boom box, tapped the "Play" button, and sat beside it staring at the man as the strains of "Don't Worry, Be Happy" filled the room.

Jeff laughed and leaned back, patting his legs. "No matter how bad it gets, you always make me feel better, Satch." The tabby leaped into his lap, turned once so the softest part of the worn jeans were under his paws, and settled down purring.

They'd been together for five years, through good and bad times. This last six months since he'd been laid off at TechWorks and had lost his investments through lousy advice was the leanest stretch they'd had. Love interests for Jeff had dwindled to nothing because of his peculiar hours, leaving him very lonely.

The cat stoically accepted his partner's frustration, exhaustion, and erratic hours working whatever jobs he could get. In return, Satch offered companionship and entertained them with a zany selection from Rath's CDs. How and when the cat had learned to dig the disks from their folders and work the boom box Jeff couldn't recall. It was part of Satchmo's magic.

He combed the cat's brindle coat, remembering. Rath had known that Satch was uncommon from the moment they met. Five years ago he'd been walking across the parking lot of TechWorks, the area's largest computer hardware and software development firm, when an escaped Rottweiler had taken a fancy to his ankles. Jeff had butted the dog in the side with his briefcase and sprinted for the building. A gray blur streaked between them, and the Rott veered after the cat.

Panting, Jeff slid his security pass through the slot outside TechWorks' huge door. The feline wheeled and charged full-speed toward the building, the dog slavering three paces off its tail. Rath slipped inside. Something made him look back. He spotted the cat flying for safety. Jeff awaited his rescuer, holding the door just wide enough for the kitten to squeeze through. He let it shut just in time for the Rott's nose to smash into thick plastic.

"What am I going to do with you?" Rath had looked at the bedraggled, half-grown kitten and met a pair of intense peridot-green eyes. The bond between them was instant. "You could sit on my desk."

The tabby "Yowwed" silently as Jeff picked him up and carried him to his cubicle. On the desk, the kitten washed and settled into what Jeff called the "loaf" position—lozenge-shaped, head up, eyes slitted, tail and paws tucked beneath his body. He accepted admiring pats with grace, but his aloof mien announced his affection centered on his desk mate. When lunchtime came, Jeff shared two cold-cuts sandwiches with his hungry new friend.

That afternoon, Sheila in the next compartment had switched the radio station to elevator music. The kitten's eyes sprang open, his head whirled around, and his agonized wail cut across the melody. He jumped down, located the radio, hopped onto that desk, and began batting it.

"Your kitten's attacking my radio," Sheila shrieked.

"Change the station," Rath suggested, stepping around the partition to claim the tabby.

Sheila did so, passing one with jazz. The kitten complained and reached out a protesting paw. She tuned in the Louis Armstrong song. Jeff, hearing a satisfied purr accompany the brilliant trumpet, decided to name the cat Satchmo in honor of that musician.

Many incidents since then had convinced Rath his cat

knew good jazz. He had bought a stereo boom box with a radio and left it on a station that specialized in a mixture of Pat Metheny, the Marsalis brothers, Thelonious Monk, Charlie Bird Parker, and Lady Day, as well as cuts from new musicians. Satchmo reacted with his best cat smile to the oldies except for the more outrageous of Spike Jones' pieces, turning up the corners of his mouth and hooding his eyes in ecstacy. New musicians he divided into three groups: the good, the okay, and the walk-aways. Jeff learned that when the tabby turned tail, that person or group wasn't long on the play list. Satch seemed to hear something that made his ears flatten and his toes twitch to be gone.

Leaning back, Rath smiled and relaxed a little. Telling his mental alarm to wake him in three hours, he fell asleep to the cat's rumble matched to the body percussion and soft vocals of Bobby McFerrin.

By Friday Jeff wasn't so certain of success. He spent his afternoon as a clinic security guard trying to think of ways to quit the bet with dignity. He could not let his best friend go. He calculated his finances, thinking that he might be able to eke out the adoption fee from the local humane society if he skipped three meals before his next paycheck. Then Steve's sister's brat would have a kitten to maul and he could keep Satchmo. No other solution occurred to him as he walked to the security firm's headquarters after his stint, changed into street clothes, and hurried home.

"You know what you've got to do tonight." Jeff knelt, petting his friend and receiving a purr recalling the roar of an unmuffled Harley. "This is real important. I'll never, ever, make a bet like this again."

Satch butted his head against Rath's knee and looked straight into the man's eyes. Jeff stared back, mesmerized by the assurance he saw there. The human blinked first.

"Are you telling me not to worry?" The tabby's chin bumped over his knuckles. "I don't think I can. I'm too nervous. I should eat, but I'm not hungry. I'll get coffee at the Jazz House." He scratched Satch behind the ears.

"We'd better go." Jeff slung on his jacket, zipped it a few inches, and thumped his chest. Satchmo sprang, landing in his arms.

"Good thing you know when to use those claws." Tucking Satch's tail under his left arm, Rath let the cat's head protrude from the coat's opening. With a huge sigh he locked the door and thumped down the stairs.

The walk to the Jazz House passed too quickly. It seemed to Jeff as if they arrived there by science-fiction transporter instead of by his feet. He hesitated, one hand on the door, then pushed into the Jazz House. "Basin Street Blues" enveloped him and the cat.

"There you are." Steve stepped up to meet them. "I thought you might not show. Where's your—oh, there. Sit down, the coffee's on me tonight. Two, Gloria," he ordered. "The first set doesn't begin for half an hour."

Jeff let Satchmo out of his jacket onto the bar, where the cat shook to rid his fur of damp. Steve frowned, watching the tabby's ears twitch. The cat paced down the long curving oak bar and stopped again, listening. "What's he doing?"

"Probably finding the best place to listen." Rath chose a stool, perching on the edge, noticing the fog at the edge of his vision. Things were getting strange again. "He went straight to the corner where the sound balances."

Satch sat, head up and tail wrapped primly around his feet, as Wynton Marsalis wailed. The cat's ears pricked. "Maybe he does know about jazz," Steve admitted. "But that's an established artist, a sound he's probably familiar with. The trio's only been working together a few weeks."

Nerves scratched Jeff's throat, making his tone harsh. "I don't think Satchmo's ever been to a live performance. At least not with me." He sipped coffee that seared his tongue, and grimaced.

"My sister's kid's looking forward to this cat," the coffee bar's owner remarked.

"I meant to ask you about that," Rath began. "Would it be all right if I bought her one? Satch and I have been together a long time, and I—"

"Then our bet's off and you welched," said Steve. "I

want to see the feline do the things you talked about. It's worth a little risk."

Jeff twisted his cup. "You're risking nothing." His insides knotted and the room seemed to warp.

"Here they are," said Steve.

A tall, dark-haired young man walked to the piano as a bass player and a guitarist took nearby chairs. The pianist waited a few minutes for his partners to get comfortable and then struck a tuning A. When the bassist nodded satisfaction, the young man sat down at the upright and began stroking his long fingers over the keys without pressing.

Steve rose to turn off the stereo, waiting until Pete Fountain finished "Way Down Yonder in New Orleans" before he stepped to the microphone.

"Tonight the Jazz House welcomes you with a new group. And there's an added attraction." He pointed at Satchmo. "See the big cat on the bar? There's a bet. He's supposed to know good jazz. The person he lives with says the cat will have an unmistakable reaction to these musicians, particularly if they're good." He turned to the trio. "Make it hot, men, the cat's watching."

The pianist caught ready-nods from the others as Steve moved through the tables and sat down. Plunging his fingers onto the keys, the young man slammed into Fats Waller's "The Joint is Jumpin'."

The music sounded a little ragged at first, but the audience yelled moderate approval as the triad wound to a stop and swung into the next tune. Jeff glanced at Satchmo. The cat had assumed loaf position, but his head was high and his ears twitched as if he listened for something elusive. His intent green eyes stared past the musicians. Rath crossed his fingers, noticing as he did the sense of unreality taking over again.

"Don't let us down, Satch," he pleaded.

The third song gathered howls of favor as the pianist blasted into Jelly Roll Morton's "Ballin' the Jack." The young man's demeanor changed—eyes slitted, head thrown back, half-smile on his lips, his fingers caressed the keys as he gave away his lead to his partners and took it back without faltering. The sweating bassist watched him closely, but the guitarist displayed a Cheshire cat grin. People ignored coffee and conversation to listen. Some even clapped in rhythm.

They played "Old Man River" by Cole Porter, followed by Cannonball Adderley's "Mercy, Mercy, Mercy" and Brubeck's "Blue Rondo a la Turk." Following another classic, the trio rollicked into a playful version of "The Birth of the Blues."

Steve grabbed Jeff's arm. "Where's the cat?"

Rath glanced at the curve in the bar. The big tabby was gone. "I—I don't know," he stuttered. He felt as though someone threw magic into the air and was trying to suffocate him with it.

"He's probably under a table," Steve sneered. "Or someone dropped him out the door."

"Hey, look at the cat!" someone yelled.

Jeff and Steve whirled. Rath grinned in relief as the bar's proprietor lost his chin somewhere around his knees.

"Way to go, Satch," Jeff whispered.

Satchmo stood with the trio, his attention on the guitar, the tip of his upright tail dipping to the strong beats. Round and intent, his eyes looked greener than normal in the spotlights. The tabby's gaze switched to the bassist and he paced over to the big instrument as if assessing its vibrations.

"Looky there," Gloria said. "You've lost this bet, Steve."

Jeff squinted at his feline. "He's not smiling."

Steve frowned. "What do you mean?"

"The guitar player barely passed. Satch smiles when he really likes something." Jeff finished his coffee, feeling somewhat better. "I think the bassist'll pass, too. But I really want to see Satchmo with the pianist, the make-or-break man."

"Explain that."

"He's cueing the leads and setting the pace. And Satch saved him for last."

"Two more, Gloria," Steve ordered, sounding sour.

Satchmo disappeared behind the upright piano while the group played "Ain't Misbehavin'" and "St. James Infirmary." He sat close to the pedals during "Honeysuckle Rose," his striped head tipped to the left. The intent pianist didn't notice. When the trio began their hot version of "Mack the Knife" led by the bassist, Satch leaped to the top of the upright and stayed there, the upward quirk of his mouth plain to see.

"That's his seal of approval," Jeff announced, reveling in the cat's magic.

The young keyboard player struck the last chord and looked up, straight into Satchmo's wide green eyes. Neither moved for long moments. The pianist finally broke the stare and turned to his cohorts.

"Game to try a new tune?"

"Sure," grinned the guitarist. "If it goes as well as the rest of this gig." The bassist nodded.

"You'll pick it up easy." The crowd quieted as he held up a hand for attention. "One, two, one, two, three, four!"

He slapped down a few chords, broke the pattern with a short run, and returned to chords again. The rhythm resembled a cat's prowl. The bassist came in smoothly with a walking bass, and the guitarist found his part high in the soprano. The sound solidified as the musicians played off one another. People in the coffee bar jumped to dance or sat clapping in time, thoroughly enjoying themselves and the original music.

The set ended. Wild applause followed the trio as they stumbled to the bar, drunk with the heady mixture of good music and appreciation. Steve ordered coffees.

"Wow," the guitarist said. "It's never happened like that before."

"No kidding," agreed the bassist.

"It was the cat," said the pianist. "The piece seemed to jump out of his eyes right into my head. Who does he belong to?"

"Me," said Jeff proudly, putting an arm around Satchmo after the tabby leaped onto the bar.

"Will you bring him for next Friday's jam?" the keyboardist grinned. "I'll throw in some tuna. That cat's fine, he's one with jazz, man."

Steve nodded. "You win. Give me a few days to set up the meeting, all right?"

"Sure. We'll be here on Fridays." Jeff looked down

at his purring buddy. The room was upright again and the fog gone, but everything sparkled. The tabby tickled him in the ear with his tail and blinked slowly as if to say "See? Nothing at all to worry about."

Several days later Jeff's phone rang, startling him awake in the easy chair. He dumped Satchmo off his lap and rose to answer, feeling lonely and achingly weary.

"Yeah?" His voice was raspy with sleep.

"Rath, this is Steve. I'm paying off our bet. Can you get here right away?"

"I've got to work, sorry."

"Tell them you quit. And bring the cat."

Reality skewed suddenly. "What?"

"Terry McCormack's here. See you in a few minutes." The line clicked dead.

Jeff stood looking at the handset for some time before movement caught his eye. Satchmo hit the "Play" button on the boom box and Louis Armstrong's gravelly "What a Wonderful World" floated out.

"I really ought to quit?" Rath asked. The cat danced. Feeling silly about taking advice from a feline, Jeff made the call. Distinctly light-headed, he took a quick shower before zipping Satchmo into his jacket and heading for the Jazz House.

He pushed open the door with sudden jitters. The interior sparkled with phantom glitter. "Steve?"

A single light gleamed over the far side of the bar. One person sat there, facing away from the entrance with a steaming mug, disguised by a hat and raincoat. Les Paul's "Moonglow" wafted everywhere, cloaking the figure in magic.

"Jeff Rath?" A melodious voice, definitely female, cut through the music. It sent goosebumps up his arms and neck. His world tilted. "Did you bring Satchmo?"

"Yes."

The figure turned, taking off the hat. Though not pretty, her face was striking, all pale angles under a wild tumble of auburn hair. "I'm Terry McCormack, producer of Top o' the World Recordings. I've heard good things about you and your cat."

Satch squirmed. Jeff unzipped his jacket, letting the feline hop onto the bar. "From Steve, I suppose."

She watched as the tabby stared in her direction, flipping his tail. "To tell you the truth, I checked with your current employers. They say you're overqualified, but conscientious. I'm offering you something better."

Jeff's breath deserted him. "What?" he croaked.

"Talent scout for my company."

Rath dipped his head as Satchmo's tail began switching in huge arcs. "It's not me that has the talent. It's my cat. He hears something special in certain musicians. And he loves music, especially jazz." Jeff patted Satch's back. "So it's really the cat you want, not me." A chill sluiced through him. Would this be the second time in less than a week he could lose Satchmo?

"If the cat becomes the scout, he'll need a keeper. You're experienced." She smiled slightly, just the corners of her mouth and eyes turning up. The expression reminded Jeff strongly of Satchmo's smile. The tabby was already strolling down the bar toward her waiting hand. "I've heard that you two make such a great team that I'd be reluctant to take one without the other." She listened to the music for a couple of seconds as she scratched the cat's chin. He purred. "Are you free for dinner?"

"As long as Satchmo comes with us."

"Of course."

Paced by Satch, Terry McCormack rose and strode along the bar. She started to take Jeff's arm. For the first time he looked into her face. Shock staggered him. Terry's eyes were the same vivid peridot-green as the cat's.

She ignored his discomfort. "I know a little place not far from here."

He took a deep stabilizing breath. The sense of magic did not dissipate. "Great. C'mon, Satch."

Zipping the tabby securely into his jacket, Jeff offered his arm to Terry. She curled her hand through his elbow, and the three of them walked out of the Jazz House into chill mist.

The door closed, cutting off the remainder of Louis Armstrong's "I Get Ideas."

Don't Miss These Exciting DAW Anthologies

SWORD AND SORCERESS
Marion Zimmer Bradley, editor
☐ Book XIII   UE2703—$5.99

OTHER ORIGINAL ANTHOLOGIES
Mike Resnick & Martin H. Greenberg, editors
☐ SHERLOCK HOLMES IN ORBIT   UE2636—$5.50
☐ WITCH FANTASTIC   UE2640—$4.99

Richard Gilliam & Martin H. Greenberg, editors
☐ PHANTOMS OF THE NIGHT   UE2696—$5.99

Martin H. Greenberg, editor
☐ CELEBRITY VAMPIRES   UE2667—$4.99
☐ VAMPIRE DETECTIVES   UE2626—$4.99
☐ WEREWOLVES   UE2654—$5.50
☐ WHITE HOUSE HORRORS   UE2659—$5.99

Rosalind M. & Martin H. Greenberg, editors
☐ DRAGON FANTASTIC   UE2511—$4.99
☐ HORSE FANTASTIC   UE2504—$4.50

Katharine Kerr & Martin H. Greenberg, editors
☐ ENCHANTED FORESTS   UE2672—$5.50
☐ WEIRD TALES FROM SHAKESPEARE   UE2605—$4.99

Norman Partridge & Martin H. Greenberg, editors
☐ IT CAME FROM THE DRIVE-IN   UE2680—$5.50

Buy them at your local bookstore or use this convenient coupon for ordering.

PENGUIN USA   P.O. Box 999—Dep. #17109, Bergenfield, New Jersey 07621

Please send me the DAW BOOKS I have checked above, for which I am enclosing $_____ (please add $2.00 to cover postage and handling). Send check or money order (no cash or C.O.D.'s) or charge by Mastercard or VISA (with a $15.00 minimum). Prices and numbers are subject to change without notice.

Card #_____ Exp. Date _____
Signature_____
Name_____
Address_____
City _____ State _____ Zip Code _____

For faster service when ordering by credit card call 1-800-253-6476

Allow a minimum of 4-6 weeks for delivery. This offer is subject to change without notice.

FANTASY ANTHOLOGIES

☐ **ALIEN PREGNANT BY ELVIS**   UE2610—$4.99
   Esther M. Friesner & Martin H. Greenberg, editors

Imagination-grabbing tales that could have come straight out of the supermarket tabloid headlines. It's all the "news" that's not fit to print!

☐ **ANCIENT ENCHANTRESSES**   UE2677—$5.50
   Kathleen M. Massie-Ferch, Martin H. Greenberg, & Richard Gilliam, editors

Here are timeless works about those most fascinating and dangerous women—Ancient Enchantresses.

☐ **CASTLE FANTASTIC**   UE2686—$5.99
   John DeChancie & Martin H. Greenberg, editors

Fifteen of fantasy's finest lead us on some of the most unforgettable of castle adventures.

☐ **HEAVEN SENT**   UE2656—$5.50
   Peter Crowther, editor

Enjoy eighteen unforgettable encounters with those guardians of the mortal realm—the angels.

☐ **WARRIOR ENCHANTRESSES**   UE2690—$5.50
   Kathleen M. Massie-Ferch & Martin H. Greenberg, editors

Some of fantasy's top writers present stories of women gifted—for good or ill—with powers of both sword and spell.

☐ **WEIRD TALES FROM SHAKESPEARE**   UE2605—$4.99
   Katharine Kerr & Martin H. Greenberg, editors

Consider this the alternate Shakespeare, and explore both the life and works of the Bard himself.

Buy them at your local bookstore or use this convenient coupon for ordering.

PENGUIN USA P.O. Box 999—Dep. #17109, Bergenfield, New Jersey 07621

Please send me the DAW BOOKS I have checked above, for which I am enclosing
$_____ (please add $2.00 to cover postage and handling). Send check or money order (no cash or C.O.D.'s) or charge by Mastercard or VISA (with a $15.00 minimum). Prices and numbers are subject to change without notice.

Card #_____ Exp. Date _____
Signature_____
Name_____
Address_____
City _____ State _____ Zip Code _____

For faster service when ordering by credit card call **1-800-253-6476**

Allow a minimum of 4-6 weeks for delivery. This offer is subject to change without notice.

GAYLE GREENO

☐ **THE GHATTI'S TALE:**
Book 1—Finders, Seekers UE2550—$5.99
The Seekers Veritas, an organization of truth-finders composed of Bondmate pairs—one human, one a telepathic, cat-like ghatti—is under attack. And the key to defeating this deadly foe is locked in one human's mind behind barriers even her ghatta has never been able to break.

☐ **MINDSPEAKER'S CALL**
The Ghatti's Tale: Book 2 UE2579—$5.99
Someone seems bent on creating dissension between Canderis and the neighboring kingdom of Marchmont. And even the truth-reading skill of the Seekers Veritas may not be enough to unravel the twisted threads of a conspiracy that could see the two lands caught in a devastating war . . .

☐ **EXILES' RETURN**
The Ghatti's Tale: Book 3 UE2655—$5.99
Seeker Doyce is about to embark on a far different path—a ghatti-led journey into the past. For as a new vigilante-led reign of terror threatens the lives of Seekers and Resonants alike, the secrets of that long-ago time when the first Seeker-ghatti Bond was formed may hold the only hope for their future . . .
